the
SPACE
BETWEEN
SECRETS

SHERI LANGER

Unlocking New Worlds

For my wonderful husband, Brad

My knight in shining armor

My dashing prince on a white horse

My happily ever after, 143.

Chapter One

Before Rachel could even let out her last ecstatic moan, Phil rolled out of bed. He yanked her long blond hair under his armpit as he got up.

"Ouch!" Rachel massaged her wounded scalp. "Where are you going? It's Saturday." She considered dragging him back into bed but raised the plush comforter to her chin instead.

"I know what day it is," Phil said as if he'd invented the calendar. He pulled a shirt from his closet and hung it on the doorknob as he put together the rest of his outfit. "We're Zooming with Akinowa at eleven, and Jeb needs me on the call."

"Of course. When doesn't Jeb need you for something?" Rachel sat up and propped Phil's pillow against the white satin tufted headboard. Feeling more exposed than sexy, she pulled her nightshirt over her head.

"Quit bitching." Phil patted the blanket over her crotch. "As bosses go, Jeb's decent. You know, it's kind of funny. Our damn investors couldn't care less if I... come, but they'd never let me go." Phil winked, impressed with his pun.

Rachel ignored him and reached for the body lotion on her night table. She rubbed a squirt over her hands while noticing how dry they were.

"Anyway, I thought I told you." Phil admired his naked perfection from several angles in the oversized mirror above the long, white-lacquered dresser.

Do it. You know you want to. Go on, kiss yourself, she thought before he disappeared into the bathroom.

Rachel scanned the colorless room. What it lacked in charm, it compounded with sterile functionality. She would have preferred some warmth, but Phil insisted on everything being black and white. "Color clutters the mind," he'd said as he signed for the Danish set from an up-and-coming group of new designers. At the time, he was in a new position at work and needed to stay focused. She saw no reason to argue, especially since he'd said that apart from his office, the rest of the furnishings were up to her. It had been a fair compromise, but now, she was sorry there weren't more touches that made it her bedroom too.

After a glance at the clock, she quickly threw her legs into the air, propping herself up to facilitate fertilization, a tip she'd learned from *Good Morning America* a few weeks earlier. Twenty minutes seemed like a ridiculously long time, but she was limber and could handle it. Something had to give. She and Phil had been trying to get pregnant for over a year, and nothing was happening. Much of the time, she felt like crying, but negative energy was not going to aid conception. Neither was Phil singing "I'm Too Sexy" at the top of his lungs from the shower.

He's a freaking narcissist. Rachel could hear her sister Beth's words screaming in her head. Beth was pissed that the last time they met for dinner, Phil had told Rachel to park because it was raining and he didn't want to get his new suit wet. Rachel explained it was no big deal. Silk could stain, and she didn't mind the extra steps. Beth had made a joke about it at the table. "Phil, we know you love your dick, but as *Seinfeld* taught us, shrinkage doesn't work that way." They'd all laughed, but Rachel knew Phil had dropped a few more pegs from grace that would never be recovered.

Unfortunately, Beth wasn't entirely wrong. Phil did seem more self-centered every day. Little things, like not taking out the trash and forgetting to call if he was working late, which felt like always, were hard to ignore. But Rachel was resigned to dismiss them, just like the negative pregnancy tests that were now part of her monthly trash. Staring keenly at her forty-third birthday, she didn't have time to indulge in petty disappointments. According to her calendar, she was ovulating, and that meant she could get pregnant if she made the most of the moment. Nothing else mattered.

Somewhere in the middle of Rachel imagining making love as a redhead and Phil being too sexy for his shirt, she realized the phone was playing her sister's assigned ringtone. Twisting toward her night table, she used a box of Kleenex to push it out of its cradle and onto the bed, all while keeping her legs erect. Rachel wasn't about to lose the troops just to chat.

"Hi, Bethie," she answered breathily, shaking as she readjusted herself.

"Are you in the middle of sex?" Beth asked without hesitation. Her younger sister had no filters.

"No! Do you think I would have answered the phone if I was?"

"For me, maybe—hold on," Beth muttered. "Joshie, stop calling your sister a vagina-head. You're making her cry. Yes, she does know what a vagina is, and you're making her cry. Evan! Evan! Please come watch the kids for a few minutes so I can talk to my sister. Jesus. Thank you!" Rachel could hear Beth take a deep, cleansing breath. "Still sure you want children?"

"Yes. I have my legs practically touching the ceiling to prove it."

"Ah, so you already screwed, and now you're doing the *Good Morning America* thing. It's a long shot, you know. But I admire your ambition. Are you coming to the shop today?"

"Well, here's the thing—"

"So, you're not," Beth cut in.

"I need the day."

"Plans?"

"I was thinking of getting a Brazilian wax with the gift certificate you gave me."

"You just had sex. Why would you bother?"

"It's kind of kinky, and since we're celebrating our anniversary tonight, I would—"

"Do anything to get Phil's attention?"

Beth's words stung. She was right. Rachel could feel Phil pulling away, especially since their sex life had become work with a clear agenda.

"Give it up, Rach," Beth continued. "Even if you got a lightning bolt trimmed down there, I doubt Phil would notice." Scary how Beth could read Rachel's thoughts. "He's always been in his own world, but lately, he doesn't even seem to *visit* yours except for mandatory sex at your insistence."

"It's just the baby thing. I can deal with that." Rachel felt a defensive knot growing in her gut. She wanted to say, "Shut up, Beth. You can get pregnant just by announcing the desire." But she held her tongue.

"I understand how much you want to be a mother," Beth said. "You've always been like one to me, but I'm worried you and Phil aren't in the right place for it."

"Don't worry. Once I conceive, I know things will be different. Phil's just busy with work and frustrated, like me."

"If you say so. But I'm not convinced."

"Jesus! Between you and Mom, I can't catch a break. Phil is fine. He and I are fine. It's a rough patch. Circumstances, like every marriage."

"True, but as depth goes, this marriage was ironically 'I do'ed' on a pond, not an ocean. The first words out of your mouth when you told me about Phil were, 'He's gorgeous, cut, and man is he well—'"

"Enough! Beth, stop."

"I was going to say heeled."

"And I was still going to say stop."

"Fine, fine." Beth relented.

A stream of laughter came from the bathroom just before Rachel heard Phil turn off the music. If she hadn't known better, she could imagine him being in there with someone else. Maybe a ginger who had perfect boobs and a snarkier sense of humor than hers.

"Okay, I'll admit, you're a little right. I was angry at Dash. And, yes, I've made some historically poor choices when I was on the rebound," Rachel admitted. "But, at this point, does it really matter why I married Phil?"

"It might," Beth answered.

A crash that sounded like a window hitting concrete exploded on Beth's line. "Aw, geez, hold on." A normal person might have hung up, but in Beth's life, cleaning up broken glass was like wiping a runny nose. Rachel pressed the phone to her chest and shifted her hips to maintain a ninety-degree angle in what yoga professionals might have called the insemination pose.

She audibly asked herself if Beth was right and her marriage was, in fact, a misguided case of gratitude after an unbearable breakup. She'd spent seven long years with Dash Flynn, only to find out he had a wife and kid in Chang Mai, Thailand. That devastating discovery had nearly led her down a rabbit hole but had instead led her to a business cruise, where she'd met and married Phil. Even Rachel knew it was a spontaneous leap of faith, but sometimes, thinking was overrated. Her rationale had always been, much to Beth's objections, that everything happened for a reason. Rachel was certain that Phil showing up at the right time and place was kismet.

"Are you still there?" Beth shouted over the receiver.

Rachel quickly released her thoughts and again readjusted her bottom. If Phil's sperm wanted to escape, they would get no help from her.

"Yeah, I'm still here," Rachel said, hitting the speaker mode on her phone. "You know, you're being harsh, Bethie. I married Phil because I fell in love with him the moment our eyes locked."

"Are we still on this?" Beth replied. "I just had to clean up a huge broken jar of honey that fell into a sea of dog pee."

"Well, as gross as that sounds, and Jeter should see the vet, I'm still annoyed, and I'm telling you, I married Phil because I fell in love with him."

"Yes, I remember it all. You regaled me with every detail from sitting at the captain's table every night to the champagne and caviar before hitting the sheets."

"You're making it sound ugly," Rachel said.

"No, I'm just not catering to your delusions of this being some mighty, important love. It's not like the two of you got together and discovered a way to save a third-world country from the clutches of an evil despot."

"What the hell are you even talking about?"

"I don't know," Beth admitted. "I've been binge-watching something on Netflix. But the point is that five minutes after you met, the captain was pronouncing you and Phil man and wife. And seven years later, that is still the definition of insanity."

"It was not five minutes," Rachel insisted.

"Whatever, it was my fault anyway," Beth said. "I drove you to Bayonne, handed you condoms and Dramamine, and forced you to go on that business trip. You were so vulnerable. I don't know what I was thinking."

Rachel could hear Jeter barking and Beth barking back at him, probably Beth's substitute for barking at her.

"It was a week after we met," Rachel said, feeling empowered by correcting her.

"Yes, a very short, dreamy week," Beth continued. "The only reason I forgave you is because I don't have some hideous maid-of-honor dress embarrassing all the other clothes in my closet."

"I'll admit, it was a passionate decision," Rachel said confidently.

"It was an impulse buy," Beth shot back. "Like when I got my Sub-Zero refrigerator and had to lose the broom closet because the damn thing was too wide."

"I don't get it. When you met Phil, you said you liked him."

"There was a time I liked parachute pants. Times change. And so did Phil. He stopped making you happy."

Beth was more on point than Rachel wanted her to be. She saw through Phil's charm and bullshit when others believed he could coax the wind to blow from one direction to another.

"Bethie, can you please do me a favor and get over it already? So Phil happens to be great-looking and majestically endowed, which, in fact, I only told you about after a vat of margaritas." Rachel cleared her throat and continued. "And his pedigree is flawless. His mother was a CEO for Bell Telephone, and his father was a poet laureate." She paused at how effortlessly the defense tumbled from her lips, then she glanced at the clock. "I have to stay in this position for another few minutes, but if I were a contortionist, I would hang up on you."

"Why? I'm not telling you what to do," Beth argued. "I think it's great that Phil has stellar genes, but parents only tell half a story."

"I have to go, Beth."

Rachel heard Phil laughing again as he turned off the shower. The imaginary mistress she'd given him seemed to be working overtime.

"You just haven't seemed like my Rachel in a while. And not just because you haven't gotten pregnant. You seem distant and distracted."

Rachel pondered her sister's claim and realized it had validity. It was hard to be open when she feared the kind of criticism and judgment Beth was dishing out. Maybe that was why Phil was so vacant. Rachel was subconsciously judging his commitment to their marriage, criticizing his work schedule, and being indifferent to his priorities. Under those circumstances, if he wanted to be upset with her, he had every right to be.

"I'm speaking to you from a compromised position, trying to keep the sperm at this party long enough to nail the hostess. Believe me. It's all-consuming."

"Fine. I'll keep my mouth shut."

"Ha, I'll take 'promises that can't be kept' for two hundred." Rachel giggled.

"Well, I'll do my best. Anyway, have fun. I'll take care of the Muppet collection. Hayli is in, so she can open and close. Oh, by the way, the superhero costumes came in right after you left. I know it's coming up on Memorial Day, but it turns out you can never stock up too early for Halloween. We got the last of these Spidermans, and they're super cute."

"I'm hoping we did the right thing. I mean, we've been strictly vintage, and I don't want to become just another toy store."

"Stop worrying so much, or I'm going to start calling you Mom. It's a lure. We get customers in the shop, and they'll buy for the holidays. It's good business."

"I guess you're right." Rachel propped her legs a little higher. "You want to meet for coffee or something later?"

"Can't, sorry. Evan's working. I have to drop Jeter off at the groomer. He humped the crap out of Courtney's stuffed panda, and now he has fuzzies caught all around his balls. I had to throw the friggin' thing out, and Courtney ripped me a new one. I promised to take her shopping. Hopefully, she'll choose a less attractive stuffie this time."

"Sounds like you're booked. I'll call you later." Before she could hang up, Rachel heard Beth yelling at Courtney to stop smearing cupcake frosting all over Joshie's hair. Beth could be crass, but she was totally the earth mother type. It was understandable that Beth was attracted to Evan. He was exactly what a software sales guy would look like, cute in a sweet, boyish way. Much the opposite of Phil, who could thrust his masculinity inside her until she begged for breath. For all Beth's talk, she was pretty quiet about her sex life, and although she never seriously complained, Rachel often wondered if she had much to talk about.

Phil came out with a towel wrapped around his waist, his full head of dark hair glistening. He was stunning, and the more than ten years he had on her were unnoticeable. That face, chocolate eyes, straight nose, and full lips that lived in an almost smile, with a strong chin covered by just enough stubble to give him an edgy Calvin Klein underwear model look, was impossible to resist. He was pure sex, and though she could have him whenever she wanted him, she was troubled that lately, it was more about need than want.

Another nod to the clock informed Rachel it was time to get out of her upside-down seven. Her conversation with Beth had left her feeling confused and oddly self-conscious. Still in her flimsy cami, she was about to get up to put on her robe but opted to stay in bed. A fly crawling up and down Rachel's arm commanded her attention. It was all going to work out. She was just letting everything get to her. She would tell her gynecologist since it was probably hormonal.

"So, what are you up to today?" Phil dropped his towel.

One look at his perfect penis, and Rachel shook off her doubts to move back into the moment.

Phil sat on the edge of the bed, doused in the cologne that made her wriggle. She ran her hands through his thick hair and gave him a soft kiss on the cheek.

"I'm... shopping," she said, wondering if Phil realized she was still in the mood.

He leaned in and kissed her deeply. The tension in her body dissipated. Maybe he did want intimacy. She responded by stroking his bare chest and covering his neck with hungry kisses. She was ready to fling off the covers when he leaped up.

"Sorry, babe. Maybe later. Dr. Love has to go make the big bucks." Phil pointed to his watch before quickly throwing on his pants and a light cotton sweater. He was dressed faster than a high school boy caught with his girlfriend. Rachel saw her pained expression in the mirror.

After a quick peck on her forehead, he was out the door. *Good. Go,* Rachel thought to herself, angry that she had felt a moment of affection. And there she was—back in that vacuous space where nothing felt right or normal.

Rachel noticed a pair of Phil's pants on the closet floor that hadn't made it onto the pile for the cleaners. As she picked them up, a receipt fell out of a pocket and onto the carpet. It was from the Hilton Woodcliff Lake for a room registered to him smack in the middle of a workday.

Chapter Two

Rachel took the last long sip of her Virgin Bay Breeze. Gattanella's always made the best mocktails, and she was ready for another. The bad news was her crotch was still stinging from that stupid wax—she would thank Beth with a root canal gift basket she would find on Etsy—but not enough to sway her thoughts from that damn hotel receipt she found. It appeared different from the usual. This one was stamped with some kind of code and didn't indicate a dollar amount. It was probably a special business promotion. Rachel decided to dismiss it. Phil often had meetings at hotels. For those, he usually wore suits, not Dockers, but maybe he had back-to-back appointments, and one was more casual. There was a logical explanation, but she didn't need to hear it, and so she'd slipped it back into his pocket as if it had never seen the light of day. Now, she was obligated to forget about it and concentrate on anything else.

Though it was supposed to be their anniversary dinner, Rachel had been sitting at the table alone for so long that the waiter, Nicola—a tall, thin man of about forty—had taken pity on her and laid a "complimentary" cheese-and-cracker board next to her mocktail. After one more square of cheddar and two sizable grapes, it would be finished. Phil's text saying to meet him at eight sharp was proving to be as reliable as her ovulation-predictor kits. It was creeping up on nine, and after leaving several messages, she still couldn't reach him.

Rachel wondered if he'd been in an accident and immediately had a vision of Phil in a wheelchair, with a groin injury and a compromised sperm count. She shuddered at the thought. Then a flush came over her. A normal wife would've been worried about her husband being hurt, lying in a ditch off the side of the road. But that would require a marriage that didn't involve a receipt from a stay at a local hotel without her. Rachel blamed the rush from the sugary drinks but still asked Nicola for another.

After reviewing the crowded, dimly lit room, Rachel confirmed she was the only party of one. Wanting a diversion, she took out her phone and checked out the latest eyeliner hack on TikTok. When Nicola returned with her drink, she kept him there.

"Do you have fresh *tagliatelle*?" Rachel asked, trying to sound authentic.

"*Ah, bella, non lo so. Controllero,*" Nicola answered in a very thick Italian accent.

Rachel shrugged, certain she had gone down a path from which there would be no return. "I'm sorry, I don't really speak Italian."

"Oh, my mistake," Nicola apologized. "You speak natural. It's good. What I said was, 'Beautiful woman, I don't know. I will check.' I know we have some pasta specials, but tonight, everyone is hungry like bears."

Rachel giggled like a flirty teenager. "Where do you come from?"

"Down the block," Nicola answered earnestly. "I can walk here, and my wife can use the car." Nicola looked at Rachel's hand. "You're married, too, heh? Where's your husband?"

"I've been asking myself the same question for almost an hour," Rachel replied.

"He'll be here soon, bella," Nicola said. "A man in love never makes the mistake of leaving a beautiful woman alone for too long." Another waiter near the kitchen caught Nicola's attention, and he excused himself.

Rachel shifted uncomfortably in her seat. Though it was reassuring that Nicola didn't seem to think she was a loser, the new thong she'd bought seemed to have decided she was and continued to mercilessly ride up her butt. Though she gave herself props for buying something fun for the evening, Beth was right, lace after a Brazilian wasn't a good idea. Though less like dental floss than most of the others she'd considered, the damn thong was still making her irritable.

She shifted in her seat a few times and decided she would toss it and go commando. Rachel was grateful the ladies' room was only a few steps away from her table and even more grateful she had the room to herself. She was in no mood to swap war stories about period cramps, bladder leakage, or cosmetic procedures gone horribly wrong. She was up for a conversation about inconsiderate husbands, but she wasn't likely to find one.

A few tugs later, Rachel managed to fix the thong and emerged from her stall a new woman. She was feeling more confident, but a quick glance at her face in the mirror advised a fresh stroke of Passion Pink blush was in order. Then a quick whiff of her underarms suggested a spritz or two of Tahitian Vanilla. She was approaching the door to exit when an enormous walking womb of a woman entered and nearly knocked her over.

"Rachel! Rachel Schein! I thought that was you in there sitting alone with a drink!" It was Macy Daniels, who still chortled exactly like the impudent schoolgirl Rachel had met on the debate team decades earlier. The girl was so full of herself she'd handed out nightshirts with her face emblazoned on them as her sweet sixteen party favors. Rachel heard the guys got jockstraps with the same image.

"Sutton," Rachel offered without batting an eye.

"What's a Sutton?" Macy asked, confused.

"My name now," Rachel explained. "I'm sure you've met Phil. Tall, cut, full head of hair, gorgeous." Rachel chuckled to herself, knowing that Macy's Freddy had lost his hair and, quite evidently, his will to exercise.

"Oh, maybe I have," Macy responded, sounding disappointed. "I heard you were divorced."

"Well, I'm happy to report all is deliciously hot as hell under the Sutton roof."

"Yes, well, one can never be too sure these days. Men are such dogs. Except for my Freddy. He's as loyal as a basset hound."

So a dog himself then. Rachel controlled another giggle. Macy was still a pompous idiot.

"I'm sure that's a comfort to you," Rachel offered.

"Oh, it's not a comfort. It's a fact, Rachel," Macy said, staring her down.

"I'm glad you're happy, Macy."

"My husband and I have always been happy. Always. We live in Camelot Elms. You know, the two-acre custom estates in New City." Macy paused. Rachel assumed it was to give Rachel the chance to soak in Macy's success and charmed life. "You know, by our old high school."

"Yes, lovely area. We're not far from you." Rachel turned to the mirror, knowing full well Macy was not done. It was a simple case of insecurity. And, in all fairness, that wasn't totally unfounded. Macy's then-boyfriend, now-husband, Freddy, had made it clear to Rachel, while he was seeing Macy, that he wanted her. While Macy was in Utah skiing with her family, he'd offered Rachel "the best sex of her life." Still a virgin, Rachel had been sure being with Freddy was not the way she wanted to be indoctrinated and had turned him down. She'd never said a word, but Macy had found out and freaked.

The betrayal had sent Macy over the edge and straight into therapy. She took a leave of absence from school and made it her life's mission to punish Rachel whenever the opportunity arose. No matter how many lunches Rachel spent trying to reassure Macy that nothing had happened between her and Freddy, Macy remained reluctant to be anything but Rachel's nemesis. And here was dear Macy, standing before her, as pregnant as Rachel wished she could be.

"Twins. We're calling them three and four until we decide on names." Macy snorted. "What can I say? Freddy just can't keep his hands off me, and I'm a fertile Myrtle. I can get pregnant if he waves to me from across the room."

"Oh." Rachel smiled. "You're pregnant? I didn't realize." Rachel flew out of the bathroom before Macy had the chance to utter a single word.

Rachel returned to the table to find a fresh bread basket and a new bottle of garlic-flavored olive oil. She caught Nicola's attention and ordered a tray of giardiniera, hoping the brine would quell the bad taste left in her mouth.

The room was a lot less crowded than it had been when she'd first arrived. A group of several couples from the other side of the room rose to leave, and she caught a glimpse of Macy, donning a cocoa-colored Pashmina shawl, lumbering toward the exit. The thought of another stream of bullets spewing out of Macy's mouth was making Rachel's left eye twitch, and she quickly took cover. In seconds, her head was buried in the *frutti di mare* section of the menu.

Relief was in sight as Rachel watched Macy blow a half-hearted kiss in the air to some woman in a tight leather jacket before walking out the door. *Maybe it's time for me to leave too.* Any more mocktails, and she would start pooping maraschino cherries. She was just about to ask for the check when she saw Phil making a beeline for the table.

"I swear, it wasn't me," Phil said, holding his hand in the air. "Please don't give me a hard time. I had no choice. Akinowa didn't call until late, and I had no way of getting out of the conference. As soon as it ended, I hopped in the car."

Rachel had a quick flash of him in bed with a Victoria's Secret model and struggled to keep herself from throwing the last of her drink in his face. A reminder of his good genes and her present mantra, "You're ovulating," kept her in check. In truth, it didn't pay to admonish him anyway. Phil, believing he could do no wrong, was not a fan of the words "I'm sorry." There was always an excuse for any indiscretion, and since nothing was ever his fault, it always somehow managed to be hers.

"Honestly, Rachel, if you weren't so stuck on Tony's puttanesca, I would have been happy with curry chicken and a movie at home," Phil said, right on cue. He sat down and adjusted his tie, took a breadstick, and slathered a glob of herb butter all around its sesame frame. "What's with you?" Phil scowled. "You haven't said a word."

"Happy anniversary," Rachel said stoically.

"Yeah, I know," Phil said, softening. "I didn't forget. It's just that business is in high gear right now." He gave her hand a squeeze and searched her eyes until she saw him catch his reflection. "I promise I'll make it up to you... later."

Rachel picked up a breadstick and brushed it provocatively against her lips. She knew exactly what Phil meant. Maybe an odd period of sexual pragmatism, with Phil's work schedule on overload and her basal thermometer dictating when they should be in the mood, was what they needed to stay connected.

"I'm counting on it," Rachel replied, ready to be bought.

Phil called Nicola over and asked him to bring out a jar of Beluga from their private stock. Nicola grinned like a Cheshire cat, and Rachel assumed he was already beginning to compute his tip. Before he walked away, he gave Rachel a grateful nod, probably happy there actually was a husband and he hadn't given the freebies away in vain. She turned her focus back to Phil, who was torn between lobster fra diavolo and osso buco.

"You should get the lobster," Phil decided. "This way, we can share."

"Have it all worked out, huh?" Rachel said. "But I want the puttanesca."

"You get that all the time." Phil shook his head. "Just order the lobster."

Nicola brought over the caviar and was about to leave when Phil said they were ready. Rachel was so stuffed from the appetizers that when Phil said, "Lobster for the lady," she simply handed Nicola her menu. With a quick nod, he was gone.

Phil cocked his head and grinned at her like an impish four-year-old. He lifted his drink and motioned for Rachel to do the same.

"A toast to my lovely wife. Thank you, Rach, for these past few wonderful years. I just want to say—damn!"

Phil's cell phone was ringing "Shining Star," and he immediately dug into his pocket to retrieve it. He checked the number, and his eyes widened. A lion having just spotted its prey, he motioned to Rachel that he had to take the call and sprinted to the alcove in the front of the restaurant, away from the small but steady stream of dinner conversations.

Nicola looked at her with sympathy as he put a heaping plate of mussels on the table next to hers. Rachel shrugged at him and took a sip of water. Phil was so engrossed in his call, Rachel wondered if he would remember she was there when he was done. She took out her cell phone and started playing Wordle with Friends.

After more rounds than she cared to count, Phil was back.

"So, where was I?" Phil asked.

"You were saying, 'I just want to say.'"

"Right. Right," Phil said, holding up his glass. "Rach, I think you know me better than I know myself."

"Not really." Rachel sighed involuntarily.

"No—really, you do," Phil insisted as he put his glass back down on the table. "You probably already know I had no clue what to buy you this year."

"I thought you said you didn't want to exchange gifts." Rachel shifted in her seat. "We're going to Paris next month instead, remember?"

"We always say we won't exchange gifts, but we always do," Phil said. "You have something for me, don't you?"

"Well, yes," Rachel said, pulling a small gift bag and a card out of her large pocketbook and placing them on the table. "But it's not a big deal."

"I knew it! You're so predictable. I always know what to expect." Phil eyed the gift but didn't pick it up.

"I'm thrilled. I sound like your Car-Vac."

"Well, you do suck," Phil teased.

Rachel rolled her eyes and snatched an olive from her plate.

There was a sudden silence that seemed to indicate Phil hadn't gotten the laugh he'd expected. Unwavering, he quickly added, "But in a good way. The best way. And even though a Car-Vac is a good thing, you're a lot prettier."

"Whew, what a relief." Rachel let out a deep sigh.

"Rach, you're getting this all wrong. I wanted to get you a real gift, but I don't know *you* like you know *me*. It's a guy thing."

Phil handed her a small bag. She took a peek inside and saw a Visa gift card. She took a moment to contemplate her disappointment then continued.

"Thank you, Phil, but you know me well enough to know I don't care about presents. I just want us to finally spend some quality time together. We are still going to Paris, right?"

"Rach—"

"Aah! I should have known." Rachel was fuming and folded her arms across her chest. "You know who's predictable, Phil? You are. Why would I even think that a second honeymoon was important to you?"

"It is, and we will go. Just not yet. I have to deal with the Franklin merger first. I'm the guy, Rach. There's no clone, and no one else can handle a deal like this."

"So, when? When do I get *my* time?"

"I don't know. But soon. Why don't we go home and make that baby you keep talking about?"

The baby *she* kept talking about. Phil's truth was staring her in the face, but so was her fear of being childless. *Tick, tick, tick…* If she didn't play her cards right, she would end up with a house full of perfect furniture, limited simple carbs, and deafening silence.

Rachel turned to Phil. "Sounds wonderful. I guess we can always name the baby Paris."

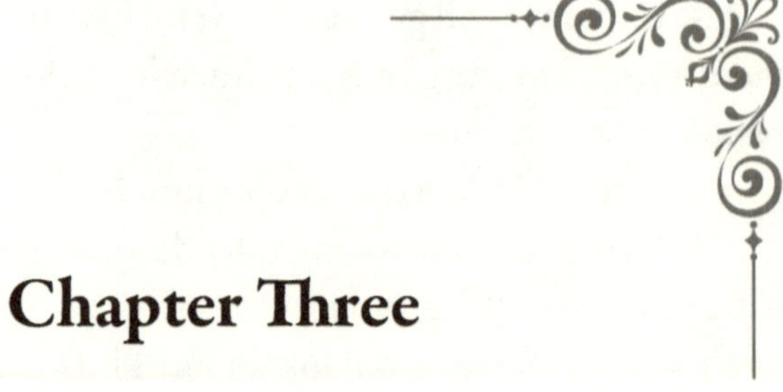

Chapter Three

Rachel sat anxiously in the bland gray seat planted in front of Dr. Rose's clean-but-cluttered desk, kicking her foot against the wooden leg closest to her. She'd missed her period, and a positive home test had her cautiously over the moon. All she wanted was confirmation and a due date, but the doctor was taking forever, leaving her with nothing to do but stare at the gallery of photos from his daughter's beach wedding. She took out her cell phone and started playing Boggle. Much to her chagrin, she realized that just because she could make the word *infant*, it wasn't a definitive sign that she was having one.

Finally, the door flung open. Rachel could feel her heart pounding against her blue shirt. Dr. Rose, a short, handsome senior with a displaced, unruly mustache, sailed in and gave her a look she couldn't read as he took his seat.

"Rachel," Dr. Rose said in a tone that made her feel like she'd been stabbed, "I'm sorry, dear. The test is negative. You're not pregnant."

"But that's impossible," Rachel cried. "I'm telling you, impossible. The home test said I was. Clearly. There was a smiley face."

He checked her chart again. "You were taking Valium for a pinched nerve?"

"Yes, but so what?"

"It's rare, but sometimes that drug can result in a false positive," Dr. Rose explained.

"Are you kidding?" Rachel grabbed a tissue from her purse and dabbed at her teary eyes.

"Wish I was." He went into a cabinet and pulled out a container. "Here. Take these. They're organic vitamins."

Rachel put the bottle in her pocketbook.

"I have a load of samples. They're completely natural, and they'll help level out your hormones."

"Will they help me get pregnant?"

"Maybe, indirectly. Rachel, I know you've been trying to conceive for at least several months—"

"Longer than that," she interrupted.

"I'll be frank. You're over forty. The chances of conceiving on your own get slimmer as you get older. You might want to consider your options. I can recommend a specialist."

A specialist. She had suggested that to Phil months ago. For someone who only cried out to the Lord while in the throes of passion, he'd been a man of faith during that conversation. According to Phil, having children was God's will, and any assistance would be tampering with nature.

"I'll discuss it with my husband."

"Good. Call and let me know if I can help."

"I will, thank you," Rachel said, closing the door as she left.

Tears ran down Rachel's face as she headed for the car. Brakes squealed.

"Hey! Watch where you're going!"

The Jeep only inches away made her jump. She stopped at the man's window. "I'm so sorry."

At the sight of her doleful eyes, he simply patted her arm and took off. Rachel wondered if Phil would offer a fraction of that kindness when he got home from work. Who was she kidding? Phil ran hot and cold, but he had too great a need to protect his heart to fully give it to anyone.

She drove home on autopilot, mindful of nothing but her biological clock. She wasn't ready to go inside and sat in her driveway to make a call. "Beth?"

"Rachel, you just called *me*. Who else would it be?"

"Please don't kid around right now."

"Sorry. I'm having sinus trouble." Beth let out a long sneeze. "So? Tell me! When are you due?"

"I'm not." Rachel's voice trembled as she struggled not to cry. "Rose said the little smiley face was there because I've had a happy little reaction to the Valium I took for my back."

"Aww, Rach, I'm so, so sorry. That really blows."

"It sure does."

"Want me to come over with a quart of chocolate brownie chunk?"

"No, I'm fine, just disappointed." Rachel clicked the remote for the garage and saw Phil's car. "I'll call you later. Phil's home."

"So early? Maybe there's a psycho in your house, holding him hostage."

"Goodbye, Bethie."

"And if the psycho happens to be cute..."

"Goodbye, Bethie."

Rachel slung her bag over her shoulder and, with Beth's mention of a psycho, was spooked enough to go through the back door with mild trepidation. "Phil?" she called into the hallway.

There was no answer. She headed back to the kitchen, poured herself a large glass of iced tea, and popped a vitamin into her mouth.

Before she swallowed, Phil danced into the room, singing "Night Fever." Sweating in his preppy jogging suit, he didn't look much like Travolta, but the deep dimples helped. "This was such a great present, babe," he shouted over the music. "I love them." AirPods still in his ears, Phil came up behind Rachel and began kissing her neck.

Without even realizing it, she flinched.

Phil turned off the music. "What's wrong with *you*?" he asked as he took a bottle of water out of the fridge.

"Nothing. It's no big deal. I'm just not pregnant."

"Sorry, babe. I know you're disappointed, but look at it this way—we get to keep trying. We're having fun. That's a good thing."

Rachel couldn't get a clear read on what Phil was feeling. At times, he was totally into the idea of having sex, yet other times, he dismissed her like a boring series on Hulu.

"Phil, I'm getting too old for this. I'm afraid it's never going to happen. And Dr. Rose isn't so sure it will either."

"It will, when it's supposed to, and don't call my old lady old."

Rachel decided to leave the conversation about a specialist for another time, preferably after a few drinks, when Phil was feeling relaxed and agreeable.

"What are you doing home anyway?" Rachel asked, taking out a container of roasted almonds.

"Now you're complaining that I'm home?"

"No, of course not. I just didn't expect you to be."

"Franklin left for the Philippines, so I have some downtime while he's en route. Wanna grab a bite and catch a movie?"

"Sure."

As if Alexa were eavesdropping, Phil's cell phone rang the moment they made a date. He greeted the caller with his usual charm and mouthed to Rachel that he could be a while.

That night, Rachel tossed and turned for hours, drifting from one exhausting dream into the next. First, she was being pursued by a herd of cattle then a bubbling cauldron of snakes. She managed to escape into the arms of an ancient sheik who claimed he had a magic penis and could get her pregnant, but only if she would agree to be his wife and change his diapers. By the time Rachel woke up, Phil had already gone to work, leaving nothing but an unflushed toilet and his receipt from an oil change.

Rachel quickly threw on a pair of jeans and the black sweater Beth had said made her look like a twig. When all else failed, she was grateful to have the shop to keep her occupied. Golden's Toy Palace had become her sanctuary, the place her grandparents had made safe with their expansive stock of vintage dolls, games, and novelties from a time when, as they'd put it, "life was simpler and people didn't need the *chazerai*, trash, of the modern world to keep them entertained."

By the time her grandparents retired, the shop, located in Nyack near the New York State Thruway, had become a gem in the Tristate area. Rachel's mother, Sandy, an artsy divorcee with a penchant for Mediterranean men, took charge. Preferring to run the administrative end from her villa in Greece, Sandy asked Rachel and Beth, both of whom had grown up in the business, to physically manage the shop. Rachel was hesitant, but Beth insisted it would be a blast. "What could be more fun than stocking every Scrabble game known to man or choosing which Barbies to place next to which Kens? That's power. And think of all their clothes and accessories."

Beth had Rachel at Barbies, her childhood obsession.

For Rachel, the shop offered security, not just financially but also emotionally. The nostalgic atmosphere was like a hug. Naturally, she pushed back when Beth wanted to modernize. Change meant losing the one familiar vestige of safety she could always rely on. It was something Beth, being younger and happier, couldn't understand.

Rachel felt a little chill as she thought about the past and went to the closet near the front door. Carefully housed on the top shelf was a brown chenille scarf that had been her grandmother's. She wrapped it around her neck and immediately felt protected against whatever demons the day had to offer.

As Rachel headed to work, the Thruway was clear, and even the Palisades Center parking lot looked empty. Rachel toyed with the idea of stopping to surprise Phil at his office with a quick hello kiss. It would be a daring move, and she didn't dismiss the idea that she might be the one sadly surprised. Phil had said early on work was hands-off, much like *his* car and *his* computer. "Why would a woman sabotage her husband's efforts by breathing down his neck?" he'd said after hearing a couple bicker at a company function. Rachel typically honored his wish to keep their personal life away from the office, not wanting to be one of *those* wives Phil spoke of with such enmity—especially since, bottom line, he was doing it all for them.

At least that was exactly what he'd promised her on their first anniversary, the day he'd started working for Jebbling Enterprises. It was, Phil had explained over Korbel and filet mignon, an opportunity of a lifetime to work for a company that could boast more takeovers in a year than most could in ten.

As Rachel strained to understand Phil's executive lingo over a series of puzzled shrugs, he finally explained that Jebbling did the same kind of thing Richard Gere's company did in *Pretty Woman*. With that, they clinked glasses and agreed to never again bother with pesky details.

As Rachel sighed at the thought of Phil being underwhelmed by her visit, an older man, with a scruffy beard, in a white Lexus honked furiously as she meandered carelessly into his lane. She swerved back quickly, mouthing an apology, but the guy replied with a bellowing "Fuck you, lady!" before speeding away. Rachel turned on the radio, hoping she might drown out her thoughts before causing any serious damage. The shop was only a few lights and a couple of songs away.

Annoying ads interrupted the music, but the one for couples counseling caught Rachel's attention. She fumbled with her phone to jot down the number of the therapist but got an incoming call instead. It was her mom, telling her that a new cleaning crew, Charlene's Angels, would be coming, so she and Beth could close the shop a little earlier. The call ended amid a flurry of phone kisses while a quick glance at the clock informed her it was too late to visit Phil even if she wanted to. Relieved the decision was made for her, Rachel headed to work.

It was still early, and the parking lot, once a massive front lawn, was predictably empty. Despite the gray clouds, Rachel marveled at how Golden's Palace always looked cheery. A large, two-story converted house that shared a driveway with a pool and garden center located in an adjacent building, Golden's was a successful blend of modern and classic architecture. The beige bricks played well off the white columns, achieving the eponymous regal effect her grandparents had desired. In recent years, during the holidays, the shop would partner with their neighbor to create the kind of display that often garnered media attention. It was expensive, but her mom felt drawing a crowd was money well spent.

When Rachel entered the shop, she took a sweeping look around as if she were seeing its magic for the first time. For instance, she remembered playing dominoes with her grandfather in the room off the stock area, enjoying the smell of the cherry cough drops he let melt in his mouth one at a time. Rachel couldn't help but feel like that same little girl, hoping those precious memories could last for more than a fleeting moment.

Getting her head back to business, Rachel decided to review the merchandise that had come in before she'd left. She was thrilled to find that the wooden shelves around the perimeter of the lower level had already been stocked with the new shipment of board games initially expected at the end of the week. There were several rows of Monopoly from six different decades, and Scrabble, in classic and special versions. Life, Mystery Date, Careers, and Trouble in the sixties and seventies editions were stacked near a collection of first board games, Candyland and Chutes and Ladders. It was so tastefully organized, Rachel did a little jig to celebrate. As she checked further, she was delighted to find an enormous collection of classic and career Barbie dolls. Rachel thought Beth had said Bratz dolls, but these were far more impressive.

The tweeting of the vintage cuckoo for Cocoa Puffs clock hanging on the wall grabbed Rachel's attention at the same time Beth wandered in from the stock area in the back. She handed Rachel a stack of papers. "We have a new shipment of Beanie Babies from Provence coming next week."

Before even realizing it, Rachel let a few tears loose.

"What the hell did I say?" Beth asked, pointing at Rachel's watery eyes.

"Provence. Made me think of Paris." She wiped away her tears. "We're not going."

"What? Why not?"

"Work, of course. There's a new client, and Phil is the only one this guy will deal with. It's not that I don't understand, but it's always work."

"Rach, why are you letting him do this?"

Beth began to scan the solid wood tables arranged throughout the center of the floor, putting check marks next to the *Alvin and the Chipmunks* puppets, the Colorforms, the Etch A Sketches, and several other items on the list Rachel couldn't make out as she followed along.

"Where's Hayli?" Rachel asked, trying to get Beth to talk about anything else.

"Class. But she came in early." Beth was climbing up a small stepladder. "I gave her the rest of the day off." She moved a few cartons and turned to look at Rachel. "So how did Phil take the no-baby news?"

"There was news?" Rachel asked facetiously. "No, for him, there was no news. He was fine about it. Now we 'get to' keep trying."

"Well, if nothing else—and I do mean nothing else—he is being practical," Beth said. "If I were you, I'd just lay back and enjoy it."

"You're incorrigible," Rachel argued. "Stop making me sorry I tell you everything."

"Geez!" Beth sounded offended. "My point is, when he's around, you'll have more sex. And since you like sex, I don't see a big problem here."

"But it's not just about sex. Every day that goes by is another day that makes me feel like…" She paused, trailing off as the phone rang, and Beth started down the ladder. "A barren woman," Rachel whispered.

"That's got to be the new manufacturer," Beth said, reaching for the phone. "Luckily, they're in Bern, hours from Provence, so buck up, kiddo, and no more tears."

Before Rachel could supply a comeback, a stocky woman in a denim jacket and skinny jeans entered the shop, pushing a stroller with a baby in the seat. Rachel quickly studied her face and surmised that her youthful appearance belied her age.

"Hi. And what can I do for you and this little angel?" Rachel spoke cautiously, unsure of the relationship between the two.

"I'm looking for a very specific doll," the woman explained, retrieving a piece of paper from her pocket.

"You've definitely come to the right place." Rachel was letting the exchange lift her mood. "We have many."

"This one has some kind of certificate—of authenticity. My sister is an avid collector and sent me here to look for it." The woman tried to shush the child, who was starting to fuss.

"Let me," Rachel said, handing the little girl a monkey-shaped rattle to play with.

"Thank you," the woman replied as she handed Rachel the slip of paper. "Your children are lucky. You're so patient."

Rachel winced a bit at the woman's assumption but didn't correct her.

"It's a Tiny Tears doll," the woman said, "with platinum hair."

"Your sister has very expensive taste," Rachel teased. "It's part of a rare collection, but we do have her."

"Terrific!" the woman exclaimed. "Fortunately, my sister can afford to have expensive taste, and she has searched absolutely everywhere with no luck."

"Just give me a minute, and I'll get her for you," Rachel said, heading to the stock area.

Beth was on her way out when Rachel met her in the middle and told her about the doll. Beth said she knew exactly where to find it and told Rachel to go back to the front register to complete the sale.

"My sister's in back, getting the doll," Rachel explained, bending down to play with the baby. "She is just beautiful!"

"Thank you. Nessa—that's her name—is my miracle," the woman said in a hushed voice. "I'm fifty-five, and she's the only child I ever delivered."

Rachel's eyes widened as if her own dreams had been validated. "Well, I think that's wonderful!"

She was completing the sale and insisting the baby keep the rattle when Beth came back. After a brief discussion about the joys of motherhood, Rachel carefully wrapped up the doll, and the woman left.

"You friggin' sold the platinum Tiny Tears!" Beth applauded. "Madonna wanted that doll in the eighties, remember?"

Rachel had some recollection of her mother saying they had spoken but that Madonna had opted to buy Eleanor Roosevelt's Raggedy Ann from a competitor instead.

"It's pretty unbelievable." Rachel shook her head.

"I know. Eight thousand dollars! How are you going to celebrate?" Beth asked, going back to examining the shelves.

"Truly unbelievable," Rachel whispered as if she were revealing government secrets. "That woman is fifty-five, and the baby is hers. Biologically hers."

"I thought the kid looked kinda like Adam Sandler."

"You're nuts. She was adorable."

"So is Adam!" Beth argued. "Anyway, I guess it can happen. Janet Jackson had her first at fifty, and Brigitte Nielsen had a daughter at fifty-four." Beth flicked her fingers under her chin. "Take that, Rambo."

"Encouraging. Bethie, according to my predictor test, I'm in the ovulating zone. I started taking the supplements the doctor gave me, so maybe I'll get lucky. I'm out of here. Time to go home to have practical, let's-conceive-already sex."

"Have fun," Beth said. "I'll see you in the moaning. Um, I mean morning."

Chapter Four

Phil wasn't going to be home for a while, and Rachel decided to use the time to relax and get in the mood. She lit a few lavender-scented candles and lined them up along the perimeter of the Jacuzzi. She clicked on Pandora and found her favorite jazz station. There was certainly nothing wrong with trying to be in the mood. She even considered checking out one of the many "toys" Phil used to buy her from his countless trips out of town.

It was fun remembering the way he would call her in the middle of the night just to be a tease, describing what he would do to her with the toy he'd bought in Bangkok or the sensual oils he'd found in Detroit. In the early days of their relationship, he always knew how to turn her on, and he'd seemed dedicated to pleasing her in ways no man had ever tried. She decided to nix the artificial assistance. Maybe if she focused on the way they used to make love, she could be ready when he stepped in the door.

What nagged at her was the fact that things were not the way they'd been before Rachel had announced she wanted a baby. Phil couldn't even do it that first night, and that had never happened before. He'd made a joke of it, saying that as long as the stock market kept it up, he didn't have to, but it made her wonder if something about her request was keeping him down.

After that, she'd felt their sex life cool. It wasn't that Phil had stopped being into her, but the toys and the kinky conversations had begun to wane. Sometimes, she got the distinct impression that their intimacy was in jeopardy and that down the line, she, too, could be uttering the same frustrated lament as every unfulfilled soccer mom doomed to cliché. Maybe sex wasn't the strongest basis for a healthy relationship, but for her and Phil, it had been one of the most compelling.

The tub was ready, and Rachel let the warm, sudsy water swirl away her doubts. Of course Phil wanted a family. He was getting older. He would be too vain to have people think he was their baby's grandfather, even though it would be a plausible assumption. The smartest thing she could do was to leave the baby discussion out of the bedroom. Maybe then, things would fall into place more naturally. She also had to let Phil get used to the idea of fatherhood.

Relaxed and ready, Rachel went into her dresser drawer and pulled out a lacy red negligee. A few sprays of Prada here, there, and everywhere. She was ready for a night of details that would shut her sister up about the merits of "a nice, good boy like Evan." Rachel envisioned him in Fruit-of-the-Loom boxers, crying, "May I?" before letting himself touch his wife. She didn't have anything against Evan, but lately, Beth's insistence that she had the all-around ideal husband was driving Rachel crazy. It was like Beth and Macy Daniels lived to compare notes.

Rachel heard the garage door open and quickly jumped onto their king-size bed. She posed herself provocatively, propped on one arm. Her pulse quickened as Phil's steps drew closer. She wondered if she'd left the room too dark and sighed for not bringing the candle in from the bathroom.

"Rach?" Phil asked from the doorway.

"I should hope so," Rachel teased.

"What are you doing?"

"Waiting for you to make love to me."

"I just got home." He turned up the dimmed light.

"I know." Rachel, undaunted, continued. "I've been wanting you all day." She was sure not to say a word about the older mother she had spoken with at the store.

Phil shook his head and disappeared into his closet.

Rachel wasn't sure how to respond. She kneeled on the bed, checked the mirror, and adjusted her nightie. Maybe she was being too eager. She sat up in bed, opting to look more casual than alluring.

When Phil emerged, he was wearing a jogging suit. "I'm going to go for a run."

"Really? Now?" Rachel wondered if she looked dumbfounded.

"I prefer daylight so the schmucks in their Vettes don't run me over."

"I understand. I just wanted to—"

"What? What do you want from me?"

Rachel took a deep breath, trying to let the sting of humiliation pass. Phil had an uncanny way of making her feel small and undesirable. She was always told she was smart, attractive, and witty and that she made incomparable chicken soup. That he didn't understand or appreciate her was puzzling. But despite the knot in her stomach, Rachel needed this moment to go her way.

"Come. Sit here." She patted the empty space on the bed next to her. "Tell me about your day."

"Oh, if only you cared."

"Of course I do. I'm your wife."

"Yes, yes you are." Phil sat down next to Rachel. "If you want to know, my day was shit. I work like a fucking dog, and it never matters. Jeb wants what he wants, and I give it to him, hoping it will eventually pay off."

"I know how hard you work." Rachel wanted to add that she wished he worked half as hard on their marriage, but she refrained. Instead, she planted soft kisses on Phil's ears and neck then proceeded to undress him. He wriggled a bit as she slid him out of his jacket then his T-shirt. "You're the best, Phil. Everyone in the company knows it." Rachel rubbed his shoulders, all the while whispering sweet, manipulative nothings in his ear.

Finally, he let out a small moan and passionately pushed her down on the bed.

"I want you!" she cried.

"Do you, baby?" he asked.

She was caught off guard when Phil suddenly got up.

"What are you doing?" Rachel asked.

"Taking my time," Phil answered, walking out of the room.

Rachel tried to remain calm, all the while wondering if her hopeful preparations had been a wasted effort. She was about to get dressed and call it a night when Phil walked in with a small tray. From what she could see, there were two glasses and a bottle of wine. Then she saw a fat line of cocaine.

"What the—?" Rachel exclaimed. "I thought you quit!"

"Calm down. I did." Phil patted her shoulder. "This is nothing. Just a little tension reliever." He put the tray on his nightstand. "Want some? *You* could use it."

"No, Phil, I don't want any." Rachel resisted her urge to cry. "Never have and never will. You know that."

"Suit yourself." Phil poured them each a glass of wine.

He picked up his pants from the floor, dug into one of the pockets, and pulled out a fifty. With expert precision, he rolled the bill into a thin tube, bent over the tray, and quickly inhaled the line.

Rachel was about to get up, but Phil grabbed her and drew her into him. She struggled to get out of his hold until she saw tears in his eyes.

"Rach, do you have any idea how much I love you? You're my world." He wiped his wet face. "You're my whole world, Rachel, my everything. I know you'd never leave me. Please don't ever leave me."

He brushed his lips against her mouth then eased her onto the bed. He began caressing her with his tongue from head to toe, repeating his devotion with each kiss. She could feel her body yielding to his words as much as to his touch. He entered her with unfamiliar, quick rhythmic motions that made her wonder if he'd been watching internet porn during his downtime. Rachel had just climaxed when Phil rolled off her onto his side of the bed. She was too stunned to remember to keep her legs in the air.

"Wow," Phil said, "that felt like our honeymoon. I'll have to remember what I did." Phil turned and kissed Rachel on the forehead.

"You did coke" was what she wanted to say, but what came out was "You stayed in bed and didn't jump up to go to the office."

"Actually, I do have a file to look over for tomorrow. You don't mind, do you?" Phil got up and started to get dressed.

"Would it matter if I did?" Rachel replied, finally shooting her legs upward.

"Yeah, it would make me feel bad. I know you like all the cuddling stuff to linger in the moment."

Rachel could feel the tension building in her body. Phil's comment made her feel like a clearance item in a sales bin. Maybe she did want too much from him. She knew he didn't have the capacity to share his emotions with the same energy he used to share his penis.

"Oh, that nonsense. Nah, don't worry." Rachel blinked hard to force away a tear. "Go do your thing."

"Hey, I'm not an idiot. You got what you wanted."

Though Rachel knew he wasn't totally wrong, she still hoped the connection she longed for wasn't completely out of reach. "Really? And what do you want, Phil?"

"I want you to be okay with me working for a little while."

Rachel forgot all about housing Phil's troops and leapt out of bed. She threw on a sweatshirt and didn't bother with a bra.

"Where are *you* going?" Phil asked.

"To the shop," Rachel snapped as she grabbed a pair of jeans.

"Why? It's late."

"It's not late for you—"

"Come on, Rach. It's different."

"Why?"

Phil walked over to her dresser, opened the bottom drawer, and pulled out a long, blue velvet box. "Remember this?" Phil asked, shaking the box like a maraca. "This is why."

Rachel nodded. It was an apology diamond necklace he'd given her after not making it home in time for the surprise fortieth birthday party Beth had planned for her. "Geneva is unpredictable," he'd explained when he'd given her the box. Despite its showstopping dazzle, Rachel associated the gift with disappointment and resentment. She didn't suffer a moment of compunction for hardly ever wearing it.

Phil tossed the box onto the bed, grazing Rachel's arm. Pissed more than hurt, she shoved the offending reminder back in her drawer.

"Am I supposed to be grateful because you work ridiculous hours?" Rachel tried to control the hurt in her voice.

"Yeah!" He shot back while zipping up his fly. "Because I speak to countries in different time zones. And because I make deals worth millions."

"You're right—I'm impressed." Rachel clapped. "But now, let me tell *you* something. Today, I sold a doll that cost almost eight thousand dollars. And you know what? I have paperwork. I have inventory. And I make people smile. I make Christmases and birthdays."

"I know, very important stuff. And me? I just make us the big bucks. So sue me, Mrs. Claus. I don't have time for this." Phil threw on his jacket in a huff, but he still took a few seconds to check himself out in the mirror above the dresser. "Don't bother waiting up!" He stormed out, muttering vague obscenities.

Rachel glanced at the clock. It was late and hardly worth the effort to go to the store. She went into the kitchen and grabbed a protein bar for dinner.

—⁙—

"So, when he went down on you, was it long and lingering, or was it just prep work?" Beth frantically munched on a breakfast biscuit while arranging a series of Dr. Seuss books on a wooden display rack at the front of the store.

"I just told you we had an awful fight," Rachel said, "and *this* is what you're asking me?" She sat Raggedy Ann and Andy on a miniature bench on a nearby table then eyed a big carton of Duncan yo-yos and Spalding balls that needed to be arranged in an adjacent bin.

"I know, I know," Beth replied. "And I will definitely get back to that, but can you please answer my question before we have to open?"

"I don't know, Bethie. Probably a little of both. Why?"

"Isn't it obvious? One way, it's for your benefit. The other way, it's for his."

"Bullshit, little sister," Rachel said. "A man that prepares you to receive him understands that getting you ready enhances the experience. Making love is for both of you, not just him."

"Right, straight out of old-school Dr. Ruth," Beth said. "Do you really believe Phil has the best intentions?"

"You're impossible!" Rachel shook her head. "Can this not be about how right you think *you* are? Can this just be about how upset *I* am?"

"Sorry," Beth said through a deep breath. "You know I'm always here for you. Honestly, I just wanted to hear about the sex. Lately, it feels like I either can't get enough or don't want it at all. I've been a hormonal mess since I weaned Courtney."

"That was almost two years ago."

"Things take time."

A knock on the window ended the conversation, sending Beth to the stock room and Rachel to the door.

"Anna!" Rachel greeted the striking middle-aged woman, who carried a soft red leather briefcase. "It's been such a while. How *are* you?"

"Fine, dear," Anna replied in a gentle British accent. "I'm launching a new magazine for doll collectors, *Simply Dolling*. We really must talk. In the meantime, I need a favor." Anna scanned the shop as if looking for something. "Can you find me that Betsy Wetsy in the gingham dress we spoke about last time? It's for a friend."

"Shouldn't be a problem. Let me check." Rachel consulted the computer at the front counter and frowned. "Sorry, I'll have to order her. I thought we had her in back, but it was her cousin."

"That's fine," Anna assured her. "I need it shipped to London anyway."

"London?" Rachel asked. "Is it for a friend back home?"

"She's not exactly a friend, per se, but I'd like her poor grandbaby to have something special. It's a complicated story," Anna said in almost a whisper.

Rachel moved her head closer to Anna, expecting to be entertained. Anna had a flair for drama, and Rachel imagined her latest tale would not disappoint. The mere thought of someone else having to deal with complicated issues made Rachel feel better. It wasn't that misery had a passion for company, but it did level the playing field.

Anna took a breath and licked her frosted, tawny lips. "This woman, who used to work for me, had a child recently with her"—Anna used air quotes— "lover." She continued, "He's a dreadful man."

Rachel took a sip of her lukewarm coffee. She hadn't the time to watch *General Hospital* last week, and Anna's story was promising to make up for it.

"Truly off his trolley," Anna said. "He refused to stay if the baby stayed. Well, she made her choice, and of all things, dropped the baby off straightaway on her mother's doorstep. Then she vanished. Connie, the baby's grandmother, is understandably heartbroken and snookered over it all. There's more, of course, but I can't be asked to tell it all right now."

"Snookered?" Rachel asked, not wanting to miss anything.

"Sorry, sometimes I forget I'm not home," Anna said. "Stuck. Connie feels like there's no way out of the situation. And from my view, she's right."

"That's awful." Rachel shook her head in disbelief. "Who could abandon a baby like that?"

"It's criminal. But desperate women make desperate choices."

"I'm desperate to have a baby, and it isn't happening," Rachel shared without thinking.

"I'm so sorry, dear." Anna offered a sympathetic nod and patted Rachel's hand. "That's criminal too. How is that handsome husband of yours?"

"Handsome," Rachel repeated. "That, he is. Though I haven't had the chance to look at him much lately. He's always working."

"If he's neglecting a stunning woman like you, he's a fool, and if he doesn't know it yet, he will one day."

"Thanks, Anna." Rachel finished the order on the computer. "The doll should be in next week."

"Lovely. Just give me a bell when she arrives. I'm sending Connie other things as well, so I'll pick her up myself." Anna clutched her briefcase and swiftly walked out the door.

Feeling surprisingly shaken by the story, Rachel decided to call and share it with Phil. She wasn't sure how he would react, but something in her needed to know. She was disappointed to get his voicemail. "Hi, I called to ask if you'd like me to get a pizza on my way home. Call me back. Or starve. Just kidding."

Chapter Five

Rachel was folding laundry and watching *The Surrogacy Trap*, a movie that reinforced her decision never to buy another woman's womb to house a child of her own. Rather than pick up a pizza, she had already made a vat of pasta primavera for dinner. It was a more seductive choice, a subtle way to show Phil that she was thinking of him. It was also a practical choice, since she counted on inviting Beth over for leftovers when Phil would be away on his next business trip. He had already been around for an entire week, so she knew he would be due for one soon.

Rachel was putting away Phil's underwear as the evil blue-eyed surrogate was trying to off the naïve biological mother by pushing her down a flight of stairs. There was, of course, a great commotion, and it was tough to figure out who was going to stab whom with the Williams-Sonoma butcher knife. Rachel's eyes were glued to the television as she closed the drawer, and the naïve mother was cornered against the wall.

Suddenly, an arm was enveloping Rachel at her waist. She let out a piercing scream and instinctively jabbed her elbow into the opposing force. Flowers and chocolate truffles went soaring into the air then decorated the carpet. When she turned around, Phil was on the floor, confused, as the surrogate ranted that the naïve mother had stolen her family.

"Oh my God, it's you!" Rachel cried.

"Who were you expecting?" Phil groaned, holding his stomach.

"I don't know. A deranged brunette with sinister eyeshadow? I was watching a movie," Rachel explained as she turned it off with the remote. "And considering it's only just after six, I figured it was anyone but you."

"Don't be snide." Phil scooped up his gifts from the floor. "I even bought you these." Phil handed her the flowers, minus some baby's breath that had remained clinging to the carpet. Then he laid the box of chocolates at her feet.

"I'm really sorry." Rachel picked up the remnants of the flowers. "Are you okay?"

Phil nodded, looking perplexed.

"What's all this for?" Rachel inquired.

"I was kind of a dick last night. It's work. I'm under a lot of pressure." Phil gazed into Rachel's eyes. "It was wrong of me to guilt you that way. I shouldn't have left like that."

"I get it," Rachel said. "I wish it was different."

"Me too, but so it goes. Bottom line is I want my wife to be happy to see me and glad that I thought of her." Phil kissed her cheek.

Rachel softened, partly because Phil's gesture was reminding her of the old days and partly because she had an agenda of her own to consider.

"Thank you. That means a lot to me." Rachel held the flowers up to her nose and sniffed their perfume. "I'm not used to you bringing me gifts anymore."

"Well, I'm sorry for that," Phil replied. "And for a lot of things."

Rachel was almost cheery as she laid the presents on her night table. She heaved a sigh of relief. Maybe she was finally getting through to him. Maybe her marriage wasn't such a joke after all. She watched Phil take off his jacket and hang it in the closet.

"I'm thrilled you understand." Rachel gave him a hug as though he had pardoned her from execution.

"I do," Phil replied, returning a small squeeze.

Rachel cocked her head with uncertainty.

"Can we eat?" Phil asked. "I'm starving." He headed to the kitchen.

Rachel stayed behind and finished putting away the folded towels. As much as she wanted to bask in his sudden affection, something wasn't adding up. Phil hadn't been in "thoughtful mode" in longer than she cared to remember. Now, after one forgettable night of arguing, he was not only coming around but also listening, even after she'd elbowed him onto his ass. Still, she wanted to give him the benefit of the doubt. Maybe he was capable of soul-searching and was finally willing to hear her. Suspect or not, Phil was being uncharacteristically open, and she didn't want to squander an opportunity that could set their relationship on a better course.

When Rachel got to the kitchen, the table was set, and Phil was sipping a Heineken. She plated the pasta and, as usual, served Phil first. She wasn't sure why, but she no longer wanted to tell Phil the story Anna had told her earlier. She was still processing how any parents could even think of abandoning their child and didn't want that negative energy to touch her circumstances.

"I know I've been a little crazed about wanting to get pregnant," Rachel admitted through a bite of garlic bread. "Maybe that's not fair to you. I just want a baby so badly. You do, too, don't you?"

"Of course I do." Phil twirled his spaghetti against a spoon, a move he'd once told Rachel was reserved for worldly gourmands. Though that was a fallacy, Rachel contained her urge to correct him. It was amusing to know he lacked the cultural awareness he was so sure he possessed.

"Hey, remember Dana?" he went on with his mouth full. "The assistant that looks like a horsey Olsen twin?"

Suddenly, the hotel receipt she found in Phil's pocket flashed across Rachel's thoughts. She'd met Phil's new assistant, Dana, a couple of times. Nice body, but not much to look at. Rachel had never given her much consideration as a threat. "The curvy kid?"

"Is she?" Phil asked. "I hadn't noticed."

He sounded earnest, and Rachel breathed a surprising sigh of relief. Phil and his penis had standards. Neither would consider sex with someone deemed physically subpar. If he was having an affair, it likely wasn't with the strikingly underwhelming Dana.

"Anyway, she told me quite a story today about Rob Steele."

"Rob Steele," Rachel repeated and took a sip of water. "Isn't he heading the project you're working on?"

"Yeah, him," Phil replied with more than a hint of contempt. "Anyway, while I was out of town, he had some issues. Seems Rob's been a bad boy. His ex-stripper wife, Brandi, got a hold of some photos that didn't please her. She busted into the conference room during a pivotal meeting, got up on the table—mind you, the woman's not exactly small—and started throwing pictures of Rob being *friendly* with different women all over the room. Rob went to slug her, but Jeb grabbed his arm. Dana called security, and Akinowa stormed out." Phil broke into a hearty laugh. "Man, I am so sorry I missed it."

"Why are you laughing?" Rachel stifled her own grin. "That sounds horrible."

"Oh, come on. You know what an ass Rob Steele is. He earned Brandi."

"Yeah, but—"

"But nothing. I spoke with Jeb today. Rach, he offered me Steele's job."

Rachel's heart flipped. Visions of Phil saying an endless stream of goodbyes as her pregnancy predictor kits remained sealed danced in her brain.

"Wow. That's really something. But Rob was traveling even more than you do."

"Barely. And once I set things up my way, I can travel less."

"I don't know, Phil. The timing doesn't feel right."

"Rach, there's no such thing as timing when it comes to opportunities. You just take them." Phil stroked her cheek. "Let's finish this upstairs."

Phil sat at the edge of the bed and drew Rachel toward him. The soft glow of a jasmine-scented candle cast a shadow on his cheeks that Rachel thought freed his face from the fine lines of stress around his mouth. Lines or no lines, nothing could diminish Phil's boyish smile.

She searched his eyes for the welcome to assure her she wasn't just another obligation he had to endure during the course of an average day. Surely, she would find some trace of her value to him if she studied his gaze long enough. And for an instant, there was something there, a spark, a memory, or perhaps a simple moment of peace. She wasn't sure what it was, but it was enough to make her believe they were still a couple who, at least at one time, had been in love.

Phil closed his eyes, and Rachel planted whisper kisses on his lids. It reminded her of their honeymoon when they were getting to know one another, and every touch, no matter how small, was appreciated. She continued kissing his face then moved her mouth down his belly. He stopped her and brought her face to his, kissing her in a way that made her feel their marriage was worth fighting for.

They made love over and over again, and Rachel felt for the first time in ages that they were in sync, lovers and mates truly meant to be together. She wanted to call Beth and tell her how wrong she was about Phil and their marriage, but that would invalidate the moment. It would also be a lie. Rachel knew the chasm between her and Phil was deeper than a night of passion could remedy, no matter how much she wanted to believe otherwise. She started to moan, hoping her reaction would catch up with the action. But she was a little late.

"Rachel, Rachel," Phil groaned like a mantra as he finished. "Promise you'll always be mine. God, I love you so much."

He rolled off her, turned the other way, and went to sleep.

Chapter Six

"Morning, Beth," Rachel yawned into the phone. Phil had already left for his morning run. "What's up?"

"Me, unfortunately," Beth griped. "You sound chipper. You guys did it all night again, didn't you, you slut?"

"Thanks, Bethie. Will that be all?"

"Um…"

"Do you want me to pick up balloons or something?" Rachel felt compelled to offer something to help.

"No, Evan's getting them." Beth paused.

"How about the cake?" Rachel tried again.

"Joshie, stop it!" Beth yelled loudly enough for Rachel to have to hold the phone away from her ear. "Stop sitting on Jeter. He's growling, honey. That means he doesn't like it."

Rachel laughed. "Having fun yet? Sounds busy."

"Busy is a foot massage compared to this. I hate kids' parties, especially the ones I have to make. I'm a bad mother." Beth sighed.

"You're not a bad mother. You're a tired one."

"You can say that again, and again, and again."

"So, what do you need?" Rachel asked, distracted by a new text on her phone.

"Xanax—Courtney, put mommy's lipstick away. No, don't color Jeter's tail. He's growling, honey. That means he doesn't like it."

"You should get that on a bumper sticker. What color?" Rachel snickered.

"Shocking Violet. Can I interest you in a friggin' purple dog?" Beth begged.

"I'll be over there within the hour. Promise."

The Kramer yard that day could easily have passed for the Xanadu of the toddler set. Between the cotton candy and snow cone machines, the enormous Cinderella bounce castle, the elaborate jungle gym complete with an ark to rival Noah's, and the section designated for live pony rides, any child with even a modicum of intelligence would refuse to leave.

"Have you lost your mind?" Rachel asked, munching on a wad of pink cotton candy.

"Ages ago," Beth retorted as she set a balloon centerpiece on a long table. "I'm just grateful Evan took the kids with him so we could finish setting up. I love that man."

"Have you forgotten that Courtney is only turning three?" Rachel held up three fingers in the air. "She's not even going to appreciate all this."

"She will, eventually. Someday, she'll look at the pictures and feel obligated to speak of us more kindly to her therapist."

"How goal-oriented of you." Rachel straightened a tipping blown-up bunny.

"I complain, but the truth is Evan and I do what we want to do for us. The kids are just an excuse to redo our childhoods."

"I guess I can understand that." Rachel ate the last bite of cotton candy and threw the empty paper cone in a mammoth trash bin rented especially for Courtney's pre-K soiree. "I'm sorry Phil couldn't make it. He texted me during his morning run. Some meeting. Must have been important. He didn't even come back to change."

"It isn't a problem for *me.*" Beth swiped a handful of pink and purple M&Ms from a bowl on the tiki bar. "Is it for you?"

"You know I'm used to it." Rachel stared at a bird effortlessly building a nest in a tree. It was so easy to make a home, but hers was still empty, housed by two posers unwilling to fly. Relationships were complicated, and with Phil, she had become skilled at winging it.

"Bullshit. No one gets used to being disappointed all the time." Beth popped the candy into her mouth. "I know you're having perfunctory sex whenever you can, but do you think he's having an affair?"

Rachel tried to cover the surge of emotion welling up inside of her. There was no way she could tell Beth about the hotel receipt and her suspicions. As much as she believed her sister was on her side, sharing such potentially damaging information would be hard to come back from if she stayed married.

"With his iPhone, definitely. With a woman, I seriously doubt it," Rachel said a little too adamantly. She was immediately sorry her delivery hadn't been softer.

"What makes you *so* sure?" Beth pressed.

Rachel thought for a moment. If she told Beth about the receipt, they could discuss the possibilities. Maybe Beth would agree Phil had been there for a conference and had needed a quick place to freshen up. That was what executives did. Maybe Rachel could convince herself of that scenario, but Beth would be a harder sell.

Rachel continued more strategically. "Phil's favorite word is *me*. A girlfriend's favorite word is *me*. He could never put up with that."

"But *you* can?" Beth said.

"I want a baby, badly. I deal with what I have to." Rachel swatted away a mosquito. "I don't think Phil is a lost cause. Yes, we're going through a difficult time, but being a family could change everything for the better."

"Look, I want you to be happy," Beth said. "But I think you need to get a better handle on what you really want."

Just then, a small white van screeched to a halt in front of the Kramer yard. Rachel let out a sigh of relief, as if a knight on a white horse had shown up to save her. Instead, it was a delivery man wearing a brown uniform and sporting a long ponytail that registered more 1960s than 2020s. Rachel gave him an innocuous once-over before deciding he had too much hair for his slim frame. He caught her gaze and smiled, keeping his eyes fixed on her as he retrieved a carton from his trunk. Rachel, still processing the state of her troubled marriage, licked her lips and flashed him a hint of a grin. He nodded and seemed reluctant to leave their tacit connection when Beth walked over and led him into the house.

Rachel saw herself in a field somewhere, near wherever Carlos Santana had played at Woodstock. She was wearing a long flowery dress with thin stringy straps that hung over her otherwise-naked body. Delivery Man was in tight jeans and shirtless, showing clearly defined biceps. He slung his arm over her shoulder and let his fingers brush against her nipple. Feeling aroused, she let him lead her down onto a soft mound of dirt in the middle of a small crowd. He lifted her dress and lay on top of her, covering her neck with kisses. They made love to the electrifying chords screaming from Carlos's guitar until they let out cries of their own. He held her as she quivered and kissed the sweat on her brow. She was relaxed in his arms when he asked, "Is there anything else I can do to make you happy?" And when she said, "Just stay and hold me," he did.

"Rachel!" Beth screamed, barely an inch from her sister's face. "Where the hell were you? Didn't you hear me calling you? I need your help with the chocolate fountain."

Where am I? Rachel felt herself blush a deep shade of what she assumed was crimson when Delivery Man walked past her and headed for his van. He opened his door and gave her a wink before getting in and driving away.

"Sorry," Rachel managed to whisper, still reeling from her fantasy.

"Whatever. If I weren't so crazed, I wouldn't give a shit."

Beth started walking back into the house, checking to see that Rachel was behind her.

Rachel followed, feeling more like a lost puppy than she cared to.

"By the way, why did that delivery guy ask me if you were single?"

Rachel hesitated to try to contain her amusement. "I have no idea. Did he say anything else?"

"Seriously?" Beth shook her head. "You were just talking about Phil not being a lost cause. What are you thinking?"

"I'm not thinking anything," Rachel said.

"That's probably truer than you know."

"Can we just set up?" Rachel pleaded. "The party is going to start soon, and you're going to bitch and moan that every pink napkin isn't where it's supposed to be."

"When you're right, you're right," Beth said.

Rachel was tired of thinking. It was crazy to send out vibes she would never honor and wrong to fantasize about making love with a strange man in a crowd of peace signs and Birkenstocks. She had no explanation other than that she missed having a deep connection. Someone who was a generous lover and a compassionate partner. She wanted Phil to be that person and decided to figure out a way to make that happen, hopefully before pregnancy would overcome the desire. In the meantime, to dodge a scrutinizing inquisition, she would do everything exactly the way Beth asked.

There were thirty boisterous kids running around the yard, and Rachel thought it was heaven. She did have a moment of hoping the poor ponies weren't being run ragged, but they seemed happy enough munching on carrots and some extra-high pockets of grass.

If this was the epitome of motherhood, Rachel couldn't have it fast enough.

"I can't tell you how much I appreciate all your help," Beth said, picking up a mini slice of pizza.

"Don't be silly," Rachel said. "I'm your sister. I owe you."

"Why?"

"You put up with me... my dazing, my whining, my constantly bringing up the baby thing all the time. I'm sure it's annoying."

"Frustrating, not annoying. Because I want it for you." Beth finished the pizza in a quick gulp. "Especially now."

"Why especially?"

Beth gave her a guilty, doe-eyed look.

"You're kidding!"

"Not according to the zipper on these jeans or the pregnancy test I took this morning."

"Oh my God, that's incredible!" Rachel grabbed Beth for a hug.

"It sure is." Beth took another slice of pizza. "Once. That's all we had time for in—I'm not sure how long."

"I should have your water tested."

"Are you okay about this?" Beth was cutting through a hunk of Jarlsberg cheese.

"Of course! I'm more than okay. I'm completely excited. I love your kids." Rachel poured herself a purple plastic cup of seltzer and stared at it. She felt her eyes get misty when she realized it was the same color as the layette she'd chosen years ago.

"It's weird. Do you remember what today is, besides Courtney's birthday?"

"I always remember." Beth sighed. "It's the same date."

"She would have been a woman by now," Rachel said under her breath, letting a tear go.

"She?"

"Yeah. I was convinced it was a girl. I named her Charlotte and bought her little bows and barrettes. I didn't have it in me to return them, so I gave them to you when Courtney was born."

"Oh man, I feel awful." Beth pressed her forehead. "Jeter ate those."

Rachel chuckled. "It doesn't matter anymore. I just had no idea how much I would still miss her."

"I did. You've always wanted to be a mom."

"How would you know?"

"How would I know? Because Mom was always working or painting. I felt like your baby, the brat you always yelled at for getting my clothes dirty."

"Some things never change." Rachel giggled as she wiped a tomato sauce spill on Beth's shirt. "And I thought we were having fun."

"We were. I liked being your brat." Beth took a sip of Rachel's soda. "I never admitted it, but I was jealous when Mom told me you were pregnant. I'm not sure why she did. Maybe a cautionary tale, but I wasn't even eight years old. There you were, my big sister, seventeen, in college, and having a baby. I knew you'd be a great mom, but I was still shocked."

"So was Mom. She was ready to yank me out of school and send me to a convent."

"She got used to the idea, and Dad was always cool, especially after their divorce."

"Maybe. But I lost my girl anyway. Pregnant for twelve whole weeks, and a miscarriage took her. And the part that kills me now—I was relieved."

Rachel couldn't sleep. It was after two in the morning, and Phil was still out. He hadn't even tried getting in touch with her. The TV was still on, and she stared at a faux-fur backpack being presented by someone who had never taken a modeling class. There was little in the Susan Lucci collection on QVC that Rachel didn't already own. She turned off the television and vowed she wouldn't do anything stupid like call Phil or touch herself and think of Delivery Man. A wise decision since moments later, she heard the garage door open. Rachel couldn't hear him walk up the stairs, but Phil didn't make a point of being quiet when he came into the room.

"It's late," Rachel said, sitting up in bed. "Where have you been?"

"Celebrating my promotion at Jeb's." Phil took off his jacket and hung it in his closet.

"You accepted the offer?" She tried not to sound disappointed. "Why didn't you call me? I would've gone with you."

"Yeah," Phil said. "This was a guys' thing. He had a surprise for me. Look." Phil dangled a set of car keys in the air.

"Oh, Phil! The minivan we wanted! That's so great." Rachel sat up propped against the headboard. "So—which one? The Honda? Beth swears by hers... or—"

"The Porsche."

"They make a minivan?"

"Rachel, screw the minivan. This is *my* car. It'd be nice if you'd think of *me* once in a while." Phil flung his tie over the handle of his armoire. "I'm picking it up when I get back."

Rachel winced at his accusation. She wanted to say he'd already cornered the market on putting himself first, but she went the practical route and muttered, "Back from where?"

"Rio. It just came up. Jeb asked, and there was no way I could refuse. Car service is picking me up at eight." Phil kissed her on the cheek nonchalantly before heading into the bathroom. "I knew you'd understand. You're my girl."

Rachel touched the spot on her face Phil had kissed. Maybe he was manic or growing a brain tumor. Clearly, they were living different realities, and his seemed way out of touch. She couldn't think of a thing to say that wouldn't send them into yet another battle, so she stoically put her head on her pillow and tried to sleep.

Another look at the clock—3:42 a.m.—convinced Rachel not to bother. *A Porsche. Please. The quintessential antifamily car.* It was almost like handing her divorce papers signed "Fuck you, Rachel." Then tossing in his international business trip like some inconsequential aside was a real thoughtful topper.

"Breathe, Rachel," she whispered to herself. Anger could upset her pH balance or throw off her estrogen level.

Rachel flipped her pillow over as if that might bury her dizzying thoughts and offer a clean slate. She inhaled the fresh scent of the organic lavender detergent she'd used and decided to go with the flow. If she could focus on the positives and even invent some if she had to, things would have to work out.

She went to the bathroom and got the basal thermometer. The ovulation predictor stick she'd taken earlier indicated she would be ovulating. Her temperature confirmed she was in the range, but Phil had partied pretty hard, and she wasn't sure she could get him awake enough to have sex. She could wait a couple of hours for a goodbye tumble, simple, straightforward doing it that didn't feature dawdling over erogenous zones.

Rachel watched Phil sleep for a few moments and studied the smirk still plastered across his face from when he'd waltzed in with his big news. There was a thin line between the love and the hate she felt while watching him gloat, even unconscious. For better or worse, she'd decided to hang in there. There were always compromises.

Rachel blew into her hands and rubbed them together. She examined Phil as if he were a specimen in a rat lab and sensually ran her hands up and down his back. It took him seconds to react.

"Rachel?" he asked in a foggy stupor.

Seriously. That was a question. Okay, not what she was expecting, but rather than assign herself an amusing alias, she continued to try to get him interested.

"Who... Wha, time is it?" Phil asked.

Rachel waited to hear if he would add a "Tiffany" or a "Bambi" at the end of his question, but he didn't. "Four," she answered drily.

"Four!" Phil pushed her off him and rolled onto his side. "Are you nuts? Take care of yourself."

Rachel sighed and fell back to her side of the bed. *What an idiot.* He really thought all she wanted was to get off after he'd spent the entire night not giving her a moment's consideration. Maybe Phil was right. Maybe she was nuts. She knew he wouldn't be into it. It was almost as if she wanted him to reject her, as if she needed yet another reason to resent him.

After a while, Rachel managed to doze off and didn't wake until the sun cracked through the verticals. Phil was gone, and he hadn't woken her up to say goodbye. She felt around her night table, but there was no note, no anything expressing that he was going to miss her. She went to her closet and threw on a pair of black jeans and the same gray sweater she'd worn the day before. She wasn't in the mood to even smell Phil and used the guest bathroom to get ready for work.

It was too early to open the shop, but there was always inventory to check and board games and stuffed animals to rearrange. The important thing was to keep busy, and since she had already told the ever-puking Beth she would handle the morning, she would have the space and extra time to herself. Before she left the bathroom, Rachel caught a glance of herself in the mirror. She wasn't sure how much longer she could convince herself that having a baby with Phil was worth the emptiness.

Chapter Seven

The early ride down Route 9W to the shop wasn't the kind of distraction Rachel was hoping for. The whipping winds and electric skies made her nervous and kicked the knots in her twisted gut into high gear. The last thing she needed was another reason to be anxious. A clash of thunder and a relentless downpour convinced her that despite her nausea, it would be more prudent to sit in an endless drive-thru line at Starbucks for a nonfat caramel macchiato than to hydroplane her way to work.

"Sorry. I forgot to use soy milk," the very pregnant kid admitted, handing Rachel her consolatory brew.

"Did I ask for soy milk?" Rachel hoped her tone didn't come off as bitchy. She truly wasn't sure what she'd asked for.

"Maybe?" the teen said. "Baby was kicking, and we're short-staffed. I probably just forgot." The girl tugged at her tight shirt. "I'm real sorry."

"Don't worry about it. Don't worry about anything. It's not good for the baby." Rachel handed the girl a twenty and drove off without waiting for a reaction. There was no need. She did it for herself to score brownie points and gain favorable karma. Eventually, something had to work for her instead of against her.

The rain subsided, and the rest of the drive was uneventful. A radio news bulletin warned of flash flooding and high winds, but that was for later in the day. Rachel saw no reason to panic, especially since she'd wrapped herself in the protection of a good deed.

The lot was empty. Rachel parked and bolted into the shop to avoid getting soaked. She immediately saw the sizable carton of new and vintage Fisher-Price infant toys that had been plopped in front of the counter just before she closed. Though she usually enjoyed setting up new stock in just the right places, she eyed it aloofly. The only thing she could think of to help was chocolate. And PopChips. Maybe extra calories would help her be productive, if not reproductive.

A huge crash of thunder sent a bite-sized dark Milky Way firing out of Rachel's mouth clear across the stock room and onto the floor. *Another spit like that could make me a Yankee.* Then the lights flickered and went off.

She rushed over to the fuse box, but nothing appeared to be wrong. The few windows didn't let in much natural light, and the space was dark. Another crash up at the front of the shop grabbed her attention. She knew it couldn't be Beth, who was scheduled for her first sonogram and wasn't due in until later in the day. And it wasn't Hayli either—she'd called earlier to say she had to make up a psych exam and couldn't be in until after lunch.

That only left the possibility of an intruder, there to take advantage of the storm. Rachel thought of calling out and asking who was there. But if it was a psychopathic lunatic with an axe and an overwhelming penchant for blood, she would be in deep shit. Instead, she quietly hid behind a tower of boxes and hoped the maniac would help himself to their inventory and leave before sniffing her out.

No such luck. As the footsteps drew closer, Rachel's heart was beating loud enough for her to hear it thumping through her sweater. She couldn't figure out why this was happening. She'd given the pregnant kid a healthy tip. It was unreasonable of the powers that be to want more from her before noon.

"Rach—what the hell are you doing?" Beth said into the back of Rachel's head.

"Bethie!" Rachel shrieked.

"Nope, it's Emma Stone. Lovin' life. Being an award-winning actress was so friggin' boring."

Embarrassed, Rachel jumped up from her hiding place. Suddenly, an unstable carton was hurtling toward Beth.

"Watch out!" Rachel screamed.

Beth immediately used her enormous diaper bag to divert the blow. "Are you out of your freaking mind?"

"It was an accident!" Rachel cried as the lights came on. "Are you okay?"

"My sister is certifiable," Beth said. "*You* tell me if I'm okay."

"I thought you were—"

"Phil?" Beth asked.

"No! Why would you even say that?"

"Because he's an asshole. So what *were* you thinking?" Beth picked up her leg to look at the bottom of her shoe. "Dammit! Some schmucky clerk tossed a candy bar on the floor."

Rachel opted not to correct her.

"You know what," Beth said, wiping the chocolate off her sole with a baby wipe, "I don't even want to know."

"Good." Rachel sighed. "Aren't you supposed to be having a sonogram now?"

"Power outage," Beth said, tossing the wipe into a trash drum. "Crap, I have to pee again. They didn't call to cancel until after I downed a gallon of Evian."

"Sorry... I'll open," Rachel said, walking toward the front.

"It's too early," Beth said, checking the red Coke Classic clock on the wall.

"Right. Um, then... I'll take care of, um... the new shipment first," Rachel stammered.

"Good, but leave the Rock 'Em Sock 'Em Robots alone. You don't need any new ideas." Beth playfully shielded her face with her arm. "Oh, and call Anna. Her doll is in."

The lights were back on, and the store was bustling for a midafternoon. It was as if everyone wanted to hoard classic checker sets and Parcheesi boards in case an immobilizing storm would coax families into old-fashioned entertainment. Rachel was grateful for the rush since it kept Beth from pumping her for more information about Phil. He was becoming even more arrogant and self-serving, the kind of egoist no one, except Beth, of course, had expected. There was no longer a list of pros and cons to determine if it was worth it for her to stay. Rachel knew it likely wasn't, but she still clung to the notion that despite his self-indulgent muck, Phil really wanted a family and would be a changed man the moment he discovered he was going to be a father.

Rachel was rearranging an assortment of thousand-piece jigsaw puzzles and stacks of Venus Paradise colored pencil kits when the phone rang. Beth said she would take the call in the back office as a customer entered.

Rachel was in the middle of extolling the fine craftsmanship of a furnished Victorian dollhouse when she heard Beth's voice escalate. Curious, Rachel handed her customer a catalogue then excused herself. Rachel could hear Beth struggling to get a word in as she approached.

"Anna, Anna—this is Beth. Slow down. What's wrong?"

Beth's eyes were bugging as she spoke. "Anna, please, calm down. Of course you can speak to her."

"What's up?" Rachel asked.

"Don't know." Beth shrugged, holding the phone against her stomach. "But it's *urgent*, and she *must* speak with *you*."

"Weird," Rachel said, taking the phone.

Several customers, including the prospective dollhouse buyer, left as another came in holding a Jerry Mahoney puppet with a broken hand. Beth raised her eyebrow, leaving Rachel and the mysterious phone conversation to help him.

"Anna? It's Rachel. The doll came in."

"Right, the doll," Anna said quietly. "I almost forgot. Rachel, it's simply awful."

Rachel braced herself for whatever news was going to darken her already-somber mood. "What's awful?"

"The baby. Rachel. That beautiful, innocent little girl."

"What happened?" Rachel felt panicked, as if she had a personal investment in the unknown child.

Beth mouthed to Rachel that she'd closed the store and wanted to hear what was going on. Rachel motioned for her to sit and put the phone on speaker. Beth pulled up a tiny tot chair, parked herself, and proceeded to eat the largest granola bar Rachel had ever seen.

"Her parents are nowhere to be found." Anna sniffled.

"But you said her grandmother"—Rachel let the name come to her—"Connie, was watching her."

"She was. But she had a terrible accident. She was cleaning the light fixture above her bed, fell, and shattered her foot. Now, she can't take care of the baby, and she can't afford to hire help."

"So what is she going to do?" Rachel asked.

"Find the baby a new home."

Rachel sighed deeply.

Suddenly, Beth retched, and a thread of vomit trickled down her mouth onto her shirt. She jumped up and ran toward the bathroom.

Rachel shook her head. *So much crazy in one afternoon.*

"A new home," Rachel repeated. "How is she going to do that?"

"Connie needs cash, especially since she helped out her good-for-nothing daughter. Her nephew is a lawyer. He said he knows people willing to pay for a private adoption. It can all be quite quick, and legal."

"You're saying the baby is available?"

"It's a difficult situation to digest, but I suppose so." Anna cleared her throat. "Perhaps you might consider giving her a bit more money than what she's asking for?"

Rachel's heart was pounding so fast, she wondered if it might take a flying leap onto the very clean, newly polished wood floor.

"I'm not sure what to say."

"Rachel, I called you because I know how much you want to be a mother. This child needs someone with your heart. Please don't take too long to decide, or this conversation will be for naught."

"I will digest all this and let you know."

Rachel ended the call but continued holding the phone against her chest. She was so absorbed in her thoughts, she was surprised to see Beth sitting back in the tiny seat.

"So, what did I miss?" Beth asked, shoveling gummy bears into her mouth.

"The baby," Rachel uttered almost inaudibly.

"What baby?" Beth asked.

"The baby in London. Beth, you were right here when we were talking."

"Rach, I feel like I'm barely here when *I'm* talking." She took a big swig of water. "Just tell me the upshot."

"The baby has been abandoned and needs a home."

"So? What does this mean to you? Is the baby up for grabs?"

"Yeah."

"Just like that?" Beth stared at a banana peeking out of what Rachel jokingly called Beth's feedbag. It was like a mini 7-Eleven and, similar to an EpiPen, was always within reach. "Wouldn't there have to be an adoption and all kinds of legal stuff? It's not like clutching a fumble."

"Yes, but from what Anna said, none of that would be difficult to arrange." Rachel picked up a La Newborn doll from one of the nearby displays and held it as if it were an infant.

"So, who has the baby noooow?" Beth asked as she sounded a long burp.

"The grandmother. But she's struggling."

"How long will she be able to keep her?"

"Well, she's her grandmother. She's not going to toss the baby out on the street."

"But she'd toss her to a total stranger like you?" Beth asked. "If the situation is so burdensome, wouldn't she give the kid to social services?"

"Not if she can make money on the deal." Rachel hated how callous the words sounded as they left her mouth.

"Ugh! Babies for sale like condos. Ticks me off."

"Yeah, but the woman doesn't seem to have many options." Rachel put down the doll. "Bottom line, if I want the baby, I have to pony up the cash and get her now."

"You're serious about this?"

"Totally. It's been months, and I'm no more pregnant now than I was then."

"Phil's away a lot," Beth said. "Verizon Wireless isn't going to get you pregnant."

"So maybe when everything is said and done, *this* is my answer."

"I get it, but it still seems kind of nuts to me. What do you think Phil's going to say?"

"Don't know. He's in Rio."

"So you're going to go to London, fork over your retirement fund, and bring home a baby while Phil is away on business." Beth got up and took a Gund catalogue from a shelf behind the counter. "For the record, Rach, I have no problem with your marriage ending, and this should be a surefire way to do it."

"I know it sounds unreasonable, but I don't care. Phil told me he wants what I want, and I want this baby."

"I'm not sure what to say."

"Saints be praised." Rachel glanced at Beth and let out a determined sigh.

Rachel stared into the pantry and toyed with the idea of making baked ziti and freezing it so Phil would have dinner whenever he got home from his business trip. It was only fair, considering she was coming back with another mouth to feed. An earlier conversation with Anna about finances had cemented the deal. When all was considered, it would cost Rachel some of her savings and her entire retirement account. The money was a pittance if it meant she could finally be a mother.

Then it dawned on Rachel that ziti or no ziti, she had no idea how she was going to explain any of it to her husband without sounding like a nineties sitcom character.

"Hi, honey. I'm back. Did you see what I did? I'm a really good wife. I left you baked ziti, which I see you're still eating. Oh, the noise outside? That's just our new baby. She's for after the ziti." Canned laughter. *"You're going to love her. She's in the car. I figured I'd bring in my suitcase and say hello first before the two of you get acquainted..."* *Raucous canned laughter.*

Rachel nixed the pasta idea and focused her energies on more practical concerns. She had to pack if she was going to be ready to leave in the morning. It amazed her how quickly she was able to book a flight. One lucky cancellation and the seat was hers. That things had fallen into place so easily convinced her she was doing the right thing.

Rachel went to the storage closet next to the garage and grabbed two pieces of luggage with her initials artfully engraved on metal plates, then she rolled them into the bedroom. Relaxed-fit jeans, simple shirts, neutral flats, and a light jacket—the quintessential wardrobe that would scream, "Rachel Sutton is a soccer mom!" and prove to anyone looking that she was ready to cover the goal. Nearly done packing, she went into the kitchen to get a bag of new toiletries she'd left on the kitchen island.

"Son of a bitch!" Rachel shrieked as the flimsy plastic gave out and the contents of the bag dropped from her hand and onto the floor. She was on her hands and knees, retrieving everything, when the deck door slid open, and Phil came in holding a stack of mail.

"Phil? What are you doing home?" Rachel asked, reaching her arm up to put a bottle of vanilla musk on the table.

"I live here. See?" Phil teased, waving a letter addressed to him in her face. "Rio became an afternoon meeting in Chicago. Quick flight. Why are you always so surprised when I show up?"

"If I answer that truthfully, we'll end up arguing again, and I don't want to argue," Rachel said, gathering the last armful of items from the floor.

"You sure? Because we always end up making love after a round or two." Phil winked.

Rachel ignored him and set her things down on the table.

"What's all that?" Phil asked, tossing the mail on the counter.

"Stuff."

"Yeah—I got that part." Phil picked up the body spray and examined the bottle. "You going somewhere?"

Rachel wasn't sure if his question was inquisitive or accusatory, but something in his tone made her uneasy. "I may as well just tell you."

"Just tell me what?" Phil pressed. "Are you cheating on me?"

"Cheating? No, I'm not cheating!"

"Well?" Phil's eyes were bulging, and his lips were pursed.

"We're having a baby," Rachel blurted, uncertain why those words tumbled out of her mouth that way.

"You're pregnant!" Phil's face turned an ashen shade.

"I didn't say that... exactly."

Rachel poured Phil a drink and asked him to sit down. She hoped she didn't sound completely crazy as she quickly filled him in on everything. Judging by Phil's furrowed brow and the persistent twitch of his left cheek, she surmised she had definitely failed.

Phil got up from the table and walked over to the deck door. "I can't believe you wiped out your retirement account. And you made these plans without even asking me how I feel about any of this."

"I told you. I spoke with Anna, and we worked it all out. It happened too fast to... think," Rachel explained.

"Doesn't that tell you something?"

"It tells me that I'm almost as good as you at making decisions on the fly."

"But I'm your husband, and you're changing our life."

"You know as well as I do, you're gone more often than you're here. I had to think quickly." She proceeded to down her first glass of pinot grigio and quickly poured herself another.

"And you don't think this is the slightest bit insane?"

"Insane would be waiting to get pregnant. You know I've always wanted a baby. Now, by some random act of fate, I can have one. And I'm not going to pass up the chance." Rachel took a sip of wine and swallowed hard. "I believe you're the one who said that there's no such thing as timing when it comes to opportunities. You just take them."

"You know I can't go with you. Jeb has a client for me to meet in Chile. We'll be assessing property in some remote village. I'll be gone a while and probably won't even be able to reach you most of the time."

"No problem," Rachel said. "Obviously, I wasn't planning on you coming."

Phil shook his head. "You really would have just gone and done this without me."

"Yes and no," Rachel answered, finally feeling a wave of liquid courage from her last slug of wine. "Last time we made love, you swore you want exactly what I want. So you tell me—is it my fault if you're not around when I can get it?"

Phil was pacing from one side of the kitchen to the other. "No, but I thought it would take a little more time. There's so much going on now. You know there is my promotion to consider."

"I agree, there *is* a lot to consider. My feelings, in particular. And I have had plenty of time to think while you've been going everywhere."

Phil continued to pace but stopped abruptly as if he'd had an epiphany. "I understand. I haven't been a model husband these days. I'm gone a lot, and I guess the pressure has been getting to me." He stopped to take a sip of his drink. "But it's important to me to do right by us. So if this adoption is what you think is best, for you, for us, go for it." Phil looked Rachel square in the eyes. "I'm not going to argue. Give me all the information. Names, numbers, whatever, I want it all."

Rachel stared at Phil, trying to assess what had just happened. He seemed to have agreed to getting the baby and becoming a family. He even seemed interested in her feelings. It wasn't what Rachel expected, but she wasn't going to trample on the gift. If Phil was coming around, maybe there was hope for them. "Really? You mean it?" Rachel beamed from ear to ear. "I'll give you anything you want. You'll see. I promise this is going to be great for us." She kissed him on the cheek and continued to pack.

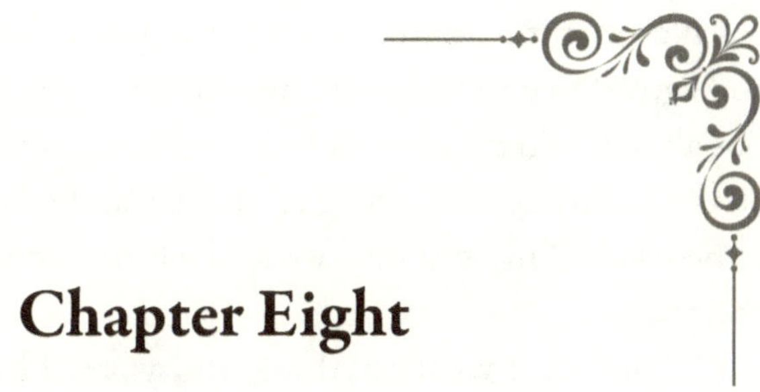

Chapter Eight

The airport was too crowded for the clock to be reading four in the morning. Rachel plunked down a five-dollar bill at a newsstand for a copy of *Oprah* that swore to teach her how to buy the best bras, have the most spiritual orgasms, put on her makeup in under ten minutes, and conquer her innermost fears. It seemed like money well spent, especially since she needed to overcome her dread of flying, pronto. Beth had offered to get her an Ativan, but the only thing Rachel feared more than flying was taking a pill that might make her feel like she was already airborne.

It wasn't the fear of crashing—that would be logical, almost reasonable. No, it was the fear of being stuck. The fear of not being able to bail if she decided she'd had enough of being trapped with a group of strangers oohing and aahing over postcard-picture views of cities and waters she would probably never visit. It was the fear of having no way out and realizing that if she did succumb to a panic attack, everyone would know her secret—that she was a neurotic lunatic.

Phil waved to her from a long line at Dunkin. After their conversation, he'd offered to take her to the airport. It was on his way to the office anyway, and he had a lot to do before leaving for Chile. He was being so agreeable that for a split second, Rachel wondered if he was really going away on business or if there was a Desiree, an Amber, or an Eboni waiting for him in that hotel room Rachel had promised herself she would forget about.

Not that it mattered. Rachel was going to be a mother, and Phil had agreed to be a father. Being a family was going to help them iron out all the wrinkles that had collected over time. One way or another, their marriage was going to change, and whoever might be going to bed with Phil right now would be history once he fell in love with their baby.

"You didn't want anything, did you?" Phil asked, cupping his Dunkaccino with both hands.

"No. Just *Oprah*," Rachel said, holding up the magazine.

"Yeah, that's what I figured." Phil smiled. "You've never been big on flying. Coffee probably wouldn't help that much."

"Nope, it wouldn't," Rachel agreed, trying to appear calm.

"I don't even remember the last time you were on a plane."

"Thanksgiving. Two years ago. Orlando. When Beth and Evan were taking the kids to Disneyworld and I went with them instead of going with you to investigate that company for sale in Denmark," Rachel rambled nervously. "You said you'd be busy the whole time, so it was either go with them or prepare Danish turkey for one, which made me think of those sad unpublished Greenwich Village poets with a cat in one hand and a clove cigarette in the other. So yeah, I exchanged Hamlet's castle, Kronborg, for Cinderella's castle and a week with Mickey and friends." Rachel finished and finally took a breath.

Phil nodded, his mind obviously elsewhere.

"You know, the next time I see you, you'll be a daddy!" Rachel cheered through a quivering smile, hell-bent on not being the only one uncomfortable.

"How 'bout that," Phil responded flatly.

"You sound really excited," Rachel said.

"I am, I am," Phil said. "Hey, I'm going to be a dad. It's cool." He did a little two-step while sipping his coffee. "I just have tons of shit to do before I leave."

"Tell me you're going to miss me," Rachel said, sounding more like a soap opera diva than she'd intended.

"I'll miss you," Phil said as he fished his phone out of his coat pocket. He viewed it briefly then put it back.

"Glad to hear it." Rachel opened her bag and handed Phil a sheet of paper. "Here is all the information you wanted—again. I also left you a copy of everything at home by the office phone like you asked. The grandmother's name is Connie Smith."

"Thanks." Phil glanced over the information then crammed the paper into his sleek briefcase.

Rachel checked the time. "I have to go through security."

"Beats going through insecurity," Phil quipped.

Rachel searched his face for feelings she knew weren't there.

"Nothing? Come on, Rach, that was funny."

"Yeah. It was." A thought came to Rachel, and she tapped her head. "What if we don't like the baby's name? We never discussed what we're going to call her!" Rachel cried.

"We will," Phil said. "You better go."

"Call me."

"As soon as I can. Have a nice trip."

"You too."

Rachel fumbled for Phil's lips, catching a little splash of coffee as they shared an awkward kiss goodbye. A part of her was afraid to walk away, not sure of what she was walking toward, but most of her was ready to shake up the status quo. She looked back, hoping with all her heart that her eyes would lock with Phil's in some tacit, deep understanding, but he was already on his cell phone.

The plane was bigger than the one Rachel had been on to Orlando, which was somewhat of a comfort as she mapped out a path she could take to do anything but sit and watch time drag by in the bottom-right corner of her laptop. She sat near the aisle, praying that the empty seat next to her would stay that way, and placed her bags on it to help her wishes.

She took out her copy of *Oprah* and began reading about why Barbra Streisand and James Brolin had a successful marriage. Nothing like rubbing salt in the wound, celebrity style.

"Excuse me," said a flight attendant with short auburn hair and an obvious nose job. She was trying to usher a smiley, pink-lipsticked woman in her early seventies to the seat next to Rachel's. "Can you please move your bag?"

"Oh, sorry," Rachel said, sorrier than both women could know.

The attendant dashed away to get ready for takeoff, leaving Rachel to fend for herself.

"Nervous?" the woman asked politely.

"Are you psychic?" Rachel asked, wondering if she sounded as angsty as she was feeling.

"You're clenching your fists, dear."

"Oh," Rachel uttered, trying to ease up. "Yeah, I'm nervous. Like Meg Ryan at the beginning of *French Kiss*. Which means nothing to you if you haven't seen the movie."

"It's one of my favorites, and I can assure you nothing is going to happen to you or this plane on my watch."

"So you *are* psychic—or something."

The woman was about to speak when the captain introduced himself over the speaker. A few announcements later, the plane began heading down the runway at what Rachel's stomach decided was warp speed. She closed her eyes and clutched the ends of her shirt-sleeves as they soared into the air.

Someone was patting her arm, interrupting her date with fear. Rachel opened her eyes, unsure if she was grateful or annoyed.

"I'm Edie." The woman smiled broadly. "And you are?"

"Still terrified."

"In answer to your question from before, I do have the gift. You're going to be just fine—" She opened her hand toward Rachel, obviously seeking a response.

"Rachel."

"It's very nice to meet you, Rachel." Edie took out a large deck of cards from her modest-sized carry-on. "Would you like me to read for you?"

"Oh, those are tarot cards, right?" Rachel said. "Thanks, but no thanks."

"A lot of people think it's hooey. But since you're already doing something out of character..."

"I guess it's hard to hide terror."

"I'm not much of a flier myself, but my daughter lives in London, and if I don't fly, I don't get to see her. She's an actress."

"That sounds exciting."

"It would be more exciting if she didn't need my help to pay the rent."

"The price of being an artist."

"I'm just glad she's finally found herself," Edie said. "Most of us grow old long before we grow up. Like my son, for example. He's a real intellectual, like his late father. He's in his forties and still has no family. He was planning to come with me until his schedule had other ideas." Edie sighed.

Rachel nodded, her head still swimming in the dread of the hours before landing.

"I have a thought," Edie said, struggling to contain a too-big piece of candy in her mouth. "Have you ever tried meditation?"

"No, thank you. My sister wanted to give me some pills, but I'm not the type."

"No, not medi*cation*," she corrected. "The butterscotch tripped my tongue. I said medi*tation*.

"Oh," Rachel said. "I've tried it, but my head ends up in double-fudge brownie recipes or how I'd finish a final season of *Good Girls*.

"Well, I think we should give it another try." Edie handed Rachel an earbud and placed the other part of the pair in her ear.

Rachel obliged and curiously waited for whatever was going to happen next.

"You'll like this." Edie pressed Play.

Rachel was immediately whisked off to an island with exotic flowers, lush greenery, and a beach all her own. The guiding voice was calming, and as directed, Rachel turned thoughts—in her case, Phil in bed with different supermodels—into colorful balloons she released into the atmosphere.

When it was over, Rachel yawned.

"Nice, right?" Edie asked.

"Yeah, very. I don't mean to be rude, Edie, but I think I'm actually falling asleep."

"I can have that effect on people sometimes," Edie teased. "By all means, take a nap." Edie eyed the magazine on Rachel's tray. "May I?"

Rachel nodded and let herself succumb to sleep, until the plane started doing jumping jacks and woke her.

"Where is she? Where did they go?"

"Where did who go, dear?" Edie asked, closing the magazine.

"I must have been dreaming," Rachel said, still hazy. Another dip of the plane nearly tossed her into the aisle. She gasped. "Edie, you swore!"

"It's nothing," Edie said with a wave of her hand.

"Sorry for the bumpy wake-up, folks," a man's voice said over the speaker. "This is your pilot, Captain Bob, and I think Michael Jordan's come out of retirement to dribble our plane. But no worries. This is very typical, just a simple, temporary dip in pressure, but I'd avoid a beverage for a bit. We'll be heading into smooth sailing momentarily."

"See," Edie said, "I told you."

Despite Edie's assurances, Rachel began antianxiety deep-breathing exercises she'd found on YouTube and hadn't had time to practice. She didn't even care if Edie was watching. Given the woman's self-proclaimed powers, she'd already known she was going to be sitting next to a nut before they'd even made their introductions.

"Rachel?" Edie asked after one of Rachel's long puffs. "Why don't you let me read your cards? It'll make you feel better."

"Okay, but if it's anything scary, keep it to yourself." Rachel yielded, beginning to hyperventilate.

"I'll make it a light reading," Edie assured her.

"What if the cards won't let you?" Rachel asked.

"They're not children," Edie said. "They'll do what I tell them to do. Anyway, we're going to land soon."

"We are?" Rachel asked.

"You slept a while."

Edie took out the cards and shuffled them. "You cut the deck."

Rachel did as she was asked, and Edie laid out three cards on Oprah's face.

"Very interesting," Edie mused.

"What? Why?"

"The moon, the tower, and the ten of wands."

"That doesn't sound good," Rachel said.

"Don't be silly." Edie shook her head. "The cards never tell you anything bad. They show you what's going on and help you make things better."

"Oh. So what do they say I should do to fix my life?"

"Well, it isn't quite that easy either, or I'd be out of business."

"Business?"

"We'll talk about that later," Edie insisted. "Let me tell you what I'm seeing."

"Go for it." Rachel sighed again, this time more deeply.

"It appears you've been spending a lot of time soul-searching lately. A strong feminine energy is at the core of your thoughts and decisions. Maybe even why you're here. Either there's already been or there's about to be an unexpected event, something that might seem totally surprising, given where you're at. But as long as you do the work that's coming with it, you'll be right where you want to be." Edie turned to look at Rachel. "Does any of that make sense to you?"

Rachel nodded. "H-H-How did you do that?"

"Do what? The reading? It was nothing." Edie picked up the cards and put them away. "I've been at this for years. The cards like me." Edie pulled a package of thin mints from her bag. "Want one?"

"No, thanks," Rachel said. "I miss my island."

"Want to do another meditation?" Edie asked. "I loaded my laptop with everything."

"Yes, I'd love to," Rachel said, grabbing an earbud.

Chapter Nine

The porter, a very young, very gorgeous man with cocoa eyes and a few stray moustache hairs, set Rachel's luggage down as soon as she opened the door to her hotel room. Anna had recommended the Caesar Hotel for its convenient access to the Underground and all the exciting attractions Rachel wasn't there to see. No matter. It was a place to park her things until she was set to take her daughter back to the States. She handed the kid a tip, which he seemed to appreciate. He then offered to "serve her in any way necessary to make her stay pleasant." Rachel smiled innocently, hoping she hadn't come off like some desperate cougar. The kid acknowledged her efforts with a quick nod and took off.

The room was spacious, with exposed brick and modern furnishings. If she'd been there for romance, she might have been disappointed by the sleek lines and neutral palette. But since the space was the closest thing to a womb she was going to experience waiting for her baby, she assigned it warmth and character of her own design.

One thing was certain, terror was exhausting. Even though she had managed to survive the plane ride, thanks to the watchful eye of her psychic fairy godmother, Rachel was still trembling inside and didn't feel ready to conquer the streets of London. Even as her luggage beckoned, she was too tired to move, until her eye caught the cover of a magazine left on the desk next to a booklet of hotel amenities. A mother and her baby were all smiles in "Outfits from Stella McCartney's New Line of Casual Wear," and they were apparently off to check out "The Top Five Parks to Add Greenery to Your Week-end."

A rush of stress-related tears caught Rachel by surprise. In just a few short hours, she and her new five-month-old daughter could be visiting one of those parks before going back home to begin their new life together. It was all so sudden and amazing, it was hard to think straight. A flash of them on the plane floated in her head. *Oh no! I don't have a car seat.*

She grabbed her bag off the top of her suitcase and pulled out a little memo pad. She had best make a to-do list, or she might forget to breathe. Connie Smith's information was on the front page. It was past dinnertime, but maybe there was a chance she could arrange to pick up the still-nameless child sooner rather than later. If it was just a matter of paperwork, it could easily be taken care of if the solicitor was willing.

"Mrs. Smith?" Rachel felt her voice quiver as she spoke into her phone. "This is Rachel Sutton. I just arrived, and I wanted to make plans to—"

The woman cut her off to explain that "Jemima" was sleeping and that Rachel shouldn't arrive earlier than eleven the following morning to meet her. She was in touch with her solicitor, but the papers were yet to be drawn up, and it was likely to take several days before the adoption could be considered official. After a few indignant grunts and moans about the paltry compensation for all her hard work, the woman ended the call before Rachel had the chance to say a proper goodbye.

If there was a moment to process anything, Rachel was grateful the baby was too young to be used to the name *Jemima.* Between *puddle-duck* and pancakes, there was no way her child was going to be subjected to an infinite host of wisecracks and needling. Until she and Phil made any decisions, their baby was Jane Doe.

As Rachel went to put the memo pad back into her bag, a business card fell to the ground. It read READINGS BY EDIE, with a New York number listed at the bottom right. The mere sight of it made Rachel's face brighten, and she let herself feel a reprieve from the madness that had suddenly become her life. It was comforting to know her psychic fairy godmother was somewhere nearby watching out for her.

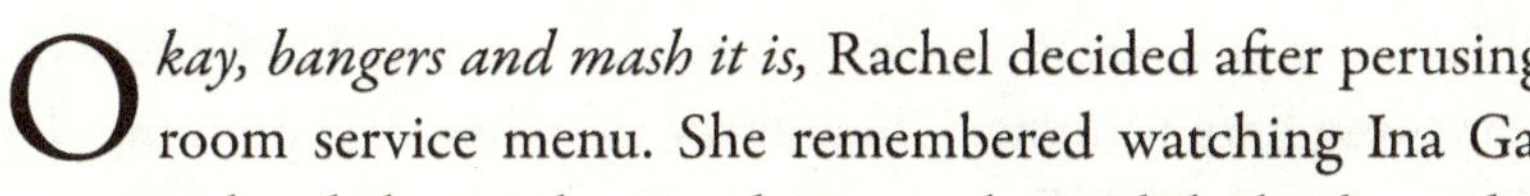

*O*kay, *bangers and mash it is,* Rachel decided after perusing the room service menu. She remembered watching Ina Garten prepare the dish on the Food Network a while back, and even though it had looked majestic on television, she was questioning if the hotel restaurant would give it the same love. *Probably not.*

With her bags as unpacked as they were going to be, Rachel quashed that idea and decided it was as good a time as any to get acquainted with her surroundings. A quick stop at the front desk was bound to steer her in the right direction for a decent meal and maybe even a pint of ale to calm her nerves.

The crisp night air felt good as Rachel walked slowly, stopping at an antiques shop window showcasing tea sets ornate enough to have been used by the Tudors. To the right of that shop was a tattoo parlor with a healthy panoramic display presenting design options. If she were in a better place with Phil, she could get an "anklet" of his name at a discounted rate.

She decided to pass and continued on to the café the hotel's night manager had recommended. A few feet away, she was drawn to a diamond necklace around the swan-like neck of a black felt-covered bust set in the window of Hawthorne's Jewelry. It was the kind of gift she fantasized about getting from her version of a newly refurbished Phil upon her return home with their new daughter. In her heart of hearts, she knew there would be no such gift, but she walked away before the sadness could set in too deeply. The café was a block away, and she was starving.

A stocky young woman with shocks of dark-red hair and a tattoo of a fairy with an enormous wingspan that spread across her chest showed Rachel to a table beside the window. "You'll enjoy the show," the woman promised. "Heaps of odd ones out there."

"I suppose so," Rachel agreed, trying not to stare at the girl's inked boobs.

"Do enjoy your meal," the hostess said, handing Rachel a menu. "I'm Lizzie, and I'll be taking care of you this evening. I'm doing a bit of everything here tonight. Oh, and try the Yorkshire pudding. It's fab. I'll be right back." Then she turned to the door to greet a party of eight holding a bouquet of "Happy Birthday" balloons.

Rachel opened the menu, trying to determine how hungry she was, when a tap at the window grabbed her attention. A tall, thin man wearing a charcoal-gray suit and carrying one long-stemmed red rose offered a broad smile and pointed to the empty seat across from her. She was studying his face, trying to find familiarity when a very short but very large woman came up beside him and clocked his shoulder with her purse. He broke into laughter and waved to Rachel as the unlikely pair walked away.

"Ah, so now you've met Irma and Harvey." The hostess pointed her chin toward the couple crossing the street as she set a bread basket on Rachel's table. "Just out of the oven."

"Thanks," Rachel said, eyeing a scone. "Irma and Harvey?"

"Yeah. They've been married for years, even seem happy, but he's always flirting with pretty women, and she's always smackin' the poor sod for it. It's like their private little game." The hostess shook her head and filled Rachel's goblet with water.

"I see," Rachel said, still examining the menu.

"Would you put up with that from a man?" Lizzie asked. "'Cause I sure wouldn't."

"I don't know," Rachel confessed, taken aback by the question.

"I tell her all the time she can do better, but she's a stubborn woman. And he's—well, you see what he is."

"So you know them?"

"They're my parents." Lizzie sighed as she headed back to her post.

Rachel started to wonder if her little girl would someday be advising her to dump Phil for being a poor excuse of a husband. It wasn't a pretty thought, although it comforted Rachel to know that at the very least, her daughter would have an unshakable bond with her like-minded Aunt Bethie. Rachel checked her watch. It was too late to call New York.

"Rachel?"

A smile blossomed across Rachel's face as she recognized the soft timbre.

"Edie!" Rachel didn't conceal her delight. "You knew I was here!"

"Honestly, I was... yes, sure, Rachel. I knew you'd be here." Edie took off her coat and sat in the empty seat. "How are you doing?"

"I'm all right, just a little disappointed my plans for tonight didn't materialize." Rachel picked up a scone and motioned Edie to help herself.

"Things are bound to work out, but—"

"Oh no, there's a *but*?" Rachel asked, putting down her nibbled piece of scone.

"Never fear the *buts*. Life would be dull without them." Edie took a quick sip of water. "The thing is... Wait—" Edie closed her eyes tightly.

"What's wrong?" Rachel asked.

As Edie opened her eyes wide, Rachel made a deduction. "Migraine, huh? I had one once. It was awful."

"No." Edie shook her head and looked at Rachel. "We're connected. It came up in a read I did earlier, and I just felt it very intensely now. I can't explain it. Yet. But I can tell you to stop fretting. Something you've wanted for a long time is coming. Just not the way you're expecting."

"That is a significant *but*." Rachel's stomach was growling, and she motioned for a thin, blond waitress to bring more bread. "For the record, I feel connected to you, too, but that could have everything to do with you saving me from making an idiot of myself on the plane."

"You're far from an idiot, sweetheart."

"Oh, you have no idea how many mistakes I've made."

"I say revel in mistakes. Without them, there would be no need for aspirations."

"The thing is, I might be making another one on this trip."

"All the more to learn." Edie patted Rachel's hand. "For better or worse, your work is just beginning." She returned to the menu then shifted her gaze directly above it to look at Rachel. "Get the Yorkshire pudding. It's wonderful."

As if on cue, Lizzie came over with another basket of scones and rolls, ready to take their order. She looked at Edie. "So, what'll it be for you ladies?"

Rachel spotted the blond waitress leading the infamous and still bickering Irma and Harvey to a cozy corner table. *Guess they got hungry,* Rachel mused. *Funny, they don't look unhappy.* Maybe that was how marriages worked over time. Couples were bound to argue, even disappoint one another, but somehow, they managed to stay together.

Lizzie appeared to notice Rachel's gaze. "Oh, just ignore 'em, love. Lord knows I do."

"Two cups of tonight's chowder to start and two Yorkshire puddings," Edie said.

Lizzie stole another glance at her parents and skulked away before Rachel realized she hadn't done any ordering.

"You were preoccupied, so I ordered for you." Edie took a sip of water. "Rachel, my daughter's show is opening tonight. The theater is only a few blocks from here, and I have an extra ticket. Join me."

"That is so sweet of you, but I don't think I'd be very good at a show," Rachel explained. "You saw it for yourself. I'm so distracted, I couldn't even order my own dinner."

"You're dwelling in negativity. I can feel it." Edie took a deep breath.

"I'm not sure I asked for this reading."

"I know," Edie said. "I'm sorry. It's just that I can't shake this feeling. I'm compelled to help you get through whatever it is you're going through."

Rachel glanced over at Harvey and Irma. They were sipping wine and laughing. Judging by the way Harvey's gaze was locked on to Irma, no one would think he could even look at another woman. It was all perspective. Maybe Edie was right. Maybe it was time for Rachel to change hers.

"Harvey and Irma," Edie said, catching Rachel's attention. "He's a raging narcissist. And oh-so charming." Edie took a roll from the bread basket and put it on her small plate.

"How do you know them?" Rachel asked. "Did they just come to you now, in the bread or something?"

"No, they didn't just come to me. I'm a psychic, not a superhero. My daughter has lived here for a while. I know the locals. Sometimes more than I'd like."

"Fascinating." Rachel took a big bite of her roll in case Edie was wrong and uber-insight could be culled from gluten. "Tell me, what do *you* make of them?"

"It's pretty sad." Edie sighed. "Irma doesn't think much of herself, and Harvey thinks only of himself. That's the danger of the narcissist.

He is in constant odds with the universe, always bucking to absorb the energy no one person is entitled to. Ultimately, they lose to karma."

"So what is the wife to do?" Rachel asked.

"Go to the theater."

Chapter Ten

Rachel scanned the theater, which she guesstimated was significantly smaller than her local Panera's.

"Tiny," Edie said, reading Rachel's thoughts as they approached their seats. "Everyone has to start somewhere. I'm going to the ladies' room. You?"

"No, I'm good."

Edie left, and Rachel sat in a less-than-comfortable seat. Though the crowd was small, each seat was filled, and Rachel was happy for Edie's daughter. Maybe this would be a fun evening after all. Edie returned just as the show was beginning. It was a riveting series of vignettes that explored the possible course of marriage between oddly paired icons. Rosie O'Donnell and Gertrude Stein shared a good deal of witty banter and a healthy affection for one another. And the relationship between Cher and Henry VIII suggested that his having one exciting marriage may have been sufficient.

Rachel found the concept fascinating, until Charles Dickens was in bed with Marilyn Monroe. For Rachel, that was when the tone of the entire play changed. All she could see was Phil as the brooding, driven Charles Dickens, trying to make her feel like his inferior underling. Rachel completely identified with the yielding, loving Marilyn Monroe, whose soliloquy described how lonely she felt while trying to be intimate with a man who invested more in his characters than in her. If only he could consider being a father more fulfilling than being some horny conquistador. If only they could triumph over their seven-year itch and fill their bleak house with something other than hard times. The intimate London crowd found the puns scrumptious, but they left Rachel queasy. She was done being full of the dickens and tried to control the tears that wanted to splash down her face.

Part of her wanted to bolt out of the theater, but the thought of creating a scene was a strong deterrent. She closed her eyes for a few moments, hoping the feelings would pass. She dug into her bag for a tissue but decided she was strong enough to save her self-soothing Cadbury fruit-and-nut bar for a more critical situation.

Rachel returned her attention to the show. In the end, Marilyn realized she needed more than Charles could give her. He craved space and distance to pursue his professional, artistic goals. Distraught and feeling like one of the misfits in London, Marilyn made plans to travel to Niagara. Charles, ever a fixture in the old curiosity shop, also left town to investigate the tale of two cities. The show finally ended, but Rachel was still dabbing at her tears with a withered Kleenex.

"I am so sorry, hon," Edie said, handing Rachel a new pack. "The way Faith described the story, I assumed it was a comedy."

"It was." Rachel sniffled.

"I know. Why else would they have a flat-chested, boyish brunette with a deep husky voice play Marilyn?"

Rachel shrugged.

"I love my daughter, but if I'd been the director, I would have sooner cast her as Dickens."

Rachel couldn't stop herself from laughing.

"You laugh, but swear you will never share that thought with anyone."

"My lips are sealed," Rachel promised. "Don't feel bad. I think I'm just exhausted. It's been a long day."

Edie pressed on. "Why don't you come to the after-party. Faith wants to introduce me to a Sean Connery look-alike, but judging from his headshot, he's a ringer for Christopher Walken."

Edie took out her phone and showed Rachel his photo.

"He's cute, sort of," Rachel said. "Sorry, Edie, but I need a hot bath and to watch *Notting Hill* to restore my faith in men."

"I'm sorry, you're right—you do need to relax. I can handle Christopher."

Before Rachel walked away, Edie gave her what felt like a maternal hug. Then she cupped Rachel's chin and looked into her eyes. "Sweetheart, whatever comes next, I wish you wisdom."

"Wisdom?"

"Yes. Luck is elusive without awareness."

Edie's pithy aphorisms might have called to mind an overpriced new-age deck of platitudes, but her earnest delivery touched Rachel, just as intended. Edie pulled another business card from her bag and pressed it into Rachel's hand. "I'm here if you need me."

"Give me the damn hammer, and I'll hang the picture myself!" Rachel bellowed to a three-foot tall Phil, who was dressed in nothing but a diaper. He glared at her and continued pounding at the wall until Rachel opened her eyes, finding herself wrestling with a pillow to a persistent knock on her hotel room door. She blinked a few times to adjust to the sun, grabbed a robe she had slung over a chair, and lumbered over to answer it.

"Room service," said the same attractive, enthusiastic young man who had brought in her luggage hours earlier.

"Ummm..." Rachel muttered. "I didn't order breakfast. Did I?"

"Oh, well perhaps you didn't, but you should have," the boy stammered. "These waffles are nothing short of spectacular, and I didn't want you to miss out."

Rachel met the eager gaze of her admirer. "Thank you. That was a very kind gesture, but if I take a bite of anything right now, I'll puke." She decided it was better to turn him off completely than tempt him—or herself—with a decorous reply.

Undeterred, he responded, "If you're not feeling well, I can—"

"I'm fine," Rachel interrupted. "It's just that I have a big day—what did you say your name was?"

"Howard, Ms. Sutton. My name is Howard."

"Howard, how do you know my name?"

"You're a guest. I make a point of knowing our guests, especially the lovely ones."

Rachel took a deep breath as she tried to decide how to handle her young suitor. On the one hand, she was flattered he found her desirable, considering she could easily have been the same age as his mother, which was also precisely why she wasn't the slightest bit interested. Still, she had to play it cautiously. She wasn't about to switch hotels, and in a strange new city, she didn't want to make an enemy when she needed a friend.

"Thank you again. You certainly know how to make an old, married lady feel like a million bucks." Rachel snickered.

"You're not old," he said, sizing her up from head to toe.

Rachel wished she believed that with as much conviction. She saw Howard catch a glimpse of her hand. She had forgotten her rings at home.

"Nor do you seem married. At least not happily so."

"Why on earth would you say a thing like that?" Rachel felt wounded and had completely forgotten her resolve to play things out diplomatically.

"Your demeanor. Forgive me, but you lack the confidence and spirit of a woman who is well-loved."

"That's a horrible thing to say," Rachel chided. "How do you know I won't have you fired for that?"

"Because if you didn't believe I was right, you wouldn't be upset. And because you're wondering what it would feel like to be kissed by someone who finds you utterly irresistible."

Rachel swallowed hard. She was being systematically wooed and disrobed by Harry Potter. "I have a lot going on, Howard. And as insightful as you may believe you are, you won't be getting lucky here."

"Luck has nothing to do with it, but I'm going to leave you the waffles anyway." Howard pushed the cart into Rachel's room. "You're hungrier than you think." He winked as he turned away from her then strode down the corridor.

Rachel closed the door and stared at the plate of waffles. The insolence of that cocky, gorgeous little shit. *What gave him the right to say any of those things to me?* She picked up a fork and speared at the waffle until she carved out a manageable bite. Eyeing the whipped cream, she created a little igloo before shoveling the whole concoction into her mouth. A small shiver rolled down her back. *Damn. Despite his audacity, Howard was a forward-thinking epicurean.*

It was a little past nine when Rachel decided to give Connie Smith a call. She picked up the phone and anxiously pressed the numbers. No answer. Connie was probably showering or bathing the baby. She had said to arrive no earlier than eleven, and Rachel knew she was being overanxious. She was always being overanxious. She decided to implement a practical plan to wash, get dressed, then call again. Chances were by the time Rachel was ready, Connie Smith and little Jane Doe would be waiting for her.

Rachel must have changed her outfit half a dozen times before settling on a pair of stretch denim jeans and the purple sweater she'd worn when she won the mandoline slicer at Beth's Pampered Chef party. Granted, other fashion choices had garnered greater successes, but she had felt particularly out of sorts that night and somehow managed to attract good luck anyway. To complete the look, she dabbed on just enough sheer rosy gloss to encourage her chapped lips to grin, uttered a short breathy wish, and once again called Connie Smith.

Still no answer, and it was now nearly eleven. Rachel began to panic. Maybe the baby's mother had fought with the father, decided he was scum, and left him to run straight to Connie and demand her child's return. Or maybe Connie had fallen while dressing the baby and they were both on the floor next to the crib, yards away from a phone. Either way, Rachel needed to get there, even without confirming with Connie.

Rachel was not ignorant of the advantages of having an admirer. She made a quick call to the front desk and gave a brief explanation that she was visiting an old friend. Howard not only arranged for a car service but also supplied the driver with the quickest route to Rachel's destination. Howard had an aunt who lived in a small home nearby, and the short, mismarked street signs could get confusing. Rachel thanked him for his help and graciously declined his invitation for "a quick pint" when his shift was over.

When Rachel exited the hotel, the fog was so thick that she could barely make out the car door being opened for her.

"Here, Miss," the balding driver said with a zealous nod.

"Thank you," Rachel said, somehow managing to slide into the back seat. "This fog is terrible!"

"One of London's many charms," he said. "No worries. I'm accustomed to the challenge. I'll have you there as quickly as traffic permits."

"That's good to hear."

"Miss, would you mind a bit of Talksport?" he asked. "I fancy meself a rugby geek, and they're interviewing Jack Clifford."

"No problem," Rachel said. "Listen to anything you want."

The last thing Rachel was interested in was making small talk. Any other time, she may have been curious about Big Ben, Buckingham Palace, Harrod's, or the other tourist spots. Under normal circumstances, she would want to know which sites were most coveted by natives and who made the most authentic crumpets. But that would be a different trip. All Rachel wanted was to focus on her family and how complete life would be once her daughter was safely wrapped in her arms.

After more bends in the road than Rachel's stomach cared to handle, the driver pulled up in front of a small brick apartment. The old building had more wear than charm. With two large but sparse trees flanking the front doors, it reminded her of Mrs. Reichman's house in the Bronx, where her grandmother played mahjong while Rachel would build domino fortresses to keep out her parents' fighting. If she closed her eyes, she could smell the Pledge-shined coffee table proudly showcasing a glass-cut bowl filled with Brach's chocolate bridge mix.

"Here you are, ma'am," the driver said, holding the door open.

"Thanks," Rachel said, getting out of the car and handing him a generous twenty pounds. "You can wait here, right?"

"Yes, of course, as per my instructions."

She offered the driver a grateful nod and hurried into the building. Connie Smith's name marked the door on the immediate right, and Rachel tapped lightly on it in case the baby was napping. With no answer, Rachel knocked again but more assertively. No answer. She rang the bell several times then pressed her ear up against the door. There was nothing to hear.

A gaunt elderly man with a ruddy complexion, wearing a gray sweater that looked like something his wife had knitted with her toes, entered the hallway from a side door that must have led to the basement.

"Excuse me, sir, does Connie Smith live in this apartment?" Rachel nodded toward the door.

"Not no more, she don't," he said, pulling an envelope out of his pants pocket.

Rachel gasped. "What? What do you mean? What happened to her?"

"Couldn't say," the man replied. "She up and left. I didn't see her. Quiet one, she was. Found the rest of her rent this mawnin' under me door." He waved a wad of bills in the air. "Place looks like she never lived there at all."

"But what about the baby?" Rachel murmured.

"Cute little bugger." He chortled. "Gone with her, I guess."

"Do you have any idea where they may have gone?" Rachel asked, fighting the impulse to break Connie's door down to find clues.

"No, ma'am, not a one. Sorry."

"Hyram!" bellowed a sharp voice at the top of the stairs. "Did you find me curtains?"

"Shite," the man muttered under his breath. "Workin' on it, love," he called. "Sorry, ma'am, the wife needs me." He turned away from Rachel and exited through the same door he had entered from.

Rachel stared at Connie Smith's apartment door as if doing so would force the woman to reappear with the baby. Rachel's feet held firm to the floor beneath her. Moving them meant she would have to leave, and leaving meant her hopes were destroyed. She dammed the ferocious torrent seeking to escape her and turned her head toward the car. The driver, true to his word, was still there, but she wasn't ready to go.

Maybe with the promise of new money, Connie was settling into a place of her own and was planning to come back with the baby. None of it made any sense. Connie could have misplaced her phone or lost Rachel's number. Not everyone was skilled at making firm plans, and it was possible Connie was flighty enough to think Rachel would be waiting for her somewhere.

Rachel was about to begin her search when the skinny man reappeared and approached her.

"Ma'am, I just found this stuck in me door," he said, waving a ratty-looking envelope in the air. "Says, 'From Mrs. Smith to Rachel Sutton.' That you?"

Rachel nodded hesitantly. She couldn't imagine the letter was going to bring her anything but pain.

"I didn't read it or nothin'," he said, handing it to her.

"Hyram!" The wife shrieked like a banshee. "Get your good-fer-nothin' arse up here."

"I best be goin', ma'am.

"Yes, thank you," Rachel said as the man skulked away.

She leaned against Connie's former door, trembling as she tore the flap of the envelope. She found a neatly folded sheet of computer paper tucked inside and shook it open.

Sorry dearie, nothing personal, but one must do what one must do. I received an unexpected fortune, from a tosser no less, and quickly departed. I shan't share the particulars, but now Jemima and I can have the life we deserve. My parting thought is that you do not allow anyone to mistake you for a muppet.

Have a good life,

Connie

With tears pouring down her face, Rachel read the note over and over, trying to process what had happened. One moment, she was going to be a mom, and in the next, her dreams exploded. Connie had explained the situation concisely, but not to Rachel's satisfaction. And the bit about Rachel being Miss Piggy or something made even less sense. Something had gone down, but whatever it was remained a mystery.

A car screeching reeled Rachel back to her surroundings. It was foggier than it had been earlier, an ironic twist of nature Rachel found amusing despite her sadness. She'd lost all sense of time, and as she walked to the car, she imagined her driver napping at the wheel. Maybe she would go back to the hotel and pack. She was in no mood to sightsee, and there was little else for her to do alone in the chilly, gray city that had just broken her heart.

As she neared the car, Rachel had a thought. Maybe Connie was lying and was still in town. An older woman with a baby and a foot injury couldn't make arrangements to leave her life that quickly. Unwilling to accept her misfortune, Rachel decided to wander the local streets in what she knew were delusional hopes of seeing them somewhere.

She quickly hid her despair between a spritz of body spray and a light comb of her fingers through her hair. She forced a stoic front and walked over to the driver.

"I've decided to stay on and walk a bit," Rachel explained as the driver removed his earplugs. "Are there any pubs or cafés in the area that you know of?"

"Going to be rather hard to find anything in this fog," the driver said. "But you might want to check out Worthington's or Scotsby's. Fine tea, and they're not far." He stuck his head out the window to scout the area. "And best of all, their signs are lit," he added with a chuckle. Before he closed the car window, he handed her a company card. Then he darted into the street, prompting a line of disgruntled drivers to respond with a series of annoyed honks.

Rachel turned back to the street and pushed her hands deep into her pockets. It wasn't that cold, but her insides were chilled beyond cause. Most of her was ready to give up, but another part was willing to be too hopeful to yield. She walked back to the front door of the building and tried to peer inside the window the janitor had indicated was Connie's apartment. It was hard to see through the grime on the windows and even harder to make out whatever was behind the tiny sliver of light allowed by the curtains.

A noise on the street caught her attention. A toddler and an older man she assumed was his grandfather were walking a dog that, upright, could have easily towered over both. They were laughing at something the dog was doing, but Rachel couldn't make it out through the dense mist. A few short barks later, the older man told Joshua it was time to go home. Rachel wasn't sure if he was addressing the dog or the child, but the three of them disappeared, having never even noticed her presence a few feet away.

Dutifully accepting the small scene as a sign, she took out her phone, which she'd wisely prepaid the day before, and dialed Beth.

"Huh?" Beth answered instead of a proper hello. "Nee-Nee, why is your face in your brother's butt? Joshie, are you telling her to smell your farts again? Go play nicely and leave me alone for five minutes... Rach? I'm so sorry. What's going on? How's the baby?"

"There is no baby," Rachel cried, allowing herself a few more tears.

"What are you talking about? What do you mean there's no baby?"

"Just what I said. It's a nightmare. One minute, I was going to pick up my new daughter, and then I got there, and there was no daughter! No anyone! Just some note from Connie saying she came into a windfall and took off with my almost kid."

"Well, where the hell did they go?" Beth demanded.

"Your guess is as good as mine. Probably better than mine. I'm not thinking straight."

"Do you want me to catch a flight and bring you home? I have the time," Beth offered. "Mom closed the shop. Her advisor said she should renovate and use the time to build up the online business."

"Great. Another change to add to my list." Rachel sighed. "But no, Bethie, I don't need you to come here. You have a family to take care of."

"You're my family too."

"I know. I'm upset, but I'll find a way to get over it."

"What did Phil say?"

"I haven't spoken to him. It's just as well. I'm not really in the mood to yet."

Chapter Eleven

The fog and Rachel's waning optimism kept her from wanting to experience most of what the streets of Queensway had to offer. She knew Kensington Square Park was somewhere nearby, but she didn't care. She wasn't interested in seeing where Samuel Beckett had once slept or where Agatha Christie had once done her dishes. That Connie Smith no longer seemed to reside anywhere was Rachel's primary concern, and despite her resolve to search for a place the woman might be found, she knew deep down there was little chance Connie would ever resurface.

Rachel weighed her options and decided on a soothing cup of Darjeeling tea before she went back to the hotel to find an earlier flight home. If Rachel had the slightest belief Phil would share in her despair, she would try to get in touch with him, but in her moment of stark clarity, she knew not to bother. He'd said more than once he would be unreachable, and Rachel decided he'd meant that both literally and figuratively.

Desperately wanting to get off her feet, Rachel followed the din of voices emanating from a café at the end of the block. Once inside, she saw the place was packed, and though that would normally be a good sign, it was not what she wanted to contend with for a cup of tea. Just as she turned to leave, Rachel's foot caught the wheel of an adjacent stroller, causing her to buckle and notice the baby girl and ornately dressed doll within. Rachel felt herself blush as she saw the striking woman beside the stroller, sitting at a table, eating a particularly plump scone.

"I'm sorry to be so clumsy," Rachel murmured. "That's quite a unique doll you have." She maintained her footing as she was being inadvertently pushed by a party reluctant to lose their table. "It looks like an original Bru Bebe. They're not usually toted about."

"Fascinating that you should know that," the woman exclaimed. "Her name is Charlotte—she was a gift. And no worries at all about the pram, love. I kick the bloody thing all the time."

Rachel felt the color from her face drain. Her baby, Charlotte, had been gone for years now, but the mere mention of her name felt like a fresh wound to her already-tender gut. She took a moment to breathe and return to the conversation without further spiraling.

"It was a very expensive gift," Rachel noted.

"Yes, and quite a lovely one," the woman said, handing the baby a piece of her scone. "You're from the States, aren't you?"

"Yes, I am."

"My guess would be... New York?"

"Born and bred," Rachel confirmed, wide-eyed. "How could you possibly tell so quickly?"

"Would you care to join us—"

"Rachel."

"Rachel. I'm Rena," she offered, touching Rachel politely on the shoulder. "And don't worry—Jane, Charlotte, and I are quite alone."

"Thank you," Rachel said, still adjusting to hearing her baby's name spoken of the doll. She took a seat next to Rena, leaving Jane's stroller between them. "She is beautiful."

"So you've said."

"I meant your daughter." Rachel blushed again.

"Thank you. I knew what you meant. I was just teasing you a bit. Reckless for a stranger, perhaps."

Rachel snickered and immediately began playing peek-a-boo with Jane.

"You know, it's a bit odd, but Jane resembles you," Rena mused. "Same color hair, eyes."

"Me and a million others," Rachel said. "So how did you guess I'm from New York?"

"I studied a bit at a college there not long ago. There was a wonderful pub nearby that served the most exquisite Yorkshire pudding. Perhaps you know the place. Thaxton's?"

"I've heard of it, but I've never been there."

A waiter with a hoop nose ring and a mop of unruly dark curls came to the table, carrying a large tray. While fumbling with another plate, Rachel noticed him haphazardly place their bread basket on top of Jane's kitten rattle.

"Then you must go try it. It's a lovely place to make memories." Rena moved the basket away from the edge of her plate, appearing perplexed as she scanned the table.

"Did you lose something?" Rachel asked.

"I can't find the damned rattle."

As if on cue, the baby started to fuss, pushing Rena into a full-table scan. She searched under napkins, shifted plates, cups, and flatware, then checked all around Jane's stroller.

"Give me a minute." Guessing that Rena had unknowingly knocked the rattle off the table when she moved the basket, Rachel squatted and looked past the crossed ankles of a very large man, where she spotted the toy. In a quick move, she snatched the rattle and apologized to the patrons at a neighboring table. Seeming amused, their party of seven gave her a round of enthusiastic applause when she held up the toy victoriously.

Rena giggled. "You have the spirit of a warrior and the gift of Saint Anthony. Thank you—from both Jane and me. It was going to be a long night."

Rachel handed Rena the prize and returned to her seat. Rena swiftly wiped the toy with a napkin and handed it back to an appreciative Jane.

For a moment, Rachel felt Rena's eyes studying her face.

"Oh my, you've been crying! I hadn't noticed."

"You weren't supposed to," Rachel said. "Not a great morning, I'm afraid."

"I know about those, as well. A man?" As if suddenly realizing the possibility, Rena quickly added, "Or a woman?"

"No," Rachel said. "Neither, although I suppose I could always cry over my marriage." Rachel took a sip of water. "I'm not sure why I said that. We've known each other five minutes."

"Time is a meaningless construct, love. You need a shoulder."

Jane began to whimper, prompting Rena to run her hand over the baby's fine hair.

"Rachel, my flat is a short walk from here, and Jane needs a nap. Why don't you come over? I can put something together for dinner in no time."

"That's incredibly kind of you," Rachel said taking out her wallet. "But I don't want to impose."

"No imposition at all. We're women, the struggle is shared, and I would adore the company. And please put away your purse. You had a cup of tea. Allow me," Rena said, putting money down on the table.

Rena stood at her door, trying to extract the keys from the diaper bag Rachel had offered to carry.

"So I'm here in the heart of London," Rachel explained as Rena continued to find everything except the keys, "and Phil is in Chile, or it could be Singapore by now. Frankly, I'm not even sure where he is, and we're no closer to being parents now than we were when I left."

"That *is* incredibly sad," Rena said. "Had you already paid the woman?"

"No, thank goodness."

"Ah, COD, the one saving grace." Rena held up the keys in triumph. "Or I suppose, in this case, one could call it 'babies on delivery.'"

"But I really wanted her. I never thought about her as a purchase."

"Forgive me," Rena said. "That wasn't a judgment, just a silly quip. I fear I tend to speak sometimes without the benefit of prior thought." Rena jiggled the key in the lock. "It's likely the product of limited interaction."

"I wasn't offended," Rachel assured her. "I just want you to understand my perspective."

The moment Rena opened the door, Jane spit up all over her clothes.

"Oh dear! Rachel, my apologies. Please make yourself at home," Rena said, wheeling the stroller into a small foyer. "Bath time seems to be warranted sooner rather than later. It might take a bit. The water's been down to a trickle the past few days. They claim to be working on it." She reached for Jane and walked down a short corridor.

Looking around Rena's home, Rachel realized it was as warm and cozy as she had envisioned. A mauve couch with black and beige throw pillows and two club chairs both in a floral pattern of the same color were arranged around a light oak coffee table with a bottom shelf that housed baby books and cooking magazines. At the far end of the room, near the kitchen, a dinette set faced a window with a garden view. It was a small but elegant space with a brick wall, complete with a fireplace serving as the charming backdrop. The style was more old-world than modern, but a few touches of glass and chrome here and there gave the room balance.

If she weren't so confused, Rachel could almost feel happy. Sitting on Rena's couch reminded Rachel of her college days, when she could make friends after offering a "bless you" to a sneeze. Some people were just meant to be friends. Maybe it was their New York connection that allowed Rachel to feel so comfortable with Rena, but whatever the reason, Rachel was grateful to have someone to talk to while trying to sort out her feelings.

She was thumbing through a coffee-table photo book of world castles when Rena walked back into the room. She put Jane down on a plush throw rug surrounded by colorful stacking cups, a ladybug teething ring, and a menagerie of little stuffed animals.

"I'm actually hungry," Rena admitted. "How about you?"

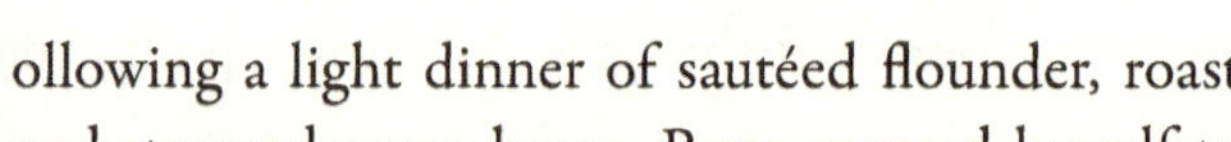

Following a light dinner of sautéed flounder, roasted potatoes, and steamed green beans, Rena excused herself to put Jane to bed. Seeming anxious to host favorably, she left Rachel with a bottle of pinot noir, a cheese board laden with a few small bunches of grapes, a carafe of water, and a bowl of mixed nuts.

Rachel used the time alone to check her phone. If it had rung, she hadn't heard it, but it was possible Phil had called and she'd somehow missed it. A glance at her call history earned a heavy sigh. She reviewed her emails, but there was nothing of particular interest.

"Sorry, it took several lullabies to knock her out," Rena explained, coming back into the room. "Poor thing was wired from all those nasty carbs."

"I could probably use a lullaby or two myself." Rachel tossed her phone into her bag.

Rena pushed the cheese over to Rachel's side of the coffee table. "I don't believe in decadent desserts. I usually indulge in an insulin chaser and call it an evening."

"Well, frankly, my hips thank you."

"No worries, dear. You're lovely." Rena popped a peanut into her mouth. "Please, tell me more about Phil."

"It's a fairly typical story."

"I doubt that," Rena said. "You don't strike me as typical, no matter how you'd like the world to see you."

Rachel flinched a bit at Rena's insight but didn't let it stifle her. "We met on a cruise ship the day after I discovered my boyfriend of too many years was married to another woman." Rachel sighed. "I have a complicated relationship history." She stopped short of disclosing everything about her miscarriage in college. There were some things she could still choose to keep to herself.

"If only we had inner compasses to steer us clear of the bastards." Rena kicked off her sensible black flats and folded her legs up on the couch. "Please, go on."

Rachel took what a yoga video had taught her was a deep, cleansing breath and explained in large detail how she and Phil had become a couple.

"What do you think drew you to him?" Rena asked, grabbing a small bunch of grapes.

"I don't really know. When I saw him, my knees almost forgot to hold up my body. I'd never felt that kind of painful attraction before. It was like it wasn't up to me. I was driven to do whatever was in my power to have him, to commit to him. I suppose it helped that I was hurt, vulnerable, and ready for another mistake. Phil was exactly the guitar-playing, emotionally stunted man-child that was destined to cross my path. For all his dysfunction, he was a bright light that promised to awaken my numb spirit."

"This conversation calls for chocolate," Rena said. "I have a stash of sugar-free peanut butter cups. Can I interest you in some?"

"No, thanks," Rachel said.

Rena got the bag of candy and set it out on the table. "Did Phil ever tell you why he wanted you?"

"He said I spent too much time breathing out instead of breathing in. I let out too much and took in too little. My guess is he found me to be a challenge, sort of like Eliza Doolittle to his Henry Higgins."

"I think women tend to be wired that way," Rena said. "We enjoy sharing both our thoughts and feelings. It's not exactly a crime."

Rachel poured herself a healthy glass of wine. There was something to be said for spilling life sitting at a stranger's table. It was refreshing to hear a new point of view. "Tell that to Phil. He wanted to open my heart up to lust, passion, and selflessness on a higher plane to stimulate my growth. And I suppose I wanted to take his wounded child and make him the powerful chord of blazing glory I decided he was meant to be. We were teachers in our heads and lovers in our souls."

Rena sat up a bit straighter. "Insecurity is the mother of intention. People often find each other when they're in the midst of need." She crossed her legs. "And then they get naked to cement the deal. I quite understand."

Rachel wondered if she would ever be as wise and evolved as her new friend. If disappointment were the emotional equivalent of Miracle-Gro, she would already be a sage.

"At the very beginning, we really clicked and had fun together, even doing stupid things. We used to play this word game we'd become addicted to, and we played it everywhere we went. The strippers were confused." Rachel noted Rena's quizzical expression. "Phil's best friend managed an exotic club. Like I said, we played it everywhere."

"That could be adorable, albeit impractical."

"Another time, Phil and I got trapped in an office building for hours after it had closed for the night." Rachel picked up a small square of cheese from the board. "After we had sex in front of the wall mirror in the men's room, Phil's thirst for adventure waned. He found a weighty extinguisher and threw it out the front glass doors so we could escape. It was in the local papers, but we never owned up to anyone until years later."

"With that colorful past, what has gone so incredibly wrong?" Rena asked, putting her legs up on the couch.

"Turns out Phil is exactly the man he's always been. I want him to be someone else."

"That could be a problem," Rena said, shaking her head slightly. "Many men profess to be one thing before we sleep with them but prove to be quite something else after," Rena said matter-of-factly as she filled Rachel's glass with wine. "As a rule, I prefer to get a taste of a man *before* I invite him into my mouth."

"A code to live by." Rachel raised her glass, starting to enjoy her slight buzz.

"But true love is different," Rena said. "True love is born of understanding, acceptance, and an insane willingness to compromise."

"I know. That's why I'm confused." Rachel shifted in her seat. "One morning, recently, I was watching Phil sleep. He really does have an exquisite face, strong jaw, cleft in his chin, and full lips. But for all his looks, I realized I was lying next to the emotionally stunted and appallingly shallow Tin Man. What am I supposed to do with that?"

Rena giggled. "Scrap metal? Buy low, sell high."

"Seriously, work and money mean everything to him. Our fun has been replaced by whatever serves him in the moment." Rachel patted a throw pillow. "I keep hoping to call what he and I share love, but I'm not sure it is. Whatever I convinced myself was there has evaporated into particles of resentment and indifference. Our relationship is like a cruel joke, forcing me to question what I want. Especially these days. When I look into his eyes, even when we're having sex, I don't see any sign of me."

"Love is difficult," Rena said. "We all want what we want, and sometimes, the package throws us. There are no shortcuts to a meaningful connection. If we don't choose to suffer together, our joys are destined to feel incomplete."

"I suppose you're right," Rachel said. "We've been leading very separate lives as of late."

"What about passion?" Rena asked.

"Passion. Phil is passionate about his goals." Rachel took another sip of wine. "It's challenging to get off on someone else's ambition."

"I understand," Rena said. "Forgive me for being bold, but if you're unhappy, why are you there?"

"Maybe a part of me believes that if I wait long enough, the old Phil will come back." Rachel shook her head a little, surprised by her own admission.

"What does the other part of you believe?"

"That I'm delusional," Rachel admitted, getting teary. "But more than anything, Phil or our marriage, I want a baby, and at my age, I can't afford to waste time searching for someone who may not even be out there."

There, Rachel had finally admitted it out loud. She was willing to put up with the hollow timbre of Phil's declarations of affection and the searing emptiness of their marriage, which had been predicated on a complete misunderstanding of needs and desires. The clock was ticking, and time was more precious than pride, ego, or even love.

"Would you be willing to go from shop to shop for just the right shoes to go with your favorite dress?"

"I'm not that hard a fit."

"My point exactly." Rena shifted in her seat. "You know, you could go it alone, pick the dad from a hat."

"True, but I don't have the money." Rachel took the pillow and held it against her. "And I still get glimpses of Phil that make me believe a child will turn him around. A little one to love could bring him the kind of joy he's never experienced before. With a little more effort, I really think I can have the life I want." As foreign as that sounded, Rachel would continue to believe it was possible.

"I understand." Rena straightened up a few intrusive toys at her feet.

Rachel sighed and walked over to the bay window facing the garden. "What about you? Are there shoes in *your* closet?"

"We all have shoes, Rachel." Rena took a sip of water. "My husband left me. And rightfully so."

That was when Rachel realized why she felt so connected to Rena. She was a wiseass straight shooter without censors. Sans the ex-husband and chic accent, it was almost like having dinner with Beth.

"Jane isn't his," Rena continued, "and when he found out, there was nothing left between us."

"I'm so sorry," Rachel replied.

"You needn't be," Rena said in true Beth fashion.

"But here we are, fast friends. I should be offering you some words of comfort and advice."

"Dreadfully unnecessary. Our marriage was one of convenience and necessity. When I was eighteen, there was an accident. A fire. I wasn't there, but I lost everyone. My entire family."

Rachel sat back down on the couch, wide-eyed. Such tragedy was on an entirely different plane than the misery of failed love. Yes, Rachel had lost two babies she'd never had the chance to hold, but there was still a path forward. Rena's life was molded by the kind of devastation Rachel never wanted to imagine.

"With no one left to count on, and a small settlement to invest for the future, I turned to a friend who got me a job at her company. Reggie was the very seasoned, very wealthy CEO. He drank in my youth like an elixir sent from the gods. He could have adopted me—he certainly had the age and the means—but since he'd never had a wife, he chose to marry me instead."

"That's all kinds of appalling," Rachel responded.

"I suppose it was, but he needed looking after, and so did I. So in some strange way, it worked until—"

Jane began to fuss, and Rena went to check on her. She returned holding the baby against her chest. After a few gentle rocks, Jane was drowsily sucking her thumb.

"Until what?" Rachel was sitting at the edge of her seat.

"Reggie had lengthy business abroad. I had local friends that had relocated to New Jersey, close to New York, and I arranged for a long visit. Reggie was due back sooner than I, but he thought a trip to the States would be good for me."

"Do you think he was seeing someone else?" Rachel probed.

"It's possible, but I hadn't given it a thought. I was ready for a change to break up the monotony of our routine." Rena stroked Jane's hair. "It took effort to contain my glee when he offered to extend my stay."

Jane began to whimper.

"She needs a bottle," Rena said, handing the baby to Rachel.

Rachel happily held Jane close. She smelled like heavenly flowers, and the way her curls framed her face, Rachel decided she resembled an exotic begonia.

Rena made her way to the refrigerator as Rachel followed.

"Were you ever in love with him?" Rachel asked.

Rena took the bottle out of the refrigerator and placed it in a warmer. "No." Rena laughed. "But I'd been a virgin when we married, and he wasn't an awful lover. There wasn't much to fuel the experience, but 'shagging,' as Reggie fancied referring to sex, wasn't unpleasant. I think at one point early on, I mistook climaxing for loving."

Rachel sighed empathetically and artfully steered the conversation to a less distressing subject. "So, what was it like when you got to the States?"

Rena took the bottle out of the warmer and tested the formula on her wrist. "Ah, just the way she likes it." Rena positioned herself on the couch, and Rachel handed her the hungry baby. "I had a great time with my friends at first, but they were newlyweds. Very busy newlyweds. It wasn't long before I started to feel like I was intruding. So, as I mentioned, I decided to take classes at a local university. And that's where I met the Professor."

"The Professor?" Rachel asked. In an involuntary flash, she thought of *Gilligan's Island* and decided Rena, with her auburn hair and seductive curves would have unequivocally been Ginger, the movie star.

"Jane's father." Realizing Jane had fallen asleep on the bottle, Rena paused. "I'm going to put the munchkin in her crib. I'll only be a minute."

Rachel scanned the room for anything that could tell her more about Rena's life. For someone so young, she'd endured so much grief. Rachel felt almost ashamed to continue to burden the poor woman with her drama. On the flip side, perhaps Rachel's issues were a welcome distraction.

Rena came back in the room, still looking fresh and beautiful despite the turmoil that Rachel imagined had to lurk within.

"Tell me about the Professor," Rachel said, curious to know the kind of man who could touch Rena's soul so deeply.

Rena practically fell onto the couch, perhaps mimicking the way love had knocked her off her feet. "He was a beautiful man. Perhaps not the classic type. He wasn't rugged and muscular, quite the opposite, actually. He was portly, much like a teddy bear, but ever so handsome. He had soft, lovely eyes and the warmest smile. He was irresistible, and I couldn't help myself."

Rena clutched a stuffed animal caught between the couch cushions and pressed it against her as if invoking the Professor for a long-awaited hug. "Our connection was like everything you read in novels that you're certain could never exist beyond the pages. I knew it was wrong—I was married. But the Professor convinced me that true love is not just glorious—it's virtuous and needs only to answer to a power higher than we possess."

Rachel helped herself to a handful of nuts.

"Want more?" Rena asked, holding up the empty wine bottle. "I do." She retrieved a bottle of pinot noir from the cabinet of a small rolling bar, opened it, and poured herself a healthy glass.

"When I finally agreed to be with him," Rena continued, "it was fiercely sublime. We didn't just 'shag,' as I had become accustomed. No. In his bed, the earth moved, the angels wept, and I was enraptured beyond reason. A few weeks later, he proposed."

Rachel took a deep breath and poured herself more wine. After a few sips, she felt a warm calm wash over her. "You were really going to leave Reggie and marry the Professor?"

"Yes. In fact, I was moments away from telling him my decision when I got the call. Reggie suffered a massive heart attack back in London."

Rachel let out an unexpected shriek.

"I know," Rena said. "He'd be requiring complicated surgery and a protracted recovery. You can only imagine my guilt. I left a brief note of explanation for my friends, but I had no time to tell the Professor. No one had even met him. When I got home, I resolved to concentrate on Reggie and our marriage."

"That must have been so difficult for you, especially when you were so in love with the Professor."

"It was a struggle, but I'd made a decision I wouldn't renounce. A couple of months later, morning sickness became a keen engrossment."

"I wish I could relate." Rachel put her hands together as if in prayer and placed them against her lips. "Did you know Jane wasn't Reggie's?"

"I suspected, but everything was going well. I didn't want to spoil it. Reggie was feeling strong, so much so that he decided to ramp up his business efforts. He acquired a new American-based company and rented us a temporary place in Denver, Colorado, so he could oversee the process of restructuring."

"How pregnant were you?" Rachel asked.

"More than I thought," Rena answered. "Reggie flew to a conference in Wichita. When he was due back, a snowstorm in Denver kept him from returning."

"Uh-oh."

"Exactly. I went into labor nearly a month early. A kind neighbor called an ambulance, and in moments, Jane was born. I was in shock at how quickly everything happened."

"I can't even imagine," Rachel said, tearing up. "You must have felt so alone. All that pain and joy with no one to share it with."

"You're very kind. But once you lose pieces of your heart, there's less to feel."

"That's a very sad thing to say." Rachel dabbed at her eyes with a tissue. "And then what?"

"Reggie finally returned. He was so upset that I'd gone through everything alone; he was quite nurturing. It was lovely, but soon, work beckoned, and he had to get back to London. He called in a few favors, got Jane's papers in order, and we flew home as soon as the pediatrician said it was permissible."

"How was Reggie with Jane?"

"He happily accepted her as his miracle," Rena said. "Which was quite magnanimous since I'd forgotten to list him as the father on her birth certificate."

"That was an interesting oversight."

"Quite unintentional," Rena said. "At least I thought it was."

Rachel stared into her wine glass before taking a sip. "So, go on."

"As I said, I was terribly dizzied by the circumstances."

"Of course," Rachel said.

"Reggie was nothing but understanding. He was planning to fill out the necessary documents to formally claim Jane, but one delay after another, and then—"

An alarm sounded from Rena's phone. "Sorry to leave you hanging, but I must take my medication. I'll only be a moment."

Rena went to her room, and Rachel once again checked her phone. She had concluded no one was interested in her life or whereabouts. Feeling sorry for herself, she decided to text Beth.

Hey—have met a new friend. She reminds me of you with a much more alluring accent. You'd love her.

Rena came back into the room and crossed over to the bay window to gaze at the starry night.

"So what happened?" Rachel retrieved and unwrapped a chocolate she didn't want. "Why did you break up?"

Rena turned to face Rachel. "Jane took ill, nothing serious, but they checked her blood type in the event she needed—or would need—surgery. Fortunately, she didn't, but the results proved conclusively that Reggie was not her father."

Rachel cupped her hand over her mouth, covering a gasp.

"Needless to say, Reggie didn't take the news very well. He went barmy—"

"He went what?"

"Barmy, bonkers."

"Oh, I get it."

"He was throwing vases, glasses, even the chicken dinner I'd prepared, all the while calling me unspeakable names. I'd never seen him like that. It was quite frightening. He vowed that Jane and I were dead to him, forever expunged from his life. We left that night and moved in with friends from this area who have since moved to New Zealand. I got this place a few months ago, just before they left. Luckily, it was furnished. Save the divorce papers, which included a healthy leave-me-alone-forever bulk payment, I haven't heard hide nor hair of Reggie since."

"Unbelievable! Does the Professor know about Janie?"

"Janie," Rena repeated. "How cute. I like it."

"Well, does he know?"

"No. No one knows. Except Reggie and now you. I must have written him a hundred letters informing him, but they were destined for the rubbish bin. I could never bring myself to send any of them."

Rena took a tissue from a box next to a copy of *Curious George* on the coffee table shelf and wiped her nose.

"Rena, you have to tell him. Janie deserves the chance to know her father, and you deserve the love of your life," Rachel whispered. "Come back home with me. One of us should have a happy ending."

"I can't. Our time has passed. It's too late," Rena said.

"Janie's not even walking yet. You have nothing here to leave. Except your fear."

"This is my home, Rachel. I can't just exit my life."

"That's exactly what you should do."

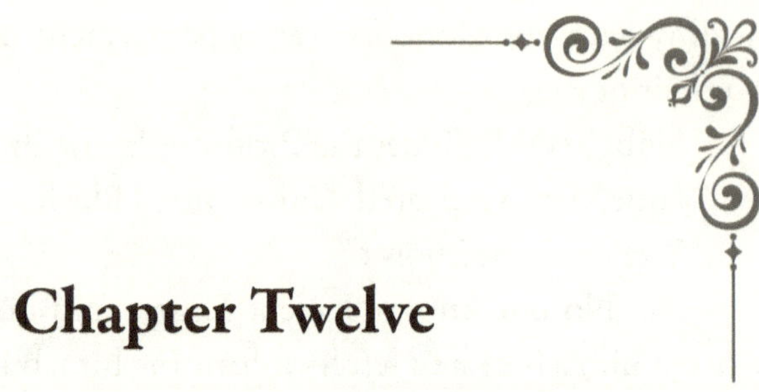

Chapter Twelve

The rich aroma of freshly baked cinnamon rolls wafted through the half-opened window of Rena's guest room. It had become one of the simple pleasures Rachel had grown fond of from the moment Rena pressed a spare house key into her hand and insisted Rachel be her guest "until the States beckoned." Rachel had hesitated initially, but then the thought of Howard, her intense bellboy paramour wannabe, bringing her room service every morning popped into her head, and she quickly dropped the key into her purse. So much had transpired in the short week she'd been there, and it was hard for Rachel to believe her trip was ending. Soon, she would be on a plane, traveling back to her reality.

The thought of leaving Rena and Janie made her queasy. Despite the brevity of their connection, Rachel believed they belonged in her life. Rena felt it too. She told Rachel she wouldn't be surprised to discover they were long-lost sisters who "had been kept apart by a random act of folly." There were few women Rachel truly admired and even fewer she considered friends. But Rena was now among them.

Rachel marveled at Rena's courage and determination. Despite her losses and disappointments, Rena had managed to persevere and build a new life. She was strong, resourceful, and despite an occasional flirtation with negativity, exceedingly optimistic. Rena would never allow the past to corrupt her present. She was the consummate fighter, and her daughter was her world. That bond was easily read in every exchange between the two of them. For all her troubles, Rena understood how fortunate she was to have Janie, and there wasn't a day they all spent together that Rachel didn't feel a palpable sense of longing to experience that same connection.

After a quick shower, made even quicker by the rebelling pipes, Rachel dressed for what Rena had promised would be a lovely day. Their ride on the Tube was a dream compared to the subway at home. Then Rena led the way to Jubilee Gardens, a sweet spot replete with lush lawns, colorful flowers, and a playground offering the kind of baby swings Janie could appreciate. It wasn't crowded, and Rena parked the stroller at a bench adjacent to a bed of aromatic lavender.

"Thank you for everything, Rena," Rachel said, gazing at the grounds. "It's beautiful here."

"You're quite welcome," Rena said. "I come here often. The fragrance clears my head, and the colors make me feel less lonely, if that makes any sense."

"It makes sense to me, but maybe that's because you and I are cut from the same cloth."

"My cloth requires wider hips." Rena used her hands to show the difference in measurement.

Jane was beginning to whine steadily.

"Teeth are like men." Rena pushed a chilled teething ring into the baby's mouth. "The first is the hardest to break in."

"I don't think the ones that follow are any easier." Rachel smoothed a section of her hair that had blown into her face from a sudden breeze. "Is it okay if I say it bothers me that you're lonely?"

"Of course. It bothers me too," Rena admitted. "But I prefer having a small life with minimal drama to a larger sphere of layered complications."

"Just say what you really mean," Rachel insisted.

"Fine. I don't need men," Rena blurted out.

As if she understood, Jane began to giggle, and the three of them laughed until small tears rolled down their faces.

"Lovely, my girl is getting a grand education, and she isn't even near a year." Rena cleared her throat. "I don't know about you, but I'm parched. Do me a favor—watch Jane, and I'll get us some drinks."

Rachel nodded, and Rena walked toward the concession. Rachel scanned the park, hoping to absorb the serenity, but instead was overcome by her pain. There were several mothers pushing carriages along the path around the flowerbeds, and everything in the universe screamed to Rachel that she should be one of them. Janie might have been sensitive to her moment, because at that very instance, she motioned that she wanted Rachel to pick her up. Rachel assumed she was hungry and wanted a snack, but Janie pushed away the cereal bites, opting instead to comfortably rest her head against Rachel's chest.

It was a small act of Janie's natural affection, but it cemented Rachel's resolve to make things work with Phil. Having a family meant having security, the kind of bond that would nurture and heal no matter what curveballs life hurled. Rachel decided even Phil, for all his bluster, would want that.

When Rena came back with two Diet Cokes and apple juice for Janie, Rachel put the sleeping baby back in her carriage.

"I know we've been doing a lot of talking, so I need to tell you." Rachel hesitated then said, "I've decided to save my marriage."

Rena smirked then rifled through the diaper bag Rachel decided earlier in the week commanded its own zip code. She found a wrap and offered it to Rachel.

"Don't be a kidder," Rena chided. "I am not amused."

"I'm serious," Rachel insisted.

"Really? Clearly, you're not looking at the big picture," Rena said through a bite of a large sliced mushroom. "Phil's not right for you, even if his chopper is the best you've ever had. And despite all your talk, you've conveyed you haven't had many."

"Neither have you, but this isn't about that. I don't care about sex anymore," Rachel swore with hesitation. "Well, at least not that much."

"Bollocks," Rena said, crumpling the paper lunch bag.

Rena let out a grunt that Rachel determined was laced with a hint of disgust before she went over to a trash bin down the path. Rena and Beth had so much in common, it was downright scary. Maybe they weren't altogether wrong, but it was Rachel's life, and she had to do what she thought was best.

Rachel was musing about getting a dachshund when Janie woke up, restless. Rachel combed through the magic diaper bag and pulled out a bag of teething twists, a move that made Janie squeal and clap. Rachel bent down to hand a cookie to the baby and, when she rose, found herself standing next to a pregnant woman in a tight blue shirt.

"Your daughter is darling," the woman gushed. "And she looks just like you. You're so lucky. I hope this little one looks like me." She pointed to her belly. Suddenly, the woman's phone blared from a pocket she couldn't find, and she quickly walked away.

"Who was that?" Rena asked when she returned.

"Some woman who thought Janie was mine."

"A logical guess," Rena said. "So, you were in the middle of lying to yourself about your marriage. Do go on..."

"I must have a child. It's that simple."

"So have a child. As I've said, you don't need a man for that, just sperm. And that can be gotten without all the nonsense that accompanies it."

"Cynical talk for someone who was once madly in love," Rachel remarked.

"'Once' being the operative word, and he *wasn't* my husband."

"Touché." Rachel snickered.

"Granted, motherhood is challenging, but—"

"Stop right there," Rachel said. "No buts. I want the package. Phil may be more malleable than we're assuming."

"Have you even heard from him?" Rena asked.

"No. As you would say, the *sod* still hasn't called."

"Don't you think that's concerning?"

"If you're asking me if I think his plane crashed or something like that, no."

"Hardly. Aren't you the slightest bit curious to know if he has someone else on speed dial?"

Rachel immediately pictured the hotel receipt she found in Phil's pocket. Despite her resolve to forget about it, she still couldn't. It gnawed at her like a paper cut. Maybe Phil was with that woman or someone else, sitting naked on some tropical beach while sipping frozen margaritas. Maybe they were in love.

Rachel tossed and turned in her bed. Rena's question and Rachel's imagination were just cause for insomnia. If she relinquished her faith in Phil, there were boundless possibilities for his infidelity. Without trust, all there could be between them was endless doubt. Either she would let go of her suspicions and move forward, or she would dwell on them and live in constant agitation. He hadn't asked for a divorce, which logically meant he wasn't in love with anyone else. He was still her husband.

A sharp knock at the bedroom door interrupted her thoughts.

"Rachel, are you awake?" Rena asked.

"What's wrong?" Rachel said while opening the door. "You look upset."

"Upset doesn't begin to cover it." Rena was seething. "I just got an emergency call from my landlord. You know how there's been a problem with our water flow?"

Rachel nodded.

"They found the issue and have to lay new piping immediately. It could take six weeks, and we can't live here during construction. Pretty bloody inconvenient."

"You know what this means, don't you?" Rachel smiled. "Square pizza at Di Fara's in Brooklyn. You're never going to want to leave New York."

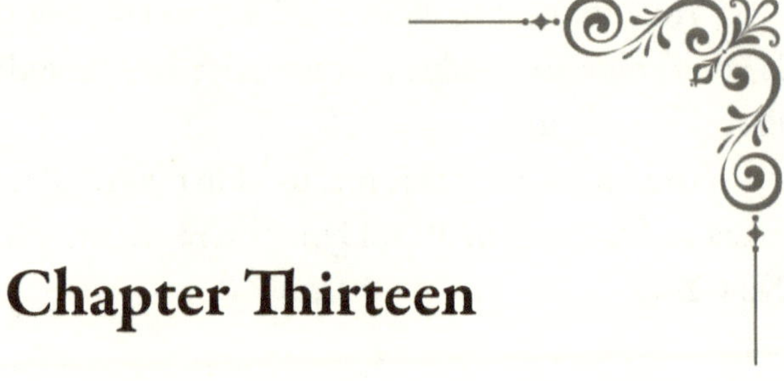

Chapter Thirteen

"I love curbside check-in," Rachel said, holding a Barbie-like replica of Queen Elizabeth. "Gives us extra time to browse before we have to board." She was pushing Janie's stroller as she continued to peruse the shelves of the duty-free shop.

"Rachel, put that dreadful thing down," Rena teased. "Our late queen needn't serve to scratch anyone's back, or anything else."

"Well, I have to bring home some kind of souvenir," Rachel griped.

"You're bringing us. Don't you think that's quite enough?"

"That's true. You guys are fairly authentic. And a bargain."

"Yes, that we are," Rena agreed. "And thanks for manning the carriage. All that frenetic packing got to me." She rubbed her arms and glanced around the store. "Would you mind watching Janie for a few minutes? I could use a pair of gloves, and I see them down by the scarves."

"Mind? It's been a very long week. You should know me by now."

Rena grinned and went to shop.

Rachel took her phone out of her bag and sent a quick text to Beth: *On my way home—with a big surprise!*

Janie started to fuss, and Rachel found a picture book of New York for her to look at. "This is the world-famous Bronx Zoo," Rachel said, bending down beside the baby to show her a page full of penguins. "See, these guys are always dressed for a party. For them, black tie is never optional."

Janie was trying to pull the book out of Rachel's hands when the manager came over holding a small stuffed teddy bear. "Before I bother putting this on clearance," he said in a thick and surprising Flatbush accent, "I thought your kid might like it. The thing laughs when you press its stomach."

"Oh, how sweet, thank you." Rachel took the toy and put the book back on the shelf. "Janie, look what the nice man has for you."

Janie grabbed the toy and immediately stuck it into her mouth.

"Oops, sorry," Rachel said. "She's teething."

"No prob. It's yours anyway." The manager was clearly enjoying Janie's inquisitiveness. "My kids are long past those days, but it doesn't get any easier. And she's a beauty. You're gonna have your hands full."

Rachel was about to correct his assumption when a man in a black leather coat interrupted them, asking for a price on a pair of binoculars. The manager excused himself, and she figured it was as good a time as any to check if Phil had called. Her heart started racing as she pulled out her phone. Still nothing.

For all her thoughts about wanting to work things out with Phil, maybe it was too late. Maybe she was only imagining she could have his love and a family on her terms. It would be some kick in the head if she got home to find he'd left divorce papers on the kitchen counter. Then she would have no choice but to start over. At her age. *Stop! You're creating a diversion because you hate flying.* Phil was out of range. Plain and simple. Unless he'd gone to hell. She'd been sending him there in her mind all week.

Janie started to whimper, and Rachel fished through the diaper bag to get her a pretzel. Food wasn't supposed to be used as a calming device, but it always made Rachel feel better. She surmised it wasn't the time to question her parenting skills. As long as Janie was content, her job was done.

Before Rachel could invest in further rumination, Rena came back, showing off her new soft black leather gloves. "Feel them." Rena brushed the material against Rachel's hand.

"Ah," Rachel said. "From the baby butt collection."

"You're a good woman, but I fear insanity runs in your family." Rena took off the gloves and put them in her bag. "Oh, good! You found the pretzels. Janie's been teething like mad, as I'm sure you've noticed."

Rachel let out a small sigh of relief. Maybe her maternal instincts were not as deficient or misguided as she presumed.

Rena inspected the diaper bag and busied herself organizing the contents. "Rachel, are you certain this whole idea isn't as crazy as I think it is?" She haphazardly ate a teething wafer then cleaned a few of the baby's toys with a wipe.

"What idea?" Rachel rechecked her emails, still ruminating on Phil's silence. No matter how much she soul-searched, she couldn't understand why her marriage had to be such an abysmal Molotov cocktail.

"Your mind is a million miles away," Rena said. "And from the look on your face, I am certain I can't compete."

"Don't be silly," Rachel chided. "I was just thinking that it's getting late. We should head to the plane."

"Fine, but you still haven't answered me."

"Right." Rachel paused until she remembered Rena's question. "Crazy is relative, as you have so aptly pointed out to me on a number of occasions this week, but I think you're making the right decision."

"Thank you. I needed to hear that. Again."

"And even though it was my idea, I have to say shipping all your stuff ahead was genius," Rachel added. "It's enough to have Janie's luggage to worry about. Besides, you won't need more than your carry-on anyway. I plan to take you shopping for an incomparable New York wardrobe."

"Genius or not, that sounds truly frightening." Rena laughed as they left the store.

"Only if my sister comes along," Rachel remarked. "But like you, she's the sane one."

"Sane," Rena said, seeming to try it on for size. "But seriously, I think you're right, Rachel. I do believe it would be best for Janie to know her father. I adored mine, and she has the right to adore hers. Yet I'm still not sure about this."

"Someone just a few hours away loves you and will love your daughter with all his heart. You need to do this."

"What if he's married?"

"What if he isn't?"

"That wasn't the question."

"Okay, if he's married. First, he'll take one look at you and kick himself at his unavailability. Then he'll still do the right thing and take care of his daughter. And next, you, my dear, will fall blissfully in love with someone else."

Rena grinned. "Glad one of us has everything figured out."

An announcement over the speakers calling their flight for an early departure took them by surprise.

"We better go," Rachel said, maneuvering the carriage to clear them an easy path to the terminal.

"Have you decided what you're going to tell Phil?" Rena asked from the window seat, her eyes appearing fixed on a cloud.

"I don't think it'll matter," Rachel said as Janie slept in her arms.

"He's expecting you to bring home a child. It'll matter." Rena massaged her sore arm. "Rachel, do you love him? I mean really love him, not the sexual adoration of teenagers, the real deal."

"I know I used to, but I'm not sure I do anymore. Do you still love the Professor?"

"Madly. Perhaps more than ever."

"That's wonderful." Rachel sighed. "We'll be landing soon." She studied the flight map on the screen in front of her. "Very soon."

"I'm a bit queasy." Rena got up and began to walk toward the bathroom, then she suddenly turned around. "Oh, can you find Jane's dummy so her ears don't pop when we land? Thank you, Rachel. You really will be a wonderful mother. I swear, if anything ever happens to me, I want Jane to be yours."

Rena turned and walked to the back of the plane as Rachel patted Janie's head. Amazingly, despite her teething, the baby had slept almost the entire flight without so much as a whimper. Rachel rifled through the diaper bag and proudly found the dummy, which she'd learned was a Brit term for pacifier. Janie instinctively began sucking without even opening her eyes.

"Oh, she's darling," said an older blonde with a Southern drawl, walking by. "You're so lucky to have a little one. Be sure to count your blessings." She tapped her chest a few times to show Rachel how that was done and went back to her seat.

The pilot announced that all passengers should buckle up and prepare for landing. Rena returned, looking peaked.

"Nervous knots?" Rachel asked.

"No, terrified knots, but I'm not to be blamed. Anyone in my position would undoubtedly feel the same." She buckled her seat belt. "Coming here like this is making an enormous assumption."

"How so?" Rachel noticed Janie was still asleep. "You're simply doing what's best for your daughter by acknowledging the truth."

"Rachel, I don't think I could bear it if he's with someone else." Rena dabbed at her teary eyes with her right knuckle. "All I've ever wanted was his happiness, but I suppose in my mind, I imagined that would begin and end with me."

"I understand, but everything will work out, either way," Rachel said. "One thing I've learned about you is that you're enormously resilient."

"Perhaps, but right now, I feel like a haughty, possessive bitch."

The plane jolted, and Rachel held Janie closer to her.

"Come on, take a deep breath." Rachel patted Rena's hand, and suddenly a light bulb turned on in her head. "I know exactly what we need right now. We're going to meditate."

Chapter Fourteen

Rachel was on autopilot as she shifted Janie in her arms and rang Beth's doorbell. She barely noticed how oddly quiet the house was as Beth opened the door.

Her body trembling, Rachel blurted out the words she had yet to say out loud. "Rena's dead!"

"What?" Beth screeched. "What are you talking about?" She pointed to the baby. "And who is this?"

Rachel couldn't speak. Everything was a little out of focus, except the horrified look on Beth's face, reminiscent of Edvard Munch's *The Scream*. She touched Beth's mouth to check if it was real or one of the pieces in the Mrs. Potato Head collection they'd received last month. It felt like a mouth.

"What the fuck are you doing, Rach?" Beth swatted Rachel's hand away and pulled her into the house. "And whose baby is this?"

Rachel's head raced with one thought after another, then she offered the only answer that made sense to her. "I think Janie's mine now."

Rachel wobbled as if she might collapse, and in an instant, Beth took the child and sat her in a fully stocked playpen.

"What does that even mean? She's yours now?" Beth asked.

"It means she has no one else."

"I'm really trying to understand all this."

"I know, I know," Rachel whispered as tears poured down her face. She was moving in slow motion, like if she wanted to, she could vomit and catch the puddle before it hit Beth's Rooms To Go abstract rug.

"Hey, Rach, next time you say you're coming over with a big surprise, do me a favor—make it reasonable."

Rachel nodded as she continued to cry.

Beth handed her a box of tissues and a shot of tequila that appeared out of nowhere. "Drink this!"

Rachel let the liquor slide down her throat in one gulp.

Beth poured her another.

Knowing she was a lightweight, Rachel could feel a welcome calm wash over her as she downed the second shot.

"Evan is with the kids, having a sleepover at the school... a reading marathon," Beth said. "I suggest we use this time wisely."

"Okay," Rachel said.

"What the hell happened?"

Rachel swallowed hard. Her head felt too heavy to be supported by her neck, and she let it hang forward. A small garbage pail appeared under her mouth.

"I'm not going to puke," Rachel said.

"Good. Start talking."

"I don't even know where to begin."

"Fine, I'll help you," Beth said, taking the pail away.

Rachel sat up straight and tried to collect her thoughts.

"Rach, listen to me very carefully." Beth was looking straight into Rachel's swollen eyes. "Did you do something we should be worried about?"

"I don't know. I hope not."

"Okay, not the answer I was hoping for." Beth opened her mouth like she was going to say something, then she closed it again. "How about this? Did you kidnap that baby?"

"Of course not!" Rachel said. "Well, not exactly."

"I'm going to lose it, Rach. We're not Abbott and Costello. Give me something here!"

Rachel let out a low guttural cry, allowing the liquor to help her speak. "Janie is, um, was… Rena's baby."

"Okay, good. That was good." Beth wrung her hands then put her clenched fists against her mouth. "So, when you said Rena is, um, no longer with us, um, you didn't have anything to do with that, right?"

"Oh my God, you think I killed her?" Rachel shouted.

Rachel and Beth both turned to the playpen when Janie whimpered in her sleep.

"No, of course not." Beth paused for a moment. "I mean, you know, like, probably not."

"Bethie, if that's what you think of me, why am I even here?"

"I wasn't thinking anything. I was just, um, checking."

"As much as I'd like to leave right now—" Rachel stopped to sob. "I can't."

"You're right—you can't." Beth was wringing her hands. "But you do sound a little better. How about I order a kitchen-sink pizza with extra anchovies, and you tell me the whole story."

Rachel nodded. Something about getting their favorite pizza made her feel comforted and safe.

Beth texted the order, then she went to the kitchen and brought back two big bottles of water.

Rachel took a deep breath. "It started on the plane to London when I met this woman who turned out to be a psychic. It's almost like she knew something big was going to happen."

"How about we talk about *her* later," Beth suggested. "Tell me more about what happened to your friend Rena."

"She had no one, just Janie. And almost the Professor."

"You're really going to make me work for this, aren't you?" Beth sighed deeply. "I want to know who the Professor is, but for right now, what the fuck happened to Rena?"

"I'm not exactly sure," Rachel said. "I heard the paramedic at the airport tell someone dressed in a uniform it was insulin shock."

"How did you end up with Janie?"

"Rena had no one." Rachel took a tissue from a flower-printed box and wiped her nose. "I convinced her to come home with me so she could find the Professor, Janie's real father, and put her family together."

"Lovely plan, but how did you end up with Janie?"

"Rena and I got close," Rachel explained. "I told her how badly I wanted a baby and that Connie reneged on our agreement. She understood my grief, and the whole time I was with her, she let me play mother to Janie. I think she also enjoyed having a little break here and there."

"Oh, yes. I do get that," Beth interjected. "So, then what?"

"Rena hurt her arm while she was packing," Rachel continued. "She was having trouble with it at the airport and asked me to take care of Janie. So I did."

"Right, but there's... more."

"I wheeled Janie through the airport and had her on my lap the whole flight," Rachel said. "Everyone assumed she was mine."

Beth got up to peek at Janie. "Weird." Beth glanced at Rachel then at Janie again. "She does look like you."

"I know," Rachel agreed. "Even Rena commented on the resemblance. Anyway, once we landed here, Rena was still hurting. She seemed super anxious, and I continued to take care of Janie."

Rachel was parched and took a few sips of water. She was just about to continue her story when the dinging of the doorbell took her by surprise and made her jump.

"Relax," Beth said. "It's got to be the pizza kid." Beth was shaking her head as she walked to the door.

Despite the tequila, Rachel's heart was somewhere in her gut as she considered the possibility Beth was wrong. Maybe it was an official from the airport—or worse, whatever that could be. She watched Beth peer through the small windowpane to check out the visitor.

"Hey," Beth said, greeting a kid holding an extra-large pizza box. He was struggling to hand it to her over a cluster of suitcases.

"Oh, crap!" Beth carefully took the pizza from him and put it on a nearby end table. "Hon, can you do me a favor?"

The kid eyed her like she might be interested in giving him more than a tip.

"You can stop all that," Beth said, making a circle with her finger in the air. "Bring in the luggage. I'll pay you."

The kid chuckled, obliged, and left a ten-percent-off-the-next-order coupon on his way out.

Beth brought the pizza over to the large coffee table. "Wow," she said, clearly delighted they'd included plates and plasticware in a paper bag taped to the box. "I don't want dinner to get cold, but I also want to hear the punch line before we eat, okay?"

"Yeah." Rachel's hand shook as she poured herself another shot of alcohol. Something had to calm her down. She noticed a tiny spill on the coffee table, wiped it up, then continued. "We landed in Newark. I got our stuff from baggage, which included Janie's car seat carriage thingum. I already had her bag and her passport."

"It doesn't look like you had much." Beth pointed to the bags. "Are any of those things Rena's?"

"Just her carry-on. Before we left, she was so busy with last-minute details, I arranged to have her things shipped here. They'll be arriving at my house any day. The rest was easy. I had all of Janie's papers, and I guess with divorce being so common, no one questioned our names being different. We got to customs, and one, two, three, we were through. The Uber was waiting for us."

"You were exceptionally methodical." Beth sounded impressed.

"I can be," Rachel said, "when it matters." Rachel smelled the pizza and was annoyed at herself for being hungry.

"I know," Beth said. "Can we—"

"Just before we were ready to leave, Rena said she felt queasy and needed the bathroom. I sat with Janie and all the stuff, including Rena's bag, and waited," Rachel explained.

"For how long?"

"It felt like a while," Rachel said. "Then suddenly, a woman who said she was a doctor came out calling for help. As officials came over, the doctor said a young woman appeared to have expired due to insulin shock. The woman had Rena's medication in her hand and said the body was on the floor of the ladies' room."

Rachel took a few breaths and continued. "The rest is mostly a blur. People in uniforms were everywhere. Someone in a suit asked for flight information, but someone with a badge said there was a glitch in the system, and it couldn't be retrieved. There'd also been a problem with security footage on the plane and in the airport. It took every ounce of self-control I had not to lose it altogether." Rachel started tearing up again. "I knew I had Rena's identification, but I thought about Janie, and I panicked."

"Oh, Rach, I can't even."

"I was just about ready to tell someone—I'm not even sure what I was going to say—when a security guard came over. He said the situation was getting intense and that if I had no further business in the area, I should take my baby and leave. So I did."

"Un-be-friggin-lievable!" Beth heaved a sigh. "I'm starving."

Rachel watched Beth grab the last slice of pizza as if she might not eat again for weeks. Since Beth had already downed most of the pie, Rachel couldn't imagine what that kind of hunger might feel like. Maybe one day, she would know. It was still possible, but in this moment, she took note that she didn't care.

With a glob of cheese taking up most of her mouth, Beth shook her head. "Are you sure Rena has—" She stopped then continued with "Had no other relatives?"

"Yes," Rachel said, cleaning up the remnants of dinner. Despite the food, she was still a little buzzed. "Rena made a point of saying she and Janie were alone in the world."

Beth took a long swig of water. "And the ancient ex-husband?"

"As far as I know, he's disinterested and long gone." Rachel could imagine Phil handling the situation similarly had he been in Reggie's shoes.

"What about the Professor dude, the daddy?" Beth asked. "Is there a possibility he knows about the baby?"

"Not a chance in the flames of hell," Rachel said. "Rena and I had a fast, deep closeness. She said I'm the only one besides Reggie who knows, and I believe that."

"Do you have any clue who the Professor is?"

"No, I don't," Rachel said. "Rena only referred to him as the Professor. She said he was teaching at a university around here, near some restaurant I forget the name of."

Beth got up for the first time in a while. Rachel assumed she had to vomit, but Beth walked over to the counter and grabbed a box of donuts instead.

"I understand how you feel about Janie." Beth was searching through the confections as if she were mining for gold. "But don't you have to tell someone? Some authority?"

Rachel wiped her mouth with an oily piece of napkin. "And then what? Have this beautiful girl caught in a ball of endless red tape? No way. I'm not doing that. Rena wouldn't want Janie to be a system's baby."

Rachel dabbed at her eyes with her sleeve. "It's hard to explain, but it felt like Rena almost knew. I think her health was a bigger issue than she shared. That may have been why she let me bond so intensely with Janie. One of the last things she said to me was that I'd be a wonderful mother and that if anything happened to her, Janie was mine."

"Wow!" Beth's eyes looked wider than her hips. "What are you going to tell Phil?"

"There's no reason to tell him anything. He knew I was going to London to bring home a baby. And I did. So, aside from my life, nothing has changed."

"But there could be ramifications."

"Why? You, and I assume Evan, will be the only ones who know," Rachel said, sounding a little more frantic than she wanted to. "I took all the luggage, I have all of Janie's documents and records, and as I said, Rena's stuff is being shipped to my house. There's nothing that can screw this up except human error, and I will make sure that doesn't happen."

"What if Janie gets sick?" Beth asked.

"I'll take her to a pediatric urgent care," Rachel said. "I could keep her records in a safe for my own reference but say they were destroyed in a flood. Then there'd be little to question about anything."

"Geez, you've really thought this through." Beth cocked her head and studied Rachel as if she were a lab specimen. "I never knew you could be so devious."

"Don't look at me like that! I'm not devious. I'm prepared," Rachel said. "I know Rena would've wanted me to put Janie first. That's what I'm doing."

"Not for nothing, but if Rena has no identification on her, what will happen to her... her body?"

"I don't know," Rachel said, "and it makes me sick to my stomach thinking about it. But everything has to be about what's best for Janie. I don't feel like I have a huge variety of pleasant options."

"And what about the baby's father?"

"I'll try to find him. Eventually."

"Eventually?"

"I need time to sort things out."

"I'll say," Beth said, watching Janie sleep.

Rachel bent over the playpen and kissed the top of Janie's head.

"The guest room is already made up," Beth said. "I still have Courtney's crib in there. We have a lot to think about. Stay the night, or for as long as you want."

Rachel couldn't sleep. Unlike Janie, who, after downing two small bottles, couldn't keep her eyes open. One thought after another raced through Rachel's mind. If she'd accidently left something incriminating at the airport, she could be arrested for kidnapping. On the other hand, would it be considered kidnapping if no one could claim Janie as theirs? Maybe, if she got caught, they would go easy on her since she was saving the system from having to deal with another orphan and more paperwork. Rachel continued driving herself crazy until she couldn't take it anymore. She grabbed her phone and brought up Temu, hoping she could shop her head out of spinning.

She was just about to pay for a diamond-studded Minnie Mouse spoon she knew she would never buy if her head was on straight when she heard footsteps in the hallway. She opened the door to find Beth looking distressed.

"I knew the pizza was going to be a mistake," Beth moaned. "I'm going to make a cup of chamomile. Want something?"

"If only I could find it in the kitchen." Rachel was leaning against one side of the doorframe.

"Come on," Beth said. "I'll make you my famous hot spiked apple cider. It may not knock you out, but it'll make you happy."

Rachel decided to save her wallet from "I took my newly dead friend's baby from the airport" purchases and followed Beth.

"You just want me to drink it for *you*," Rachel teased, taking a seat at the granite-topped center island in the large but inviting kitchen.

Beth turned on the light over the counter and took out two mugs. "Tea or cider?" Beth asked. "Your choice. I'm not going to impose my desire to be inebriated on you."

"In that case, make it a double."

"You got it," Beth said, pouring the cider into the taller mug. She reached into a top cabinet and took out a liter of butterscotch liqueur. "This is the magic." She poured in a hefty shot then a bit more before putting the drink in the microwave.

"Um... I'm going to have to get up with Janie in the morning, remember?"

"I'll take care of her. I'm used to sleep deprivation, and you look exhausted." The microwave beeped, and Beth set the drink in front of Rachel.

"What I can't believe, on top of everything else, is that you still haven't heard from Phil." Beth poured more honey into her tea. "Evan can go on a business trip for a day and call five times because he misses me or because he can't decide which breath mints to buy or how many squirts of hair gel he needs—but whatever."

"We both know very well Phil and I don't have the same relationship you and Evan have, and to be fair, he did warn me he wouldn't have phone service."

"Oh, come on." Beth groaned. "He isn't an idiot. Well, wait a minute. Let me take that back because he could figure out a way to reach you if he wanted to. He's a dick, and he doesn't deserve to be your husband much less that sweet little girl's father."

"Are you done?" Rachel asked after taking her first sip of the cider. "'Cause I could bring this heavenly liquid gem into my room and finish it there."

"I knew you'd love it," Beth said. "So, speaking of reaching you, get this. Anna called."

"Uh-oh." Rachel swallowed hard.

"Yeah. She wanted to check up on you and the baby. And she was also wondering why she hasn't been able to get in touch with Connie Smith."

"Oh no! What did you tell her?"

"I said that you and the baby were finer than tea with clotted cream and that I had no info about her lovely, barely-a-friend, Connie."

"Okay. Good girl. That works."

"For now, Rach. But how long do you think this can go on until someone pieces everything together?"

"We'll just have to deal with it one day at a time." Rachel got up and took her mug. "I'm finally tired. Let's talk more in the morning."

Rachel was still half asleep when she heard Beth arguing with Evan about letting the dog back in the house before his butt was clean. Apparently, Joshie, in the throes of his obsession with poop, had taken his sister's comb to make sure Jeter's ass was spotless. Beth nearly fainted when she'd picked up the comb to do Courtney's braids, only to be overwhelmed by the foul smell.

Rachel went over to the crib and saw Janie asleep with a note at her feet. Beth had changed her, fed her, and let her play until she was ready for a nap. Rachel checked her phone. It was almost noon. She hadn't stayed in bed until noon since her honeymoon, and in that case, she hadn't been sleeping all morning.

She let out a long yawn. The voices were quieter, and Rachel suspected Beth and Evan had moved into the negotiating stage. Their argument, Rachel mused, would likely end the way all her sister's fights with Evan ended. He would apologize. It appeared such was still the case.

Rachel heard Beth say, "Ev, sorry shmorry. Go to CVS and buy a new fucking comb!"

Beth had never been soft-spoken, but this pregnancy had turned her into a salty sailor. Maybe it was deliberate, a tool Beth needed to add some spice to their otherwise-bland relationship. Or maybe Beth was just that ornery. The garage door opened, and Rachel assumed Evan would be home soon with a comb and, likely, some form of chocolate.

A glance at her reflection in the mirror above the dresser made Rachel shudder. She'd aged ten years in a day's time. If she let herself think about everything that had happened, she might age ten more. Instead, she got up, got dressed, and put on enough makeup to be slightly unsure that she would be recognized in a lineup.

She let Janie nap, quietly closing the door behind her before going to find Beth.

"Hey, sleeping beauty," Beth said, standing next to the fridge, eating a bowl of corn flakes.

"I heard this place doesn't charge extra for sitting." Rachel noticed there was still coffee in the pot and made herself a cup. "As much as I'd love to hang here and hibernate from the world, I think I need to go home and start figuring out my life."

"You heard the Jeter-doody fight, huh?" Beth grimaced.

"Yeah."

"Thankfully, all the kids are napping."

"Definitely yeah."

"I sent Evan out," Beth said.

"I heard," Rachel said. "A new comb is a very sensible choice."

"Yeah, but I also sent him to your house."

"What? Why?" Rachel asked.

"Because you have a baby who needs things in place for her."

Rachel plopped into a seat at the counter. She hadn't even thought about all the things Janie needed. "Oh, Bethie, I've been a mom for five minutes, and I already suck at it."

"Don't be ridiculous! You've experienced more trauma in the past twenty-four hours than Paris Hilton has in her lifetime."

"Now I feel much better."

"All I'm saying is, don't be so hard on yourself." Beth took a slow sip of tea. "You love Janie, and for now, that's what matters most. That, and she needs a fucking crib. Which Evan is setting up along with a high chair, a changing table, and a Diaper Genie."

"Bethie, thank you so much, but I don't even know how much I owe you."

"More than you can fathom, but we're good." Beth was putting dishes away in the cabinets behind the island. "I had some things here, doubles from my past baby showers. You know I can't part with anything."

"Yeah, you're a mush." Rachel chuckled. "No one would know it, but you really are."

Beth's phone buzzed. "It's Evan," she said as she read the text. "He's at your place setting everything up." Beth sat down.

"I can't thank you both enough."

"That's true," Beth teased. "Oh, and before you ask, Evan didn't see any signs of Phil."

The sound of Phil's name made Rachel's heart sink. If they were off-kilter before she'd gone to London, there was little chance much would improve. "I wasn't going to ask."

"Rach, I know we've been doing a lot of talking and kidding around, but are you going to be okay?"

"You know I never think I'm going to be okay, but somehow, I manage. This will have to be one of those times."

"This is bigger than those times. You didn't just go too ashy on your base coat or drunkenly friend-request Macy's husband what's-his-name on Facebook. And for the record, I still don't understand why you did that even buzzed, but anyway—this time, you brought home a baby to raise that isn't really yours."

"I'm aware." Rachel poured more almond milk into her coffee.

"Just so you know, I'm on your side, always, even when you've turned your face into a palette for Revlon." Beth got up suddenly and ran to the bathroom.

Rachel cleaned up her dishes and finished just in time to hear Janie cry, "Mama."

Chapter Fifteen

Rachel had barely gotten the baby settled into her little play area when the doorbell rang. Her heart started to race as she once again feared it might be someone trying to track her down for information about Rena or Janie. She took a few deep breaths and tried to compose herself before opening the door.

"Delivery, ma'am." A tall, skinny man who looked anything but official stood by two large trunks and a suitcase.

Rachel guided him into the house and offered him a twenty to put everything in the attic. He enthusiastically complied and was out the door in moments.

After a mac 'n' cheese dinner, Rachel took Janie into the nursery to decorate. The first touch was finding just the right spot on the shelf for Charlotte, the coveted doll that made Rena light up almost as much as Janie did. Once the doll was comfortably seated next to Jasmine, Elsa, and a talking Tinkerbell, Janie seemed content and quickly drifted off to sleep.

Rachel stayed in the room to hang a group of pictures she had picked up at a yard sale she'd gone to with Beth. At the time she'd bought the soothing collection of animals and fairies playing in lush forests, she and Phil hadn't even begun to talk about starting a family. It might have been a premature purchase, but Rachel liked the prints and figured they would find a place on a suitable wall someday. She was sticking on the last picture hook when she heard a loud crash on the other side of the house. Rachel firmly gripped the hammer she hadn't yet used or needed.

She tiptoed out of the room and closed the door behind her softly. Once downstairs, she heard noises coming from the office and noticed the door was closed. She opened it very slowly, trying to keep most of her body away from the entrance.

"Oh Christ, it's you!" Rachel cried. She tried to catch her breath as Phil got up from the floor, holding the box where he kept business receipts.

"Ah, my usual welcome-home greeting. At least you're consistent." He eyed the hammer. "I see you've been playing in my toolbox."

"You scared the shi... crap out of me. I had no idea you were home or when you were coming home. You never called or emailed. Nothing."

"It was a crazy, backward place. There was a small generator keeping things going. I'm lucky I was able to get anything done. So, do I get a hug?"

Rachel was too numb and confused to argue. She gave him a perfunctory hug as much to stall as to keep things amicable.

"Well, that was as tepid as my dinner on the plane," Phil complained.

"I'm sorry," Rachel lied. "You just caught me off guard."

"Why do you need to be on guard?" He pushed her against the wall and started to touch her over her clothes.

"No, not now," Rachel said. She had no clue what made him tick. They'd had no contact for a couple of weeks, and now that he was home, the only thing he was feeling was amorous.

Phil backed off without a word and went back to some papers on his desk. "Actually, I thought you'd be at the shop," he said, looking up from a stack of papers. "I was going to shower and then come by and surprise you, take you out for a late supper."

"My mom closed the shop," Rachel said flatly. "We're renovating. But that aside, what exactly were you thinking? I wanted this moment to be special."

"Me too. I'm home. I'm safe. It's special."

"That's not what I'm talking about."

"Then, what are you talking about?"

"The baby, Phil. The baby. Don't you remember why I went to London?"

"Um, yeah, sure," Phil stammered. "Sure, I remember."

"Well, don't you want to see her?" Rachel tried to get a read on Phil's reaction, but he offered nothing but surprise, which, given the circumstances, baffled her.

"See her?" Phil emphasized the word *see*.

"Yes, Phil, *see* your daughter, our daughter." Rachel felt like she was dealing with an amnesiac.

"She's here?"

"Of course she's here. Sleeping in her crib. Why do you sound so surprised?"

"I'm... I guess... I just... I guess I kind of... didn't realize she'd be here." Phil's face was white, as if someone had shown him his actual birth certificate claimed he was eighty.

"What did you think? She'd get herself a room at the Ritz?" Rachel wasn't sure why Phil was acting so strange. There was no way he could have found out about Jemima. They hadn't had any contact the entire time she was away. Maybe he was still doing coke. That would explain some of his obvious brain fog.

"Come on, Rach. I've had a really busy time with work. Cut me some slack."

"Slack? You have a daughter now. There is no more... slack." Deciding to go the passive-aggressive route to address his cocaine use, she added, "I think it's time for you to grow up."

Phil shook his head. "When did all this happen?"

"While *you* were cocktailing with slumlords, *I* was making us a family."

"Enough already. I got the message. Let me see the kid."

"The *kid* is asleep."

"I won't wake her."

Rachel led Phil up to the nursery and walked over to the crib with him.

"She's... cute."

"She's wonderful." Rachel watched Phil stare as the baby slept, not quite sure what to make of his expression. "I've been calling her Janie."

"Janie. Okay. That's a decent name."

"Glad you're okay with it."

"And you got her just like that?" Phil snapped his fingers together. "No problems, no paperwork?"

"Everything was taken care of before I left London. Papers are in a vault I got there for safe-keeping." Rachel was crafty to make sure Phil didn't think there was easy access to information about Janie. "She's officially ours," Rachel declared, oddly enjoying her story.

"Okay then. I have to—"

"Work. I know. I'm going to bed."

"I'll be up soon."

"I won't hold my breath," she mumbled to herself.

Chapter Sixteen

Rachel woke up the next morning to find Phil's side of the bed untouched. In the wee hours, she'd awakened briefly to him screaming on his office line at someone she was grateful not to be. Moments later, he'd slammed the phone down harshly, then a car door had slammed. She'd been too exhausted to investigate and decided the whole incident had been a dream. From the looks of the smooth comforter and the undeniable calm in the atmosphere, she was pretty sure Phil had taken off at some point between wanting to have sex with her and being shocked that he was now a father.

Phil's reaction to Janie had clearly been halfhearted, but in all fairness, his extensive travels could've left him wiped. It was also possible he'd thought an adoption would take longer. Regardless, Rachel couldn't think of anything she'd said or done to make Phil angry enough to take off without a word. He'd always been somewhat volatile, but recently, his behavior had been even more unpredictable.

A steady stream of babbling from the nursery jarred Rachel out of bed. She was a mother now, and keeping her baby safe and happy was infinitely more important than making Phil the romantic lead in her unscripted movie. At some point, staying married to him might not be worth the angst.

After Janie was dressed, fed, and rocking in her swing, Rachel had the time to be anxious. She wasn't sure she could keep her secret without slipping, but she also couldn't let Janie be subjected to the constant fear that this whole plan would blow up. Rachel had to fight her impulse to hide. She needed to go out into the world, introducing Janie as her daughter.

"Hey, Beth," Rachel said, realizing her phone was crusted in baby oatmeal. "Janie and I are up and ready to conquer the day."

"Good timing," Beth replied. "I've been fantasizing about broccoli-cheddar-stuffed potatoes and an extra-large chocolate shake all morning. When this pregnancy is over, please remind me I'm a size six."

"Sure, I'll even beg your jeans to comply. You've been through this before, and you've always bounced back. I wouldn't worry."

"This time, I might be bouncing for a while." Beth sighed. "When can you"—Beth retched—"get here? Uh-oh! Gotta puke."

Rachel gave herself a huge pat on the back when she managed, yet again, to get the baby into the car seat without breaking a nail. Janie was enjoying the ride, especially when Rachel put on the classic Disney soundtrack and sang along. By the time she got to the restaurant, Janie was in no mood to be interrupted and put up a slight fuss when Rachel took her out of the car.

"Sorry, honey, but the drive-thru line is ridiculously long, and we have to get Aunt Bethie lunch quickly because she's still working on needing a forklift to get her out of a chair."

Janie continued to squirm until she realized she was going nowhere except against Rachel's chest. Someone leaving as Rachel was entering held the door open for her. It was a small gesture, but it nearly made her teary since she'd always been the one without the baby holding the door open for someone else. There was no line to speak of, and she ordered quickly.

"Rachel?"

That voice. Good lord. No. It was like that scene out of *Casablanca.* Why here? Why her? Why now? But there she was, Macy Daniels, more pregnant than ever, munching on french fries.

"Macy, well, don't you look great." Perhaps flattery would deter questions. "You're carrying so well. How are you feeling?"

"Good. Very good. The twins are coming along." Macy rubbed her enormous belly. "And Freddy got another promotion. Life couldn't be better. Is this one of your sister's kids?"

Uh-oh. The inquisition is starting. Rachel didn't have the necessary arsenal to fend off the onslaught. She needed to think. All Rachel could muster was "No. No, she isn't."

"Oh. Are you working as a nanny?"

Rude. And intrusive. Rachel had no reason to expect anything less. "No. Beth and I still manage the shop. We're temporarily closed for renovations."

"Right, sorry," Macy said, clearly anything but. "Then who is this cutie-pie?"

"She's my daughter." Rachel knew that telling Macy was like putting up a billboard on the Jersey Turnpike. But she had to do it. Anymore tap-dancing would've raised suspicion. Despite that it hurt Rachel's heart for Macy to be the first outsider to know, at least the die was cast, and the only direction to go was forward.

"But you don't have any children."

"Well, I do now."

The kid behind the counter handed Rachel her order, saving her from further explanation. "Sorry, Macy, gotta run," Rachel said with a half wave.

Beth's house was less chaotic than usual. The kids were at preschool, Jeter was at the groomer's, and Evan was working out in the field instead of from home. Rachel had fed Janie and put her down in Courtney's old Pack 'n Play, surrounded by toys.

"You don't have to worry about Macy Daniels," Beth said, relishing a swig of her shake. "When push comes to shove, that 'c-u-next-

Tuesday' is way too enamored with herself to invest the time of day in you."

"I know," Rachel said, "but running into her and being deliberately sketchy made me feel guilty. Not because I owe Macy anything but because I owe Rena something."

"You're taking care of Janie. Isn't that enough?"

"No, unfortunately, I don't think it is. I think I have to find Janie's father," Rachel whispered. "I don't think I'll have a moment's peace until I do."

"This is like a one-eighty from yesterday," Beth said, devouring her first potato. "Are you sharing my mood swings?"

"It's crazy, but when Macy started talking about Freddy's promotion and life being wonderful, all I could think about was Phil and the mess I'm imposing on Janie."

"I knew Phil wasn't going to give you the Hallmark homecoming you were hoping for," Beth said, wiping her mouth with three small napkins at once. "I keep telling you, the man's a dick. I think at some point, you're going to have to accept it."

"Maybe, but I think it would be best for me to take a little more time to adjust to the situation before I kick my husband to the curb."

"Let me ask you this—are you really ready to find Janie's daddy?"

"No, I'm not. I may never be. But that's why Rena was coming here, and if I'm the person I want to think I am, I have to honor that."

"So, what's next?"

"I'm not sure."

"You know you could end up losing Janie."

"I know. I can only hope that doesn't happen, because finding him is the right thing to do."

More tossing and turning. More binge-watching *Sex and the City* on Max, a part of the past that felt more snuggly than an afghan. Rachel still wasn't sure what to do about Phil—ride out the rough patch or part ways and hope for civility? He'd been home for a couple of days, but then last night, he'd called to say he was staying at the office. It happened from time to time, especially when he was consumed by a deal. There was no sense in arguing if she wasn't sure there was something worth arguing about.

She was airplaning a spoonful of applesauce into Janie's waiting mouth when Phil walked into the kitchen through the deck door.

"Morning." He waved.

Rachel waved back, trying to get a read on his mood. It was likely a long night. His color was off. He was paler than usual, and there were dark, puffy circles under his eyes. He made a beeline to the refrigerator, took out the orange juice, and chugged it from the container. Then she saw a rolled-up hundred sticking out of his shirt pocket and knew he'd dipped into his cocaine stash again.

"Hey," she said, ignoring her deduction. "You're just in time to watch Janie taste carrot pudding. I made it myself, and I must admit, it isn't bad."

"Well, if you made it, I'm sure it's delicious." He kissed her forehead. "Sorry I had to work last night. I missed you."

Maybe it was wishful thinking, but somewhere in their exchange was a glimpse of the Phil she'd fallen in love with. It made her insides twist that drugs made him more open to his feelings. It was an old pattern he had pretty much given up, but every so often, it reared its ugly head. She wanted to believe that with her unwavering support, he would see who he could be and would want to change. Maybe if this project went his way, he would feel confident enough to stay clean and be a true husband and a good father.

"I'm really glad you're home now, Phil," Rachel said, finding herself meaning it. "I want everything to work with us. I want to be a real family. We can have that now."

"I'm sure we can." Phil put the almost-empty container back in the refrigerator.

"Want me to make you breakfast?" Rachel offered.

"Listen, I know I haven't been around, and I'm sorry, but Jeb needs me to..." Phil took a deep breath.

Rachel turned to face him. "Please don't say it. You've been home for ten minutes."

"I can't help it, Rach. I have to work. You know how it goes."

Rachel went back to feeding Janie. "I'm sure Jeb can get someone else. He's a father. I'm sure he can respect that you are too."

"I keep telling you. No one else can do what I do."

Rachel tried to catch the carrot mess running down Janie's chin but missed. Despite her intentions, she felt her anger mounting. "You haven't told Jeb about Janie, have you?" She got up and ripped off a sheet of paper towel from the holder, knocking it down.

"For what, Rachel? So he could send us a year's supply of bibs after he fires me?"

So much for my fantasies of marital bliss.

"Doesn't it amaze you how much everything has changed between us?"

"Don't be so dramatic. We're busy. Everyone's busy. You've just had it so cushy that you're having a harder time accepting responsibility."

"Cushy?" Rachel thought of throwing carrot glop in Phil's arrogant face. The possible consequences stopped her. "Oh, please stop being an asshole. Raising a child is the biggest responsibility anyone could possibly have, and I'm accepting it just fine. How about you?"

"Me? I'm a man, the real breadwinner in this family. I know you like playing house and dressing up dolls. I get it, but there was a lot more that made you a woman back in the day." Phil ran his hands over his thick mop of hair.

"Oh, what was that, Phil?" She cupped her hands over Janie's ears. "Twenty-four-seven sex? Your suits neatly hung and organized in the closet after every business trip?"

Deep lines formed in Phil's forehead as his disappointment yielded to anger. "Maybe. What was so bad about taking care of me?" Phil demanded. "You have a problem being a good wife?"

"No. I don't. But I do have a problem with you being my husband." Rachel wiped her tears then Janie's mouth. She walked over to the cabinet to get a sippy cup. "Maybe this trip to wherever you're going this time is a good thing. We could use the separation. We both have a lot to think about."

"Who the hell do you think you're talking to?" Phil glared. He grabbed her by the shoulders and steered her out of the kitchen and against the adjoining wall. "You listen to me. And you listen good. I was there for you when you were nothing but a simpering little slut."

"Slut? Are you that high? The man I loved for years had just dumped me." Rachel tried to wriggle out of his grasp, but she couldn't break free.

"No more of this crap, Rachel. You and I are married, and we're staying that way." Phil pressed his mouth against hers.

She was pushing her head to the side, but the weight of his body against hers made it impossible. "Get off me right now, Phil!"

He squeezed both her wrists, pinned them to the wall, and pushed up against her. His hold was overpowering. Rachel feared she was walking a fine line between asserting herself and getting him upset enough to hurt her.

"Please, Phil, stop," she cried. "You're going to break my arms!"

"More drama. Give it up, and repeat after me." He kept her pinned to the wall. "We live in a nice house. We drive nice cars. We wear nice clothes, and we're not doing anything to change that. You got me?"

Rachel could feel him getting turned on and tried to control her desire to vomit. "I hear you," she said through a stream of tears.

"Good," he whispered into her ear. "Now, how about a little bon voyage time before I go?"

"I can't. The baby."

"Sure you can," Phil sneered. "It's nap time."

Phil took Janie out of the high chair, cooing in her ear and cuddling her as if he might have the capacity to love someone. As Phil headed to the nursery, Rachel thought about running out of the house, but the thought of leaving him alone with Janie made her shiver.

Out of options, she sat on their big bed and fought back tears. Maybe there was something heavy she could clobber over his head. Her eyes took a desperate tour of the room. The sconces were mounted, and the phones were plastic. The heaviest thing in the room was Phil's extra-plush terry robe.

She was about to dutifully strip naked when the doorbell rang. Rachel nearly tripped over her own feet as she darted out of the room with the speed of a cheetah. She was younger than Phil, and as she made her way down the stairs, she could hear him scrambling to catch up to her.

He was shouting unintelligibly, but here and there, she could make out his threats to do something or other to her if she dared to answer the door. She was halfway down the stairs when his footsteps neared. She kept her wits about her and maintained a steady pace while silently thanking her YouTube workouts. Phil was about to push her to the tiled floor when she grabbed the door handle and flung the door open.

"Macy!" Rachel cried, breathier than she'd anticipated. "How absolutely incredible to see you!" Without a moment's hesitation, Rachel embraced the woman as if she'd given her a kidney.

Out of the corner of her eye, Rachel could see Phil shuffle to the door. He was crouching, and she hoped he'd thrown his back out when he was chasing her. It gave her pleasure to find him belittled, even weak. She knew she had won in every sense of the word, and she reveled in the knowledge that Phil not getting his way was going to gnaw at every crevice of his colon.

"Rachel!" Macy said, breaking free from Rachel's overzealous hug. "Are you going to invite me in?"

Phil grimaced and let out a small but detectable snicker when he saw Macy's huge belly.

"Of course, please, come in," Rachel insisted, taking Macy's enormous jacket.

Macy entered gazing around as if she were a reporter for *Better Homes and Garden*.

"So, who's this guy?" Macy asked, as if uncertain he and Rachel had anything of substance to do with one another.

"This is Phil." Rachel paused. Maybe Macy thought he was her accountant. "My—uh, my—uh—"

"I'm her husband," Phil said flatly. "If you'll excuse me, I have to pack."

Phil held Rachel in an intense gaze until she offered him a triumphant smirk that sent him away.

Rachel led Macy to the den and directed her to an ample love seat.

"Did he say he was packing?" Macy asked.

Rachel thought about it for a moment. Given the excitement in her voice, it was possible Macy thought Phil had a gun in his pocket, but she doubted the woman would entertain such unconventional thoughts.

"Yes, that's what he said." Rachel licked her dry lips nervously.

"Oh no, I'm so sorry, Rachel."

"Why?"

"Is he leaving you?"

Rachel wanted to say, *I certainly hope so*, but now that she was able to breathe and return to her saner self, she decided divulging that truth to Macy was not necessarily in her best interest. "No, at least not today." Rachel pushed back a few strands of hair that had fallen in front of her face. "He's going on a business trip."

"Oh, well, that's good, I guess," Macy said. "I assume you just adopted, and it would be really hard to be a single mom at this point."

Seems I'm about to find out. "Can I get you something? Water? A quart of chocolate chip cookie dough and a spoon?" Rachel asked.

"You're funny," Macy said stoically. "No, I came here because the shop was closed, and I want to register with you. I don't even know if you do that."

"Oh, how lovely—and surprising! Sure, we can do that for you." Rachel wanted to question why Macy was being so kind, but she had too many more pressing thoughts to entertain. She pulled a Lenox candy dish filled with chocolates from the cabinet and put it on the coffee table. "We're not fully set up online yet, but that's part of our expansion plan."

"Good," Macy said, shifting uncomfortably in her seat. "I may not have ever told you, but I love your shop."

"That's very nice to hear." Rachel sat in a chair adjacent to Macy. "We aim to please."

There was an awkward moment of silence that Rachel wasn't sure how to fill. She certainly didn't want to bring up Freddy, or pregnancies, or houses, or money, or the utterly forbidden topic of high school. She got lucky, as Macy was gearing up to say something.

"All right, that's not the only reason I came here," Macy admitted.

Rachel's heart started pounding. "So what else can I do for you, Macy?"

"I think it's time for us to move on." Macy eyed a chocolate but didn't take it.

"Really? I thought we had."

"No, we haven't. We've been insulting each other for decades."

Rachel wasn't sure what to do with Macy's sudden honesty. After her interaction with Phil and his continued clamoring upstairs, it was hard to focus. "Maybe we've always misunderstood each other," Rachel said, figuring her true feelings—*You've always been a colossal bitch*—wouldn't do much to manifest a truce.

"You made a play for my husband," Macy shrieked. "It wasn't a misunderstanding, but it was a long time ago."

Rachel wanted to set the record straight with Macy once and for all, but she wasn't sure how it would be received and decided on a different approach. "Macy, you and Freddy are the most perfect couple I know. I have never and would never do anything to come between the two of you. And even if I tried, I couldn't possibly succeed."

Rachel was laying it on thick, but she knew the ego she was dealing with. "Freddy worships and adores you. No one else would stand a chance."

Macy lifted her head, and a tear rolled down her round, puffy face. Maybe it was Macy's hormones, or maybe Rachel had struck a chord. "I appreciate that, Rachel. I really do."

"I have to ask. Why bring up all this now?"

"My therapist said I should." Macy took a chocolate and unwrapped it. "She said being a mom to two toddlers and soon adding a set of twins to the mix was tough enough and not to let the past drain me."

Rachel had to admit Macy had already begun to look more relaxed.

"Well then, I hope this chat helped."

The sudden bang of a door slamming upstairs made them both jump.

"I think I should leave," Macy said, struggling to get up.

A few more slams later, Phil's cursing grew steadier and louder.

"Macy, please don't go." Rachel wondered if her desperation sounded as intense as it felt. "I'll make iced tea and show you our new line of antique ceramic dolls."

Rachel hoped Macy wouldn't force her to say more. Maybe this old new friend didn't know exactly what was going on, but she had to know something was up. It was too benign to call the police but too disconcerting to go unnoticed. The look on Macy's face made Rachel feel like her former enemy was seeing her for the first time.

"Sure, Rachel, I'll stay." Macy sat back down and took another chocolate. By the time Phil left, she had eaten almost the entire bowl.

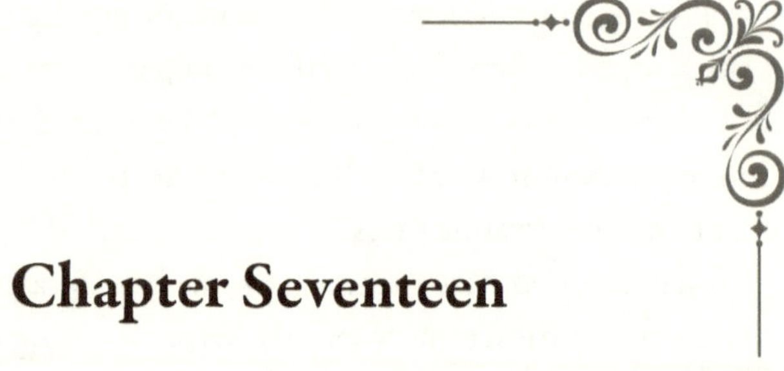

Chapter Seventeen

The temptation to call Beth to tell her what had happened was overwhelming. Phil was out of control, lost to whatever demons were now in charge of his soul. There would be no return to any kind of normal, no trying to be a family and make things work for Janie's sake.

After some internal debate, Rachel returned to logistics and made an appointment to have all the locks and the security system changed. Phil was potentially dangerous to her and Janie, and Rachel had to make sure he could never get into the house on his own. Though she had no clue how he would react to being locked out, it was a risk she was willing to take.

Having devoted far too much energy to Phil, Rachel was ready for a distraction. The dishes were done, the laundry was folded, Janie's food was prepped, and all the new shows on her watch list were set to record. Still, she needed to get something done while the baby was napping. Then she remembered Rena's stuff was in the attic. Maybe there would be keepsakes for Janie.

The big trunks were like the ones that had belonged to her grandfather when he was in the navy. Rachel's mother had repurposed them to store seasonal linens that were kept in the basement when Rachel was a child. Although Rena's trunks were cumbersome, Rachel was determined to move them to an area that made going through the contents more accessible. A few hard shoves was all she needed. Opening the first chest was relatively easy. It was filled with

Rena's wardrobe, a variety of conservative and funky shirts, pants, and skirts that made Rachel smile. This was the woman she'd known, full of whimsy and practicality, each with its own place in her life and, evidently, her drawers.

Rachel held up a few things against herself, but nothing worked. Rena had been smaller-framed, fuller-hipped, and shorter. For a moment, Rachel thought about something for Beth, then she laughed out loud, remembering how Beth had scarfed down a late-night Domino's pizza on her own. Instead, Rachel saved a few classic blouses for Janie then began making piles for the nearby women's shelter. It was comforting to know that many lucky recipients would be well clothed.

The next chest Rachel opened held shoes, belts, toys, some clothes for Janie, and a few hats, but underneath everything was a medium-sized fabric keepsake box. At first, Rachel was hesitant to open it. Whatever was inside was personal, and she still didn't want to trample on Rena's privacy. But if she was going to find Janie's father, she had an obligation to seek out any information available. She took a breath and opened the box.

Lying on top was a letter addressed to Rena from someone named Jackie Benson. It was postmarked from New Jersey, and the date suggested it had been written right around the time of Rena's visit.

Dear Rena,

It was so good to hear from you! Dennis and I would love for you to stay for a visit. Please let us know the date so we can have the guest room ready. Right now, you'd be sleeping on a toaster oven and an espresso maker. I'm so excited that you're coming. It'll give me the incentive to finally put our gifts away!

Love, Jackie

Rachel thought for a moment and realized the letter was from the busy newlyweds Rena had told her about. Rachel put the note aside and opened another right beneath it. This one had no post-mark.

My Dearest Rena,

I cannot tell you how much these past few weeks have meant to me. I don't think I have ever been happier or more certain of love. I understand your loyalty to Reggie, but what about us? Don't we deserve a chance? Marry me, Rena.

All my love,

Your Professor

Rachel couldn't help but sob. This was him. Janie's father. His words were in her hands, and his daughter was in her heart. She gave herself a moment then wiped her tears and began to review the letter for clues. As far as she could tell, there were none. He hadn't signed his name. A look through the rest of the letters proved to be equally unhelpful. Nothing was postmarked, and there were no signs of the Professor's identity anywhere.

Tomorrow, Rachel would drop the baby off at Beth's. She had no choice. It was time to meet the Bensons.

"Thanks again for watching Janie." Rachel adjusted the Bluetooth to get a clearer connection. "How's she doing?"

"She's fine. Courtney is finding her things to teethe on. Don't worry, none of them involve electricity. Are you there yet?"

Rachel checked her GPS. "Almost. A few more miles."

"Do you know what you're going to say?"

"Sort of, but who knows? It all might change when I get there." Rachel checked the map. "It's saying I should make a right, but I can't. There is no right turn."

"It's Jersey. There's no logical way to get anywhere."

"I better go." Rachel sighed. "I think I'm lost."

"Okay, go, but chances are all you have to do is make a U-turn, and you'll be fine," Beth suggested. "Call me as soon as you leave their house. Before you get back on the road."

Rachel turned off the Bluetooth, looked at the GPS, then figured she had nothing to lose and made a U-turn. The Bensons were two miles away on the right.

Rachel parked in front of the Bensons' neighbors' house, a small white replica of all the Cape Cods on the block. She knew it wasn't making her appear any less conspicuous, but she needed to stay in the car for a few minutes to calm down. Psychologically, she felt the less blatant she was, the better. She once again reminded herself she was there to find out as much as possible about the Professor. She would say she had something for him from Rena's belongings and ask them where she might locate him. Rena had said they'd lost touch and knew nothing about the baby, so there would be no reason to bring up anything else.

Rachel wiped the soles of her shoes against the Mother Goose on the welcome mat and gripped the brass doorknocker. The name engraved at the top informed her she was at the right house. She paced a little when there was no answer, then she knocked again. A lanky brunette in jeans and a sweatshirt answered the door hesitantly.

"Hi. Listen, thanks, but we already have a religion we're content with." For a Brit, the woman had almost no discernable accent.

"Oh, great, but, um, no. I'm not... That's not why I'm here. I'm a friend of Rena's. Rena Stanton."

"Oh! Well, now I feel stupid. So, you're Rena's friend." The woman held open the door. "I'm Jackie. Please, come in."

"It's nice to meet you, Jackie." She extended her hand. "I'm Rachel."

"I've always liked that name."

The Bensons' house was small but cheery with sand-colored walls and touches of yellows and muted greens. The entrance was in the living room, and Rachel followed Jackie to a little conversation area consisting of a light-brown couch and two beige wing chairs.

"Have a seat. So, Rachel, how do you know Rena?" Jackie asked.

"We became friends when I was in London not long ago. Unfortunately, I'm here with some sad news."

After the initial shock had worn off, Jackie was ready to share a few stories and insisted Rachel join her for a cup of tea. Rachel finally felt comfortable enough to broach the topic of the Professor but opted for a different tactic than the one she'd planned.

"Do you know if Rena had any other friends in the area? Someone else I should tell?"

"No. Not really. I know she was seeing someone, but she didn't talk about him much. Barely at all. Maybe she felt too guilty since she was still married. I know she called the guy the Professor. And she said he made her happy, but that's all I know. She was always smiling—until the call about Reggie, and that was that. She left, and we never heard from her again. We tried, but I guess she moved or something."

"I know she was taking classes." Rachel took a slow sip of tea. "Did she ever say where?"

"No, she didn't. She kept her private life to herself." Jackie took another oatmeal cookie from the tray she had put out with the tea. "Just someplace in the area. I think in Westchester, because she mentioned the constant traffic on the bridge. I'm pretty sure that's where she met him."

"Do you know what he taught?"

"English. Literature, that I remember. And I also remember her saying something about a pub near the campus she'd go to after class. Thaxton's? I'm pretty sure that was the name of the place. I don't know if it's still there, but it's a fairly short distance away. Right off the Garden State to the thruway. Sorry, I wish I could be more helpful."

"No, you've been great," Rachel assured her as she got up to leave. "Thank you for your time."

Since Rachel was frustrated to begin with, fighting traffic on the parkway made her seethe. All she wanted to do was check out Thaxton's and see what the crowd was like, but the traffic gods were being woefully uncooperative. Unlike her usual take-it-as-it-comes road etiquette, Rachel had given the finger to several rude motorists who'd cut her off.

When she started to cry, Rachel realized her anger was meant for Phil. She was livid. He had demeaned her in ways she'd never imagined possible. Every night, she spent the minutes before drifting off to sleep dreaming of redemption and justice. There was no other way to deal with her rage. Still, in her heart of hearts, Rachel believed in karma. She assumed Phil would eventually get his without needing any intervention from her.

Rachel felt calmer as she approached the exit for Thaxton's, which was a few miles farther from the Parkway than Jackie had said. The local road to get there was more twisty and bendy than Rachel had anticipated. It was possible she would get there but never be able to find the place again. She continued on until she came to a big brick house. According to the red sign with gold lettering, this was Thaxton's. *Odd.* With the exception of one car, the lot was empty. Maybe the attractive, burly guy standing by the entrance was the manager.

Rachel parked, figuring she would ask him their hours and when they were busiest. Before she was even halfway to the door, the man turned around. He was wearing an expensive suit, and she decided he was more the banker type than a restaurateur. He was walking with his head hanging toward the ground as if he'd been dared to watch his shoes until he reached his car. Rachel was impeding his route, and he flinched when he saw her.

"Sorry," Rachel said. "I didn't mean to—"

"Oh, no, it wasn't you," the man said. "I was knee-deep in my own world."

"Does your world happen to serve fries?" Rachel asked. "Because I was all set to order a heaping plate of them."

"Bummer. I'm a lousy cook, and the sign says, 'Welcome to the Grand Not Reopening Yet.' They're still working on the place. You can sign up online to get a date."

Rachel guessed he was in his forties, and she liked his kind eyes. "A date?"

"Yes, for when they actually open."

Rachel blushed. She was sensitive about misunderstandings.

The man glanced at his watch. "I'm really sorry about the fries." The guy checked his watch again. "If I didn't have a previous engagement, I could ponder them with you further."

Rachel wasn't sure what the vibe was between them, not that it mattered. But the guy kept fidgeting with his keys.

"No worries, thanks!" Rachel said. "I'll go online and sign up."

"Great. Enjoy your day."

"You too."

By the time Rachel pulled into Beth's driveway, she'd resigned herself to the idea that finding Janie's father was not going to be an easy task. She took a couple of minutes to freshen her makeup, something she learned from her mother, who had a palpable fear of corner-of-the-eye goopies. She walked in to find Janie in the family room, playing with a few toys as Jeter stood guard by the Pack 'n Play.

"Beth?" Rachel called.

"Hey, I'm in here," Beth answered. "Just a minute."

Rachel couldn't help but laugh when she saw Beth juggling more snacks than she'd seen the last time she'd been to a carnival.

"Seriously?" Rachel continued laughing.

"I must be carrying a linebacker." Beth set the food on the coffee table and parked herself on the couch. "I should really stick our blow-up mattress next to the refrigerator. It would make my life easier."

"For now, you're lucky the couch is only a few feet from the pantry," Rachel teased. "Where is everyone?"

"Evan took the kids to a birthday party." Beth surveyed the table and chose a fresh bag of Veggie Crisps. "They should be gone for a while." She opened the bag, took a handful, then somewhat reluctantly offered some to Rachel.

"Oh, no thanks," Rachel said.

Beth looked relieved and took another handful of crisps. "So? You never called me. How did it go with the Bensons?"

"Sorry, my phone was down to one bar, and I forgot my charger." Rachel snatched a chocolate-covered pomegranate from an almost-empty bag. "I'm basically at square one. Except for a pub called Thaxton's. I went—like us, they're closed for renovations. But I was almost invited for fries."

"Huh?"

"Nothing, really. Some guy there was bummed they were closed."

"Okay, so that's it? That's all you got?"

"Pretty much, although the woman did confirm Rena was quietly involved with someone she referred to as the Professor."

"So what are you doing here?" Beth closed the bag of crisps and picked up a package of cookies. "Janie will be napping soon, and you'll have time to do more research."

Rachel got up to look at Janie, who was already asleep.

"You're sure you didn't give them any inkling about the baby?"

"It was just the wife, and why would I?" Rachel snapped. "Janie is my daughter now. The only one who needs to know the truth is her father."

"You don't have to bite my head off." Beth picked up a Tootsie Roll. "I can see you have all kinds of objectivity on your side."

Rachel rolled her eyes. "I'll find the college that's nearest to the pub and go from there."

"Maybe you should take a class," Beth said. "You always liked school. Maybe child development."

"That's actually not a bad idea," Rachel mused. "And even though I know it's a long shot, I'm thinking of calling the woman I met on the plane."

"The fortune teller?"

"Yeah, but she's more legit," Rachel explained. "She gets feelings, hunches, and she also reads cards. It's an art."

"How is she going to help you?"

"I don't know," Rachel admitted. "Maybe she can help me find Janie's father."

"That would be one hell of a hunch."

"I know, but I don't have very much to go on." Rachel took a Twizzler. "I should probably consider any lead I can get."

"If you say so, but just in case, try not to send her any energy about Janie."

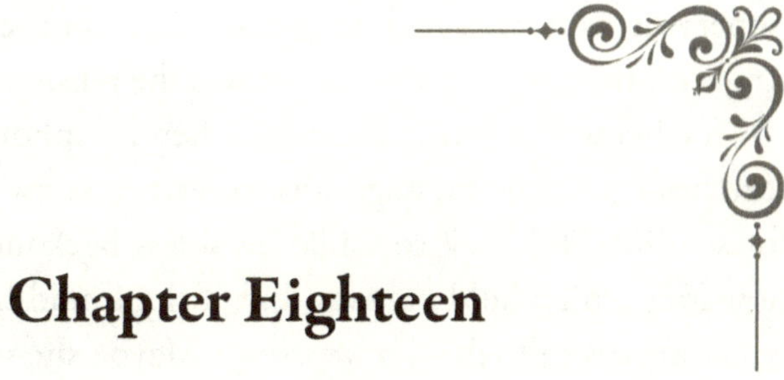

Chapter Eighteen

It was nearly four in the morning, and Rachel had spent the last half hour feeding Janie and being urged to buy a new Dorian Gray-type skin serum, a magic potion that promised to keep any signs of maturity a deep, dark secret between Rachel and a patiently waiting telemarketer.

These days, the only one close enough to scrutinize her face was Janie, and she apparently didn't mind what Rachel looked like as long as it was well after midnight and there was a bottle. For the past several weeks, it seemed certain that Janie was not only destined to grow up on late-night TV and lengthy infomercials but to also have a penchant for working the graveyard shift. The child simply couldn't manage to keep her eyes open during the day, no matter how hard Rachel tried to tire her out before nightfall.

Janie drained her bottle and was finally ready to go back to sleep. Rachel rocked her in her arms from the family room to the nursery and put her in her crib. Janie instinctively stuck her thumb in her mouth while patting her soft, stuffed giraffe. Rachel watched her for a few minutes, wondering how it was possible to be so crazy in love with this child. Janie wasn't biologically hers, but every fiber of Rachel's being believed she was regardless.

Rachel went back to her room, pulled off her robe, and collapsed into bed. There was no getting around Janie's stubborn nature or her boundless desire for affection. The fact that it led to exceptionally long nights and yawn-filled days wasn't wonderful, but it wasn't as unnerving as Rachel had imagined when she'd considered life as a single mother. With Phil gone, so was the tension.

Rachel was enjoying the calm when her phone buzzed. It was a text from Jeb. His message was to let her know how sorry he was for sending Phil back to Chile. Business beckoned. Jeb wasn't sure how long Phil would be away, but if she found herself in need, she could always call Jeb—*for anything*. Maybe she was reading into it, but the *for anything* part made her skin crawl. At seventy, Jeb reeked of privilege, the kind of old money he seemed to think could buy him anything or anyone. He was in for a rude awakening if he thought Rachel was interested in being another of his many possessions.

To compound her disfavor, Rachel believed it was partly Jeb's influence that made Phil the mess he was today. But that story was becoming so old that Rachel didn't want to invest another moment in it. Her new life didn't have room for narcissistic, controlling men who viewed power as their divine right. Not now. Not ever again. She was finally free to do things her way. She just wasn't sure what her way looked like yet. The one thing she did realize was that it was becoming increasingly difficult for her to get serious about finding Janie's father.

"Thanks for these, Rach." Beth's eyes lit up as she opened the bag and pulled out a huge everything bagel. "I would have gotten them after I dropped the kids off at school, but I had to walk Jeter." She took a bite that was too big for her mouth and continued to speak while chomping. "Poor dog is pissed that I'm having another kid, and when he doesn't get time with me, he pees right next to the toilet in my bathroom. He knows how much time I spend running in there." Beth scoffed. "Typical spiteful male."

"Want a drink?" Rachel put Janie down on a large play blanket in the family room and went to the fridge.

"A Pellegrino, thanks." Beth stretched out on the couch. "What's going on with Phil? You haven't mentioned him lately."

Rachel's heart flip-flopped, and she was glad Beth couldn't see her face from where she was sitting. She forced a smile and brought in the drinks. "I would imagine he's fine," Rachel replied, setting the bottles on the coffee table.

"Imagine?" Beth repeated.

"I told you. He went on a business trip."

"To the bowels of Nepal?" Beth snickered through another bite of bagel. "People who travel can still communicate."

"It's not polite to talk with your mouth full," Rachel chided.

"It's not polite to be full of shit either," Beth shot back. "There's got to be something you're not telling me."

Rachel took a swig of water to stall. Janie was sleeping, and waking her just to avoid dealing with Beth didn't seem fair. With nothing else readily available in her arsenal, Rachel went to her bag, pulled out Edie's card, and handed it to Beth.

"Right, the fortune teller. What did she say?" Beth took a sip of water and burped.

"I still haven't called her."

"Well, I'm sure she knows you want to, so go ahead."

"Now?"

"Janie's sleeping, and it's quiet." Beth yawned, and in an instant, her eyes closed.

Rachel picked up the card and studied it. Edie had been attentive and helpful. Maybe she would, without specific knowledge, help Rachel decide if finding Janie's father was the right thing to do. Rachel was ready to take out her phone when she heard Beth snoring. Rachel took the uneaten half of the bagel from her and put it on the coffee table. Janie was still asleep, and even Jeter was dozing.

Finding nothing but support, Rachel went into the kitchen with her cell phone and called Edie.

"Hello?" she heard herself say in a tiny voice.

"Hello. Who's this?"

"Rachel."

"Rachel?"

"From the plane."

"Oh, of course," Edie said. "Forgive me. My son stopped by and is just about to leave."

"Oh, no problem, I'll call you another time."

"No, please hang on. I'll be a minute."

Rachel could hear Edie saying goodbye through what sounded like the hum of a jet. "Hello, Rachel?"

"Yes."

"How are you, honey?" Edie asked. "You've been on my mind. I'm so glad you called."

"I'm fine." Rachel hesitated. "I was wondering if I could meet with you... professionally."

"Is everything all right?"

"Yes, but I think I could use a reading."

Edie's place was much easier to find than the Bensons'. It was a charming brick house with a plum-colored door and a wraparound porch. Off to the side was a detached garage that had been converted into an office. Edie led Rachel into the soothing space, allowing her time to browse and get a feel for the different trinkets, candles, and crystals. Edie found an herby-looking cylinder and put it in a large brass incense burner.

"Would you mind?" Edie asked. "Scent is a powerful resource. I think it also helps clear the air by neutralizing the properties. It can be really intrusive when a spirit overstays its welcome."

Rachel shook her head and shifted uncomfortably in her shoes. "Does that happen often?"

"It's hard to say," Edie admitted, trying to light the stubborn leaves. "I guess often enough for me to buy white sage in bulk."

Rachel rubbed her suddenly chilled shoulders. Being there was probably a bad idea. She didn't even get free readings when they were offered at parties, and forget about cracking open fortune cookies. She'd made peace with being prone to anxiety but confidently prided herself on being grounded and logical. Now here she was, ready to have her soul examined by Mother Nature in what looked and smelled like a head shop.

Edie had Rachel sit at a small table as she prepped the cards. "Can I get you anything? Coffee, tea, persimmons, Milk Duds?"

"Will they help?" Rachel asked.

"Sure," Edie said. "If you're hungry."

Rachel considered pocketing the Milk Duds for Beth. "No, I'm fine, thanks."

"No, you're not fine. You're not even sure why you're here."

Rachel swallowed hard. *Okay, that was an obvious observation.* Besides, Edie already had a sense of her from their initial time together.

"Do you want to talk about what's going on?" Edie asked.

Rachel remembered Beth warning her not to send out any vibes about Janie. It was going to take an abundance of will for Rachel to keep both her mind and her mouth quiet. "No, not really. I think the cards can do the talking. They knew what to say the first time."

"Yes, they did," Edie said. "I take it that reading was fairly accurate?"

"It was. Not that I understood it very well," Rachel explained. "But everything ended up making sense. That's why I'm here. I need some kind of direction again and figured this was worth another try."

"Well, thank you very much." Edie smiled. "When I get approval from a skeptic, I am particularly flattered."

Rachel watched Edie shuffle the cards.

"Get comfortable, and let's get started." Edie closed her eyes for a moment. "Hmmm... There's that feeling again, like you're familiar to me. It happened when we met, and I've felt it several times since. I still can't figure out why."

Rachel stiffened in her seat. "Maybe I have that look, like someone you saw picking cherries at the supermarket."

"I don't think so," Edie said.

Another chill crept up Rachel's spine, and once again, she patted her shoulders. "Okay... maybe we rubbed elbows on the *Mayflower* in a past life. Or auditioned for Busby Berkeley on the same kick line—"

"Rachel, stop!" Edie interjected. "You're freaking out for no reason." Edie opened her eyes. "Energy is always around us. Having a sense of it is never a bad thing. It's illuminating, like having a light in your closet so you don't have to struggle to pull an outfit together. Consider it a dear friend who wants the best for you."

"I'll try, but light or no light, I usually have a tough time deciding what to wear," Rachel said.

Rachel appreciated Edie, but the likelihood of her embracing the New Age was almost the same as the likelihood Phil would be waiting for her at home with an apology and news that he'd quit his job to be a family man.

Edie smirked. "Let's continue. I'm going to do an abbreviated read. I don't think you can handle more than that."

Edie instructed Rachel to cut the deck, then she laid four cards out on the table. "Hm, interesting."

"What is it?" Rachel's voice shook.

"The high priestess."

"I'm Jewish. Is that kosher?" Rachel clasped her hands together. "Give it to me straight—what does she mean?"

"Please, relax." Edie patted Rachel's clenched fist until her hands separated. "Usually, it signifies a woman keeping a closely guarded secret, either because she has to or is choosing to."

Rachel breathed deeply and pulled a Lifesaver from her bag. She sucked on it so hard, it nearly disintegrated before she could even discern its flavor.

"The ten of cups," Edie said, "typically means enduring familial love and a romantic bond that includes raising children and sharing values, which is strange because I am not getting a strong sense of marital union or harmony."

Rachel sighed. "Well, we both kind of know about that one."

"Yes, but the cards didn't, and now, they do."

"Well, I'm glad the cards have caught up with my life," Rachel said smugly. "Anything else?"

Edie scrutinized the cards more closely. "I must be right, because here's the ten of swords, which could signify a breakup." Edie shook her head. "I think you're in a turbulent phase. I do see love, but my instincts are telling me it's likely from an unexpected source. The disparity is confusing."

"If I'm being honest, this all makes sense." Rachel felt tears stinging in her eyes and plucked a tissue from a nearby box.

Edie touched each card as if figuring out how they linked together to make a statement about Rachel's circumstances. "Now, here are the twos. Twos are tricky. When a card like the two of swords shows up, it can mean there are big choices to be made." Edie eyed the cards again. "I can certainly understand why you've been feeling overwhelmed."

"How do you do this, Edie?" Rachel dabbed at her tears. "How can you plunk down a few cards and understand my life?"

"But I don't. *You* have to make sense of what the cards are offering."

"I'm still not sure what to do."

"Let me give you some good old-fashioned advice that has nothing to do with the cards." Edie patted Rachel's shoulder. "Find something to distract you for a while. Sometimes, the best course of action when you're feeling stuck is to submit to fate."

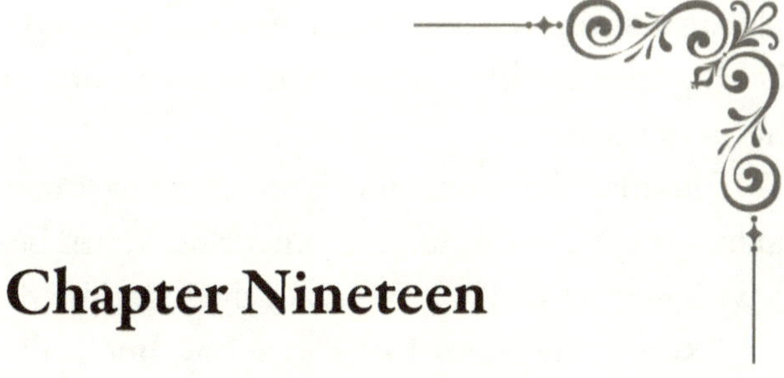

Chapter Nineteen

The cool, crisp September air felt good against Rachel's cheek as she trekked through the Purchase College parking lot, en route to the registrar's office. It was the one university that Google deemed the closest to Thaxton's, and since the school was touted as having the most extensive English department of those in the vicinity, she felt it was the most likely choice.

When she'd called earlier, a secretary with an attitude had told her to hightail it over if she wanted to enroll in the current semester. Luckily, there were rolling admissions, and many classes were still open, especially if she wasn't interested in matriculating. Rachel had to laugh. She wasn't even sure she wanted to be there at all.

Up until a couple of weeks ago, the thought of going back to school made Rachel cringe. Her BA in women's studies and minor in philosophy were more than sufficient to run the family business with Beth. If anything, finding her baby's father was much more inspiring than the promise of a certificate in the endangered haiku, a new area of study an advisor suggested she consider.

As Rachel continued walking, deep in thought, a gentle rain began to fall. She did enjoy learning, but the whole college experience had been a painful one, especially when she got pregnant. She and the father had met in a Spanish literature class, where they'd bonded over a research paper on Federico Garcia Lorca. He was a totally hot exchange student, proficient in piano, Latin cooking, and lovemaking. When he said he wanted to go between her legs and give her pleasure until she screamed, her seventeen-year-old hormones and her hips rose to the occasion. She wanted him as much as he wanted her—all the time.

The machismo dripping from every part of Jesus Lopez, not to mention the cross dangling from his neck, had been exactly what her Jewish mother had been afraid of the first time she'd met him.

"Rachel, he seems like a nice boy, but really? A sexy Spaniard whose namesake was born in a manger. What am I supposed to tell your grandparents?"

As it turned out, her mother's concerns had been legitimate. Yes, they'd been responsible and used protection, but Jesus was ample, and the condom wasn't. The semester had ended, and he was back home somewhere near Barcelona before Rachel even had the chance to tell him she was having his child.

Despite her mother's pleading, Rachel had never tried to locate him. She felt Jesus deserved to have a life in his country, and Rachel had resigned herself to the idea of raising the baby on her own. Telling him would only have complicated things for everyone. But for better or worse, none of it was meant to be.

A strong wind whipped Rachel's scarf across her cheeks, reeling her back to the present. She didn't know where the registrar's office was and picked up her pace to get anywhere warm. As she passed lecture halls and department buildings, she continued to be flooded with her own memories. The irony was blatant. She'd been in college when she'd lost a baby, and she was back again because she'd found one. *Higher learning, indeed.*

Another blast of arctic wind that had no right to invade September ran right through Rachel, making her shiver from head to toe. She heard a guy call out to another guy to meet up for lunch at D Hall, and since it was directly on her path, it was the logical place to go to get her bearings. A hot cup of coffee sounded more seductive than sex.

As Rachel entered the building, a girl with long, straight hair and no makeup handed her a flyer listing the egregious offences of the cosmetic industry. Rachel, in full L'Oreal regalia, walked past the table that touted lipstick as one of the seven deadly sins and asked a bald guy with ripped jeans for directions to the café. He pointed the way, suggested either a blueberry muffin or crumb cake, and admitted he was addicted to the snickerdoodle coffee. Rachel wasn't hungry but figured she would follow the bald guy's advice anyway. Muffins weren't real food. They were baked pillows of immense calories that did nothing to make or break one's appetite.

For such a large space, there was no line at the counter, and the tables were virtually empty. Rachel watched a tall blonde thumb through a course guide as if it were the *Kamasutra*. She wasn't sure what turned the girl off, but suddenly, she tossed the book onto a chair as if it had cooties. Snack in hand, Rachel checked the catalogue for vermin then claimed a table near the exit. After a bite of the luscious muffin, she started searching the guide for an English course.

The History of the English Language looked interesting, but it was being taught by Dr. Gloria Farrell, who had no chance of being Janie's father. She was reading the description of Courtly Love in Literature when a stream of coffee went spilling across the table, splashing a thin spray on her chin.

"Whoa, I am so sorry!" A man armed with a stack of napkins was dabbing frantically at the mess. "That was really clumsy of me."

Rachel looked up to see a wiry guy in his forties with sandy-colored hair and soft hazel eyes. "My fault." She took a napkin from him and wiped her chin. "Bad place to park a coffee cup." She moved her things and used her napkins to clean the last of the spill.

"No, I should have been more careful," the man insisted.

"Okay, truth is," Rachel said, "I'm only being noble because nothing got on my clothes."

"Noble deserves another cup of coffee. On me."

"Literally?" Rachel smirked. "Because it *can* be arranged."

"I earned that." He nodded. "Be right back."

Rachel went back to scanning the book.

The man returned with a large cup of coffee, which he carefully set in the center of the table. "Snickerdoodle, light, one sugar?" He sat down opposite her.

"An excellent presumption," Rachel said.

"Good—since I forgot to ask." The man threw a few extra packets of sugar next to her cup. "But it is the campus favorite."

"Yes, I've been told." Rachel closed the course guide.

"New student?"

"Sort of," Rachel said, unsure of how to respond. "I have a BA, but I'm ready for an academic adventure."

An academic adventure? Rachel was certain she was bringing new meaning to the word *lame*.

"Sounds spirited," the man said. "Have you decided which courses to take?"

Maybe I didn't sound that ridiculous. "I'm only taking one, and I'm not sure yet."

He pointed to an entry. "You should take this one."

"Childhood in Victorian Literature. Why?"

"I teach it."

"I see." Rachel felt her cheeks flush. "Actually, I am considering that one. I've always been interested in the Victorian period."

"Great," he said, getting up. "I'll look forward to seeing you again."

"Sure. By the way, I'm Rachel."

"Well, it was a pleasure to spill your coffee, Rachel," he said, extending a hand. "I'm Zach. Zach Jamison."

"Thanks for the makeup coffee, Zach Jamison." She chuckled. "Much appreciated."

He checked his watch. "Sorry, I'd love to chat more, but I have to run. Faculty meeting. About five minutes ago."

"Uh-oh, you're late." Rachel grinned and shook her finger at him.

"I'll see *you* in class." Zach smiled, revealing dimples.

Rachel watched Zach leave the café, feeling her stomach tighten as she thought about Phil.

Chapter Twenty

Beth's SOS call begging Rachel to go to the supermarket with her and the kids worked. Rachel was pushing the overflowing shopping cart and supporting Beth's determination not to buy everything salted, frosted, or slathered in chocolate. It was a surprisingly fun outing. Janie was enjoying the kids as they each took turns trying to make her laugh. Their interaction was so natural, the familial touch Rachel had been longing for. She could only hope when all was said and done, they would be real cousins.

Rachel watched as Beth examined her selections and apparently decided there was enough room to balance a jumbo box of Raisin Bran on top of a tower of stretch-mark cream and juice boxes. Rachel was about to applaud the feat when out of nowhere Beth groaned, "Victorian lit? Really? With all the possibilities, that's what you want to take?" Beth grabbed a Snickers bar on their way to the checkout line.

"Mooommy... I want candy like you have!" Joshie wailed.

"This is not for Mommy," Beth said. "This is for the baby in Mommy's belly."

"I got a baby in my belly too." Joshie stuck out his stomach like he was Santa Claus.

"Me too!" Courtney cried, copying her brother.

Beth growled something inaudible that Rachel didn't bother to question.

"Okay, guys, this is dessert. Remember, nothing else after dinner." Beth handed Joshie and Courtney candy bars.

"So, what's wrong with Victorian literature?" Rachel asked.

"Huh?" Beth seemed lost in other thoughts. "Um, um, oh, I remember. I think it's impractical."

"We run a toy business, Beth. We specialize in impractical." Rachel picked up a pack of wintergreen gum and threw it into the shopping cart. "Who knows? Maybe I'll learn more about our inventory or doll history. I may even get a better idea of what we should have in stock."

"Aaahh..." Beth sounded like a light bulb had turned on in her head. "I get it now. This Zach guy, the tall hottie who got you coffee, he's the one teaching the class, isn't he?"

"Why would that matter?"

"He's cute."

"Adorable. But so what?"

"I thought you were trying to find the chubby baby daddy."

"I am. But I was thinking about what Edie said, that I should allow myself to be distracted. If I'm on campus, I'm still being proactive without actually..."

"Being proactive," Beth finished.

"Exactly." Rachel wasn't sure she was buying her own bullshit, but she was going to work it just the same. "Besides, none of this matters anyway. I'm married."

"Honey, the way you're married," Beth said through a wad of caramel, "is the most single a girl could be."

Oh happy day! Or night, as it were. Janie had finally had enough of hearing about wrinkle creams and Ninja blenders and was sleeping through the night. It was ten o'clock, and Rachel could put the baby in the crib and be reasonably certain there would be no need to feed her again until breakfast. The extra time also assured Rachel that she could shower, wash her hair, and even slick on a coat or two of nail polish. Strange how motherhood had initially robbed her of her femininity. She kissed Janie good night and went to bed.

Still trying to adjust to the new schedule, Rachel wasn't tired. She tried counting sheep then shifted over to make-out sessions and how many tongues she'd had in her mouth throughout the decades. She reached some impossible number and was surprised to feel like she was getting turned on. It was troubling, given all the emotional craziness in her life. Rachel wasn't sure she had the right or will to be horny. The guilt made her uncomfortable, as did the realization that she still had the stash of toys Phil had bought in her nightstand drawer. The thought of their steamy late-night calls when he was away on business made Rachel nauseous, and she leapt out of bed to toss the few hundred dollars' worth of erotic entertainment into the trash.

She got back into bed, feeling empowered. She'd never been into solo sex, which was probably the reason she'd had so many trysts before Dash, years ahead of marrying Phil. She hadn't slept with *all* of them, but there were few penises that could surprise her. Despite what Phil had said, being experienced in male anatomy didn't make her a slut. It made her someone who had always been seeking to find true love, body and soul. She may have been somewhat misguided, but nothing she'd done was criminal, and each experience had taught her something she hadn't known before.

Maybe a glass of wine will quiet my mind. Rachel got up to go to the kitchen but ended up at her dresser, where she'd put Rena's keepsake box. She picked up a handful of letters and sifted through them for the umpteenth time. There was still nothing new. She was about to put them back when she noticed the corner of an envelope peeking out underneath the lining. Rachel tugged at the corner, and it came out easily. She slid the pink paper out of the envelope and held it under the small lamp.

Darling,

Please find it in your heart to forgive me. I was prepared to leave Reggie and spend my life with you, but fate has had its way with us. Reggie is desperately ill and needs me. I'm his wife, and I couldn't bear the guilt of causing him any further suffering. If it is in the cards, we will be together again. For now, I will treasure our memories. And though we are parted, you must be assured that our love lives on in a most beautiful way.

Forever,

Rena.

Rachel put the letter down, thought of Edie, and picked it up again.

If it is in the cards...

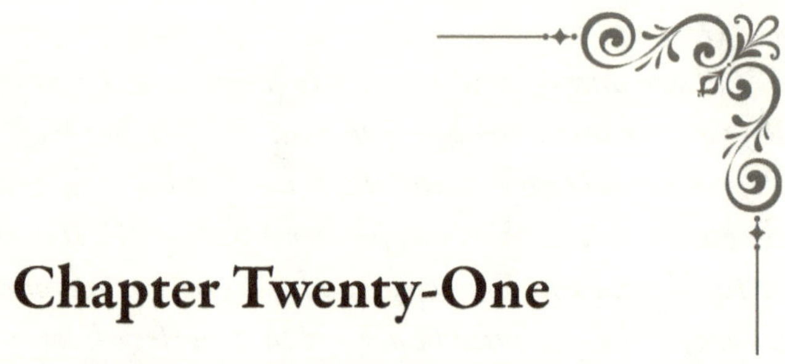

Chapter Twenty-One

Beth's griping aside, Rachel saw no reason to squelch her plans. Victorian literature was a fine subject, and even if she thought Zach Jamison might be one, too, she wasn't delusional enough to think her interest would be anything more than the distraction Edie had suggested. Syllabus in hand, she made her way to the humanities section of the student bookstore. Professor Jamison's list was long, and none of his selections were easy to find.

Out of the corner of her eye, Rachel noticed a familiar-looking guy watching her scan the shelves, but she couldn't quite place him. He began walking toward her, and she knew definitively he wasn't the gas station attendant or the guy who'd given her the finger when she cut him off in Wegman's parking lot. Maybe she would figure it out when he got closer.

"Hi," he said. "You look a little lost. Can I help you find something?"

It took a few moments, but his boyish grin was not forgotten. It was the attractive guy from the parking lot at Thaxton's. Rachel was usually better at placing faces, but her mind was so all over the place lately that she'd been stumped.

"I was hoping to blend in," Rachel confessed. "Guess that failed miserably." She decided not to say anything about their brief encounter if he hadn't deemed it worth remembering.

"No. Not at all. Everyone is in the same boat at the beginning."

"Except you?"

"I'm helping to reconfigure the store, but I'm a professor here, Wade Ryzer. I teach the Romantics."

"And the pragmatists are on their own?"

"Um..."

"Oh, please, don't. For someone who prides herself on her sense of humor, I know that was awful."

Rachel noticed Wade studying her face and wondered if he placed her.

"Wait. Don't I know you?" he said, right on cue.

"Yes, you left me at the altar several years ago," she teased. "And frankly, I've never been the same." Rachel was surprised at how comfortable she felt to be that cutesy and bold.

"No, that wasn't it." Wade laughed with his whole face. "It was... It was Thaxton's—the parking lot! You're the french fries girl." He sounded proud of himself.

"Ding, ding, ding, give the man a beer," Rachel said.

She flipped her hair and moistened her lips. *Oh geez.* There was something about being back in college that made her feel like she was entitled to be twenty again, only this time on her grown-up terms. Still, she decided it would probably be in her best interest to forget about counting tongues to cure her insomnia and go back to counting sheep.

"I'm sorry," Rachel continued, suddenly feeling self-conscious. "I'm being silly. I think it's nerves. I haven't been in school in... a while."

"Well, for starters, relax," Wade said. "This is a friendly place, you'll see."

"Hope so," Rachel said. She appreciated Wade's attempt to make her feel less anxious, but her stomach was still doing flip-flops.

"Why don't you start by telling me what you're looking for."

My baby's father. No, she wasn't going to say that.

Rachel eyed him up and down while he found and handed her several of the books on her list.

"How's that so far?" he asked.

"Looks good. Thank you."

A woman with a gray pixie cut approached Wade and asked him something about one of the books on Byron he'd ordered.

He turned to Rachel, seeming ready to conclude their interaction. "Do you have what you need? It's almost closing time."

"I believe I do." Rachel nodded, going through the stack. "I think it's all right here."

"Excellent," Wade said. "It was nice seeing you—again. If you need anything, I'm around. Have a good evening."

"Yes, thanks. You too."

Rachel watched him walk away and immediately called her sister. "Beth. I'm at the bookstore, and I'm so glad I caught you."

"Is everything okay, Rach? I really can't talk. Courtney just peed in her pants, and Evan's on the other line. If you're not convulsing right now, call me later."

"Go. Later."

The walk to Zach's class from the bookstore was longer than it had appeared on the map. No big surprise since most of the time, she couldn't navigate her way out of a strip mall. In her defense, it was getting dark. The only way Beth could watch Janie was if Rachel took an evening class. Evan would be around in case anything came up with the kids. Rachel was good with that arrangement since it gave her time with Janie during the day.

Rachel got to the humanities building and asked a group of students talking out front for directions to Zach's class. A short guy wearing a Yankees baseball cap said it was right down the hall. She walked past a row of vending machines and was a little surprised to see Zach standing against his classroom door.

"Uh-oh. Did I get the time wrong?" Rachel asked.

"Yes and no," Zach answered.

"I'm confused."

"There was a mistake in the guide. I assume everyone showed up early, except you." Zach showed her the error.

"Then, I'm late?"

"Technically, yes. I'm late, too, according to the misinformation. I'll send the class an email with the correction." Zach caught her eyes in a glance that was too long for their encounter.

"Okay, so this *is* the right time."

"Yes, it is," he said, closing the book. "The group is small. I'm glad you decided to join."

"Given your initial presentation, it was too compelling to miss." Rachel giggled.

"Yup. I have all the right moves." Zach pretended to hit a golf ball.

When Zach looked up at her, there was a warmth in his eyes that almost made her forget why she was there.

"What do you mean by 'the group is small'?"

"Not many people," Zach said. "I'm not worried. It'll pick up. There are always stragglers who find out they need credits to graduate."

"So why do they have to take your class?"

"There's usually room."

"Your popularity sounds unprecedented."

"Hey, I'll have you know my Sex and Love in the Victorian Novel is a big hit." Zach sounded proud of himself. "Why weren't you interested in that one?"

"It's at nine, and I'm not a morning person."

"Fair enough."

There was a long pause Rachel thought would feel more uncomfortable than it did.

"Whatever the reason, I'm glad you showed up tonight."

"Thanks," Rachel offered, unsure of what was left to say.

"Listen, I'm kind of hungry, and I could"—he pointed to the vending machines—"go there, but I'd much rather have a burger."

"Um, I could do that," Rachel said. *Wait. He might think this a date. It can't be a date. Dates are planned. Dates are—*

"How about Deckers?"

"Sounds good." *Anything with you sounds good. You're adorable, and my husband is an egocentric schmuck.* "I'm not that familiar with the area."

"An un-local yokel," Zach teased. "That's fine. I'll make sure you learn what you need to."

One can only hope, she thought as her cell phone blasted.

Rachel turned to Zach awkwardly. "Sorry, I have to take this."

Zach nodded in understanding as a thin woman with perfect teeth and a black updo à la Lilith, Frasier's ex-wife, walked over to him and playfully tapped his arm. If not for her giggling and cooing like a cheerleader, she could've been a strict schoolmarm.

"Yeah, Beth, what's up?" Rachel said, barely listening.

Unbelievable. This woman was all over Zach. If she could have spilled her breasts out of her plunging neckline directly into his mouth, it seemed like she would have. No big deal, but it was a bit unnerving considering Zach had just asked Rachel out on a not-really-a-date. *Ridiculous.* Rachel had to laugh at herself. She was still somewhat married, but she was feeling like a jealous schoolgirl. She knew she would have to figure out what she really wanted, but it was liberating to be in the moment.

"What did you say?" Rachel asked, remembering she was on the phone. She was still assessing Zach's body language when she heard Beth say, "We need you here—now!"

Zach walked back to Rachel as she ended the call.

"That look is telling me I'm having a pumpkin spice granola bar for dinner."

"Can I put my burger on hold?"

"Sure. Is anything wrong?"

"No. Not at all." Rachel smiled. "I have responsibilities."

Rachel walked into Beth's house, anxious to get Janie and go home. "Hey!" Rachel called, making her way inside.

"Hi. Sorry to drag you away from your guy," Beth said as she continued giving Janie a bottle. "But Joshie came home from gymnastics coughing, and I don't want Janie to get it. I sent him up to his room with Evan."

"No problem. Hope the little guy feels better. And, for the record, he is not my guy, and you didn't drag me away from anything."

"Sure."

"Cool," Rachel said, amazed by how easily Beth yielded.

"You never told me what happened at the bookstore." Beth turned Janie upright to help her burp.

Rachel unzipped her coat halfway. "Get this—remember the guy I met at Thaxton's?"

"The almost invitation for fries."

Beth's memory always impressed Rachel.

"Yeah, what about him?"

"He was at the bookstore," Rachel said. "Turns out he teaches there."

"Hmm, interesting coincidence."

"Maybe, or maybe not." Rachel took a seat facing Beth. "I think he could be Janie's father."

"What? That's huge!" Beth laid Janie down across her lap and continued to feed her. What makes you think so?"

"He teaches Wordsworth and those guys—"

"Just because he's *a* professor doesn't make him *the* Professor," Beth said, cutting Rachel off.

"I know that, but he's also good-looking, with a teddy-bear gut and a great smile."

"Is he single?"

"I don't know. I was looking for a book." Rachel picked up a flyer from the coffee table, took a quick look, and put it down. "And what difference would it make?"

"It would be good to know what you're up against."

"You mean if he has a wife, this could get even more complicated."

"It could." Beth shoved a cookie in her mouth. "When you see him again, check out his hand for a ring."

"But plenty of guys don't wear wedding rings."

"Rachel, he teaches the Romantics. If he's married, he's wearing a ring."

Luckily, the night Rachel had class was the same night the bookstore had extended hours. To do the next assignment, she needed the paperback she had on order, and since Zach had cancelled class to attend a lecture, she had the time to get it. A paper was exactly what Rachel needed, something to shift her thinking away from Zach, a Burberry-scented complication of the highest caliber. That he was occupying space in her thoughts after a few short weeks was keeping Rachel up nights now that Janie wasn't. It didn't even make sense. Zach hadn't given her the slightest indication he was interested in rescheduling their almost-dinner plans, which meant there was even less reason to allow him to stir her emotions.

Rachel knew Zach wasn't part of her mission. She simply wanted to find Janie's father, figure out a reasonable custody arrangement, and leave Phil—or work things out with him if the universe offered a cosmic miracle that insisted they were destined to stay together. Rachel was less inclined to focus on that possibility. Her feelings about Phil and their marriage had changed, but what that meant was yet to be determined.

A guy with spiky green hair held the door open for her as he was leaving the store and she was entering. There was a line at the desk designated for special orders, and she picked up a bottle of water to drink while she waited.

"Sorry I had to take off so quickly the other day," Wade said, appearing out of nowhere. "Were you able to find everything you needed?"

"I think I'm okay, for now." Rachel studied Wade while he was reaching to get a book from a crowded shelf. "Thanks for asking."

"Are you an English major?"

Small talk. She found his interest unexpectedly charming.

"No. I'm just taking one class." Rachel picked up a floral-covered day planner. "I decided to broaden my scope."

In a sudden flash, Rachel remembered Beth telling her to check out Wade's hand for a wedding band. She struggled to get a glimpse, but she wasn't at an optimal angle. Determined, she deliberately began fumbling with her water and the planner until they both dropped to the floor.

Wade, as chivalrous as she'd hoped, immediately bent down to retrieve them. Rachel got a good look at both his hands, which were large but almost delicate, with well-maintained nails, and more importantly, no sign of jewelry indicating a commitment.

"Sorry," Rachel said, taking back her things. "I'm such a klutz. Thanks."

"No harm done."

"Have you been teaching here long?"

"This is my first full year. I've filled in for others here and there, but most of the time, I taught in Ohio. Ohio and London."

Rachel controlled a gasp. Rena had mentioned something about the Professor having several friends from his early years of teaching in London.

She had to think fast to capitalize on the information. "London! I love London. All the culture... the people... the wonderful aroma of baked scones."

"Yes, it's quite a city. I once had a relationship with a Brit who spoke with a rich accent," Wade said. "Still resonates in my head." He let out a pained sigh. "Can I interest you in a cup of coffee?"

A wave of panic started at the base of Rachel's spine and coursed its way through her body, turning her insides cold. Some part of her wanted to shout, "I have your daughter," but she retained the presence of mind not to be that impulsive. She would have to get to know him much better before she said anything to suggest that might be the case.

"Another time?" She needed to collect her thoughts and sort things out. "I'm still waiting for a book."

"Sure, no problem." Wade gave her a look that was difficult to interpret then left the store.

Rachel watched him exit and stood numbly as the clerk practically put the book in her hand.

"You're done, hon," the clerk said. "You can go."

Rachel stood there for another moment until the woman behind her nudged her way to the counter.

The chilly night air encouraged Rachel to walk swiftly back to her car. Before tonight, the idea of Janie belonging to anyone else had been a faint, distant possibility. It didn't matter that she was seeking out the truth. She'd never believed she would find it. The pursuit in and of itself was enough to make her feel like she was honorable. She'd expected to fail then heroically announce that she'd tried.

Rachel dabbed at the tears streaming down her face. There was no way she could give Janie up. She'd been a fool to even entertain the possibility. Janie was her daughter, and there was no one else who could love her as much or be willing to sacrifice as much for her well-being as Rachel. There was nothing as pure as maternal love, and though it had occurred in less-than-conventional circumstances, it was stronger than any feelings Rachel had ever imagined possible.

Rachel believed fate had been at play. From the moment she'd met Rena, Rena had encouraged her to bond with Janie. Rena had even gone so far as to say Rachel and Janie looked alike, and she'd seemed amused, even pleased, when strangers mistook Rachel for Janie's mother. That Rena had immediately felt familiar made sense to Rachel. Their connection had purpose. In days, they'd become like sisters and shared a tacit understanding that Rachel would always be there for Janie. It was a promise Rachel respected and would never breach.

Maybe it didn't have to matter whether Janie had a father. Plenty of kids grew up to be successful, responsible people without one. Still, in her heart of hearts, Rachel held Rena's wishes close. She knew she would inevitably have to seek out the Professor, but for now, she would allow herself to look the other way and honor her distractions.

Rachel got into her car and turned the key in the ignition. It wouldn't start. *Dammit!* She tried playing with the pedals, gears, and dials, but nothing was working. She got out of the car and lifted the hood as if somehow, the heavens would supply her with a step-by-step manual. But that didn't happen. It still looked like the guts of a car and meant nothing to her. Although she had seen a couple of security vehicles driving around when she first arrived, it was getting late, and there wasn't much left to patrol.

The near-empty parking lot made Rachel's overactive imagination turn to a vindictive, angry Phil. She was now playing the movie version of her situation in her head, half expecting some great-looking hit man who was lurking in a family van to casually pull up alongside her and ask if she needed a hand. It could go a few ways from there. He could kidnap her and bring her to the villain to receive a threat and a persuasive, sexualized warning. Or there was always a chance she could be shot. She quickly got back into the car and tried to start it again and again.

A sharp tap at her window nearly sent Rachel through the roof.

"Whoaaa!" Zach said, jumping back.

Rachel took a deep breath and opened her door. "I'm so sorry. It's late. My car won't start. And I had myself starring in a John Carpenter movie."

Zach laughed so hard the skin around his hazel eyes crinkled and a yet-unseen team of dimples invaded his face.

Rachel tried to suppress the butterflies in her stomach, but that wasn't happening. Zach was undeniably more attractive than she had allowed herself to realize.

"You laugh, but I nearly had a coronary," Rachel said, trying to keep their exchange light.

"We certainly wouldn't want that to happen, especially since we haven't gotten that burger you promised me."

The invitation she was hoping for had been delivered. All Rachel had to do was figure out what she was going to do about it.

Zach escorted her to the passenger side of her car then got into the driver's seat. She wondered if he realized how much she was analyzing his every move. It wasn't calculated like she had some kind of agenda—it just happened because he was beautiful. It was almost surprising the car didn't start when Zach turned the key, given all the energy Rachel felt flowing. She celebrated quietly to herself, glad she would get to spend more time with him.

Clearly unaware of all her musings, Zach remained in pragmatic mode. He got out of her car, went to his, then pulled into the vacant space next to hers. Rachel watched him intently as he retrieved a pair of jumper cables from his trunk and effortlessly affixed them onto their batteries. She wondered if he was as proficient in bed. The idea of Zach's battery breathing new life into her exhausted car made Rachel weepy. It wasn't logical, but it had been a long time since a man was there for her without wanting anything in return. After a few moments ticked by, her car started up. Rachel sighed as Zach got out of her driver's seat.

"I think you left an interior light on when you left the car," Zach explained. "Should be fine now."

Rachel stood awkwardly against the car as Zach unhooked the cables and put them back into a compartment in his trunk.

"Come join me at Decker's," he said, using the moment exactly the way Rachel had hoped.

As much as she wanted to continue the evening with him, she didn't have the luxury of acting impulsively. "I thought you had a lecture or something."

"I did, but I came back. I forgot my freshmen's papers," he admitted. "Good thing, because as it turned out, I needed to be here for you."

"And I am so grateful and would love to join you, but—"

"Responsibilities." Zach said, finishing her sentence.

Rachel nodded. "I'm really sorry."

"No worries."

Zach got into his car, and Rachel could see in her rearview mirror that he didn't leave until she was moving.

Rachel sat on Beth's couch, still wearing her jacket, and waited for Beth to put Courtney back to bed after a bad dream. The little one had a point. *Monsters are everywhere. They just take on a more human form as we get older. Damn Phil.* He'd been hurting her for so long, she'd become used to it. Now a decent guy seemed interested in being friends, and she was trying to keep her distance.

When Rachel had called the house earlier, Brittany, the new babysitter Rachel had found when Joshie had strep, hadn't said she had to be home early. Janie was sleeping, and Rachel could have easily gone out for a bite to eat. But she'd let Phil and the unfinished business between them win. A strong breeze from an open window hit the back of Rachel's head. The cold pierced her as she pushed away frightening images of what might have happened if Macy hadn't shown up that day.

Beth waddled a little when she walked back into the room. Rachel couldn't tell if it was due to the baby or the weight Beth was inviting through her indiscriminate diet.

"Courtney's asleep, thank the Lord." Beth sank into the couch. "How's it going with Brittany?"

"Great. Janie loves her, and I have no complaints."

"Good. Cause I was feeling guilty," Beth admitted. "What's up? You look preoccupied."

"I am." Rachel sighed. "I think Wade Ryzer really is Janie's father."

"I know, you told me. You also said you *wanted* to find him. Why do you look depressed?"

"I know what I said, and Wade does seem like a nice guy. I'm just not sure."

"Of what? If he's a good guy? Father material? What?"

"I don't know," Rachel said. "I'm thinking of calling Edie again."

"Why?"

"A few days ago, I found a letter from Rena that she never sent to the Professor. It said something about their destiny being in the cards. And—"

"I swear, if you start carrying crystals and chanting over eye of newt, I'm going to disown you."

"It's not like that."

"I know you like Zach, but what about Wade?" Beth put her feet up on the couch. "Any chance of an attraction?"

"I guess. Possibly. He is cute and intelligent," Rachel mused. "But like it or not, I still have to deal with Phil."

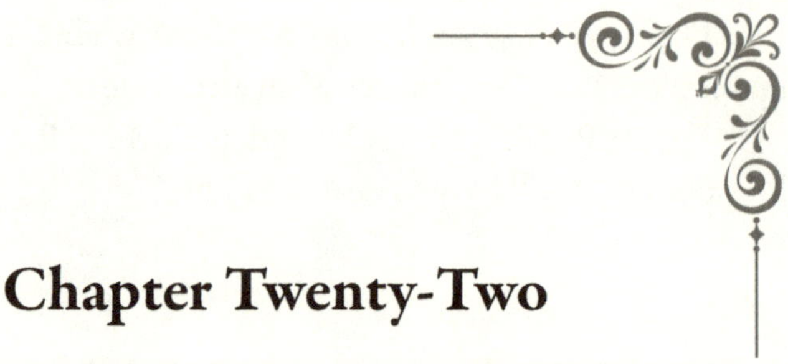

Chapter Twenty-Two

As a student, Rachel had always chosen a seat near the window so she could watch nature in action. Birds were particularly intriguing, flying from branch to branch, seeming so confident that wherever they were headed was the right place to go. It was possible some of them may have hit a wall or crashed into a tree, but not the ones she watched. They were decisive and owned the moment. Rachel was fixated on a finch whose head bobbed up and down a few times, making sure it had its last bite of nourishment. Then, just like that, it took off. She could eat an entire bag of pretzels and still have no clue what she was going to do next.

"Rachel?"

Rachel turned her head and saw Zach standing beside her.

"Class is over." He smiled. "But I am glad you find the material so compelling."

Totally embarrassed, Rachel imagined she was a deep shade of crimson. "I am so sorry. I think I got lost somewhere between Brontë and Eliot."

"You could do worse," Zach teased. "You know, you owe me a burger, and I'm not inclined to let you turn me down again."

"I didn't turn you down." Rachel got up from her seat and slung her bag over her shoulder. "I had something to take care of."

"Fine. What are you doing now?"

"Now?"

"Yes. Meet me at Decker's. It's down the road on the right. You can't miss it."

Rachel's heart was thumping. *Wait. Let me put on my big-girl panties, preferably crotchless, and get myself to say yes.* She summoned her immense attraction to Zach and nodded. "Where are you going?"

"I have to pick up a reference book from the chairman's office." Zach closed the classroom door as they entered the hallway. "Just meet me. I have a proposition for you."

Rachel stood inside the door of Decker's, waiting for the hostess. She scanned the room for an empty table, but the prospects looked bleak. Zach hadn't warned her there would be a crowd. A girl with sparkly purple eye shadow and a short blond bob walked over to her, shouted something about it being a few minutes longer, and walked away. Rachel thought about getting a drink but decided to stay put.

For a Tuesday, the vibe was more energized than Rachel had expected. It was a school night. Why all these kids were out doing shots, shooting pool, watching games on too many TVs, and dancing while some hippie relic was playing guitar made no sense. When she was in college, there were partiers, but midweek was tame except for when finals were over. That was when all hell was *supposed* to break loose.

Wow. She was officially sounding like that old lady she'd sworn she would never become, no matter how much the world around her changed. That she was even thinking of passing judgment on these kids made her want to tell herself off. They weren't her children, but as a mom, she felt concerned. One day, Janie would be in college, and Rachel wondered how she would handle the angst and drama that rounded out a proper education. Her best hope was that the wisdom she'd culled from her own experiences would serve as the guidance Janie would need as she matured. Rachel was staring at a guy doing a body shot off a girl's cleavage when someone bumped into her from behind. She turned, ready to yell at the offender, and giggled when she saw it was Zach.

"Sorry," he said, nodding toward the bald kid behind him. "Domino effect."

"No problem." *None at all.*

"This place is packed," Zach said, taking in the room. "You waiting long?"

"I don't think so. The guy with the pot belly in the *Welcome to My Whirled Tires* T-shirt is still drinking the same beer."

"Interesting gauge."

"I'm creative."

"Good. I'm counting on that."

The hostess, a ringer for Beyoncé, handed them menus and led them to a table near the end of the bar.

"Enjoy." She was about to walk away then paused. "Two-for-one Buds each inning the Yankees score."

"That could account for the beer-nursing," Zach said.

"He was drinking a Corona," Rachel replied, not missing a beat.

"You're good," Zach said.

"I try." *Oh, I'm not just good. I'm the best. You're gorgeous, intelligent, and gorgeous. My hormones are screaming.*

"What are you in the mood for?" Zach asked, looking up from the menu.

A night of relentless passion, exploring our naked bodies in your bed. Rachel tried to shake off her heat but couldn't quite get there. "You know this place, and I'm up for anything. Surprise me." *Oh, yes, please, surprise me. No one would see you touching me under the table—Rachel, stop, stop, stop!* If only self-control were on the menu.

"I can do that." He took their menus and laid them at the end of the table.

Rachel was curious to see how Zach would react to the idea of another meeting. "Maybe I can have the same opportunity next time."

She was hoping for a response, but a kid with a septum ring tapped Zach on the shoulder and engaged him in a conversation that seemed important.

That was okay with Rachel. It gave her more time to study Zach. Though she wasn't sure if they were on a date, having a business meeting, or both, he had made an effort to look good, presumably, for her. And as always, he smelled delicious. Rachel's head was about to take them to the six-hundred-thread-count Egyptian-cotton sheets on her king-sized bed when Phil, like eczema, became a persistent distraction. As much as she wanted her dinner with Zach to be a date, she had a marriage certificate sitting in a vault at home telling her it wasn't, at least not yet.

In her head, Rachel had been ending things with Phil since the moment she had the locks changed. But something was still stopping her from calling a lawyer. Maybe there was already too much on her plate. The past few weeks had been nothing short of a ravenous hurricane that had thrown her world into chaos. It was fair to need time before taking on more changes.

Then Rachel glanced at Zach's kissable lips, and all she could think was *Change is a good thing*. He was handsome, funny, smart, sexy, and her version of normal, and he still managed to be interesting. Not many men in her life could pull that off. Beyond her fantasies, Rachel considered what it would be like to really get to know him.

Zach had just finished speaking with the student when the server with a faint moustache came with waters and a basket of veggie chips. His head was rocking with the music as he took their order then danced away.

"Sorry for the intrusion. That was a student who—never mind him. Do you want a drink?" Zach asked. "I'm sorry I didn't ask. I'm just not much of a drinker."

"Me either." Rachel opened her straw and slipped it into her water.

"You're probably wondering why I asked you here." Zach grabbed a few chips.

"I assumed it was because you were hungry. And you wanted to prove that you have genuine table manners."

"All true," Zach admitted, "but there's more."

"More? What kind of more? Hit me," Rachel said, immediately fearing she sounded too salacious.

Zach took a sip of water. "It's about a book I'm writing. I need a research assistant, and I like the work you've been doing in class. I think you'd be an asset to the project."

"Thank you. I appreciate the... proposition."

I did it again. Rachel worried that her voice sounded too smoldering when she said *proposition*. But there was no way to unsay it. She knew she had to tone it down, or she was going to give Zach the impression he could have something she wasn't sure she could give him. With luck, he was too focused on his offer to have heard her not-so-subtle message.

The server came with their burgers, coleslaw, and pickles. Rachel was starving, and in very "un-date" fashion, she didn't wait for Zach before taking her first bite.

"You like?"

"It's delicious. I'm usually a salad kind of girl, but this carnivore thing has its merits."

"Good. I pride myself on being a decent recruiter." Zach took a modest-sized bite of his burger and put it back down on his plate.

"That you are." Rachel continued to eat with enthusiasm.

"I'll need you a couple of times a week for a few hours and maybe some time on weekends. We could play that by ear." Zach took a sip of his water. "What do you think?"

"I think I'll have to ask my babysitter if she has extra time." *Oh shit. That just slipped right on out. Big mistake. So not the way to tell the man you imagine on top of you about your daughter.*

"Babysitter?"

"I have a baby. A daughter."

"You do?" Zach sounded perplexed. "I had no idea."

"Why would you? I don't have it written across my forehead."

"So you're married?" Without waiting for an answer, Zach added, "No ring. Married women always wear rings."

"I'm sort of separated."

"Is that like being sort of pregnant?"

"Things haven't been good between us for a while." Rachel heard herself commit to the words out loud. "We had a nasty fight, and now he's away on business, indefinitely. Before he left, I told him we had a lot to think about."

"I see," Zach said in almost a whisper. "I guess that changes things."

"You don't want me to work with you?"

"No, I do, but I... I thought... I thought we were going to get to know each other better... personally."

"I would like that." Rachel dabbed her mouth with a napkin.

Hearing herself openly say that she was interested in Zach made Rachel's head throb. Sure, she had thought it, but a blatant admission was like the first pitch at a ball game. She was going to have to confront the status of her marriage.

"I'm not sure now." Zach squirmed in his seat. "This feels... I don't know..."

Rachel's heart sank. Even if Zach didn't know, she did, and his rejection was going to hurt. "It's your call."

Rachel picked up the check, but Zach took it from her.

"Thank you," Rachel said, collecting her things, "for the burger." She got up to leave and added, "I'll let you know about the project after I speak to my sitter."

Chapter Twenty-Three

Though Rachel's mind was jumping from one concern to another, the library was calm and quiet. A simple paper that should've taken no time at all to write had become an onerous chore, and she was determined to knock it out before finding her photo next to "loser" in the dictionary. Rachel found a table adjacent to the biographies and plunked her bag on the seat next to hers.

Two weeks, and still no word from Zach. First, class had been canceled due to a hailstorm, then he'd cancelled because of an alleged literary conference that could've just as easily meant Zach had taken the schoolmarm to a Giants game. Rachel wasn't sure why she was so suspicious of his activities, but something resembling jealousy was gnawing at her as if she were a spurned sophomore.

A kid from her class with a seventies afro gave her a nod and a smile as he passed her table. He was tall and muscular, and Rachel immediately wondered what he'd look like naked. She shook her head to fend off her own tempestuous thoughts and went into her bag to retrieve her heavily highlighted copy of *Wuthering Heights*. She opened the book and put her feet up on a neighboring chair. It was all there in black and white; people like Heathcliff and Cathy made love a living hell.

Rachel was reading when her phone, which she thought was on vibrate, rang in a strange new tune she had selected from her Verizon lineup. The number showed up as Beth's.

"Hello, little sister," Rachel said quietly.

"Hello," a man's voice answered.

"You're definitely not my sister. Who is this?"

"Wade Ryzer. I'm a professor at..."

"Wade, this is Rachel." There was no reaction, so she added, "The klutz at the bookstore."

"Ah, yes, Rachel."

That's always a way to make an impression. "Why are you calling from my sister's phone?"

"A strange coincidence," Wade said. "I was heading toward the parking lot after my class and found the phone on the ground right outside the bookstore. I called the first number that showed up. I guess it was yours."

"Why would my sister be on campus?"

"*That* I couldn't tell you." Wade chuckled. "Where are you? I'll drop it off."

"I'm at the library," Rachel said, gathering her things. "I can meet you at the entrance."

"Sounds good. Be there in a few."

Rachel flung her bag over her arm and started walking. Fate was obviously intervening. There was no other explanation for Wade finding Beth's phone. Zach was too conflicted and reluctant to give her a chance, and Wade was always managing to make his presence known. Sometimes, the universe supplied all the information necessary to make a decision. The key was for Rachel to make a firm commitment to end her marriage. Once that was done, no one could fault her for pursuing other possibilities.

While crafting a dear Phil letter in her head, Rachel careened into a passerby, sending a stack of papers to the floor. "Oh, I'm sorry!"

Another pair of hands was gathering the heap, but she didn't bother to look up until her pile was ready to be returned. She felt her face flush when she saw Zach next to her, shaking his head.

"You're not excused, young lady," Zach teased.

"Zach! I'm sorry. I don't know..."

"You were a million miles away," he said, standing up. "Hope the waves were high and the sun was strong."

"Thanks a lot. I burn easily." Rachel stood up and handed him the stack of papers.

"I owe you an apology." Zach avoided looking directly at her.

Rachel's heart started to race.

"I should have called you about the project sooner, but I've been swamped with another gig I have going on." Zach shifted the stack of papers from his hand to his arm. "But that's not your problem. Anyway, if you're still interested in working with me, the position is yours."

The first position that popped into her head was missionary, but she blinked to make it go away long enough to accept Zach's offer. Rachel blushed. "Yes, I would be happy to work with you."

"Good, can you arrange to meet me tomorrow night?"

"Sure," she said, not caring if she sounded eager.

"Say seven. My office," he said with a faint grin as he walked down the hall.

Nice butt, Rachel thought as he disappeared around the corner. *If fate is at play, it would be nice to know what it's playing.*

She had no time to ponder it, because Wade was waiting for her right inside the entrance. Rachel checked him out as if for the first time. He really was a good-looking man with his neatly trimmed moustache, just-right goatee, and big, soft chocolate-brown eyes. In his long black leather coat, he looked more 007 than double-wide, and she could at once imagine his fiery love affair with Rena.

"I'm sorry," Rachel said. "Were you waiting long?"

"No, I just got here," Wade said. "A student stopped me about an assignment."

"Oh good, because I had to embarrass myself, and it took a while."

"Pardon?" Wade shook his head a bit.

"In my inimitable fashion, I knocked into someone in the hall and had to clean up all his papers." Rachel waited for a snarky reaction like she would get from Zach, but Wade didn't offer one.

"Prerequisite for the job. It's happened to me too—on both ends. Everyone is rushing these days. I'm sure it wasn't a big deal." Wade fumbled with the long strap of his soft leather briefcase, finally setting it over his shoulder.

"I appreciate your generous perspective."

"Are you on your way to class?" Wade paused to adjust his scarf.

"No, I was just going to try to find my sister," Rachel said, scouting the immediate vicinity.

"Right. Here you go." Wade pulled Beth's phone out of his pocket and handed it to Rachel.

She immediately checked the time of Beth's last call. It was well over two hours ago, and by now, she could be anywhere.

"You think she went home?" Wade asked.

"Maybe." Rachel called Beth's landline but got no answer.

"I have an idea," Wade said. "I was planning to check out the new juice bar across from the gym. Join me, and we can try to figure out where your sister is."

Rachel was about to decline, but then she quickly realized the only way she was going to discover if Wade was decent father material was to spend time with him.

"I hear the Strawbananalope smoothie is killer," Wade added as a further enticement.

"That sounds reasonably healthy," Rachel answered. "I've been trying to wean myself off of Frappuccinos—so many empty calories."

"You look pretty fine to me."

The way Wade studied her up and down made Rachel consider his intentions. She followed him past the administrative offices and across a couple of parking lots until they came to a cute, freestanding building slightly bigger than a food truck. Wade held the door open for her and took the nearest table for two available.

"How's your class going?" Wade asked, taking off his coat.

"I think Brontë and I should part ways for a bit." She took off her jacket, and Wade hung it on the coatrack hook under his.

"So it's not going well?"

"Define 'well.'"

"A pleasant balance of comprehension and interpretation."

"That's unfortunate." Rachel shook her head. "I've yet to strike a balance. How are your classes going?"

"Really well." Wade chuckled. He went up to the counter, got their drinks, and came back with a package of cookies. "So much for my diet." He opened the package and offered her one.

"These are my daughter's favorites. She's teething," Rachel mumbled through a hefty bite.

"You have a daughter?" Wade didn't sound overwhelmed. "Lucky you. I've always wanted a little girl."

"You have?"

"I love kids. Someday, I hope I'm lucky enough to be a father. My sister has two girls, and I enjoy spoiling them. To me, they're like little dolls."

Rachel toyed with the idea of mentioning Janie's doll, Charlotte, but she decided that information might lead to a conversation she wasn't ready to have. Instead, she shifted their exchange back to academics.

"Yes, I love kids too." Hoping Wade would accept the segue, Rachel continued, "I'm curious, do you write poetry too?"

"As a matter of fact, I do," Wade said enthusiastically. "Would you like to hear my most recent?"

Rachel nodded. She had forgotten how oddly random and spontaneous college life could be.

Wade wasted no time sharing his sonnet about love and loss with her. His voice rose and fell with palpable depth and emotion. Rachel consumed each line as his words, both soft and powerful, coursed through her veins. *Oh, the passion he and Rena must have experienced in the privacy of their own bubble.* When he was done, Rachel wanted to applaud but decided that would be too trite a response.

"What do you think?" Wade asked.

"It was... beautiful and tragic." Still thinking about Rena, Rachel was afraid she might weep.

"Thank you. I think many relationships are."

"I suppose you're right," Rachel agreed.

"You're very easy to share with. From my perspective, it's refreshing."

Rachel offered a semismile, which was apparently Wade's cue to continue. In moments, he had switched gears and was rambling on about the differences between the poetry of Wordsworth and the linguistically cleaner poetry of Whitman.

She was grateful he was too invested in sharing his knowledge to notice how absent she'd become. If she weren't feeling so numb, she could appreciate his contemplations, but all that was running through her head was that in the not-so-distant future, she would have to tell him about Janie.

"Rachel!"

For a moment, Rachel was too deep in thought to recognize Beth's voice behind her.

"I'm so glad I found you." Beth's hair was in a messy bun, and despite being dressed in a sweater that was too light for a cold evening, beads of sweat framed her forehead.

Without a moment's hesitation, she pulled up a seat opposite Rachel's.

"Me too," Rachel said, handing Beth her phone.

"What are you doing with my phone?" Beth asked.

"You lost it, and—"

"Hi, I'm Beth, Rachel's sister." She extended her hand to Wade.

Rachel was relieved Beth hadn't introduced herself as "Rachel's baby sister," like she usually did. In most of their shared social situations, Rachel preferred to gloss over the years that separated them.

"Wade," Rachel continued as if she hadn't been interrupted, "found it."

"Oh, wow. Thank you so much." Beth turned to Wade. "I didn't even know I'd lost it."

"Good. Less stress, and regardless, it's a pleasure to meet you." Wade studied her face as he shook her hand. "You know, I just noticed you have the same lovely, long neck Rachel has."

"Really? Well, thank you, but she's the swan." Beth tilted her head toward Rachel. "I just need something to support my chins."

"You're ridiculous." Rachel dabbed her mouth with a napkin. "Anyway, how'd you know I was here?"

Wade sat back and silently sipped his smoothie.

"I didn't," Beth answered.

"Then what are you doing here?"

"Getting a Cocoakalata." Beth got her order and came back to the table. "A kid at the bookstore said these are amazing." She took a sip and frowned.

"How stoned was he?" Rachel asked. "But seriously, what made you come this way?"

"I signed up for a prenatal yoga workshop that promises it can make me calm." Beth took another sip of her smoothie. "I hope it works because, so far, the only things that have helped me are Oreos and bacon-parmesan subs. I'm thinking of becoming a competitive eater."

"Bethie, you're not fat. You're pregnant." Rachel took a cookie from the package and gave it to Beth.

"You're an enabler." Beth pushed Rachel's hand away. "You want to be the thin one."

Beth eyed the cookie, then she leaned in and snatched it out of Rachel's hand.

"I am the thin one. For now." Rachel took a cookie.

"This pregnancy has made me a basket case," she admitted, giving Wade the once-over. "You don't know me, but I'm really not a lunatic."

Rachel rolled her eyes at Beth as Wade let out a belly laugh.

"You girls are a treat, but I must get going." Wade got up and put on his coat. "We should do this again."

"Aah, finally, a threesome I can get behind." Beth took a sip of her drink.

Wade chuckled as he threw out his empty cup and walked toward the exit.

Beth turned to study Wade as he interacted with a pretty coed who entered the shop as he was leaving. Except for a wink and a chortle, nothing remarkable happened between the two of them. Once Wade left, Beth turned back to Rachel. "So, he's the Professor, huh?"

"Think so."

"He's pleasant. A little stiff, but unassumingly flirty. I think he probably has a fun side. And he is totally into you." Beth hiccupped and immediately began to hold her breath.

Rachel thought about it for a moment. "He is?"

"Oh yeah." Beth let her breath out in a steady stream. "The whole 'lovely neck' business and bonding with you over my lost phone. Come on."

"I guess," Rachel mused.

"And even though he's a bit stocky, he's certainly cute enough."

"Enough for what?"

"To take to bed."

Rachel sighed deeply. "Do you ever stop?"

"I'm being practical. You want to keep Janie, and if we're assuming Wade is her father, wouldn't it serve you well to get with him?"

"Yes, it probably would, and you're right, I should try, but—"

Beth jumped in. "There's Zach to consider, and you really like him."

"Definitely, maybe." Rachel sipped her drink as if she were taking a slow drag of a cigarette. "I saw him before I met up with Wade, and he asked me to work with him."

"That's great, but if you're going to try to get things going with Wade, do you really think you should?"

"Won't matter. Zach wants a strictly platonic working relationship."

"Until you seduce him."

"I won't. I can't." Rachel grimaced. "I'm... whatever... married."

"Then why do you sound so disappointed?"

"Because I don't want to be married anymore."

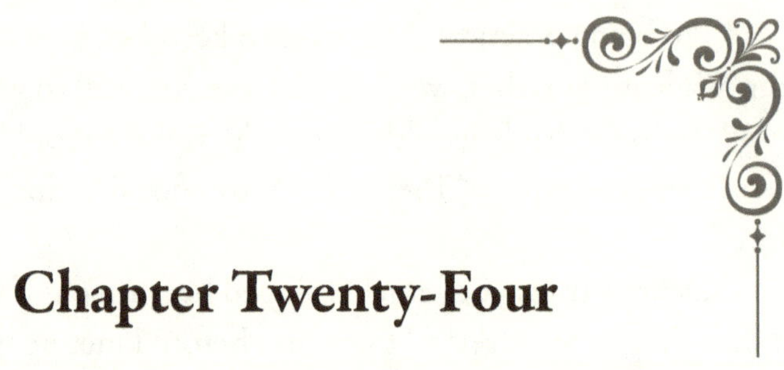

Chapter Twenty-Four

It wasn't quite six o'clock, and Rachel was primping in front of the mirror, hoping for fashion inspiration. It didn't matter how many times she told herself that it was "just work." She still systematically rejected each outfit for one reason or another. If she and Zach were to have a casual friendship, she wanted to make sure he was going to wish otherwise.

A clingy black sweater caught Rachel's eye. She pulled it out of an overstuffed drawer along with the memory of the Thanksgiving Day fight she and Phil had the last time she'd worn it—one of many battles over the trivial to mask the serious. In this one, Phil had accused her of sabotaging his favorite American holiday by serving gefilte fish as an appetizer. She quickly tucked the shirt and its consuming energy away and realized she'd stopped counting the weeks Phil had been gone.

Despite her wish to be a two-parent family, she was managing to navigate motherhood without him, and it wasn't so bad. She had Beth, who, when she wasn't trapped between the fridge and the bathroom, offered practical information, baby food recipes, and hands-on help. And there was Brittany, the godsend she'd lucked into when the bursar at the college said her kid-loving daughter wanted to babysit to save up for school. Even Rachel's mother, despite the seven-hour time difference, was a phone call away in a pinch. It was all working out. But it was still confusing.

Rachel went back to the closet and retrieved gray jeans and a newer black sweater with a semideep neckline. Pleased with her ensemble, she added a pair of small hoop earrings and the gold locket her parents had given her for her sixteenth birthday. To complete the look, she applied two coats of mascara, a soft peachy bronzer, and a shimmery slick of neutral lip gloss.

She didn't mind that Zach wasn't in his office when she knocked on his door promptly at seven. She needed the time to stare at his locked door and imagine what her role was going to be once they were working one-on-one. Not inclined to make the first move, she was reasonably certain she could keep her attraction at bay without embarrassing herself. There was always the possibility she was convincing herself she wanted him simply because he would resist her. Her heart fluttered as she imagined what winning would feel like.

Rachel was searching her bag for a breath mint when she was enveloped by a waft of familiar cologne. She quivered ever so slightly as she turned to Zach.

"Hey," Zach said, "you're right on time."

"Yup," Rachel said, struggling to come up with anything more captivating to add. *Nope, nothing.*

"Shall we?" He opened the door and led her inside.

The room was large with two oak desks set up in an L-shape designed for them to work back-to-back or facing each other depending on where the chairs were placed. Zach arranged the furniture so they would be sitting opposite one another, sharing a desk.

"Please." Zach motioned for her to sit down as he walked over to a large shelving unit housing books that took up an entire wall. His back was toward her, and all she could make out was him contemplating each selection then putting it back.

Rachel sat there, waiting for a break in the awkward silence. The last time she'd felt love-queasy like this, she was at her first boy–girl party, pining over Scott Maldanado and wondering if he was ever going to ask her to dance. It had taken nearly the entire night, but he'd finally manned up after a few winning rounds of Pac-Man with the guys. He'd even felt comfortable enough to kiss her. That unexpected treat had stayed with her long after her mother pulled up in their aging Chevy to take her back to reality.

That was a lifetime ago, yet she was still hosting the same butterflies. Rachel had yet to figure out what Zach ultimately wanted from her. In her estimation, he was exceedingly competent and didn't need an assistant to help him with his research any more than she needed one to help her shave her legs. But that was conjecture—or worse, hope. Rachel wanted to believe Zach had really requested her assistance because, despite his objections about getting personally involved because she was married, he couldn't help himself and wanted to get to know her.

"Sorry," Zach said, turning his head slightly toward her. "I'm not sure what I want to start with." Zach finally chose a leather-bound book that came from what appeared to be part of a large collection.

"By the way, thanks for coming." Zach sat down and opened the book to the front page. "I'd like to start with *Great Expectations*. Are you familiar?"

Rachel had a flashback to the play she'd seen in London. That she was going to be working on Dickens was not as surprising to her as it once might have been. "All too well. I usually start there myself."

Zach let out a soft chuckle. "I set you up good for that one."

"And I am not one to squelch an opportunity."

"I will keep that in mind." Zach reached over to the far end of the desk for a pad and a pen. "We haven't discussed anything about your fee."

"I'm willing to count this as a learning experience if you're willing to feed me from time to time."

"Really?"

"Well, I haven't told you what I'd like to eat."

Zach turned a shade of pink Rachel could match with the lip-stick in her makeup bag. "This is going to end up being a very long night if we don't get started."

"We have gotten started," Rachel said.

"I mean with Dickens," Zach replied.

"So do I."

"How so?"

"I'm Estella." Rachel looked Zach straight in the eye. "I am a temptation that can lure you to lust or, at the very least, make you question what you want from me."

"I'm very confused."

"Yes, you are," Rachel agreed. "You're Pip. Your innocence around crafty women is painfully obvious, and although you don't want to be played, you are too intrigued not to be in the game."

"So wait a minute—you've been putting me on?"

"A woman never shows her true hand until she's ready to claim the pot."

"You know," Zach said, "I do believe you have indeed invoked the true essence of Estella. I knew you were bright, but you have exceeded my—"

"Great expectations?"

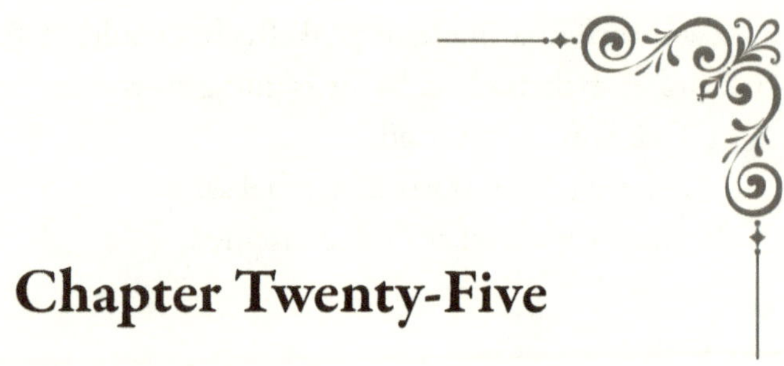

Chapter Twenty-Five

Rachel clutched the phone to her chest as she paced the hallway between her bedroom and the nursery. *I'll call Brittany and cancel for tonight. It's just one class. Zach probably won't even notice my absence.* Besides, she was exhausted. Janie was teething and had been too miserable to take a nap. Beth had told her to dab the baby's gums with Triple Sec. That had helped even more after Rachel downed a shot of her own. By early evening, right after oatmeal and a bottle, Janie had finally whined herself to sleep. Rachel put her in the crib and decided not to go to class. Okay, not just because the baby was cranky but because she wasn't sure she was up for seeing Zach.

Their first research session had been more uncomfortable than Rachel had anticipated. She wasn't sure why she'd been that boldly flirtatious. Usually, she indulged in some eye contact, a few hair touches, and a round or two of inconsequential banter. But with Zach, her moves were so blatant that she began to question her own motives.

She wasn't sure if she wanted Zach because he was gorgeous, smart, and sexy or because she needed him as the impetus to finally purge herself of her destructive attachment to Phil. Both were plausible. As for Wade, she was still trying to offer him romantic consideration, given his genetic contribution to Janie. He was also creative, attractive, and kind, and he loved kids.

The whole situation was perplexing, and Rachel didn't want her confusion to create an even greater awkwardness between her and

Zach. With a bit of time and distance, he might forget how forward she'd been.

Rachel finally stopped pacing long enough to call Brittany. During their brief exchange, Brittany had convinced Rachel to woman up, put on her game face, and share power with the world. Deciding her babysitter was an old soul whose wisdom shouldn't be squandered, Rachel kept her plans to go to class.

S printing across the parking lot, Rachel was shocked that she was not only on time but had arrived even earlier than usual. A few kids from her class were down the hall at the vending machines, exchanging thoughts about how *Wuthering Heights* could be made into a rap song about being stupid in love. She didn't know much about rap music, but that was a song she was sure she could learn quickly.

Zach peeped out from behind the classroom door and motioned everyone to enter. Rachel slipped in behind a stream of other students and took a seat toward the back of the room. As long as she kept a low profile and let everyone else answer questions instead of her usual chiming in, Zach would realize the other night had been a fluke. She was not, in fact, the feisty, boisterous tease who had probably frightened if not emasculated him within moments of sitting down to work.

Zach lectured at length about the Brontë sisters, the social climate of the time, and the concept of obsessive love. The one saving grace was that he didn't seek Rachel out while he was speaking. She made sure to keep her head squarely in her book, taking notes as he bulleted different points on the blackboard. After several pages were filled, a quick look at the clock offered relief. Five more minutes, and she would be home free.

After a brief announcement about a quiz, Zach dismissed the class. Rachel quickly gathered her things and was trying her best to blend in with the others as they exited. A sudden, firm clasp on her shoulder prevented her from going any farther. She stopped in her tracks as the last person walked out the door, leaving her alone with Zach.

"We need to talk about the other night," Zach said without a hint of reluctance.

"Okay." For a moment, Rachel considered adding an excuse or making light of the moment by playing dumb. Instead, she decided to let him do the talking.

"I'm glad you understand the content so well you were able to shape it so creatively," Zach said, collecting papers from his desk. "That energy is sure to help the project. Keep up the good work. Are you free Thursday night?"

Rachel was too dumbfounded to respond. *Energy indeed.* She'd been anxious all week, only to discover that Zach hadn't the slightest idea she'd practically thrown herself into his bed.

"Rachel, Thursday?" Zach reiterated.

"Sure." Rachel nodded. "That's fine."

"I'll bring the books, and we'll have dinner somewhere with big tables."

"Sounds good," Rachel said, still befuddled.

"Okay, then, see you Thursday." Zach disappeared out the door before Rachel could say goodbye.

Beth had called to ask Rachel to drop Janie off for a playdate with Courtney. Joshie was in school, and Beth wanted Courtney to get a feel for what being a big sister was going to be like. To make use of the unexpected time, Rachel went to the library to get a jump on Thursday's research.

If Zach found her knowledge attractive, she was going to give him every reason imaginable to find her invaluable. If nothing else, she owed it to herself to learn and get as much as she could out of their connection. Perhaps she didn't have it in her to be quite the temptress Estella had been to Pip, but there was no way she was going to miss the opportunity to be the lover he would anxiously submit to in the privacy of his dreams.

Closing yet another book of critical essays, Rachel giggled. Her uncle always used to tell her, "Opinions are like assholes—everyone has one." Some things never changed. She closed her notebook, deciding she'd earned at least a large hot chocolate before attempting to go through yet another round of analysis.

The cool autumn breeze felt refreshing against her skin as she took a leisurely walk to the café. Since it was an off hour, she had her choice of tables and selected one by the window facing a little courtyard. A couple of kids were making out on the bench outside, and for a moment Rachel thought about Jesus, her first. Young love was so blissful and consuming. She remembered how the mere thought of his lips against hers used to leave her warm and wanting. Whether she cared to admit it or not, that lust was begging to be expressed again. In her most honest moments, she wanted Zach to envelop her in the kind of heat that would leave them both enthralled and breathless.

She sipped her hot chocolate and felt the whipped cream hit her upper lip.

"Hey, Rachel," Wade said, holding a package of cookies and a diet Snapple. "Not your usual day, right?"

Feeling like she'd been caught with her skirt up, Rachel quickly assigned her desire to the more practical task of exploring Wade. "You are correct," Rachel said. *Interesting, he's noted my schedule.* "I'm doing some research." She motioned for him to sit down.

"Thanks," he said, handing her a package of cookies. "Want these?"

"Really? For me?"

Wade nodded. "I remember you said your daughter likes teething on them." His attentiveness made Rachel think about Beth saying, "The man is cute, smart, considerate, and will always wear bigger jeans than yours."

"She does, but I don't indulge her very often."

"Well, let this be one of those times if you'd like."

"Thank you," Rachel said, opening the package. "I will, as soon as I test them out."

"I'm not sure if you've noticed, but I've been making a point of getting to know you," Wade said, avoiding her eyes.

"Oh, I've noticed," Rachel replied. She took a long swig of her hot chocolate. *Damn!* The roof of her mouth was going to sting later.

"I've been wanting to ask you something." He paused and stared inside his cup of tea. "But I don't want to make you uncomfortable."

Here it is—the moment of truth. Somehow, he'd instinctively figured out she was raising his daughter, and he was going to ask her for confirmation. Or, only somewhat less terrifying, he wanted to know if she would go out with him. Her head was spinning in every direction. He hadn't even asked if she was married, and she hadn't volunteered any answers.

"Go ahead—ask, I think," Rachel said, bracing herself.

"I paint," Wade said.

"Houses?"

"Only when I really goof."

"Interesting. How so?"

"I paint nudes," Wade said.

"Nudes?" Rachel asked, to make sure she'd heard him right.

"Yes," Wade confirmed. "When I first saw you, I was struck by your presence and your spirit. Not to mention, you have magnificent bone structure and lovely skin tones."

"I do?"

"Oh, you more than do," Wade said.

Rachel felt her cheeks flush. He was going to ask her out, and she had no idea how she was going to handle it.

"Maybe I'm doing this wrong," Wade said. "I'm bad at asking for anything."

Then don't ask! Rachel took a nervous, messy bite of a cookie. As she brushed the crumbs off her chin, she wondered if she was secretly hoping to turn him off. No matter how she framed their connection, it felt like he wasn't meant to be hers.

"I'm not much of a sharer," Wade continued. "That day I recited one of my poems for you was an anomaly. There's something about you that makes me feel like I can be my truer self."

To avoid meeting his eyes, Rachel scanned the room. She thought she saw Zach in the distance, but the figure disappeared too quickly for her to be sure.

"I'm incredibly flattered," Rachel said. "Truly, I, I am, but—"

"Rachel, I'm just going to say it." Wade's eyes widened. "I'd like to paint you."

"What? Paint me?" Rachel burst out laughing.

"I know it's not a question you get asked very often—at least I don't think it is."

"Oh, this is a first." Rachel couldn't stop cackling.

"But I am serious," Wade said.

"I know. That's why I'm laughing."

"Will you at least consider it? My work has been featured at exhibits and in galleries. I even have a small following."

"I have no doubt you're talented," Rachel assured him. "Sure, I'll think about it. Since we've met, you always find a way to surprise me."

"I'll accept that as a compliment." Wade got up, put his hand on her shoulder, and gazed into her eyes. "You really are quite striking."

Rachel met his gaze for a surprisingly less-than-awkward moment. She watched as he walked out the exit past the young couple, who continued to kiss as the sun cast a glowing beam on their entwined embrace.

When Rachel got to Beth's house, a big bag was sitting in the entrance by the door.

"Hey," Beth said, waddling over to the couch. "I didn't even hear you come in."

"I think I've mastered the don't-wake-the-baby walk no matter where I am." Rachel sat on the chair opposite the couch and took a mint from a bowl on the coffee table. "Janie sleeping?"

"She fell asleep in Courtney's room while I was sorting through old clothes." She pointed to the bag. "Those are for her. They're all washed."

"Thanks, but what if you have a girl?" Rachel asked.

"If they're not trashed, you'll give them back, and if they are, we'll buy new." Beth took a sip of water from a large plastic bottle. "Don't you love when things are easy?"

"You sound chipper," Rachel teased. "Have you found out what you're having yet?"

"My tubes tied." Beth got up. "Excuse me. I have to pee—again."

Rachel went over to the bag of clothes and untied the handles. There were a few really cute outfits right at the top. One of them, a lavender shirt with jeans and a matching hat, Rachel had bought when she was with Phil at Baby Gap. He'd been bitching about weekends being for relaxing, but when Rachel had reminded him that his car was next to the mall and ready to be picked up, spiffy new hubcaps and all, he'd conceded to going with her. The more she thought about it, the more she realized everything involving Phil always required compromise and negotiation on her part. Lately, when memories would come and go, the only stand-out was how few of them made her feel good.

Rachel closed the bag and went back to sit on the couch. Even with all the complexities concerning Zach and Wade, anything was better than focusing on Phil.

Beth came back with a huge jar of peanut butter and a spoon. "It's protein. Don't judge." She retrieved a mound of the spread and sat in the chair next to Rachel.

"I won't," Rachel said as she unwrapped a mini Butterfinger. "But if *I* get fat, I'm going to hold you directly responsible."

"Listen, you got Janie. A little paunch will make the experience more authentic."

"You make an interesting point." Rachel tossed the wrapper onto the coffee table. "If I tell you something, you must promise me you won't laugh."

"I'm not sure I can do that."

"Fine. I won't tell you."

"Yes, you will."

"Honestly, you have become more impossible by the pound," Rachel teased. "Okay, I'll cave. Consider it a gift."

"This better be good." Beth grunted.

"I ran into Wade again the other day."

"Still not the boyfriend."

Rachel wasn't sure she wanted to tell Beth that Wade was in the friend zone. She would never accept it. In overbearing sisterly fashion, she would continue to point out that Wade was a good-looking, nice guy and the three of them would make a cute, sane family. A logical, compelling argument, but it omitted Rachel's heart.

"Beth, there is no boyfriend. Anyway, he explained why he's been trying to get to know me."

"Another project?" Beth asked. "I can only imagine."

"I don't think you can." Rachel shifted in her seat.

"Come on, before I deliver—please!"

"He wants to paint me."

"With what? Edible neons? Chocolate?" Beth teased.

"Nude."

"I figured that, but—"

"No," Rachel said, "he wants to paint me in the nude. You know, like in oil or acrylic."

Beth started laughing so hard, Rachel couldn't help but chime in.

"Oh man, the baby is kicking up a storm," Beth said, grasping her belly. "Amazing. So how did you blow him off? Bluntly or gently?"

"I didn't. He told me I was 'striking,' so I told him I'd consider it."

"Get out of here!" Beth was nearly choking on her laughter. "No! You didn't!"

"Yes, I did. Think about it."

"I have, and it's insane."

"Not really. I believe he's Janie's father. *We* believe he's Janie's father. I have no other way to know him outside of school."

"The smoothie date was a reasonable idea," Beth said.

"It wasn't a date. It just kind of happened." Rachel sighed. "I think this will give me a better chance to check him out."

"Except that *he's* going to be the one checking *you* out."

"I plan to keep it going without actually following through with it."

"Aah, deceptive and dangerous."

"No, Bethie—clever and calculated."

"You know, for the first time in forever, I kind of wish Phil was home."

Chapter Twenty-Six

Frustrated, Rachel threw her phone into her bag. She'd tried to get in touch with Phil several times, but as usual, there was no answer. They'd been leading separate lives for close to two months, and the arrangement was rapidly heading into forever. As long as Phil wasn't there for her, she could comfortably owe him the same.

Making that emotional transition wasn't as much a leap as it was a tap. Phil was gone because he wanted to be. Despite one excuse after another, he'd made his choice, and it wasn't her or Janie. He'd never even asked about formally adopting the baby. For Rachel, that was a good thing, but it was a clear sign he wasn't into being a parent. There was peace in no longer having to consider what kind of father Phil would be. She no longer had to bow to his whims, accept his on-again-off-again coke-addled rants, or eat the lobster he ordered for himself on her behalf.

As much as Rachel wanted to give Phil a glorious shove out of the family portrait, admitting defeat was hard. She was used to giving her all and wondered if there was something she'd missed that might have made a difference. In her estimation, they hadn't crashed and burned. This felt more like a purgatorial descent. There were some charred fragments, but it was still hard for Rachel to believe Phil had never been capable of loving her the way she wanted to be loved. Owning that would mean their relationship had been a farce. Thankfully, she had Janie, a constant source of light who filled the air with the kind of exuberance life deserved to keep her hopeful.

After a quick reality check, Rachel walked to Zach's office and let herself in. He had texted earlier, apologizing for having to postpone their dinner meeting, and asked if she could meet him for lunch in his office instead. His editor was in town and had to speak with him about a poetry series that was likely to be scrapped without funding from the university. Or he'd lied and had a date he'd chosen not to tell her about.

Rachel organized notes from their last meeting and laid a couple of highlighters on the desk. She found a jazz mix on YouTube, sat down, and tried to decompress. Zach finally showed up, looking frazzled and scruffier than usual.

"I stopped off and got us these." He handed her a bag of bagels then pulled a small tub of cream cheese out of his pocket.

"Well, don't I feel special," Rachel teased.

"Sorry, I had a meeting, and then I had to go—"

"I'm kidding," Rachel said. "I don't care about lunch."

"I do," he said, sitting down next to her. "Let's eat."

Rachel made herself a cinnamon-raisin bagel with a light coat of cream cheese. She figured it was the least likely of the choices to make her breath smell or land little disgusting bits between her teeth. "You are unusually quiet today."

Zach followed suit but slathered on the cream cheese. "Yeah. I'm tired. I didn't sleep."

"Why?"

"The sleep fairy was busy," he said snidely. "I don't know. Do you always know why you can't sleep?"

"Sometimes, it's because I get caught up in *Friends* reruns. But most of the time, it's because something is bothering me."

"Well, nothing is bothering me, and the TV was off."

"Okay."

Rachel wasn't sure why Zach was in a foul mood, but she thought it best to ignore it, at least for the time being.

"What did you come up with in the critical essays about Pip's in-fatuation with Estella?"

"The usual." Rachel took a small bite of her bagel. "He was help-less. She was an incurable flirt."

"Yeah. I think you should delve into that one a little more."

Zach was sounding particularly snarky, and it was being directed squarely at her. Rachel quickly assessed their most recent encounters but couldn't make sense of his behavior. "Wade and I were talking the other day, and he said—"

"Wade?"

"Professor Ryzer. Wade Ryzer. He teaches the Romantics. He's new, but I assumed you knew each other."

"No. I don't know Wade," Zach said, pronouncing the name with an exaggerated tone. "Listen, today isn't a very good idea after all."

"What's wrong?" Rachel asked.

"Nothing. I have to go. Here." He threw a key down on the desk. "It's yours. Lock up when you're done." He stormed out, leaving Rachel to figure out why he was so ticked off and what to do with the tub of cream cheese.

As she was getting in the car, Rachel got a text from Beth saying the girls were having a great time and that Janie could stay over. Happy that all was going well, Rachel considered how to spend her unexpected alone time. She was trying to shake off her baffling lunch with Zach, but her uneasiness was still lingering. Maybe a good soak in the tub would help. It felt comforting to finally be going home, where she would be free of literary criticism and moody people.

Rachel plugged in a flash drive of Stevie Wonder hits her mother, a Motown fan, had made for her. During a break between songs, she heard her phone ring and quickly turned down the music, activating the Bluetooth.

"Hello," Rachel said.

"Hi, Rach. It's me, honey. How are you? How's Janie?"

It was Phil. Stevie had just been singing, putting some much-needed order in her world, and now, Phil decided it was time to remember he was her husband. She couldn't think of a word to say.

"Rach, are you there?"

"I'm here," she squeaked out. "It's been a long time since we've spoken."

"I know. Please forgive me." Phil sounded desperate, much like the last time they were together. Something must have gone wrong at work. The only time he ever sounded anguished was when something or someone was in his way.

"It's been impossible to get phone service around here. I miss you, honey. I miss you so much. Are you and Janie okay?"

"Yes. We're both fine," Rachel said.

"That's really good to hear."

Rachel decided to let him know how well she was getting along without him. "Janie's teething and learning the joys of SpongeBob, and I'm back at school taking a class."

"A class, huh? That sounds good. I'm glad you're keeping busy. I can't wait to get home, Rach. I'm telling Jeb I'm done traveling. I need to be home with you and Janie. How does that sound, honey?"

"That sounds... different. Very different."

"I want to come home, baby," Phil whispered. "I have to go, but I'll call you again soon. Promise."

Rachel ended the call feeling like she'd been sucker-punched. She'd grown accustomed to despising Phil and felt comfortable wishing the worst on him. How dare he suddenly call, contrite and apologetic, seeking her forgiveness. She continued to drive until she realized she had no clue where she was and veered off to the side of the road to get her bearings. A big marquis was standing in front of a large brick building: *Thaxton's Welcomes You Back. Grand Opening. Tonight!*

This was the place. It was finally open again. Rachel pulled into the crowded parking lot just as a Jeep was backing out of a space near the door. She claimed it quickly then texted Beth to check in on Janie. For a second, Rachel thought about adding that Phil had called, but that would only invite a conversation she didn't want to have. Instead, she pulled down the visor and examined her face in the mirror.

Big mistake. The day had left her complexion dull. There was no excuse for any cosmetic company with a modicum of success to have not yet created a foundation to cover angst, confusion, and poor judgment. And she had no clue about what was up with her frizzy split ends. She thought about scrapping the whole idea of checking out the restaurant, but inevitably, intrigue usurped vanity. Thaxton's was the only place Rena had mentioned by name, and Rachel had been mysteriously led there.

Rachel brushed on some bronzer, smoothed over her hair with a small squirt of lotion, and resolved to make the best of it.

A striking middle-aged woman with long auburn curls greeted Rachel as soon as she walked in. "Are you meeting anyone tonight, hon?" the hostess asked in an unexpected Southern drawl.

"No, no one, not tonight. Maybe not ever... Who knows..." Rachel had no clue why she'd let a perfect stranger know she was struggling.

"I wouldn't worry. Pretty little thing like you won't have a stitch of trouble finding someone."

Apparently, Rachel sounded closer to devastated than disappointed. She let out a weighty sigh.

"I hear ya, hon. I do," the hostess said. "Would you like a table, or would you prefer to sit at the bar?" She cocked her head toward the bar, indicating that was the place to go if one was on the prowl.

"A table, please."

"That's just dandy." The hostess grabbed a menu. "Follow me, sweet thing." The hostess led her toward the back, past several crowded tables.

"Rachel?"

It was a familiar woman's voice, but Rachel couldn't place it until she turned around. "Edie!"

"Rachel! How nice to see you. Please, sit with me if you're free."

"Oh, she's free, Edie," the hostess said, leaving the menu on the table. "Dawn should be with you shortly, but she's on the rag, and I have no idea how long she's gonna take."

A man standing at the entrance to the kitchen shouted, "Lucybelle!" And the hostess darted off.

"You know her? Lucybelle?" Rachel asked.

"She's been a client for years." Edie opened the menu. "Her husband owns this place."

Rachel grinned. "So she has license to speak her mind."

"Always. And she's stunning, which helps because that woman doesn't mince words, ever."

"I noticed," Rachel said. "Sounds like you know a lot of people here."

"I do. I've been a customer since day one."

"I read it was closed."

"It was. They wanted to bring it up to speed for the college crowd. You know, all the flat-screen televisions, the electronics—new this, new that. New shmoo. I liked the old charm. But truthfully, there are more of *them*"—Edie waved her arm at the crowd— "paying the bills."

"You came tonight to show your support?" Rachel asked.

"It turned out that way, though I honestly hadn't given it much thought. My friend was supposed to join me, but I told her she was going to have a surprise visitor, and she canceled."

"You knew?"

"Sort of. A skunk ran into her house."

A busboy with dark-framed glasses brought over water and a basket of bread and butter. "Anything from the bar, ladies?"

"I'll have that fine-looking gentleman with the gray beard and tan sports jacket," Edie teased.

"Haha, well, I'll check on that for you." The busboy laughed as he walked away.

"I'm really glad *you're* here," Rachel said. "I didn't even know *I* was going to be here. What a coincidence."

"Rachel, *coincidence* is just a word people use to justify fate. We're obviously supposed to talk tonight."

"Maybe. You have been on my mind."

"And you on mine."

Rachel sat silently for a moment, staring more *through* than at her menu.

"How are you?" Edie said, sounding concerned. "You look like you've seen a ghost."

"You're not too far off," Rachel admitted. "My husband called out of the blue. He's been away on business, and I pretty much told him I would consider us separated while he was gone. Now, he says he wants to come home."

"And what do you want?"

"I want... I wanted him to say that months ago."

"And now?" Edie poked at a roll, and Rachel could feel the jabs.

"Now, I don't know what I want. I've been on my own, doing things for myself, making a life without him." Rachel toyed with the wrapper from her straw. "And I met someone who might be special to me. And I met someone else who also might be special to me—for an entirely different reason."

A server came over sand quietly filled their water glasses.

"I think I'm following this," Edie said.

"Well, it's good to know someone is." Rachel took a sip of water. "And there's something else."

"You should find out if you're right about that." Edie took a pat of butter. "Knowing if your husband cheated may help you make peace with the choice you want to make."

"I know you're psychic, Edie, but how did this information come to you?" Rachel asked, eyes wide with wonder.

"Not only do you wear your heart on your sleeve, but you also wear it on your face," Edie said. "I don't need the cards for this one, Rachel. I can see the pain and uncertainty in your eyes."

Rachel held back the tears that wanted to escape.

"Honey." Edie patted Rachel's hand. "You already know what you want. The key is to be brave enough to get it."

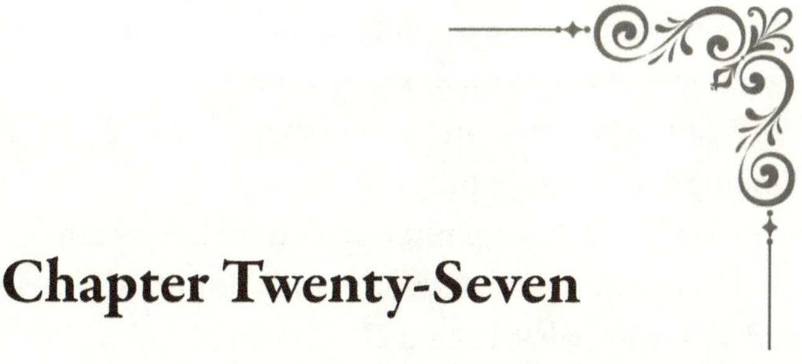

Chapter Twenty-Seven

After speaking with Edie, Rachel couldn't bear one more moment of uncertainty. She'd called Brittany at the crack of dawn the next morning and asked her to come an hour earlier to babysit. That left Rachel just enough time to swing by the Hilton Woodcliff Lake before going to her class. Anxious to get there, Rachel could feel her foot leaning too heavily on the gas pedal, and she eased it back. The last thing she wanted was a speeding ticket while she was out gathering proof of her husband's infidelity. Three lights and a downpour later, she was parking.

She took a deep breath as she walked to the front desk, hoping she had practiced her lines enough to sound convincing.

"Good afternoon!" a man in a too-tight burgundy jacket said through a broad plastic smile. "One moment, please." He had yet to look away from the computer to formally greet her.

"No problem," Rachel lied. It was all a problem. Her having to be there in the first place was a problem. It was possible that in a few short moments, she would know if she'd been deceiving herself about her marriage for longer than she cared to imagine.

"Good afternoon," the man said again as if on a loop. "How can I help you today, young lady?"

Young lady. Rachel hoped he wasn't going to hit on her. She dug into her coat pocket and handed the man the receipt. "I know this sounds a bit out of the ordinary, but our accountant is working on our taxes, and neither my husband nor I can remember if this particular stay was personal or professional. I see there's some kind of package code that may help us figure it out."

"You folks sure are impressively honest," the man remarked, looking over the receipt.

"We'll see," Rachel muttered under her breath.

"I'm pretty new here," the man admitted. "Give me a minute, and let me see what I can do."

"Thank you," Rachel said slowly, trying to control her agitation. "I really appreciate your help."

The man ignored her, too engrossed in the data on his computer to respond. "Ahh... Look here... This code... This code is..."

"Is what?" Rachel said in a tone she knew was decidedly inappropriate.

"Sorry, I was in the wrong place." The man continued to punch in an inordinate amount of material from one small receipt.

"Sorry to be so much trouble," Rachel said through a smile that belied the truth.

"No trouble at all. This is fun for me. I'm getting to practice." The man stopped and checked the receipt again.

"If it's too much of a bother, that's telling me something anyway." Rachel could feel the weight of what she was expecting to discover resting heavily on her shoulders.

"It was pleasure!" the man said like he'd struck gold. "Sorry it took me so long, but this is one of our newer specials. It's our RAP."

Rachel was trying to process what the man was saying, but he was being too cryptic for her to catch on. "What's your 'RAP'?"

"Oh, right, you probably wouldn't know." The man continued to read the description directly from the computer. "It's our Romantic Afternoon Package. Champagne, strawberries, chocolate, a couple's massage, plus the room from noon to four."

Rachel was waiting to feel stunned or nauseated and ready to expel buckets of tears. Surely, she would have some visceral response to learning that, for who knows how long, she'd been deceived. Instead, she felt intensely calm. The doubt was finally gone. The ruminating could end. Maybe the anger and other emotions would come later, but for now, she was enjoying the freedom.

"Hope this helps," the man said.

"More than you'll ever know," Rachel said.

The man smiled proudly then quickly answered an incoming call.

Rachel realized the desk clerk had no way of knowing that he was the first person to see her walk out of the Hilton and into her new life.

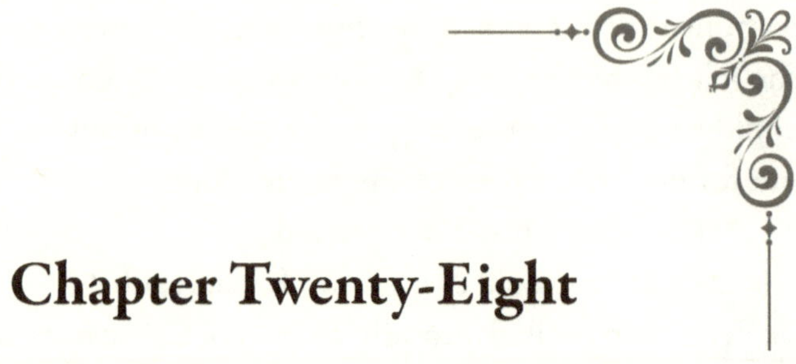

Chapter Twenty-Eight

Rachel sat at her favorite table in the dining hall. During off hours, she could claim the whole table and arrange her notes and books any which way suited her. She'd piled all the Dickens notes in different sections and her class notes on *Wuthering Heights* in others. Somewhere in the middle, she'd found a space for a cup of yogurt and a bag of almonds.

"What, no hot chocolate?" Wade took the seat opposite hers next to the notes on Edgar Linton.

"Nah, not today. But come to think of it, I should get a water."

"Here." Wade handed her a cold, fresh bottle. "I bought an extra for later."

"Thanks." Rachel twisted off the cap and took a sip.

"So, have you given any thought to our discussion?" Wade asked while skimming through papers.

"I have given many thoughts to our discussion."

Last night, as she'd drifted off to sleep, Rachel had pictured Wade sitting behind an easel, looking very intense as she stood before him covered in nothing but a soft sheet. He directed her to lie on a red crushed-velvet divan that she imagined had once belonged to Dorothy Parker. Rachel knew this session was about art, not sex, but her vulnerability was unsettling and made her giggle like a little girl. Wade seemed oblivious and continued to arrange his supplies.

Rachel was antsy and unsure of what position Wade wanted her to take. It was also frigging cold, and she could feel her nipples hard-en in response. That wasn't good. He might get the idea she was into him. She wasn't, but she was naked, and he was the father of her child, so she let herself imagine what making love with him might be like. She tried to get into it, thinking it might be for the greater good, but something beyond attraction was missing.

Despite the tepidity of her fantasy, it still felt a bit like coitus interruptus when Wade quite suddenly instructed her to release the sheet and let it fall into whatever pattern emerged naturally. Rachel obliged and blushed as Wade turned from his palette to study her. He took a few deep breaths, and Rachel wondered if he was trying to control his ardor. She didn't mean to ooze incomparable sexual energy that made him flush with desire, but perhaps it couldn't be helped. Of course, Wade was a gentleman and didn't come on to her in any way. Even in fantasy, that felt right.

"Earth to Rachel." Wade put down his papers and snapped his fingers in front of Rachel's face. "Where are you?"

Rachel heard Wade's voice faintly but was still in her fantasy, putting on her clothes and processing her total lack of romantic interest in him. "I... I'm here," she said, slowly coming back to their conversation.

"You still haven't said if you'll pose for me."

Rachel finally realized she had to offer a response. "Maybe. But I was thinking it would be helpful for me to see your studio and some of your other work and then decide. How does that sound?"

"Hmm. I suppose that's only fair. When's good for you?"

Rachel saw Zach come in from the other side of the room. Her heart fluttered as he approached the table, and as her fantasy about Wade illustrated, it was tough for her to imagine being intimate with anyone but him.

"Hi. Zach Jamison." Zach extended a firm handshake to Wade. "Victorian lit. I'm Rachel's... professor."

Rachel glanced at Wade's face to see if he caught Zach's slight pause before saying he was her professor. He didn't seem to notice, but she was pleased Zach implied he had other thoughts of who he might be to her.

"Wade Ryzer. The Romantics." Wade pointed to an empty seat. "Please join us."

Rachel winced at Wade's suggestion that she and he were an "us," but things were still too precarious for her to say anything to clarify their relationship. The interesting thing was Zach seemed determined to figure things out for himself and took the seat he was offered.

"I've been looking forward to meeting you," Wade said. "You're quite accomplished. I thoroughly enjoyed your book on the Brontës, particularly the section on *Jane Eyre*. Very insightful."

"Thank you. Rachel and I are working on another book in the series. Dickens."

"Yes, she mentioned that." Wade shifted his gaze from Rachel to Zach. "I'll look forward to it."

"I'm not familiar with your work," Zach confessed.

Wade took a bottle of water out of his pocket and took a sip. "I'm an eclectic kind of guy. I'm also a painter, and our Rachel here is going to be my next subject."

"Maybe," Rachel said quickly.

"That's a terrific idea," Zach agreed. "She has excellent features for a portrait."

"Yes, she does, but I'm more interested in her elegant bone structure," Wade said.

"I can see that." Zach gave Rachel a quick once-over from his seat. "So, it's more of a full-length painting?"

"I paint nudes." Wade cleared his throat.

"Nudes?" Zach's voice sounded almost an octave higher than usual.

"Excuse me," Wade said, noticing an incoming text on his buzzing phone. "I'm sorry. Rachel, call me. I've got to run." He jumped up and darted out of the room.

"Is this for real? You're posing nude?" Zach pointed his thumb in the direction Wade had taken to leave. "For that guy?"

"Maybe." Rachel was surprised at how confident she sounded. "I have my reasons."

"I'm sure of that. You know, you are quite an enigma."

"I don't mean to be."

"Then you wouldn't be," Zach said. "How would your husband feel about this?"

Rachel cringed. "Phil? It has nothing to do with him." Rachel took a fruit bar from her bag, trying to stave off a conversation about Phil.

"Ah, the husband has a name."

"As if that mattered."

"It might, depending on where you stand with him."

Rachel hesitated before replying. Zach's use of the word *might* conjured up worlds of ambiguity that she was not inclined to entertain.

"I don't stand or sit or eat or lie with *him*," Rachel said with even more conviction than she'd planned.

"But you're going to pose nude for a guy who teaches the Romantics."

Rachel could understand Zach's bewilderment. It did sound like an odd decision without context. "Please understand, I have my reasons, and none of this has anything to do with you." Rachel got up to leave.

"It could," Zach said.

Rachel sat back down. "How so?"

"Maybe I'll buy it."

"Buy what?"

"The painting of you."

"Why would you do that?"

Zach was about to answer when a colleague with a briefcase hanging from his shoulder tapped Zach's arm and offered his congratulations for something or other.

Rachel, unsure she wanted Zach's answer, took that as a cue to leave.

Chapter Twenty-Nine

The drive to Wade's house was taking too long. It was only eight in the morning on a Saturday, and yet Rachel could swear one car after another was determined to keep her from getting there. It was not that Wade was so far away, but those damn malls were traffic magnets, especially during the holiday season, which she'd discovered was suddenly in full swing. As she passed a billboard of a baby eating cereal, Rachel called Brittany to remind her to give Janie her vitamins before her bottle. At some point, Rachel figured she would owe Brittany a car or a degree.

Wade's studio was attached to his house, a charming, sage-green Cape Cod with a white picket fence and flower boxes on the windows. It was the kind of house that screamed *Brady Bunch*—exactly what Rachel wanted for her daughter. She let out an enormous sigh. If his place had looked more like *Animal House*, she would have been less inclined to think he was serious about having a family.

She got out of the car and grabbed the bag of donuts and box of coffee she'd bought to compensate for the myriad bottles of water and packages of cookies he freely gave her. *This is for Janie,* she told herself as she knocked on the door.

Wearing Adidas slippers, Wade was dressed like the embodiment of the weekend. He'd probably had the faded, holey, too-short T-shirt from a *Foo Fighters* concert since he was a teenager. His belly hung over his navy-blue sweats ever so slightly, giving him the look of a teddy bear that needed a makeover. He was holding a jar of paint in his hand and had a slender brush strategically wedged over his ear, where his pen would be if they were at school. After giving him a cursory review, she felt confident he wasn't after sex.

"Hey, come on in." Wade took the bag from her and led her into the open-concept kitchen. "Glad you could make it, but you didn't have to bring anything."

"My mother taught me never to go anywhere empty-handed."

"Ah, my mother taught me never to go anywhere empty-headed." He chuckled, putting down the paint and bag of donuts.

"Guess we both have wise mothers," Rachel said, looking around the spacious room. "You have a lovely home."

"Thank you. It's comfortable." Wade took out a platter from a glass-paneled cabinet. "These look unfortunately delicious. What else can I get you?"

"Oh, nothing for me. I already had breakfast," she fibbed.

There was no way Rachel could eat, especially if there was the slightest possibility she was going to get even a little bit undressed. Maybe Wade could be cute and Pooh Bear-ish with a whisper of a protruding gut, but if she were to have any kind of pouch, she'd best be pregnant. Besides, this whole situation had her stomach in knots, and a bite of anything could have set off an embarrassing result.

"Okay, then." Wade took a chocolate-glazed donut and closed the box. "Let me take you through the studio."

He led her to an open corridor at the far side of the kitchen that connected to a long hall and opened a bright-yellow door. "Here it is."

The studio was the size of a two-car garage, and Rachel figured it probably had been one in a former life. Aesthetically speaking, it worked as an appropriate space for a frenzied artist who had too many ideas to ever finish just one at a time. Yet the room also imparted an almost constipated, organized calm. Nothing appeared out of place, and each work, whether it was completed or not, felt relatable.

Rachel was struck by how many easels were standing in different places around the room. Some had pencil drawings clipped to them, while others held sketches in pastels. The canvases varied in size, and most were blank. Paints of all types and colors were neatly placed on pristine shelves, while stacks of finished paintings were lined up against walls. Some weren't nudes, which made Rachel wonder if Wade had cultivated this interest recently.

An unfinished painting caught Rachel's eye, and she stood for a moment to study what looked like an older guy pointing his penis, a chicken leg oozing mashed potatoes, into a large red-and-white pail.

"This one means a lot to me," Wade said. "It's a protest piece deriding the fast-food industry."

"I thought that was Colonel Sanders," Rachel said. "Interesting use of the bucket."

He led her over to a corner of the studio. "These are more like what I have in mind for you."

Wade showed her a series of lovely nudes. Some were abstract, and others were more defined. They weren't all young or women. He went through several more with her and invited her to continue looking when he got a call he had to take. Rachel walked down another row of Wade's work.

A few paintings with a Picasso-like feel made her laugh, and Rachel decided that if she let Wade paint her, she didn't want her vagina in the middle of her face or her lips smiling over her ass. She was nearly done looking when her eyes locked in a compelling gaze with a warm, almost-familiar twinkle that made her heart skip a beat. Forget the abstraction—it was Rena.

Rachel took a deep breath as Wade returned, and she pointed out the painting.

"This one is particularly unique. Is she a friend of yours?"

"Yes, she was, briefly. She was taking a class the summer I was teaching. Lovely woman."

"Guess you must have been close if she was willing to pose for you."

"I'm not always close with my subjects. But yes, she and I were. It was originally intended to be a gift for her husband, but things got complicated, and it didn't work out," Wade said. "So, what do you say, Rachel? Would you like to get started?"

No. She didn't want to get started. She wanted to run. It was too soon. Seeing the unbearably accurate likeness of Rena was shocking and made everything feel more real and immediate. There were decisions to be made that she still wasn't ready to make, though in her heart, she knew this lovely, gifted man deserved to be the father he longed to be.

"I'm sorry," Rachel cried as she clutched her stomach. "Must be last night's lo mein. You know takeout. I... have to go."

"That's it?" Beth asked through bites of a huge Italian sub oozing olives and bits of cheese. "You saw a painting that you assumed was of Rena, and you split?"

"Yup." Rachel picked at a salad she'd bought on her way to Beth's. "I told him I felt sick and ran out of there like an Olympic sprinter. I'm sure he thinks I'm crazy."

"As we all do," Beth said.

"Very funny, but you have no idea how I felt staring into Rena's eyes."

"When I'm fantasizing, I get confused between Bradley Cooper and Matthew McConaughey."

"I wasn't fantasizing," Rachel said. "Although you do have a point. I have mistaken Zooey Deschanel for Katy Perry."

"Exactly. Maybe you saw what you wanted to see, something to force you out of there," Beth suggested.

"No, no, that isn't what happened," Rachel insisted. "I saw the painting of Rena, and I freaked."

"Rach, I don't get it. So what if Wade is Janie's father? You like him. I think he's a little stuffy, but you take to intellectuals more than I do."

Rachel threw an olive at Beth, who caught it and popped it into her mouth.

"You're a bottomless pit."

"Shut up," Beth chided. "You're just trying to avoid this conversation, and I won't let you."

"Really? What if I promised you this?" Rachel tauntingly reached into her fast-food bag and took out a chocolate shake. "I even have a straw."

"Suck it up yourself, big sister." Beth flaunted a huge whole pickle and took a forceful bite.

"Ouch!" Rachel cried. "Poor Evan."

"Nice try at deflection, but we're going to talk about this."

Rachel took a sip of the thick, creamy shake and knew in an instant that, like Beth, she would easily succumb to all cravings if she were pregnant.

"You think Wade is smart, artistic, and tidy," Beth said. "You've also said he's thoughtful, considerate, and sensitive. In other words, he's a great catch, and since there's no wife in the picture, what are you waiting for?"

"I wish I knew, but something keeps holding me back."

"Do you find him attractive at all?"

"Yes, but not in a baby-do-me-now kind of way."

"Hell, Rach, I haven't had that with Evan since he put a ring on my finger. But I still love him like hell."

Rachel took a forkful of alfalfa sprouts and poured more dressing on her salad. "I don't know what it is."

"Okay, let's forget about Wade for now. Are you afraid Zach won't accept Janie?"

"Maybe," Rachel admitted. "He's never spent any time with her or us together."

"That would change if you were honest with him. With all of them. Cut Phil loose. Tell Wade he's the baby daddy, and let Zach in."

"I know. You're right. That's what I should do." Rachel sighed deeply. "But I can't."

"Are you afraid if you choose Zach instead of Wade, Wade will fight you for custody?"

"No. He wouldn't do that. He's fair and reasonable. He'd be willing to share her. I'm sure of it."

"Then, Rach, it's time. You have to move forward."

Finally, a night Rachel could watch Jimmy Kimmel without worrying about essays or research. Janie was asleep, and Zach was with a few of his frat brothers at someone's house for a long weekend and had told her she was off duty. If she'd felt more comfortable, she would've asked him about the particulars, but nothing had changed since their last meeting, so she had no right to that information.

That would need to be fixed, but until then, the next best thing was a tub of chocolate-fudge frozen yogurt. Rachel sat with a spoon and a can of coconut whipped cream as Jimmy made guest after guest crack up over everything from politics to animal farts. It was a gift to be able to make people crack up on purpose, unlike her tendency to elicit unsolicited laughter.

Her cell phone rang, and she figured it was Beth begging to be dissuaded from eating an entire marble cheesecake. But the number didn't look familiar.

"Hello?" Rachel asked.

Silence.

"Hello?"

"Rach?"

A wave of nausea gripped at her stomach. "Phil, is that you? The connection is terrible."

"Yeah, it's me, baby. Listen."

"Where are you?"

"The Caymans."

"It's hard to hear you."

"Rach, listen to me, honey," Phil pleaded. "I'm in trouble, and I need your help."

The tone in Phil's voice made Rachel's blood run cold. "Phil, what's going on?"

"I can't tell you, honey, for your own good."

"Don't call me 'honey'! And what can't you tell me?" Rachel thought of Janie asleep and tried to keep her voice down.

Phil let out a long stream of air. "Some shit went down, really bad shit."

"Well, that's a shame. *I* certainly can't help you."

"Rach, I'm begging you, baby. You have to. I've been hiding for weeks. It's not cool. They're gonna find me." Phil sounded both lucid and wasted.

All Rachel could muster was disgust. "Who's going to find you? Phil, what the fuck have you done?"

"Baby, you gotta wire money into my bank account."

"So this is about money?"

"Rach, listen, you have to transfer your business account over to me," Phil said. "It's easy. You could do it online."

"Maybe it's the heat, but, Phil, you've lost your mind."

"No, no, hon, listen, you have to do this."

"No, I don't," Rachel said. "It's not even my money. Beth would never go for this even if I agreed. Not that I would."

"Don't let that bitch boss you around, Rach. Stand up to her for a change."

"Tell me that you are the most wasted you've ever been in your life, or I'm hanging up right now."

"Okay, hon, you got me. I'm out of it. But you have to listen to me. Let's make this simple."

Rachel could hear the panic in Phil's voice, but he'd betrayed her, and she was unmoved.

"Call the bank," Phil said. "Turn the house over to them and transfer the funds to me."

"So you're joking, but I'm not laughing." Seething, Rachel looked at the phone. "I'm not giving up the house, and your tough luck, it's in my name."

"Cash out, for me, baby, for us. The house is worth over a mil. You could easily get a half-mil credit line."

Squelching a scream, Rachel picked up a pillow from Phil's side of the bed and hurled it across the room, knocking over a bud vase. "Phil, listen to me very carefully. I will not cash out. I will not send you a penny. There is no us anymore. We are so beyond done, you won't even find a crumb of us at the bottom of a fucking box of croutons."

"Come on, honey, this isn't my girl talking."

"You're right. This is *my* girl talking. No more phone calls. To be clear, I'm divorcing you. From now on, you can speak to my lawyer." Rachel immediately thought of the attorney who'd come into the shop a couple of months ago to pick up a Divorced Barbie for her new office. After the sale, she'd handed Rachel her business card, saying, "You never know." At the time, Rachel had believed her marriage was flawed but solid, and she had *almost* thrown the card away.

"Come on," Phil said. "Don't do this, Rach. I need you. I'm in trouble."

"I'm sorry, Phil. I truly am. But if something happens to you because you're an asshole, maybe you'll learn something. I've had it. We're done."

"That's not right, babe. I'm the guy who makes love to you like there's no tomorrow."

"You're right about one thing—for us, there is definitely no tomorrow!"

"Come on, don't be a bitch to me, Dana. You love me."

"Dana? Really? Was she your slut du jour that afternoon at the Hilton?"

"Come on. You know me, Rach. I'm a Marriott guy."

"Fuck you, Phil. Fuck you!" Without giving herself a moment to pity him, she slammed down the phone.

Still seething, she retrieved a business card from her wallet and picked up the phone again. It was late, but she could leave a message.

"Hi, Susan. This is Rachel Sutton. You came to my shop a couple of months ago for the Divorced Barbie you wanted for your new office. It appears you were right. You never know. I'm going to need your services after all."

Chapter Thirty

The planned menu was green bean casserole, tomato basil chicken, rice pilaf, and Rachel's famous meringue cookies. The meal, coupled with the fine tableware her grandmother had given her a zillion years ago, was bound to prove to Zach that she meant business.

It was the signature dinner Rachel depended on when company was coming. The prosecco was chilling, the candles were glowing, and the table was dressed in an elegant satiny white cloth. Each plate, utensil, and glass was carefully set in its proper place.

She planned to surprise Zach as much as he'd surprised her when he'd accepted her impromptu dinner invitation. He'd called a couple of hours earlier, freaking out that his editor had to present a comprehensive outline to the publisher on the Dickens book by tomorrow's close of business, or the whole project could fall apart. Zach had tried and failed to wrangle more time out of the guy. He'd asked her how she felt about working all night.

"I'll have to find a sitter," she'd said. But Beth had a Lamaze class, and Brittany was on a field trip. So she'd called Zach to say, "Sorry, no luck. The best I can do is have you come here."

The annoying decision about what to wear loomed large as she stood in her closet, wishing she had Tim Gunn to help her figure out what said "do me" without saying "do me." The red dress with the slit on the right side might have been a contender, but the memory of wearing it when Phil screwed her in the backseat of a limo after a Christmas party at Nobu made her skin crawl.

Deep breath time.

Clouding the future with the past was not going to serve her well. Zach did not have to deal with her pain, and in time, neither would she. As soon as she heard from the lawyer, she would begin divorce proceedings and dance into a welcome new chapter.

With no fashion advisor in her contact list, Rachel chose to play the evening for what it was—a business dinner. She hoped there might come a time when greeting Zach in panties scantily covered by a skirt would be just another fun night at home. But this wasn't even a real date, and she settled on a long, low-cut purple sweater and a pair of black silky leggings. Going classy felt appropriate, and if nothing but Dickens came between them, Zach could still admire her well-developed calves.

Dressed and ready, Rachel stood at Janie's crib and stroked her silky curls. Motherhood was even more wonderful than she'd imagined, and it continued to amaze her that Janie seemed content to be her daughter.

Cuddling her stuffie, Janie seemed to know Rachel had big plans and had accommodated her by falling asleep immediately after feasting on yams and pea puree. It was going to take nothing short of a miracle to get used to sharing her with Wade, but the more she thought about it, the more certain she was he would prove to be a fine father.

Rachel bent down to give Janie a kiss when she heard a faint knock at the front door. She flipped on the intercom and left Janie's bedroom. Anxious to greet Zach, she walked a bit too quickly down the steps and nearly tripped over her heels. Why she was wearing heels was a question she couldn't answer, but there was something decidedly feminine and sexy about an elongated look that Rachel hoped was in order.

Zach was at the door, holding a cake box in one hand and a bunch of assorted flowers already in a vase in the other.

"Hi! Wow, what's all this?" Rachel asked, leading Zach into the family room.

She was trying to feel safe and comfortable, but she'd never entertained a man in her home before, much less one she wanted in her bed. Keeping dinner a work meeting was going to be a challenge, especially since the intoxicating smell of Zach's aftershave was toying with her libido.

"It's a response to your invitation." Zach put the flowers and dessert on the coffee table.

"You're very responsive," Rachel said loosely then blushed at the implication.

"Never thought about it."

"Well, sure, it's not something to think about. It just is."

I'm an idiot. If she were smart, she would shut up and let him do all the talking.

"You look pretty," Zach said without actually looking at her.

"Thanks, you do too."

Zach grinned.

"I mean, you—"

"Thank you, Rachel, I know what you meant." Zach looked around the room. "You have a nice place."

"Glad you think so."

Zach took off his coat and laid it over a chair as if he'd done that a hundred times. He was distractingly seductive, wearing a blue, long-sleeved shirt and black jeans.

"I like it here. It's very homey," Zach said, helping himself to a handful of nuts from the bowl on the table. "It's very... you."

"Thank you. I've made some recent changes, courtesy of late-night home shopping."

Rachel shivered a bit at how intimate his compliment felt. Maybe he'd been trying to figure her out. As much as she wanted to believe he was that invested, she wasn't sure. He'd simply stated her home reflected her general style, neat and casual. Since they were working together, it made sense that he would be interested in how organized she kept her own space. She decided to stop overthinking his every breath and instead go to garnish the chicken.

"Can I get you a drink or anything?" Rachel asked. "I have to check on dinner."

"Water, ice, if you have it," Zach answered. "Is your daughter sleeping?"

Rachel was hoping to keep away from the subject, especially with things being so precarious with Wade. But there was no way of knowing what the future would bring, and if she wanted Zach in her life, avoidance would be unnatural. She certainly didn't want him to think she had issues about being a mother.

"Yes, she was pretty tired," Rachel said. "Be right back."

She went to the kitchen, hoping her Amanda Freitag cookbook hadn't failed her. Much to her delight, everything looked and smelled delicious. It made her wonder why she always had to complicate things even when they were going well. Zach was being attentive despite initially saying he wanted to keep his distance. She was reasonably certain once he knew her marriage was over, he'd be willing to make the first move.

Zach seemed worried about Wade, though—and for good reason. Even Rachel couldn't be sure how he might factor into the equation. But even with Wade aside, there was always the possibility that Zach was a commitment-phobe who had no intentions of pursuing anything meaningful. She had no clue about his relationship history. Come to think of it, she didn't know much about him at all.

"Candles, wine, and the good dishes," Zach said, holding out a chair for Rachel. "I'm honored."

"I don't get much of a chance to entertain these days," Rachel said as she placed the food on the table. "And you can't work on an empty stomach." Rachel passed him the prosecco. "Would you mind?"

The bottle opened with ease, and Zach poured them each a healthy glass.

"You're good at that," Rachel said.

Zach raised his glass. "To the chef."

They clinked glasses and took their first sips.

"Thanks for all this, Rachel." Zach filled his plate. "I can't remember the last time anyone cooked for me, except my mother."

"Does she live around here?"

"Yeah, not far. Your family around here?"

"My sister and her family are. My mom moved to Greece. And my dad's been gone a while."

"Sorry, mine has too." Zach speared a green bean. "So how does the family feel about your husband?"

Rachel nearly choked on her chicken. "They don't like him," she said effortlessly. "They haven't for years."

"Why? What kind of guy is he?"

"The kind you divorce."

Zach looked up from his plate to meet Rachel's gaze. "Is that what you've decided to do?"

Wait. This conversation is supposed to happen over the lovely mini cannoli and eclairs still living in the bakery box. They were only on the main course—the time for questions like "What's your favorite music, movie, color?" and "How do you take your tea?" But the mood had shifted, and suddenly, those questions seemed trivial. She really didn't care which team he rooted for during the World Series or the Super Bowl.

"Yes, that's what I've decided to do." Rachel took a sip of prosecco.

"Are you sure?" Zach stared at her intently.

"More than you could imagine. I called a lawyer." She stayed locked in his gaze.

"You did?" Zach said, sounding more surprised than she'd expected. "I thought you weren't ready."

"You thought wrong." Rachel brushed an imaginary crumb off the table. "And what about you? Have you ever been married?"

Zach shifted uncomfortably in his seat. "Yes, I was, a very long time ago. We were barely twenty-one."

Rachel decided he needed comfort carbs, and she passed him the bread basket.

"Thanks," he said, taking a seeded roll. "I was still in college."

"Wow, that must have been stressful." Rachel thought about her relationship with Jesus and imagined they would have divorced had they married back then.

"It was insanity," Zach said, shaking his head. "She was the breadwinner, a cashier at Home Depot by day and a barmaid by night."

"That must've been a lot for both of you to deal with."

"It lasted nearly two years," Zach said. "I was so grateful when she left me for the club owner that I almost sent him a gift."

"You were happy about it ending?" Rachel asked.

"Oh, yeah," Zach admitted. "I knew it was a mistake from the get-go, but I was too stubborn to listen to reason from anyone."

"And that was that?"

"Yup. Thankfully. No kids and no contact since." Zach buttered a piece of his roll.

Rachel swallowed hard when he said "No kids." Before a moment's thought, she blurted, "Oh, you don't want children?"

"Definitely not with her," he said. "Maybe, someday, with the right person. We'll see."

Rachel breathed a small sigh of relief. It was a reasonable response to a question she had no business asking.

"That was a long time ago. Anyone since then?" Rachel asked, uncertain what she wanted to hear.

"I've fallen in love a couple of times, but nothing ever took."

Zach's past sounded relatively simple. Nothing made her cringe or worry in *Let's Make a Deal* fashion that there was a zonk waiting for her behind a curtain. An impulsive marriage and a few breakups were nothing compared to Phil, whose recent call had Rachel conjuring up visions of *The Godfather*. She poured the last of the prosecco into their glasses and opened another bottle.

Two empty bottles of prosecco and many conversations later, Rachel felt an easiness growing between them. Rachel wanted to call it trust, but given all the secrets she still felt the need to keep, she wasn't there yet. Maybe, in time, that would change, but having Zach gazing into her eyes with the kind of spark she'd been hoping to see did not feel like settling.

"Can I get you something? Coffee, tea, or—me?" Rachel teased.

"Oh, I think you know my answer," Zach said as he got up and stood behind her chair.

Little goose bumps appeared on Rachel's arms as she realized dinner was about to turn to pleasure. Sex had become so perfunctory between her and Phil she wasn't quite sure how to respond in the throes of actual passion.

Zach bent down and pushed her hair away from the sides of her neck and began covering her with soft, breathy kisses. It felt so genuine and natural. Maybe she couldn't handle it. She thought about making a little joke, like *"Oooh, I smell something. I don't know, it could be flames of desire, or my neighbor really overdid it on the crème brûlée."* Or she could simply feign innocence and get up for water. None of that was meant to happen.

Zach lifted her from her seat and turned her face toward his. Tingles ran through her body as the path of his kisses led to her mouth. Rachel decided it was probably best to let whatever was happening between them happen. He pressed his lips against hers, prodding them open with the tip of his tongue. She welcomed the kiss, slowly grazing her tongue against his in small circles.

His hands broke from their embrace to move down her back and over her bottom to firmly draw her closer to him. She rocked into him over and over, finally understanding why she had been guided to wear heels.

"Where's your bedroom?" Zach asked as he moved his kisses down the line of her cleavage.

Rachel took his hand and led him up the stairs into her room. For a moment, her mind flashed to Phil and the dread that might have occurred had Macy not miraculously shown up.

As if he felt the demon haunting her, Zach held her close against his chest. "You want to try a different room?"

"No," Rachel said, looking down at the carpet. "I'm fine right here. With you."

He held her face up to his and kissed her so tenderly, she began to feel the ugliness of the recent past fade as its power was abated by lucidity. There was nothing to keep her from giving herself to Zach, and any doubts she might've had about his intentions evaporated with their kiss.

"Are you sure about this?" Zach asked, taking off his shirt.

"Hell yeah," she said, tugging at his belt buckle.

He pulled off her sweater, unhooked her bra, and lifted her onto the bed.

A blood-curdling scream echoed down the hall.

"Oh no, it's Janie," Rachel cried, jumping up. "I'm sorry. I have to..."

"Go. Of course, she comes first." Zach got up and headed to the bathroom.

Rachel threw on her robe and went to the nursery.

"Oh, poor baby," Rachel said, cradling Janie. "You're hot enough to melt an igloo." She held Janie and walked back to her bedroom to get the thermometer and baby Motrin from her medicine chest.

Zach was just coming out of the bathroom, wearing the robe Phil kept on a hook near the shower.

"She's got a fever," Rachel said, kissing Janie's head. "I'm sorry."

"I'm sorry too. Poor thing." Zach patted Janie's head. Indicating he wanted to hold Janie, he asked, "May I?"

"Of course." Rachel handed the baby to Zach, who immediately held her against his chest. He was rocking her back and forth, humming a tune that Rachel recognized as something from Disney. She went into the bathroom and came back armed like Hot Lips Houlihan.

"Hey, pumpkin, don't worry." Zach's soft, soothing tone immediately put Janie at ease. "You have the best mommy, and she's going to make you all better."

Rachel spent the next couple of hours trying to get Janie's fever down. She told Zach he didn't have to stick around, but he insisted on staying. There was something incredibly gratifying about seeing Zach take to Janie so well. He seemed comfortable with her in the same way Rachel had been from the moment she'd held her. Though she fought the idea of making comparisons, she wondered if Wade would have handled the situation as well.

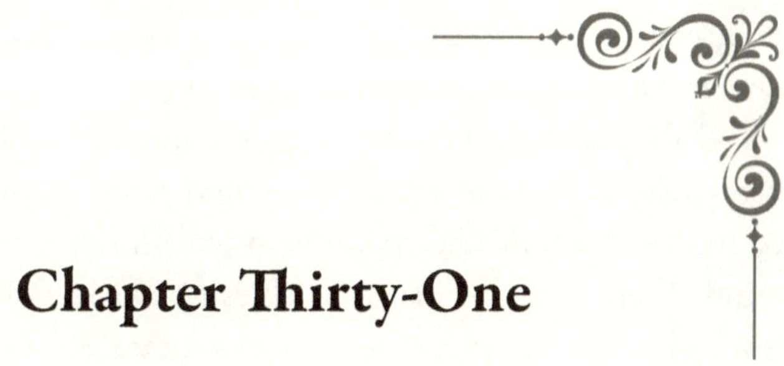

Chapter Thirty-One

Rachel stared at her tense frame in the mirror. She was too stiff. She wouldn't want someone who looked that uptight telling her she had a baby she didn't know she had. If she was going to tell Wade everything, she had to look relaxed, like she knew how to manage the situation and that he had nothing to be concerned about. She would take care of Janie to give her the kind of continuity that every child deserved, and he could be as involved as he chose to be. Maybe he wouldn't even want shared custody. There was no way to know how he would react, especially when she had no clue what she was going to say. She moved a little closer to the mirror and stared intently into her eyes.

"Hi, Wade, I came over today because... Well, you're not going to believe this, but I have something to tell you that is going to change your life."

That sounded ridiculous, and her lips were too taut when she spoke. She would have to rehearse the way she had when she was doing Sanford Meisner repetition exercises in her college acting workshop. She decided to practice some kind of structured lines, take a guess at what Wade's might be, and respond. If she had an inkling of what could be coming, she wouldn't sound flustered. Confusion and chaos would make her seem weak and lacking confidence.

This was all sound reasoning, but she still wasn't sure *how* she was going to tell Wade. She didn't want the formality of a scheduled appointment or to meet him at his office after a class. *Maybe I'll just drop by his house. That's better than calling.*

Calling would give him too much time to wonder, and wondering would make him suspect. He would probably think she'd decided to pose for him, and that would put him in a different frame of mind. There were too many variables to consider and no way of assessing how he would take to the news regardless of how she chose to deliver it.

"Wade, I know this news is somewhat shocking, but in all honesty, not much has to change. I am more than happy being Janie's mother, and you don't have to do anything that might disrupt your life."

That sounded kind of lame, too, but at least she didn't come off like an overstarched shirt.

Rachel checked the time. It was early. She was supposed to go shopping with Beth, but that wasn't until much later. Brittany was already on the clock, playing with Janie downstairs. Everything seemed to indicate that there was no time like the present to put her plan in motion. Still, most of her wanted to forget all about integrity and leave life to chance, the exact way it had come to her.

The moment Rachel saw the white picket fence, she shivered. She wasn't sure what she would do if Wade wanted to fill his house with children by starting with her little girl. She contemplated turning back. She still could. No one was forcing her to tell him, except her own damn conscience. Beth and Evan were the only people on the planet who knew the truth. Rachel could walk away and keep walking. No one would be the wiser.

Deep down, she knew if she didn't tell Wade the truth, she would never have a moment's peace. Then she would surely lose out on any possibility with Zach. Worst of all, she would be denying Janie her paternity, and for that, there would be no excuse.

Rachel knocked and stood waiting for the door to open. After a few seconds, there was no answer. Maybe Wade wasn't home. She forced herself to ring the bell and tried to keep her composure as she heard a mad dash to the door.

"Rachel! What a nice surprise." Wade ushered her into the house and led her into the kitchen. "I wasn't expecting you."

It didn't seem to matter since he was in his usual weekend casual wear.

"I just made a pot of coffee, hazelnut. Want a cup?"

"Sure." Rachel nodded. "I owe you an explanation."

"You do?" Wade poured her coffee into a large mug covered in rainbow-colored open hearts. "I bought the food-poisoning story."

"This story is a lot more complicated."

"Really? I can't wait to hear it." Wade poured himself a cup of coffee and sat down across from her.

"Well, I... I am not quite sure where to start," Rachel said.

"Wherever you feel most comfortable, I suppose." Wade took a sip of coffee and added another pour of sugar from the dispenser on the table. "Let me just say, a lot of people, especially women, have body-image issues. Usually, they criticize their bellies or their butts. They complain about their sagging breasts or think their necks are too thick."

"Oh, I don't care about any of that," Rachel said. "I mean, I suppose my breasts could be perkier and my ass shapelier, but that's not why I'm here."

"I understand," Wade said. "You're shy. Most people are. We're not taught to walk around naked and appreciate our bodies. Most of us experience the opposite and are directed to feel ashamed of how we look without our clothes." Wade poured himself more cream. "Have you ever gone to a nude beach?"

Rachel, needing a few more moments to steady her nerves, decided she was curious about where this conversation was going. "Yes, I've been to a nude beach."

"Did you feel comfortable?"

Rachel chuckled. "When I was lying down with my eyes closed."

Their exchange was interrupted by a tall, thin, attractive man in his thirties who walked into the kitchen wrapped in a towel. His hair was wet, and his mouth was agape when he noticed Rachel.

"Oh, hey," the man said with a small wave. He took a bottle of water from the refrigerator and left the room.

"I'm so sorry," Rachel said, starting to get up. "I had no idea you were working. I shouldn't have come without calling."

"No, it's okay. Please sit. I'm not working."

"But, that guy—"

Was an Adonis, and if he was Wade's brother, he didn't look even a smidgen like him. Rachel's mind raced for an answer, but she couldn't come up with one.

"That guy is Trey. My partner."

"Business partner?" Rachel asked, wondering what kind of company they were running.

"On occasion, but we're much more successful romantically."

"Wait a minute." Rachel blinked then shook her head. "He's your... He's your *guy*?"

"Yes, indeed he is."

"I'm... I'm confused." Rachel's head was spinning in every direction imaginable.

"It's simple," Wade said. "I don't publicize my private life."

"But, but... were you ever with a woman?"

Wade cleared his throat. "In the interest of our burgeoning friendship, I'll answer your question. Yes. I have been."

"Recently?" Rachel started to chew on her bottom lip.

"Um, no. Trey and I are in a committed relationship."

"And you never strayed, like with the woman that you painted from the summer you started teaching?"

"That's a weird question." Wade flashed her a puzzled look. "But since I find you interesting, I'll go with it. I had sex with Stephanie Kelley in my junior year of college. She was an art major, and we became very good friends. She insisted it was more than that and refused to believe I was gay, so I proved it to both of us. She never doubted me again."

"I'm sorry."

"Don't be. We've stayed friends," Wade said.

"If you don't mind my asking—"

"And if I do mind, you won't ask?" Wade teased.

Rachel smirked. "Who's the woman in the painting we were discussing?"

"Alana Schoenberger. I was madly in love with her brother."

"Was he the relationship from London you mentioned?"

"One and the same," Wade said. "It was quite a few years ago, but when Alana came over to study, it brought me back."

"Where is she now?"

"Alana? I'm not sure. She was having marital problems. We lost touch."

"And her brother?"

"Damian is married to Arthur now. A real estate guy from New York. They lived around here for a brief time, but thankfully, they've moved to London to be near Damian's family."

"Sounds like it's still painful," Rachel said.

"It is, but Trey is wonderful, and life goes on."

"Let me get this straight—and I'm not being facetious—there's no way you can be a father now?"

"Well, of course there are ways, Rachel, but Trey and I are not quite there yet." Wade speared a piece of melon. "What's all this about, anyway?"

"It's a long story for another time." Rachel sipped her coffee. "And just so you know, your life is your business. My lips are sealed."

"Oh, I know that," Wade said. "I knew we were going to be friends, good friends, from the moment I laid eyes on you."

"Thanks, Wade, I really appreciate that, but I still can't pose for you."

"After your last visit, I didn't suspect you would. But I have a feeling you will... someday."

Rachel tore through Beth's front door like a hurricane seizing control of the premises. Beth was nowhere in sight, and Josh and Courtney were oblivious to her entrance, seemingly transfixed by an episode of *SuperKitties*.

"Joshie! Where's Mommy?" Rachel stood blocking the television.

"We can't see, Aunt Rachel!" Joshie cried.

"I know that. Where's Mommy?"

"In the bathroom," Courtney said. "She barfing."

Rachel walked toward the bathroom and found Beth in the kitchen, making a cup of tea. "How are you?"

"Fine." Beth sighed. "I was purging for my involvement in the Ring-Ding rebellion. Want tea?"

Rachel got a beer out of the refrigerator.

"Okay then," Beth said. "I take it you saw Wade. Did you end up posing for him?"

Rachel went back to the refrigerator and got out another beer. She edged her seat away from the counter to face Beth.

"Here," Rachel said, handing Beth a beer. "Drink this."

"You want *me* to drink a beer?"

"I think this could be one of those exceptional times you might want to." Rachel opened her bottle and took a healthy swig.

"Hey, slow down," Beth said. "I don't have many of those babies left."

Rachel continued drinking.

Beth went to the fridge and took out a box of Yoo-hoo. "Okay, I'm ready. Tell me what happened."

"Wade isn't Janie's father." Rachel let out a long, deep sigh, uncertain if she was relieved or terrified that she was back at square one.

"What!" Beth dropped the little plastic straw that came with her drink on the floor. Instead of picking it up, she got another out of a drawer. "Bullshit. Of course he is! What makes you think he isn't?"

"Oh, I'm surer than sure." Rachel retrieved the fallen straw and put it in the garbage.

"You've made mistakes before."

"Not this time. He's gay."

"Gay?" Beth sounded disappointed.

"He's always been gay."

"But I swear he was so into you."

"As a friend." Rachel nearly drained her bottle of beer. "I must have a trustworthy aura."

"But the whole long-neck thing and—"

"He's an artist. He wanted me to be a subject." Rachel took a bag of pretzels out of the pantry and tugged at the top to open it.

"Unbelievable."

"I even met his partner."

"Cute? Thin?"

"Bethie, gay!"

"Please tell me your clothes were on when you found out."

"Yes, they were on. I didn't pose."

"Well, actually, now, it wouldn't be so bad."

"This kid better arrive soon," Rachel said. "I am running out of patience to deal with you."

"But seriously, Rach, if Wade isn't Janie's father, who is?"

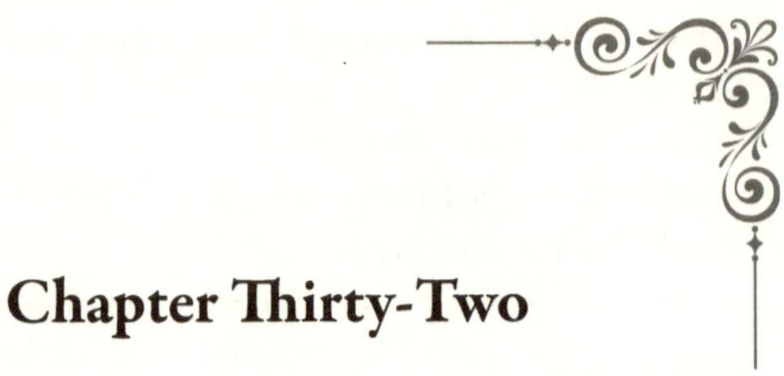

Chapter Thirty-Two

It was chilly in the attic, but Rachel was determined to use Janie's nap time to find something in the mix of Rena's things that would lead to Janie's father. It was possible she'd missed something before, like a pocket or a compartment in a suitcase or a handbag. The relationship between Rena and the Professor seemed to have had the features of a fine Cabernet—bold, complex, and definitive—but even the slightest mishandling could have disrupted its unique essence. Though Rachel was certain she hadn't missed anything overt, there was a possibility she might find something written in code. But no matter how hard she searched, nothing new turned up.

Rachel was climbing back downstairs when her cell phone rang, but it went to voicemail before she reached it. She checked her phone and saw Zach had left her a message. Luckily, the publisher had to delay, which gave them a little more time for the book. He wanted to know if she was free to go out for a work dinner since staying in was clearly too distracting. Rachel couldn't help but let her mind wander over to Zach and how good his hands felt learning each curve of her body. If it were up to her, she would skip Dickens and head straight into dessert.

A work meeting wasn't a date. It was work. In fact, they'd never gone out in the traditional sense. Their somewhat awkward attempt at sex had hardly been a date, especially since the evening had culminated in caring for her sick baby. As disappointing as it had been to miss out on an evening of lovemaking, she was grateful Zach had been nothing but understanding about the whole experience.

Rachel and Zach were sitting at what had become their favorite table at Decker's, attempting to organize, structure, and compile their myriad pages into a draft cohesive enough for submission. Zach was up to a part in the process that Rachel couldn't help with, but she was content to simply watch. He was building a pile of notes on *Oliver Twist* and looked so intense and sexy, Rachel decided he would put the *stud* in *studious*.

She pondered the possibility that she and Zach weren't meant to date. It was possible they were beyond the simplicity of dating. Since they'd already seen each other naked, their entire dynamic had been forever changed. She could no longer look at him with ferocious anticipation and wonder what his penis would look like erect. She already knew—*sublime*. For better or worse, all Rachel could think about was how much she wanted him. If they were destined to know each other better, it might happen more effectively in the context of an actual relationship.

A waitress with short pink hair came over to take their order. Zach was still looking at his menu as if he didn't know it by heart.

"Go ahead," Zach said.

"Okay, I'll have the Greek salad, light on the feta cheese," she said, handing back the menu. "And an iced tea with lemon."

"That sounds good. Make it two."

"What? No burger and fries?"

"A guy's got to watch his figure."

A busboy with tattoos covering both arms came over with water and crackers for the table then quickly walked away.

Rachel took a cracker. "Since when do you care?"

"Since Weight Watchers and my gym membership." Zach reached into his briefcase, retrieved a notebook and a folder, and laid them on the table next to his place setting.

"Are you serious?"

"Very. You can ask my belts."

"I can't picture you heavier."

"Well, I was—but now, let's talk about Estella." Zach quickly studied one of his many pages of notes.

"Okay, what about Estella?"

"Do you think she has any real feelings for Pip?"

"I think she does." Rachel took another cracker.

"Emotionally or sexually?"

Oh, so that's where we're going. The first time she'd read *Great Expectations* was in Mr. Cantor's ninth-grade honors English class. As soon as there was mention of intense yearning, the pubescent students giggled uncomfortably. From then on, the teacher dealt with the concept of lust framed as a crush in a sitcom template. Rachel's latest read of the novel offered significantly more.

"Do they have to be mutually exclusive?" Rachel asked, anticipating Zach's response.

"No, but what do you think is the basis for her feelings?"

"Well, I don't think she has a tremendous libido. Ms. Havisham has seen to that."

"Given her disappointments in life, do you think she has the capacity to return Pip's affection?"

Rachel's eyes widened. Zach's line of questioning was feeling personal.

"Probably not," Rachel said, "but that's Estella. Zach, do you have something on your mind? Because I don't think we're in Dickens anymore."

An overhead TV directly in Rachel's view flashed to breaking news and a building she recognized.

"Could you please turn up the volume?" Rachel asked a nearby server, who complied immediately.

"What's going on?" Zach asked.

Rachel's eyes were glued to the screen. "I have to watch this."

Rachel directed her attention to the reporter on the screen, but she could feel Zach's eyes on her.

Another blow to Wall Street came earlier today, when the acting vice president of Jebbling Enterprises was arrested on eight counts, including fraud, embezzlement, and possession of narcotics. The FBI identified and arrested Philip R. Sutton and Sutton's assistant, Dana Dunne, this morning at JFK International Airport as they approached customs. According to police, Sutton is linked to El Dictador, the Colombian drug lord running that country's largest active cartel and heavily responsible for the current opioid crisis.

The words in the report danced in her head as her heart raced, and her body trembled.

"Are you okay?" Zach got up and sat next to her. "Do you know that guy?"

"Do I ever," Rachel shrieked. "That's Phil!"

"Sutton!" Zach put the name together with Rachel's reaction. "He's your—"

"Husband."

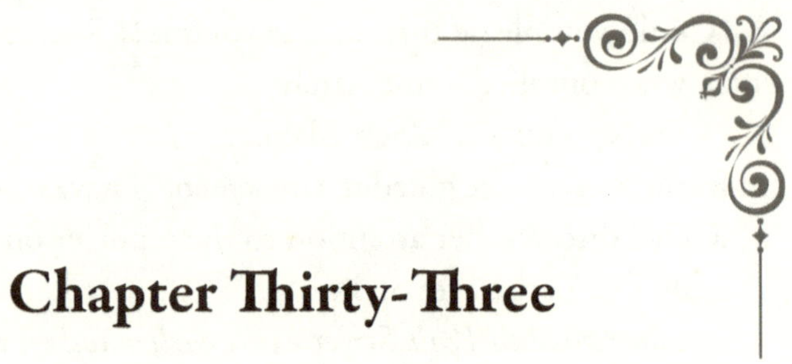

Chapter Thirty-Three

Rachel held Janie close as she rocked her back to sleep. It was four in the morning, and Rachel's head had yet to hit the pillow. It was all too impossible to process. Seeing Phil splashed across the news in handcuffs, escorted by the FBI, was not an image she could let go of easily. The man was still her husband, and now the whole world knew she was married to a criminal. In the scheme of things, that didn't matter nearly as much as what might happen if journalists took an interest in the story. The last thing she needed was hungry reporters asking about her and Janie, hoping for a byline.

Rachel took a few deep breaths and realized she was being over-reactive. Given the political climate and social situations in the country, even in her county, it was possible there wasn't much to worry about. Chances were good their fifteen minutes in the spotlight had already come and gone. Phil just wasn't that important—to anyone.

There was no doubt she would secure a divorce as quickly as her lawyer could manage, but how she would frame the situation for her own well-being was a different story. Somehow, she would have to forgive herself for her poor choices, for trying to make something of a marriage built on quicksand, and for truly loving Phil, whom she apparently hadn't known at all.

Rachel was fully invested in motherhood and was beginning to open up to a much richer, fulfilling love. Zach was everything Phil wasn't, an ethical man who appreciated her and all she had to of-fer. Since the moment they'd met, Rachel had begun to see shades of herself again, the girl who could rejoice in literature, fix a clogged drain, decorate a room, and order for herself in a restaurant. By accepting her, warts and all, Zach helped Rachel feel more confident and less intimidated by challenges. This new air was cleansing, and even though she was unsure where their relationship was headed, she was looking forward to finding out.

A couple of hours after Rachel's head hit the pillow, she was awake again. So many thoughts were still running through her head. She went to check on Janie, who was still sound asleep. Morbid curiosity and fear of a possible new development made her reach for the remote. She flipped on CNN, certain there would be more sordid details about Phil and his paramour. But there was nothing. She clicked through each channel, and when the birth of a sea lion at a Florida zoo proved to be the most newsworthy story of the morning, Rachel turned off the TV.

Trash bags. Rachel took a box from the garage and brought it into Phil's closet. He had more clothes and accessories than she did. She held up one designer suit after another, certainly nothing he would need in jail. Phil's jewelry, ties, shoes, and trinkets were doing nothing but taking up space that was no longer his. Until she sorted everything out, his crap was going to the attic.

As the day continued, one item after another found its way into a bag while Janie sat with Rachel, seeming to cheer her on. It was a little disappointing to have found nothing of significance in Phil's pockets, but she really had no need for further incriminating evidence. The only thing that made her slightly raise an eyebrow was an old prescription for painkillers from Ben Starr, Phil's friend and urologist. She couldn't remember Phil having any problems around the time it was written. He might have gone to see Ben on his own when they couldn't get pregnant, but that seemed unlikely.

Rachel had finished cleaning out the clothes hanging in Phil's closet but had yet to conquer his built-in drawers. Since Janie was happily playing with her nesting cups, Rachel decided to plow on, through the briefs and special-occasion satin underwear, the myriad athletic socks, the wifebeater shirts that had come dangerously close to being literal, and the heaping folder of papers. She found it peculiar those weren't in Phil's office. Maybe it was worth going through. Rachel toyed with the idea of possibly learning more than she wanted to know but ultimately yielded.

The papers seemed benign—receipts for office equipment, Phil's car maintenance, business credit card bills, and a few notes from pleased clients. Rachel was about to toss the whole pile into the trash when she noticed an envelope with Ben Starr's return address. Maybe Phil was treated for an infection.

Rachel opened the envelope and let out a shriek that might've made Janie cry had she not fallen fast asleep. It was a thin booklet explaining self-care after a vasectomy. A cheeky, personalized note from Ben on the back page assured Phil that despite the procedure, Phil still had the biggest pair of balls of any guy he'd ever known. A smiley face, much like the one that had lied to her about being pregnant, punctuated the message.

As if belittling her and cheating on her weren't enough, that miserable son of a bitch had sabotaged the one thing she'd truly wanted out of the marriage. Rachel didn't know whether to laugh, cry, or hunt Phil down and strangle him with her bare hands. Through tears, she decided all three would work, but murdering Phil would give him too easy an out. No, she would let the pretty boy with dimples and great hair rot in a jail cell with the likes of thieves, mob bosses, and overly arrogant politicians.

Rachel had calmed down and put Janie to bed when the house phone rang. It was Beth, likely bursting to talk about Phil being on the news without knowing the whole story.

"Hey," Rachel said. "Glad you got back early. I have—"

"A dick for a husband." Beth snickered. "I saw it on the inter—"

There was a sudden concerning silence.

"Beth?" Rachel said, hearing the worry in her own voice. "Bethie!"

More silence.

"Bethie!"

"Rachel, will you shut the hell up? I'm in the middle of a god-damn contraction." Beth panted then blew out several times.

"Oh shit, you're kidding!"

"Does it sound like I'm kidding?"

"Where's Evan?"

"On a plane to Dallas." Beth blew out. "Okay, it's over."

"Dallas? Now?"

"Well, I wasn't having contractions when he left."

"How about your mother-in-law? Is she around?"

After a sustained burp, Beth answered. "Janet's at her brother's house. She'll be back tonight."

Beth started breathing deeply again.

"How close are they?"

"I'm not sure," Beth said. "But it's too soon, and I'm never early."

"Bethie, I'll call Brittany and bring Janie over to you. I can't in good conscience let you deliver this child on a couch while your kids watch reruns of *Good Luck Charlie*."

"Okay." Beth panted. "You should come... Ow... Ow... Now!

"Hang tight. Be there soon!"

Rachel quickly took off her coat and flung it to the small sliver of space on the couch next to Beth. As much as she wanted to share *all* the news she had discovered about Phil, Rachel thought it best to wait—maybe even until after the baby was born. Beth didn't need more to stress about. It actually made Rachel breathe easier to push it all aside, at least for a little while.

"How are you feeling?" Rachel asked, putting Janie in the nearby playpen.

"Hee, hee hooo...hee hee hooo..." Beth panted until the contraction passed. "Dizzy, probably from all the breathing and puking." She let her head drop between her legs.

Rachel called Brittany but got her voicemail. "Shit, I forgot. She went to visit her grandmother in Florida."

Beth got up and circled around the room, stopping to accommodate her contractions when she had to. "So, now what?" she asked, stopping to lean against a chair.

"I'll make another call."

"Who?"

"Wade."

"You're going to call the not baby daddy to come watch our kids?"

"Do you have a better idea?" Rachel argued. "At least I know he likes kids." Rachel shook her head then called Wade while Beth had another short contraction.

"Sorry I missed your call. I'll be in Kennebunkport 'til Tuesday. Please leave a message,

after—"

"So?" Beth started pacing.

"He's out of town," Rachel said, following Beth's gait.

"Well, isn't that fuckin' inconvenient."

"By the way, where are the kids?"

"In Joshie's room, making cards for the new baby," Beth said through a small but obvious contraction.

"That's sweet."

"Yeah, Joshie showed me his first card. It said *my room* in blood red." Beth sighed. "Trust me, this isn't going to be fun. What about the boyfriend? I'm getting kind of desperate here."

Rachel continued to pace along with Beth, circling the couch then the dining table, which was covered end-to-end with folded laundry.

"He was out with his mother," Rachel said, "but maybe he's back home now."

Rachel called Zach. "Thank God! You're home!"

"I just walked in the door," Zach said as if he needed to offer an explanation. "You sound weird. What's going on?"

"I'm at Beth's, and I think she's in labor. Evan, her husband, is out of town, and I can't find anyone to watch the kids."

"She lives on Robey Court, right? Near my mother."

"Wow, you remembered."

"I'll try to keep that up," Zach teased. "Rach, relax. She'll be fine. I'm on my way."

Rachel ended the call, feeling an easiness wash over her.

Zach had never called her "Rach" before, and she liked the intimacy it implied. Feeling supported and cared for was new to her, and though Zach's words were simple, she appreciated his intentions. His warmth felt both romantic and familial, the kind of relationship she'd always wanted. Basking in this white-picket-fence moment, Rachel went upstairs to check on the kids and put them to bed.

Beth was on the floor, doing breathing exercises, when Rachel came back into the living room.

"Kids okay?" Beth moaned.

"Yeah. Courtney wanted Janie to sleep in her bed."

"I wouldn't. She wets right through her Pull-Ups, and who knows the trouble these little ones could get into."

"Not to worry. She settled on having the playpen next to her."

"Good." Beth shifted to her other side.

"Zach should be here soon."

Rachel checked her phone. Her battery was down to one bar, not the best during an emergency.

"Maybe I should go myself." Beth headed for her bedroom. "I'll pack a few things and go."

"You can't do that," Rachel argued. "Look, if Zach doesn't get here soon, we'll call an ambulance."

"Fine. I have to pee."

When Beth left the room, Rachel's phone rang. It was Zach.

"Hey, where are you?" Rachel asked.

"I hit a pothole, and I never fixed my spare. Roadside service is on the way, but I don't know how long it'll take."

"Oh, that really sucks." Rachel sighed. "What am I going to do?"

"My mother's on her way there."

"Your mother? Here?"

"She's good with kids, and she wants to meet you."

"She does?" Rachel asked coyly. "You told her about me?"

"Kind of. I didn't say much since all the stuff about... Wow, that was fast. Tow truck's here... Gotta run... Keep in touch..."

Beth came back into the room, looking calmer than she had the right to.

"So, don't freak out, but Zach's car broke down."

Beth's face immediately contorted into a look just shy of an exorcism. "Of course it fucking did!"

"Not to worry. His mother is coming." Rachel snatched a chocolate bar from the bowl on the coffee table. "He said she's great with kids."

"Fine, if you trust her, I do too," Beth said, breathing in quick, short puffs. "I'm going to pack a few things while I can still waddle."

"I trust Zach, so I know we're in good hands," Rachel said. "Want help packing?"

"Noooo! I don't even want *you* to see the size of my underwear." Beth left the room slowly, clutching her belly as she walked.

Rachel had nearly wiped out the candy bowl when there was a knock at the door. She opened it and reeled back in surprise.

"Edie?" Rachel squinted and extended her head forward. "What are you doing here?"

"My son called. He said there was an emergency, and I should get to this address as soon as possible to babysit."

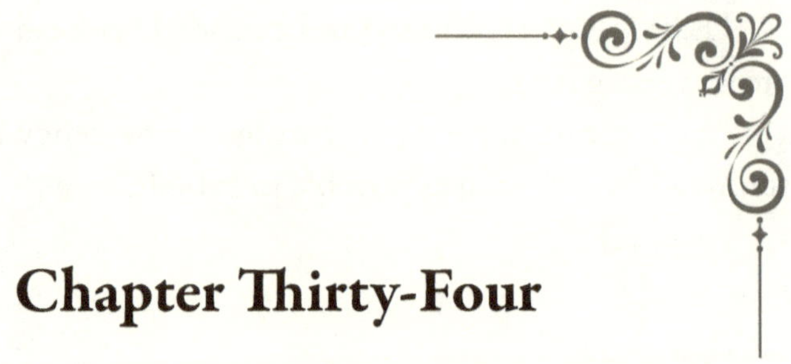

Chapter Thirty-Four

Beth bolted out of the emergency room and raced through the parking lot like she was running a Trifecta. Rachel didn't bother trying to stop her as she galloped by. There was no point. It had been false labor, but good luck trying to get through to Beth, who was letting everyone know she was much doner than done with this pregnancy.

When they'd arrived and the nurse asked for her zip code, Beth had responded, "For my stomach, butt, or boobs?" The nurse chortled and asked for the one that best represented the neighborhood. At that point, Beth giggled, but when she was told she was nowhere near ready to deliver, she lost it.

As Beth got closer to the car, Rachel clicked her key to unlock the doors. The space between the cars was limited, and Rachel wondered if Beth was going to be able to make it in. Despite a small measure of guilt, it was entertaining to watch Beth shimmy her way into the car, though not quite as amusing when she plopped down on the passenger seat like a wrecking ball, making the car bounce.

Rachel put Beth's bag in the trunk then slid into the driver's seat.

"I can't believe this," Beth cried.

"They said false labor isn't that uncommon."

"This is my third child."

"So?" Rachel pulled out of the lot and started down Main Street.

"So? I'll tell you *so*—it took half a dozen unfamiliar hands in my vagina for them to tell me I wasn't in real labor. You'd think I'd have known."

"Prodromal labor is easy to mistake for the real deal. But it's over. Let's try to forget about it."

"You can," Beth said. "It wasn't your vagina."

"Whatever you say, Beth." Rachel was just about to turn onto the highway when Beth stopped her.

"I need a chocolate shake," Beth exclaimed. "I mean it, like, right now."

"Well, I can't twitch my nose and get one for you, but I'll take the back roads and see if anything is still open."

"Drive-thrus are open," Beth said with conviction.

"It troubles me how confident you are." Rachel turned down the road and stopped at a light.

"Wait, who's watching the kids?" Beth asked as if she hadn't a clue.

"I told you. Zach's mother, Edie."

"Right, right. I forgot, the fortune teller." Beth took out her phone and opened Google Maps. "She should have known I wasn't really in labor and saved us both a trip."

"Don't you think it's kind of crazy that Edie is Zach's mother?" Rachel turned into a McDonald's.

"Honey, life has become one big full moon begging us to howl these days."

By the time Rachel got to Beth's, Evan's mother, Janet, had relieved Edie. Janet was in a floral nightgown and fast asleep on the couch. Beth groggily gave Rachel a kiss on the cheek, mumbled something that sounded like *thank you*, and wobbled into her room. She'd been struggling to stay awake in the car after getting only three sips into her shake. Everything seemed reasonably under control, and Rachel felt comfortable enough to get Janie and leave.

Zach had left her a few texts asking how the night had gone and if she could meet him at his office around six after he was done at the gym. *The gym? Since when?* He'd mentioned something about a previous membership but made it sound like it had been from a while ago.

Rachel texted him to apologize that she hadn't had cell service or time to connect but was pretty sure she could make it. She wondered if he was going to shower first or meet her au naturel. If the scent wasn't overly aggressive, a whiff of hot, sweaty athleticism was a turn-on. On a Sunday night, no one would be on campus, and if their meeting turned amorous, she was more than willing to be ready.

She was about to pull into her driveway when she noticed two men in trench coats straight out of the Columbo handbook, hovering at her front door. With all that had transpired, Rachel was too exhausted to think. She knew she hadn't been speeding, and she'd paid her taxes on time, so whoever these guys were, they had no business being there. She watched them turn toward her car as she parked.

Unless... Oh shit! What if they were from social services and had come to take Janie away from her? She said a swift prayer, hoping she was being paranoid. Her knees weak, Rachel worried she might fall while getting out of her car. She had to get it together, or they would think she was a drug addict, an alcoholic, or morbidly hypoglycemic. She took a few deep breaths and resolved to remain steady as if her life depended on it. Janie was still fast asleep in the back seat. Rachel decided to leave her there and keep a close watch while she dealt with the intruders.

"Hello, gentleman," she said, mustering every ounce of her courage. "Can I help you?"

"Are you Rachel Sutton?" the shorter of the two asked. He sounded like Mickey Mouse, and Rachel tried not to lose it.

"That depends on who's asking."

Without a shred of amusement, the men shuffled some papers between them. "I'm Detective Kessler with Internal Affairs, FBI," the taller, slightly more attractive of the two, said as they both flashed badges. "This is Detective Yeslow."

Rachel's heart raced as she envisioned Janie being yanked out of her arms. One thing was certain—she wouldn't give up her daughter without a fight. And she certainly wouldn't hand her to these automatons, no matter how many credentials they shoved in her face.

"As you know, your husband is facing serious criminal charges," Yeslow said. "We're hoping you can help us with this." He handed her a document that appeared to be a page out of the ledger in Phil's home office.

Rachel breathed a heavy sigh of relief, not caring how it would be interpreted. "What do you want to know?" Rachel asked, examining the paper. "Phil, my soon-to-be ex-husband, wasn't much of a sharer. I doubt I'll be able to help."

"You see this?" Kessler pointed to an unnamed withdrawal of one hundred fifty thousand dollars. "We can't account for the funds. Can you?"

Rachel checked the date—the transaction had occurred while she was in London.

"It seems the money may have been wired from an account originating in the Cayman National Bank, to Lloyd's Bank near Piccadilly Circus, if that means anything to you," Kessler continued.

"No, I'm really sorry." Rachel shook her head. "It doesn't." She was handing him back the paper, but he stopped her.

"Hold on to it," Kessler said. "Maybe you'll come up with something. Thanks for your time. We'll be in touch, as needed." The two left before she could say a word.

Rachel waited until they were out of sight before getting Janie from the car. She shoved the paper into her coat pocket. *Let the boys in trench coats figure things out on their own.*

Rachel's heart finally stopped racing, but she feared similar incidents were going to be a way of life until she found a plausible way to adopt Janie and make their relationship legal. It was still too risky to share the situation with anyone, especially a lawyer, when her husband was facing criminal charges. The other factor was finding Janie's father, which was still very much in play despite no longer having leads. There was no simple solution. Rachel was going to have to sit tight and deal with whatever might come next. She gave Janie an extra hug, kissed the top of her head, and put her in her crib for the night.

Hours later, curiosity about the unaccounted-for funds continued to gnaw at Rachel's gut. She had to know what else Phil was hiding from her and anyone else who stood in his way. She retrieved the document still crammed in her pocket and went to Phil's office. She'd been too caught up in her own worries to consider what the detectives had said. It all sounded very sketchy, as most things involving Phil did, but nothing regarding that kind of money stood out in her mind.

Rachel closed her eyes and systematically clicked through the last few months. Phil's obsession with work and emotionally abusive behavior had become his norm. The only stand-out was how uncharacteristically concerned he had been about the aspects of her trip to London—where Rachel would be, who the grandmother was, and where she lived. He'd gone so far as to ask Rachel for the information twice. At the time, she'd wanted to believe he'd done some soul-searching and was excited about the prospect of being a father. Deluding herself had felt better than the alternative.

Maybe he had taken out an insurance policy on her life then hired incompetent hit men who hadn't done the job. She shivered at the thought that such a scenario might have been possible then took a closer look at the document. She began rifling through the stacks of papers on Phil's desk. She was surprised the feds hadn't asked for the whole pile, but she wasn't even sure what they were looking for.

As Rachel went through the second pile, a small worn slip of paper with what could easily be an account number peeked out of a gift card envelope. Under it was the name Connie Smith. On the flip side of the paper was "$100,000" crossed out and "$150,000" written underneath it.

Rachel stared at it and went back to the document the agents had given her. The total was the same. There was another wire transfer from Cayman National Bank from two years ago, but it had gone to a bank somewhere in Iceland. She couldn't make any sense of that one, and there was no name or circumstance she could connect to it.

She went back to the small paper and stared at Connie Smith's name. If there'd been a light bulb in her head, Rachel could've illuminated the state. It was all there, hiding in plain sight—proof she'd been taken for the ride of her life by the man who'd stood in a Giorgio Armani tuxedo and vowed to love, honor, and cherish her forever. He'd even given her an exquisite diamond ring to seal the deal. Turns out her prince was a dashing con man, an epic fraud who'd strung her along about wanting a family. They might've taken the same vows, but it was obvious only she had meant them.

Drunk with rage, Rachel wanted to scream, but not at the expense of waking the neighborhood. Instead, she grabbed their framed wedding photo, smashed it with a custom-made Logan Roy paperweight, and proceeded to rip Phil into dust.

Yielding to the calm after the much-needed release, Rachel continued to piece together the fragments of her marriage. She thought about Jeb firing Rob Steele when Rob's wife stormed in on a critical meeting and nearly cost them a major client. Phil had celebrated the disaster and was thrilled when he was immediately given Rob's position. For all his talk of wanting the family she wanted, Phil simply accepted his new role along with the *fuck you, Rachel* car and basically told her to shove it.

It seemed obvious Phil had never wanted to build a life that included her. It was always about his work and what he needed to do to get ahead. He had placated her when it suited him, but all he'd needed was a marital seat-warmer he could parade at corporate parties to keep the optics *Leave It to Beaver* clean.

Rachel wondered if Phil had ever cared for her. *Maybe, maybe at the very beginning.* At the beginning, there was a chance for them to be a team and grow together. Maybe when passion was unspoiled by the familiar, when flaws were obscured by desire, he'd cared. Back then, nothing was more precious than Phil holding her in his strong arms and declaring his devotion while promising her the world. Nothing meant more to her than their private jokes, champagne toasts, and bedtime snuggles. But that was a lifetime ago. And it still wasn't the love she longed for but rather the lust she settled for.

Now, her eyes were wide open, and there was no way to get around the extent of Phil's betrayal. He'd had a vasectomy behind her back then let her go to London on a wild baby chase, knowing he'd paid Connie Smith to thwart the adoption. His egotism, greed, and selfishness were astounding. The man she'd convinced herself she loved was nothing more than a shallow grifter who'd ultimately robbed himself of the power and freedom he'd spent his life seeking.

Rachel had all the evidence she needed to cement her disgust. No wonder he'd been so surprised when she'd come home with Janie. Then an enormous wave of welcome hysteria came over Rachel, and she laughed until her throat was raw. Phil must have gone through hell when he believed he'd been double-crossed.

The phone rang, and Rachel collected herself to answer the call. It was her lawyer, with news that the final paperwork for the divorce was ready and waiting for her signature. It seemed a judge owed Susan a significant favor and given Phil's incarceration had accelerated the entire process. In a few weeks, Rachel would be free.

With so much to celebrate, she went into the liquor cabinet and poured herself a glass of pinot noir. Janie was out for the night, and Rachel needed alone time. She turned on Pandora and let smooth jazz lull her into much-needed sleep.

Brittany showed up early the next day, and Rachel put everything Phil on the back burner. Ruminating on her anger and pain would do nothing but make Janie uneasy and keep Rachel from moving on. As shocking as it had been to discover the enormity of Phil's betrayals, it was liberating. Rachel had been falling out of love for months, maybe even years. She had to accept that she'd been using Phil almost as much as he'd been using her. They'd certainly gone about it differently, but each had needs that kept them struggling bookends. There was no easy fix. In time, Rachel would accept her marriage as a lesson learned, but more importantly, the road ahead beckoned and deserved to be traveled.

A diversion seemed like a good idea, and she decided to surprise Zach with an inspiring picnic at his office. Even if they couldn't be boating in Little Venice or chilling in Hyde Park with a blanket, some wine, cheese, and a few crumpets, she could still create a vibe that would have made Dickens reflective. If she and Zach could yield to the moment, it might give them the impetus not only to create but also to seize the romance that could push their relationship forward. For an extra dose of encouragement, Rachel put on a red push-up bra that hooked in the front and a slinky dress that clung to all the right places.

True to his schedule, Zach wasn't at the office when she got there, which gave her the time to set up her intimate party. For a moment, she worried that she was the aggressor once again. It just seemed to work out that way, but nothing ventured, nothing gained. Sometimes, the promise of love was worth the risk.

She lit a sand-and-sea candle and found a loop of ocean waves to play on the computer. If nothing else came of it, he would still have to appreciate her ingenuity. The only thing missing was birth control, and if Phil had gotten himself fixed, maybe it was possible for her to get pregnant. It didn't worry her. Zach probably had condoms, and the less she had to explain, the better.

The doorknob jiggled, and Rachel turned up the sound of the waves.

Zach walked in and did a double take as if he'd wandered into the wrong office. Scrunching his face, he asked, "What is all this?"

"I thought it would be fun. You know, cross the pond without crossing it." Rachel opened the basket and started laying things on the blanket. "If you're not into it—"

"Did I say that?" Zach finally smiled. "I think you're great for doing this. It's just that I spent the last hour circuit training and—" He eyed the food. "Is any of that stuff low-fat?"

"Seriously?" Rachel studied his muscular frame.

"I told you. I used to be—" Zach put up his arms to show the enormity of his previous size. "I didn't like it. So when I start feeling paunchy, I watch myself. It's not a big deal."

He flung his coat over a chair, took her into his arms, and kissed her deeply without any reservations. She was enjoying the heat until she caught a glimpse of a brochure from a furniture store peeking out of his coat pocket. Zach had gone shopping with his mother.

"Why didn't you ever mention your mother to me?" Rachel asked, still pressed against his chest.

"I told you I had one. It's not like I was hiding her from you," Zach said. "I don't know your mother, do I?"

They broke from their embrace and sat down on the blanket.

"That's different," Rachel said. "You have no reason to."

"Okay, and you never mentioned meeting my mother until the other night."

"True, but it is awfully coincidental."

"My mother doesn't like that word."

"I know." Rachel cut the block of cheese into several slices. "It happens to be a skim-milk cheese, so go for it."

"Maybe later." Zach pushed the basket off the blanket and drew Rachel closer to him. He kissed her softly then eased her body on top of his. Her heart quickened as he stared into her eyes as if searching for something he was certain he could only find in her. He cupped her breast but remained fixed in her gaze. It was several moments before he moved her onto her back then straddled her to resume making eye contact. She knew he was teasing her, but it felt good, and for the time being, she was going to follow his lead.

Until her phone rang.

"Don't answer it," Zach said.

"I have to," Rachel replied. "It could be the sitter."

She retrieved her phone, saw it was Beth, and let it go to voicemail. Zach started to kiss her neck and let his tongue run down her ample cleavage. He was about to unfasten her bra when her phone rang again.

"Go ahead," Zach said, sounding frustrated.

"Sorry, but she might be in labor. This time, it could be for real."

Rachel answered the phone, trying not to sound like the best sex of her life had been interrupted. "Hey, Beth, what's up?" Rachel asked, breathier than intended.

Zach motioned that he was going to the bathroom.

"Oh shit. I'm sorry, Rach. You were just gonna get laid, huh?"

"How do you do that?" Rachel asked. "I think you're a sex psychic."

"No, just the queen of impeccably bad timing," Beth said. "I hate to bust up the tryst, but I need you."

Zach came back to the office, looking refreshed and ready to work.

"I am so sorry, again."

"My guess is when the time is right, it'll be right," Zach said. "You can't be raised by Edie and have none of it rub off on you. So, what's up?"

"An alarm went off in our shop, and I have to get down there."

"You have a shop?"

"Yeah, it's been closed while we're renovating. Beth has no idea what the problem is, but she can't go, so I have to."

"I'd rather you didn't go alone," Zach said. "Mind if I come along?"

"I was hoping you would." Rachel pulled her car keys out of her bag.

"Do you want me to drive?" Zach asked.

For a minute, Rachel thought about Zach at the wheel while she gave him the most intense pleasure of his life, but then she reminded herself why they were going to the shop and forced her way out of her fantasy.

"It'll be easier if I do," Rachel said. "It's close, and I know where I'm going."

Zach followed Rachel to her car without the big macho fuss Phil would have made. Phil never let her drive anywhere, insisting his stick was the only one she ever needed to worry about. At the time, she'd laughed. She'd never seen his behavior as demeaning or controlling; it was just his way. She was finally beginning to realize how much each facet of *their* life had been *his* way.

Zach patted the hand Rachel didn't have on the steering wheel. "You look upset, but I'm sure this alarm business won't be a big deal."

"Yeah, I'm sure you're right," Rachel said, letting Zach think that the shop and not a memory of Phil was her issue.

Rachel turned on music from an indie group, Cheyenne Lair, and let the songs fill the silence. She wasn't in the mood to talk, especially since she wasn't sure what to say. Juggling the disappointment of her marriage with the hopes she had for her and Zach was making her stomach churn. She wasn't even sure what it was about Zach that made her feel so convinced he was meant to be in her life, but from the moment they'd met, she'd known. It wasn't as simple as lust just because he was attractive. She'd already been there and done that with Phil. With Zach, there was a deep connection unlike anything she'd ever experienced before, even if her cheeks would flush when she thought about having sex with him.

"Listen, about before—" Rachel turned down the music.

"I know," Zach said. "I understand. You're not ready."

"I'm not?" Rachel asked quizzically.

"No, you're not," Zach replied. "And I haven't been fair."

"You haven't?"

"No. You need time to sort things out, and I've been—"

"Wonderful." Rachel squeezed Zach's hand. "That's what I wanted to say. I wanted to thank you."

Rachel pulled into the empty parking lot but left the car running. There were no police cars, fire trucks, or blaring alarms.

"What are we doing *here*?" Zach asked.

Rachel's phone rang, and she put up a finger to tell Zach to wait a minute.

"What the hell is going on, Beth?" Rachel screeched. "No one is here, and you know I have more interesting things I could be doing."

Rachel tried to listen as Beth explained the issue, but her mind kept drifting to Zach's office and his hand on her boob. She was pretty sure she'd heard the story right and ended the call. She turned to Zach, who shrugged and put his hands up.

"There was some kind of system glitch with our unit at the security company," Rachel explained. "Beth said someone should be here soon to fix it."

Zach seemed lost in thought, and Rachel wasn't sure if he'd been listening to her.

"*This* is your shop?" Zach asked.

"My family's, yeah."

"I've been here before."

"You're kidding! When? I don't remember you, and I usually remember our customers."

"It was summer before last. An older woman waited on us."

"Oh, that must have been when Beth and I were on vacation. My mother took over." Rachel paused then snickered. "How do you like that? You do know my mother!"

She turned off the engine, leaving the key in the ignition as they waited.

"*Us*?" Rachel asked as the epiphany presented. "Who was *us*?"

"It's a long story."

"Well, we have time. Let's go inside. I'd love to hear it."

"Okay," Zach said from a million miles away.

The store was in better shape than Rachel had expected. Most of the work had been done, and their new choices of shelving, counters, and flooring gave the store the facelift neither she nor Beth had realized it needed. The best part was that even though there were changes, the vibe was still homey and warm. If anything, the place was even more inviting.

"Tell me," Rachel said, running her hand over the new front counter.

"It's been a while since I've thought about her." Zach struggled to get out the words. "Meeting you has been a welcome distraction."

Rachel swallowed hard. Zach had mentioned his marriage and subsequent "loves," but her ego had dismissed those relationships as trivial. Judging by the distressed look on Zach's face, she'd been woefully wrong about this one.

"Please, tell me."

"I put it so far behind me, I didn't realize it still hurt."

"Oh, I get it. Once you're in love, it sticks to you one way or another," Rachel said. "And ultimately, that's not a bad thing. We gain perspective each time."

"I suppose you're right. I met her at the college. She was from abroad. 'On holiday,' as she would call it. We connected. Really connected. Kind of like the way you and I have. Ironic, she was married too. Some rich wiseass. We kept a low profile and never made our relationship public—to anyone. I wasn't happy about it, but I wasn't going to make her life more difficult."

The new pipes made a noise, but Zach spoke right through it.

"I felt like I needed to buy her something. Something that would always let her know I loved her even when I couldn't. She didn't want me to, but I insisted. Jewelry was out of the question. Too obvious. She said she loved dolls. She'd tragically lost the ones she'd had when she was little. I read about your shop online and decided it was the best place to get her something special."

A knock at the door stopped Rachel from falling apart on the new floor. There was no time to think about Zach's story. The repair guy from the security company arrived, anxious to fix the problem and make them "safer than they'd ever felt before." Rachel looked him square in the eyes, wishing it could only be that easy.

Chapter Thirty-Five

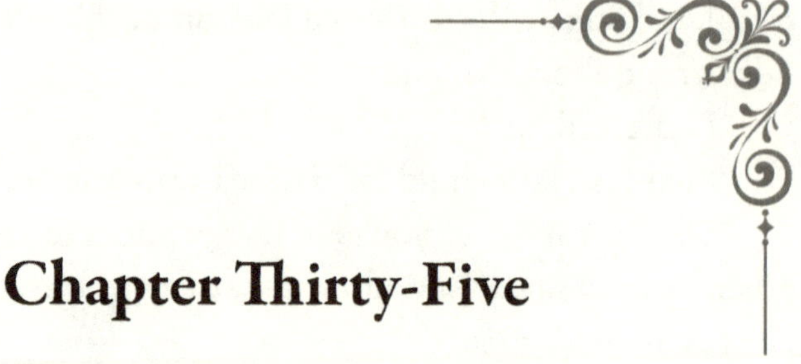

"It's Zach," Rachel cried as she flung open Beth's bedroom door and ran inside the pitch-black room.

"What the fu—!" Beth shouted. "Then why do you sound like my sister?"

"Ow!" Evan shrieked. "Jesus Christ! I swear our house is looney tunes. I'm taking a shower."

Rachel strained to see what looked like a mountain rising into the air, allowing the figure beneath it the freedom to flee to the bathroom.

"Oh man! Were you having sex?" Rachel asked, turning her head away.

"No, genius. We were playing Twister." Beth turned on the lamp on her night table to dimly light the room. She was wearing a huge nightshirt that said Conceiving Is Believing.

"I didn't think you were still doing it."

"Well, we aren't now!" Beth complained. "The midwife suggested it could induce labor."

"Sounds romantic."

"Hey, maybe you can leave and rush in again—just scare the kid out of me."

"I don't think it works like hiccups." Rachel swallowed hard. "I'm sorry, but I couldn't wait. I had to tell you."

"That's okay. I think you said something about Zach." Beth patted the bed, motioning for Rachel to sit. "What happened at the shop? And what the hell are you talking about?"

"The security system is fixed, and Zach is Janie's father."

"What the hell! Nooo! He can't be! It's impossible. Remember, the Professor is a portly teddy bear. Zach is thin."

"Have you ever heard of Weight Watchers?"

"I'm their premier client." Beth started counting with her fingers. "Maybe two percent are men."

"There you have it."

"Wow, so you're telling me Zach used to be overweight."

"Now who's the genius?" Rachel asked.

"But what makes you so sure it's him?"

They both glanced toward the bathroom as Buckcherry's "Crazy Bitch" started playing from within.

"Because he told me."

"How could he tell you?" Beth argued. "He doesn't know."

"He told me about Rena."

"He said her name?"

No, Zach hadn't said her name. It had seemed too difficult for him to connect a person to the enormity of his pain. He hadn't even tried to resume the conversation on their way back from the shop.

"He didn't have to," Rachel explained. "He told me their story."

"Wade told you lots of stories, too, and it turned out none of them mattered."

True. Rachel had misconstrued much of what Wade had shared, but the vibe between them was different. He was a platonic friend, and she'd never been sexually interested in him, whether he was gay or not.

"You're right. I should talk to Wade," Rachel said. "He's become a friend. I owe him an apology for all the times I acted like a lunatic."

"What about me? Don't I get one?" Beth reached for a chocolate bar on her night table.

"Okay, let's forget about Wade for the moment. Rach, what are you going to do?"

"I think I have to tell Zach the truth."

"Are you sure that's a good idea?"

The music stopped, and Rachel stood up.

"I'm going to go. Tell Evan I'm sorry."

"Eh, no big deal." Beth waved her hand. "Not much different than when Courtney busts in. You're just taller."

"She has much better hair." Rachel started to leave.

"Rach, I can't believe I'm saying this, but I think you should talk to the fortune teller."

Edie came in from the kitchen, carrying a tray holding two mugs of tea and a plate of biscotti.

"Thanks for seeing me on such short notice," Rachel said, letting her eyes mill about the room from her seat on a very comfortable beige couch.

Edie's house was furnished far more conservatively than her office. Considering the relaxed but practical furnishings and the subtle pastel palette, Rachel wouldn't have immediately guessed a psychic was paying the bills.

Edie took a sip of tea then put the cup down on the coffee table. "I've wanted to talk to you since I watched the kids the other night." She poured agave syrup into her tea. "But it's been one thing after another. I guess I don't have to tell you that."

"No, you don't. I'm not even sure where to start." Rachel tapped the tips of her fingers together.

"Start with the part when you and my son fell in love."

The stark reality of the statement could have, maybe even should have, sent Rachel into a tailspin, but it didn't. Her feelings for Zach were real and natural, born from a place of her own personal growth. That was an accomplishment Rachel was proud to acknowledge, but she couldn't pinpoint when it had happened.

"I'm not sure I can," Rachel said. "Is it that obvious?"

"I get a sense of things," Edie said. "That has nothing to do with hyper energy. It's human nature."

Edie shivered, got up, and turned on a large electric fireplace framed by dark wood. "But let's forget for a moment what I want to discuss." Edie rubbed her arms as if to fend off the chill. "Let's talk about why you wanted to see me."

Rachel wasn't sure jumping in was the right thing to do, but she had to trust someone, and Edie had done nothing but guide her in the right direction from the moment they'd met.

"Do you remember the woman Zach was seeing the summer before last?" Rachel asked cautiously.

"Zach has dated a lot of women." Edie sounded regretful. "And he's always been selective about what he shares."

"So he never mentioned a relationship with a woman from that time?"

"No one in particular. Why?"

Come on, Edie. Where is all that psychic juju? Rachel couldn't imagine it was her place to tell Edie she was a grandmother. The woman's job was to know these things. *She should be able to smell her own gene pool.*

"Does this have something to do with your trip to London?" Edie asked.

"Yes," Rachel answered as if they were about to play Twenty Questions.

"You seem to think I should know her," Edie said.

"She was important to Zach at the time."

"He told you this?"

"Yes."

"Honey, I'm drawing a blank here."

Rachel contemplated running to Edie's office and getting a few candles and crystals to speed along the discovery.

"They were involved," Rachel said, clasping a throw pillow to her stomach.

"I got that, but why is it relevant now? You and Zach found each other. Is this woman a friend of yours?"

"She was, briefly."

"Rachel, why are you having such a difficult time telling me whatever it is you think I should know?"

"I'm not sure," Rachel confessed. "I guess I wanted you to feel it, sense it, and know it without me having to spell it out."

Edie took a sip of tea. "You have a misconception about psychic energy. I don't have the ability to perceive random facts from the air even if, actually, especially if, they're connected to me."

"What did you think of my daughter when you watched her the other night?" Rachel asked.

"I thought she was lovely," Edie recalled. "And I thought it was interesting that her eyes reminded me of Zach's."

"Yes, that is interesting," Rachel agreed.

Edie's eyes widened, and a broad smile beamed across her face. "Oh my goodness, you and Zach had a child?"

"Not exactly."

"But there is a reason you've always felt so familiar to me, isn't there?"

Rachel nodded and put Edie's hand in hers. "Do you have those Milk Duds? We're going to need them."

Edie obliged with a tray of goodies she set on the coffee table. In her inimitable fashion, she let Rachel do all the talking. Rachel knew that as difficult as the story was to tell, it was equally difficult to hear.

Edie didn't say a word until Rachel heaved a welcome sigh of relief. Then Edie got up and gave Rachel a loving hug.

"I understand why you did it," Edie said. "It took courage and tremendous heart to act with such generosity and compassion. I can't thank you enough for being such a wonderful mother to Janie."

"That means so much to me," Rachel said. "I'm grateful for your support."

"You have it," Edie said. "Anything you need, just ask."

"Do you have any idea how I should tell Zach?"

"Anything but that."

The next morning, two delivery men arrived with a box the size of a small apartment building. It was addressed to Janie, and Rachel quickly ushered the men to the nursery, knowing she could never get it in there, or anywhere, on her own.

The men left, and Rachel noticed there was a tarot card affixed to the box. It was the High Priestess, and written on it in black marker was the message "TRUST YOUR INNER WISDOM." Edie had sent them both a gift.

No matter how Rachel arranged things, the new play kitchen was wreaking havoc in the room. The crib needed to stay where it was, but the dresser could no longer be married to the same wall. And if the shelves were to remain where they were, the heavier items had to be replaced by stuffed animals and pillow toys. There was no way around the changes, but Rachel understood how important it was for Edie to connect with her granddaughter and was determined to be accommodating.

Getting the toys and dolls off the shelves wasn't that simple. They were all wedged together, creating an intricate chain, and when Rachel moved Belle, Charlotte, the prized doll Rena had always stashed in Janie's carriage, and all the other dolls fell onto the carpet.

Nothing broke, but a small folded-up piece of paper was hanging from the bottom of Charlotte's pantaloons.

Rachel bent down, assuming it was a certificate or label of authenticity that she often packaged with the dolls they sold. She picked up the slip, which turned out to be a note.

My Dearest Rena. Perhaps this isn't the ring I wanted to give you, but it is a token of my love, and a hope for the daughter I wish to have with you someday. Love Charlotte well, as she is ours. Forever, Zach.

Rachel put the letter in her pocket, clutched the doll, and cried.

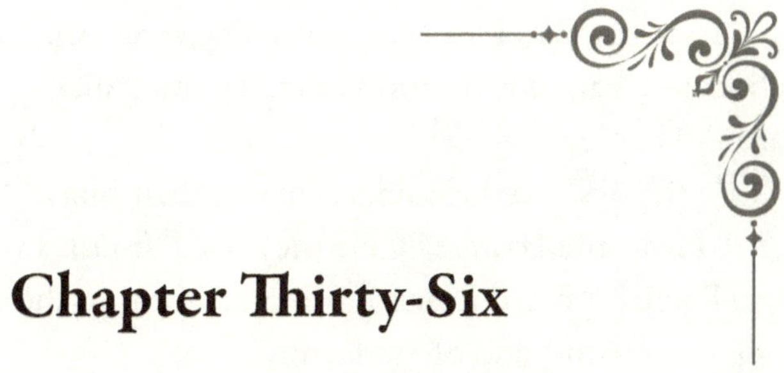

Chapter Thirty-Six

Evan called Rachel from the hospital just as traffic was starting to build on the thruway. Beth's labor was progressing rapidly, and considering it was rush hour, the irony wasn't lost on Rachel. She wasn't sure how long it would take her to get there, but since Evan said his mother was watching the kids, she didn't have to worry.

She turned on her Bluetooth and noticed Zach had called but hadn't left a message. Edie swore she wouldn't say a word—it was Rachel's story to tell when the time seemed right. The truth was, up until Rachel found the note under the doll's dress, she still hadn't been totally convinced Zach was Janie's father. But the truth was as clear as it was going to be, and the only thing left to do was tell him.

By the time Rachel reached the hospital, the lot was full. A very handsome, accommodating man at the gate gave her a salacious smile and pointed to an empty spot. If he thought the gesture was worth more than her smile, he'd blown a prime space. After she parked, she made a quick call to ask Brittany how Janie was doing then hurried to the entrance farthest from the attendant's post.

A few months back, Rachel would likely have found the guy's physique intriguing and his interest flattering. She might have even had him star in one of her elaborate fantasies, but things had changed, and these encounters were annoyances she endured to get what she wanted. Sometimes, it was hard to imagine that men and women could ever dance in sync, considering they rarely heard the same music.

Rachel walked into the maternity wing, armed with celebratory chocolate bars. Joshie and Courtney immediately threw themselves around her legs.

"Hi, guys," Rachel said, returning their hugs. "Where's Daddy?"

"He wanted coffee," Courtney said. "It tastes yuck."

Rachel spotted Evan's mother on a seat in the waiting area, talking to someone, and offered a wave.

"Aunt Rachel, guess what?" Courtney giggled. "Mommy had a baby that has a vagina! Like me!"

"Yeah. Another sister." Joshie kicked the floor with the toe of his sneaker. "I better get a brother next time."

"I knew I wouldn't get here in time." Rachel sighed. She reached into her bag and handed them each a giant candy bar. "Next week, we'll have to go shopping for big-brother and -sister presents. Would that be okay?"

"Yay!" Courtney cried.

"Sure," Joshie agreed without enthusiasm.

"You know, Joshie, little sisters are easy. They know you're bigger, and they let you be the boss. Think about that." She patted Joshie's head, and he led her to the door decorated with kids' drawings.

"She's in here," Joshie said. "I'm going to wait for Daddy."

Rachel opened the door to Beth's room, which could have doubled for a garden, considering all the flower arrangements sitting on every flat surface besides the floor.

"Aren't you popular," Rachel said.

"Not me," Beth said, holding out her arms for a hug. "These are from Evan's people."

Rachel gave Beth a hug then went over and picked up the baby. "She's absolutely gorgeous. The spitting image of Evan," Rachel teased. "How are you feeling?"

"Fine now. All ten pounds of her practically fell out of me in the bathroom. Lucky for us, we live close."

"You were right—she might become a sumo wrestler."

"Bite your tongue."

"Did you pick a name?"

"Courtney wants Barbie Doll, and Joshie wants to shove her back, so nothing yet."

"Really, nothing?"

"When we thought she was a boy, we settled on William Elliot. We're progressive, but that's not going to work." Beth took a sip of water from a plastic cup. "I'm considering South East just to stick it to Kim and Kanye."

"You're ridiculous." Rachel shook her head and kissed the baby's cheek. "Can I get you anything?"

"Lipstick and mascara. I'd like to try to be a woman again." Beth studied herself in a handheld mirror on her tray. "How about you? Anything new?"

"I'm great. Really, really great."

"Rach, I had a baby. My gallbladder won't explode." Beth patted her stomach. "You look exhausted. Tell me what's going on."

Rachel put the baby back in the hospital crib. "There's so much."

"That you haven't already told me? Why?" Beth frowned.

"I didn't want to burden you." Rachel poured water into a plastic cup on Beth's tray. "Besides, there was nothing you could do about any of it."

"That's very martyr-mom of you, but..." Beth took a breath. "No matter what, I am and will always be your best friend. Now, tell me everything."

Rachel handed Beth a candy bar, which was immediately accepted. "Phil confirmed he was cheating on me with his assistant."

"I knew he was cheating on you! He's scum!" Beth swallowed hard on a too-big bite of chocolate. She coughed a bit then continued. "No, no, he's worse than scum. He's the feces of scum. Actually, the sweat of the feces of scum."

"I don't think scum sweats or shits," Rachel said flatly.

"Well, it should." Beth resumed eating the candy. "I'm glad he's in jail, where he belongs. What else?"

"If that piece of info nearly made you choke, I'm not sure you can handle the rest."

"Rach, cut to the chase." Beth glanced at the clock on the wall. "The lactation chick is coming in ten minutes to check my cracked nipples."

"Okay," Rachel said. "I know you saw Phil on the news, so you already know he's a criminal."

Beth nodded. "Yes, and he looked nasty, like someone beat the shit out of him. He's just lucky it wasn't me."

Rachel took a sip of water. "You also know I haven't been able to conceive."

"Geez, Rach, this isn't the fuckin' prelude to *War and Peace*. Just tell me!"

"Phil had a vasectomy right before we started trying to get pregnant. And he paid off Connie Smith to squelch my plans to adopt the baby in London."

"Holy fuck! Holy the absolute fuck!" Beth's eyes were bulging out of her head. "I mean, I knew he was an asshole, but this? This borders on monsterdom. I'm so sorry, Rach. I should've gotten you away from him."

"It wasn't your place or your responsibility. Oh, and before I forget, there's this." She pulled the note out of her pocket and handed it to Beth.

Beth read the letter aloud and burst into happy tears. "It is Zach!"

The sooner Zach knows, the better, Rachel kept telling herself as she fluffed up the throw pillows on her couch. Especially since his mother was proudly toting a new the Children's Place credit card. The secret was no longer a secret, and if she didn't tell him soon, she would have to spend another day slathering on cover cream to hide the evidence of yet another sleepless night. She checked the time. He would be there shortly.

Talking wasn't going to be easy since the last coherent words she'd mustered had been the last text she'd sent Zach saying she was an aunt again. Then she'd added an invitation for champagne when she got home from the hospital, but it had gotten too late, so that didn't happen.

Rachel had just put Janie down in her crib and was singing "You Are My Sunshine" when Zach knocked lightly on the back door and, as per her instructions, let himself in. She finished the last verse then met him in the family room. He had already poured them each a glass of champagne. As usual, he looked yummy, and when he kissed her, she wished they would get too carried away to talk. But she couldn't let that happen, and before things got too intense, she broke away from the embrace and sat down on the couch.

"Thanks for coming," Rachel said, taking a sip of her drink.

"Is everyone doing okay? Bet the baby is really cute." He joined her on the couch.

"Everyone's fine, and indeed, she is." Rachel took out her phone and showed Zach a few photos.

"I was right," Zach said. "She looks like you."

Rachel normally would have gushed, but his being so nice wasn't making what she had to tell him any easier.

"Would you rather have scotch?" Rachel got up and walked over to the liquor cabinet. She eyed Zach from head to toe, taking his "before" pic in her mind. In a few moments, she would be turning his life inside out.

"Scotch? Rachel, are you ditching the project? Because please don't. If anything, I need you more now. I spoke with my editor, and

he thinks the outline is great. This book might be the best in the series, and I think a big part of that is because of you."

"Wow, thank you!" Rachel sat back down on the couch. "No, of
course I'm not quitting, but the credit is yours."

"Good, good, but something is bothering you."

Rachel gulped her drink. She wasn't sure if her angst was obvious
or if Zach had gotten to know her well enough to make secrets impossible to keep. "I have a lot to tell you."

"It's Wade, isn't it?"

"Wade?"

"You're seeing him, aren't you? I had a feeling. That guy is always
looking at you..."

"You're way off base." Rachel wanted to tell Zach everything,
but it wasn't her place, even though she'd already spilled it to Beth.
"Wade is in a committed relationship but chooses to keep his private
life very private."

Zach's eyes scrunched as if she'd told him the world was flat. "Really? Wade's in a serious relationship? He looks at you... the way I
don't want any other guy to look at you."

Rachel allowed herself a second to bathe in his declaration. "I
think it's the artist in him viewing a subject."

"So you decided to let him paint you, and now you're not sure
how to tell me?"

"No. I turned him down. At least for now." Rachel got up and
started pacing.

"Rachel, I get that you're kind of quirky. I usually find it endear-
ing. But what's going on? Tell me what has you in this vise."

She was so nervous, she thought she might pass out or puke before any words passed through her lips. It was the moment of truth,
the time to disclose Janie's paternity, the one thing that could tear her
life apart forever.

"You..." Rachel struggled. "You and another woman."

"There are no other women," Zach said. "Just you."

Rachel let the tingle she'd felt hearing his words linger for a moment before she continued. "As thrilled as I am to hear that—and I am—this isn't about me."

"I'm listening."

Rachel swallowed hard and poured herself another glass of champagne. "I'm talking about a very special, beautiful woman you loved who loved you. Very much."

"Right. I started to tell you about her the other day, but then the repair guy came. And truthfully, it's not important." Zach ran his fingers through the sides of his hair. "You have nothing to worry about. It's been over for a while, and she and I haven't kept in touch at all."

"I know that." Rachel braced herself as she headed toward the pinnacle of this rollercoaster.

"You do?"

"I do. I know all about Rena."

Zach's jaw dropped. "How do you know her name?"

"I was in London a few months ago, and she and I met."

"You're kidding!" Zach shook his head. "That's crazy."

"Oh, it gets crazier." Rachel took a long swig of her drink. "You sure I can't get you something?"

"Go on, Rachel." Zach encouraged her with his right hand.

"She and I became very close friends."

"Huh?" Zach set his drink on the coffee table hard enough for a few drops to spill over.

"She told me about you, but she didn't tell me about *you*. She never used your name. She never said where you lived or worked. She just talked about this man who meant so much to her."

"Yeah, so much so that she left. Out of the blue. Never to be heard from again." Zach stood and went to the window. "I don't get it. What's all this about?"

"She always wanted to give you this." Rachel handed him the unsent letter from Rena. "But she could never muster up the courage."

Zach read the letter aloud.

"Darling, please find it in your heart to forgive me. I was prepared to leave Reggie and spend my life with you, but fate has had its way with us. Reggie is desperately ill and needs me. I'm his wife, and I couldn't bear the guilt of causing him any further suffering. If it is in the cards, we will be together again. For now, I will treasure our memories. And though we are parted, you must be assured that our love lives on in a most beautiful way. Forever, Rena."

"How did you get this?" Zach made it sound more like an accusation than a question.

"She gave it to me. Sort of."

"Sort of," Zach mocked. "To give to me now?"

"Not exactly."

"Then what exactly, Rachel? Why are you being so cryptic?" Zach threw the letter down on the couch. "Did she say I wasn't a good lover or something? Because I swear, she always seemed satisfied. Not that I care to discuss any of this with you. But I'm out of guesses—so what aren't you telling me?"

"She's gone, Zach. She passed away."

"What?" Zach turned white. "How?"

"Insulin shock."

"Oh my God. I can't believe it! She was so young. So... alive." Zach's eyes welled up with tears. "How do you know all this?"

"I was with her." Rachel walked over to him as he stood near the window, put her hands around his waist, and pressed her cheek against his back. "She was coming back with me. To find you."

"What about her husband?"

"He left her."

"*He* left *her*?"

"When he found out about the baby."

"The baby?" Zach turned around and held Rachel by her shoulders. "What baby?"

"Your baby."

"My baby?" Zach stared into her eyes. "I have a baby?"

"You have a baby." Rachel couldn't stop her tears. "A daughter."

"Where?"

"Sleeping upstairs," Rachel said in a hushed tone. "Janie is yours."

"That's impossible. She's yours."

"I'll tell you the whole story if you promise to listen all the way through."

Zach sat on the couch. "Where's that scotch?"

Rachel went to the cabinet and poured Zach a double. Then she told him the whole story, from the beginning.

He sat with tears running down his face. "Are you saying all this time, when you and I were... You were hiding my... my kid from me? You were hiding the truth from me!"

"No, of course not. I would never do that to you... I didn't know!"

Zach got up, grabbed his coat, and stormed out of the house.

"You didn't let me finish," Rachel cried into a throw pillow from the couch. "I didn't know. I didn't know."

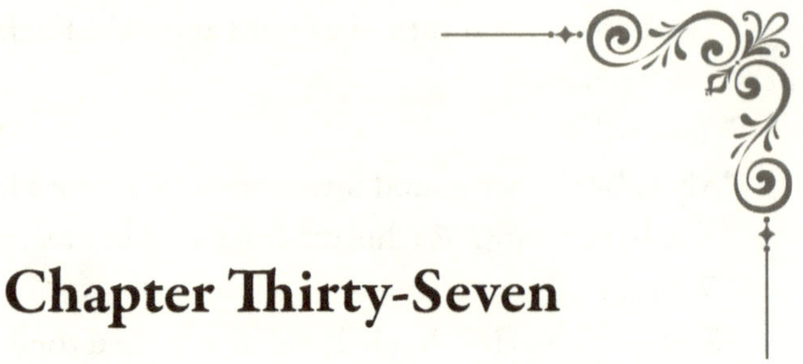

Chapter Thirty-Seven

A quick glance in the bedroom mirror on her way to the shower made Rachel cringe. Her normally big eyes were swollen into slits, and her nose looked like a mutant strawberry. It was conceivable this would be her new normal if she didn't stop crying herself to sleep every night. Yet there was no promise of anything changing. It had been a week since she'd told Zach about Janie and Rena, and he still hadn't called.

Her day had just begun, and Rachel was already feeling teary. It wasn't just Zach—it was everything. Rachel had gone from feeling like she was on top of the world to hovering at the bottom. Between Rena, her marriage, and possibly Zach and Janie, there was a lot of loss to process. As much as Rachel wanted to believe Zach would allow Janie to stay in her life, Rachel had no idea what that might look like. Edie would certainly advocate for her, but ultimately, it would be Zach's decision.

With Janie still asleep, Rachel put a cool compress on her distorted face. She'd planned to go to Beth's house to help her decorate for the holidays. It was an annual tradition, and though Rachel wasn't up to the festivities, she knew Janie would enjoy being with the kids. The mere thought of that relationship ending gave Rachel palpitations. It was possible her heart would break into irretrievable pieces if all she'd come to love over the past few months vanished into oblivion.

Despite all the potential disasters, even Rachel was getting sick of her pity party. Nothing productive or helpful would come of indulging in worst-case scenarios. They had well over an hour before they were expected at Beth's. Rachel summoned her practical side and went to the kitchen. She found her favorite tumbler, made herself a matcha latte with an extra splash of half and half, and toasted a couple of Minnie Mouse waffles for Janie. Given her very new mindset and a generous dollop of Nutella slathered on a bagel crisp, Rachel decided each day should start with a delicious reminder of how sweet life was supposed to be.

"Our house looks like turd balls," Joshie complained, tossing decorations into a plastic container. "Cooper has Santa and reindeer on his lawn. We don't have any good stuff."

He plopped in front of the television, inspiring Beth to switch recordings from *Elf* to *Shalom Sesame*.

"We're Jewish," Beth said. "Deal with it."

"How encouraging," Rachel teased.

"These kids are so friggin' spoiled, it's not even funny," Beth complained, handing Rachel one end of a Happy Chanukah banner and a Velcro strip.

Rachel tacked her side up while Beth did hers.

"Zach will come around," Beth said, apparently reading Rachel's mind. "He has to. He's Janie's father. And no matter what he said, he's glad you're her mother."

Maybe Beth was right, but there was little to indicate that was the case. When Edie had stopped by Rachel's to play with Janie the other day, she'd said Zach had a cold, which even she acknowledged as a lame excuse for his silence. Edie also added not to worry and that she was working on him, which Rachel believed had nothing to do with antihistamines.

It was not that Rachel didn't understand Zach's shock. Had the roles somehow been reversed, she wasn't sure how she would react. It didn't matter. Bottom line, she was hurt he'd accused her of deliberately betraying him. After all the time they'd spent together, that allegation made her question the basis of their relationship. There was a lot at stake and much to consider with no idea what would happen once things calmed down.

Beth interrupted Rachel's ruminations with another set of decorating instructions. "Earth to Rachel. Stop obsessing and hang this over there." Beth handed Rachel what appeared to be an endless stream of blue-and-silver-braided tinsel and pointed to one of the emptier corners of the room.

"You already had the baby," Rachel said. "Aren't you supposed to be nicer now?"

"No, she's still a meanie," Courtney complained, holding a doll upside down by its ankle. "She doesn't let *me* feed baby Casey the way *she* feeds her."

Seeming uneasy with the dangling doll and how Courtney's treatment of her could portend the future of their newest addition, Beth put down the streamer and repositioned the floppy replica in Courtney's arms.

"Your breasts are tiny and have no milk, Court, remember?" Beth said, unknotting a clump of shimmery mylar.

Courtney reclaimed her hold on the doll's ankle, shaking her as she spoke. "Well, I can buy some and put it in them," Courtney reasoned. Then she stuck her tongue out at Beth and sat down to watch TV next to her brother.

Beth turned to Rachel. "Where's the manager? *This* was not what I ordered!"

She picked up the streamer, only to be met by a stubborn beam when she tried to tack it in.

Rachel patted her sister on the shoulder. "I think it's going to take the kids some time to get used to the additional demands of those ten extra pounds around here. Casey's cute, but they sure don't want to share you."

Rachel watched Beth's attempt to hang the uncooperative decoration and yanked it from her just as the doorbell rang.

"Excellent timing," Beth said, opening the door.

Rachel cocked her head toward the new figure in the room. "Edie?" she said under her breath.

Edie stepped into the house, carrying a box of Chanukah gelt, chocolate coins, and a bag of bagels.

"Hello," Edie said. "I was near Bagel Train and figured we could have lunch while we're working."

Beth gave her a kiss on the cheek and took the bag from her.

"Edie!" the kids called out.

Edie hugged the kids and gave them the box of chocolate.

"She brang us candy!" Courtney beamed.

"Yeah, the good kind," Joshie said as he and Courtney went back to watch the show.

Rachel stood in silent confusion.

"Hello, Rachel. Sorry, but I must get to the ladies' room." Edie slung her large magenta purse over a hook on the coatrack and hurried around the corner.

"Um, Beth, since when are you friends with Zach's mother?"

"Since she watched the kids," Beth explained. "Mom's in Greece, and I love my mother-in-law, but Edie and I are simpatico. And the kids love her."

Rachel understood. Edie, much like Beth, lived comfortably out loud, a feat not many could accomplish.

Beth walked into the kitchen with Rachel in tow.

"Okay, I kind of get it, but I still don't understand all this." Rachel made a circle with her hand.

"What's to understand?" Beth asked. "People come into our lives, and half the time, we have no clue why. At least this time, it all seems to make sense. Don't you think?"

Edie came into the kitchen, holding Janie. "I hope you don't mind. Our little pumpkin was fussing, and before Courtney attempted to breastfeed, I decided to bring her to you." Edie handed the baby to Rachel.

"Thank you," Rachel said, still trying to process this new development.

Beth left the kitchen, carrying a tray for the kids.

Rachel was about to follow Beth when Edie extended her arm and stopped her.

"Rachel, I just want you to know, I don't think I'll ever be able to thank you enough," Edie said. "Without you, we might never have even met Janie. And to top it off, I couldn't have handpicked a better mother for her."

"That means the world to me, Edie." Rachel held Janie very close and kissed her head. "It's kind of weird, but sometimes, I actually forget that I didn't deliver her."

"I don't think it's strange at all," Edie said. "Love is the most powerful energy we possess, and you master it beautifully."

"That's sweet of you to say, but I think I'm more clueless about love than most. I just know that Janie feels like mine, and I hope that never has to change."

"Change?"

"She *is* Zach's daughter, and at some point, he's going to choose to do something about it."

"Just know that every attempt you make to answer your heart will always bring its own gift," Edie said. "Energy craves order and can be coaxed into being an ally."

"Sage advice," Rachel said.

Beth walked into the kitchen, grimacing. "Rach, did you bring the Happy Holidays snow globe? The one that plays 'Jingle Bells'?"

"No, why would I? You didn't ask me to."

"Yes, I did," Beth said.

"No, you didn't."

"Okay, maybe I forgot, but I want it."

"I'll bring it next time."

"We're doing decorations now," Beth whined.

"It's just a snow globe."

"Why are you arguing with me?" Beth scowled. "I've just spent months unable to enjoy margaritas, fit in my jeans, shave my legs, or do it in the missionary position, and now you're giving me grief!"

"Fine. I, for one, am grateful you have reclaimed your ability to shave. If you need the snow globe that badly, I will go home and get it."

"Thank you," Beth said, sounding exasperated.

"Will you watch Janie, please? She needs to nap and—"

"We'll watch the baby." Beth took Janie from Rachel. "Go already!"

Rachel wasn't sure why she was being chased out but was grateful for the chance to have some time to herself.

"But, of course, your highness. Anything else while I'm out?" Rachel went to get her coat.

"Rachel, stay open to whatever asks to shape your wisdom," Edie said, putting down a string of tinsel. "We like control, but most of our plans end up laughing at us. Ultimately, life is written in the stars."

"I would imagine so," Rachel said.

Edie gave her a maternal kiss on the forehead and pushed her out the door.

Rachel took another look inside the box of decorations in the attic. The snow globe was the only thing worth taking to Beth's since the banners were fraying and the lights were in unmanageable knots that refused to loosen. She put everything back in the carton, clutched the snow globe, and went back downstairs. She still had her coat on and was about to leave when the doorbell rang. She assumed the same kids she'd purchased holiday items from earlier had forgotten she'd already done her part for their school fundraiser.

A whistling that sounded like a train diverted her attention as she opened the door.

"Hey, guys, you should go to my neighbors, next door," Rachel said, turning toward them. "Oh!"

There stood a Santa holding a stack of gifts in her doorway. "Ho, ho, ho," Wade bellowed.

"You're pretty convincing." Rachel giggled.

"Hey, no pot shots about my belly," Wade protested.

"Stop being paranoid. It was your *ho ho ho* that got to me," Rachel insisted. "I was just on my way out, or I'd invite you in."

"No problem. I'm going here and there, playing Santa for the day."

"Well, you've made me a believer," Rachel said. "And what have you got there?"

"What does it look like?" Wade asked.

"Presents."

"You're awesome. You got it right away."

"Yup, that's me. Quick on the uptake," she said. "But seriously, Wade, you didn't have to buy us gifts."

"Well, the reindeer and I spoke, and we think you and Janie need some holiday cheer."

"I'm touched."

"Yes, you are, but no more so than the rest of us," Wade teased.

"Thanks."

"I'd like to think of myself as an honorary uncle."

"Uncle Wade, it is," Rachel said. "Listen, as long as you're here, I did pick up a couple of things for you too."

"I knew it!" Wade chuckled.

Rachel took the gifts from Wade and put them on the table in the hall. "Give me a minute."

Rachel went down the hall to the closet and came back with a pile of boxes that obscured her view as she walked to the door. "Sorry, some of this stuff is bulky. Would you mind giving me a hand?" Rachel shifted her weight, peered over the boxes, and froze.

"Not at all," Zach said, coming through the door and taking the stack of gifts from her while Wade stood awkwardly beside him.

"I think these are mine," Wade said, taking the packages from Zach. "Okay, I'm going to leave now... Ho, ho, ho... Have fun, kids."

Wade left with a wave Rachel didn't acknowledge.

"I'm surprised to see you," she said, trying to regain her composure.

"Listen, I don't like the way we left things—the way I left things." Zach took off his coat and slung it over a chair in the family room.

"I'm listening," Rachel said, keeping her coat on. His furious departure a week ago was still troubling. He could've taken that time to set up a life for Janie that didn't include her. Her gut told her he would never do that, but her head said anything was possible.

"Can you sit down, please?" Zach asked.

Rachel sat next to Zach on the couch.

"I want you to know I understand. I didn't, but now I think I do."

"Okay." Unsure where the conversation was headed, she started to get up.

Zach gently pushed her back. "Come on, I'm trying."

"Fine." Rachel softened and turned toward Zach.

"When you told me about everything, all I could feel was betrayed. Maybe that makes no sense, but it was like I was being punished for daring to open up again. That's why I ran. But after a few nights of Glenlivet and conversations with my mother, I realized running was a mistake."

"Why?" Rachel asked. "It makes sense to me."

"No. Running away is never the answer." Zach took her hand.

"What changed?"

"I'm running *to* you instead of away from you," Zach explained. "That's what I should have done in the first place—listened more, reacted less."

"I would've liked that. How could you think I'd want to hurt you?"

"That's where I really messed up. I should've given you the benefit of the doubt, but I didn't get the chance. First, I was overcome by grief, then I was pissed that Rena never told me. Maybe that was about my ego. I'm sure she thought she was doing the right thing."

"Don't be so hard on yourself." Rachel patted Zach's knee. "I'm not guilt free. I wasn't exactly delicate when I hit you with more than your share to sort out."

"I was shaken, and when I had the chance to escape, I did."

"It was a perfectly normal reaction. I should've been more understanding," Rachel said.

"I am so sorry, Zach. I didn't mean to hurt you, but I did."

"It seems you've been pretty generous all around," Zach said.

"You're giving me way too much credit." Rachel hugged a throw pillow. "The truth is nothing I did was selfless. I wanted to keep Janie. The thought of giving her up made me ill. I did battle with my conscience every day before I committed to finding—as it turns out—you."

"But when it came down to it, you took the risk even if losing her was possible." Zach brushed stray hairs away from his eyes. "You made the ultimate sacrifice for your principles."

"I'm no Mother Teresa, but as she said, 'Not all of us can do great things. But we can do small things with great love.'"

"Exactly. I finally realized that everything you've done has been for Janie. And for me. And it all started before I even knew you."

"All considered, you weren't that hard to find."

"Divine intervention. I laid eyes on you, and I was hooked. Damned if I could figure out why I was falling in love with you so fast. That's for movies and middle school kids. But there you were, and I couldn't get enough of you. What would you wear? How would you smell? How would I be able to control myself when I was near you? The book deal was a blessing. It was an excuse to keep you close."

"You didn't need an excuse." Rachel quivered.

"Oh, I did. I needed to understand why you were always in my head. I couldn't even eat a bagel without thinking how much better it would taste if you were sitting next to me." Zach wiped a stray tear from the corner of Rachel's eye.

"Zach, before Janie, before you," Rachel said, "my world was a sad pile of wants. There was so much emptiness, I had a more meaningful relationship with the past than I could muster for the present." She stood up and walked over to the tissue box near the window. "I thought having a baby with Phil would solve everything. We'd be a family, and I would be like every other suburban mom with a Jeep and a standing Botox appointment."

"That doesn't sound like you," Zach said.

"You're right. And when you and Janie showed up, I realized the problem wasn't Phil or our soulless marriage. The void was my doing. The problem was me."

"Maybe you're the one being too hard on yourself," Zach said.

"I'm not. It was a good thing. Remember the movie *Runaway Bride*?"

Zach nodded.

"Julia Roberts runs away from relationships because she doesn't know herself, and until she does, she can't love anyone else."

"Please don't tell me you're going to hop on a FedEx truck before we finish this conversation."

Rachel chuckled. "I don't have to. Somewhere in the middle of making pea puree and pitying Ms. Havisham, I found myself and fell in love with you."

"Baby, I love you," Zach said. "Forgive me for ever doubting you. Be with me...."

When Zach took her into his arms, all her worries and doubts disappeared. Her journey had begun with a wish that took her from her own backyard, across the pond, and back again, with each step strengthening her resolve. There was no denying life would always be a clever maze, putting her wherever she needed to be until she was ready to be someplace else. Now, that time had come. Zach kissed her with all he had to give, leaving no question of what was meant to be.

In that one blissful moment when they finally joined as one, body and soul, Rachel could swear she felt a new life taking hold inside of her. Maybe one day, that wish would be granted to further bless their union and deepen their commitment. But for now, there was just the beauty of their love, perfect in its own path as it was written in the stars.

Acknowledgments

As with children, it takes a village to raise a book.

Love, gratitude, and many thanks to my awesome team:

My editors: Rashida Breen, Stefanie Spangler Buswell, and Jessica Anderegg. My mentor: Jennifer Klepper. And my all-around RAP guide, Erica Lucke Dean

All my fellow Red Adept authors and colleagues

Brad Langer, my husband, manager, agent, and everything in between

Gloria Fishbach, my mom, for being all things glorious

My kids, Lana (who helped craft the story), Adam, Brittany, Shawn, and Hayli

Brian Sockin, my like-a-brother who always offers helpful insights

My family and friends for always being in my corner even when it pinches

And special thanks to all those whose loving light shines above me. I hope I'm doing you all proud.

About the Author

Sheri Langer is a chocoholic writer and editor who routinely feasts on romantic comedies. She's been known to spontaneously reenact scenes from classic favorites like *When Harry Met Sally*.

A self-proclaimed, moderately talented home-cook, Sheri spends a fair amount of time concocting dishes that can never be repeated. A creative rebel at heart, she has always colored outside the lines and has an instinctive aversion to recipes. To keep the calories from getting too out of hand, Sheri does step and aerobic workouts in the privacy of her bedroom, where no one has to be subjected to her lack of rhythm.

An avid word fan, Sheri frequently plays Just Words, Boggle, and Scrabble, mostly against the computer so she has excellent odds of winning. With her four kids all grown up, three of whom live in various locations across the map, Sheri and her guy, Brad, spend much of their down time watching General Hospital and football, shopping, and pursuing the best ice cream on the planet. Much to the chagrin of their waistbands, they can often be spotted sitting on a bench outside their favorite creamery, eating obscenely overstuffed giant waffle cones.

Please feel free to connect with Sheri on social media. You can help her procrastinate by engaging in spirited exchanges or viewing pics of her great-looking family and ridiculously adorable cat, Zoe.

About the Publisher

Dear Reader,

We hope you enjoyed this book. Please consider leaving a review on your favorite book site.

Visit https://RedAdeptPublishing.com to see our entire catalogue.

Check out our app for short stories, articles, and interviews. You'll also be notified of future releases and special sales.